THE LIGHT UNBOUND

C. S. WACHTER

Shadowfall Publishing

The Light Unbound
The Seven Words Book 4

Copyright © 2018 by C. S. Wachter
www.cswachter.com

Published by Shadowfall Publishing

Printed in the United States of America

Wachter, C. S.
    The light unbound / C. S. Wachter
    The seven words; book four
    ISBN: 978-0-9998861-6-8 (paperback)
    ISBN: 978-0-9998861-7-5 (e-book)

Cover Design by: Mountainview Books, LLC
Maps by: Nexgenstudio
Print formatting by: Mountainview Books, LLC

For my Lord, Jesus. I stand amazed at the ways you bless me. Even when I allow doubt and fear to creep in, you are with me. Writing Rayne's story has taught me I am never alone. You are there upholding me, loving me; I just need to trust. Thank you.

For my special friend Jan. Thank you for walking this path with me from the beginning.
You are a blessing.

ACKNOWLEDGMENTS

Thanks to those who encouraged me to begin this journey: Jan, Mac, and Peggy. Thanks to all those readers whose input and comments helped make this book what it is today. Kelly, Janae, Bryan, Marcia, Thom, Carla, Mary, Sharon, Alice, Dan, Jamie, Alissa, Matt, Becky, and the Lancaster Christian Writers. I also would like to thank all those who have been following Rayne's journey. You have blessed me with your support. A special thanks to Bree and Vicki ... love those Monster Cookies and all your special sweet treats.

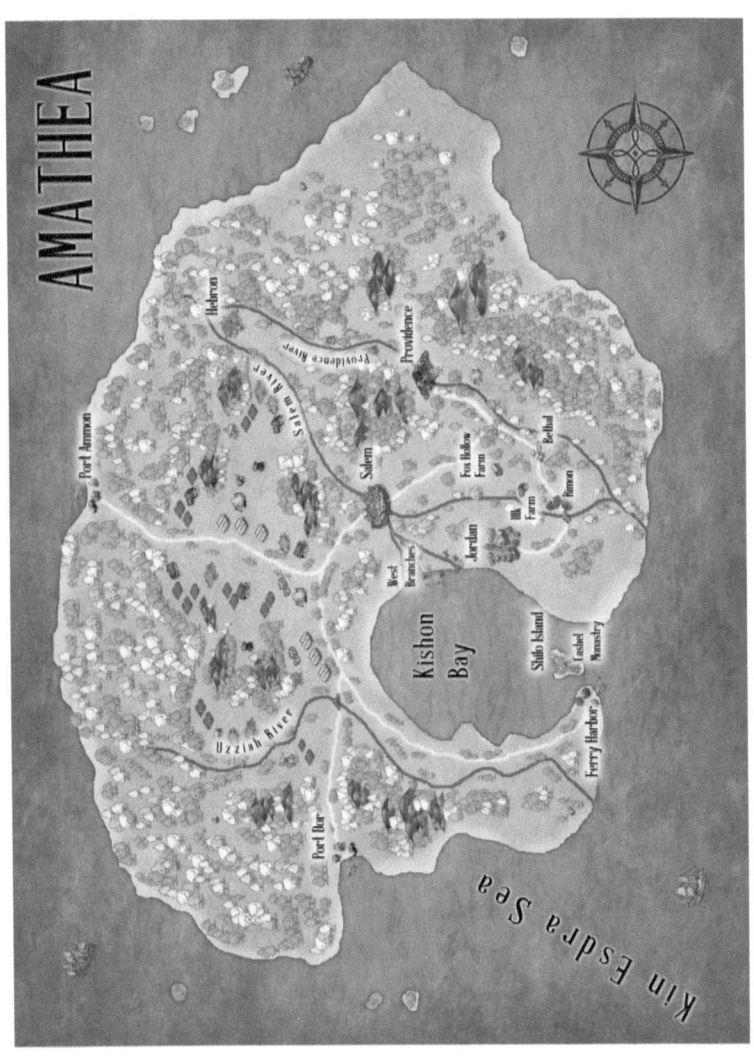

AMATHEA

Port Ammon

Salem River

Providence River

Hebron

Providence

Salem

Fox Hollow Farm

Bethel

Ammon

Jordan

Elk Farm

West Branches

Kishon Bay

Shilo Island

Ezekiel Monastery

Ferry Harbor

Uzziah River

Port Bur

Kin Esdra Sea

7

ARISIMA

Jadeth Sea

Great Desert

where the desert drinks itself

Zurayja Oasis

Oasis

Aleppo Monastry

Monastry

Oasis

CORYLUS

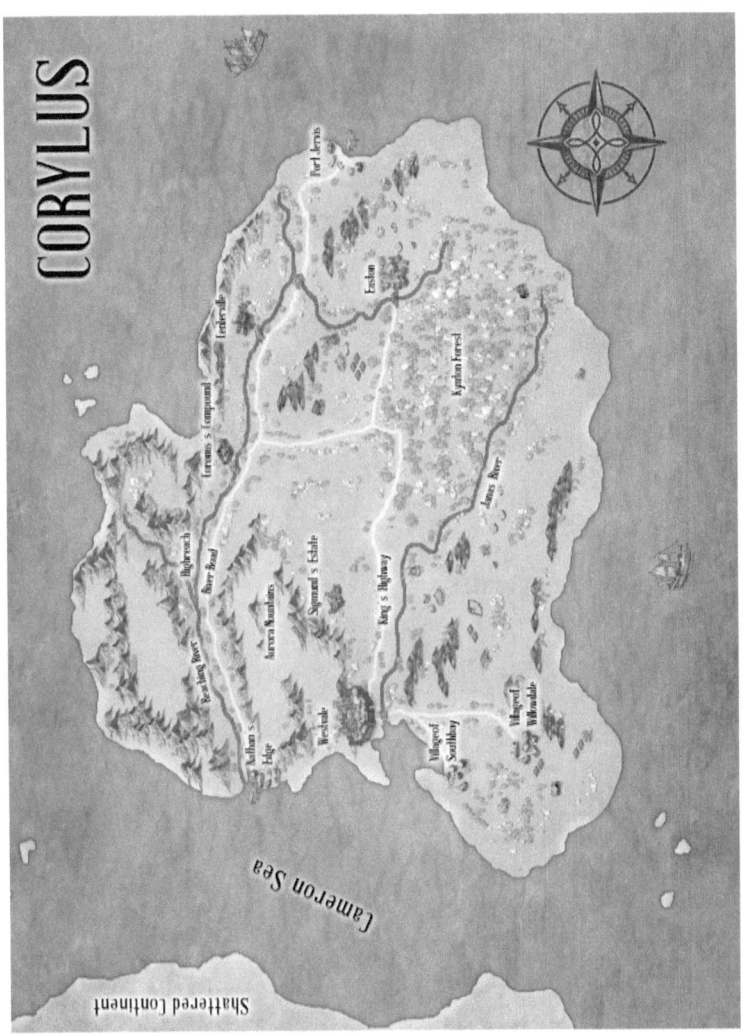

Port Jervis

Lesterville

Kovann's Compound

Highwatch

Azern Mountains

River Road

Revolving River

Sullivan's Edge

Ericson

Kyndare Forrest

Sigmund's Estate

King's Highway

Rockvale

James River

Villagord Southbury

Villagord Willowdale

Cameron Sea

Shattered Continent

11

GLACIERIA

Frozen Wastes

Wataru Lands

Khalon Lands

Swirling Bowl

Jebugra's Village

Roaring Mountain

Michi Lands

Portal Station

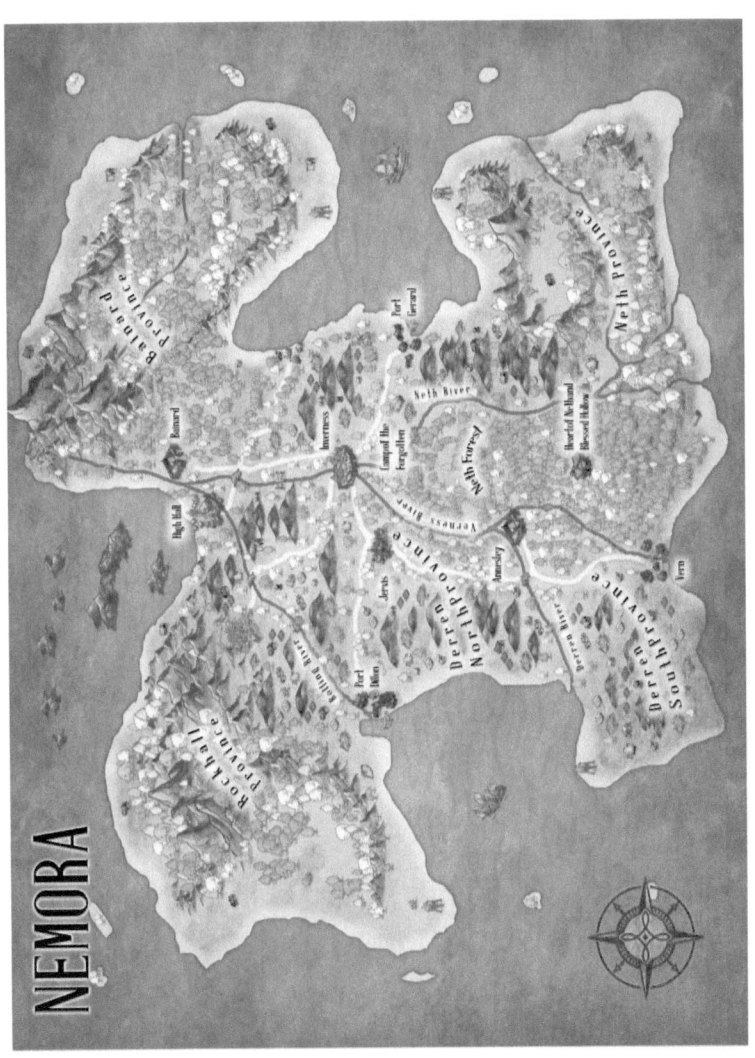

NEMORA

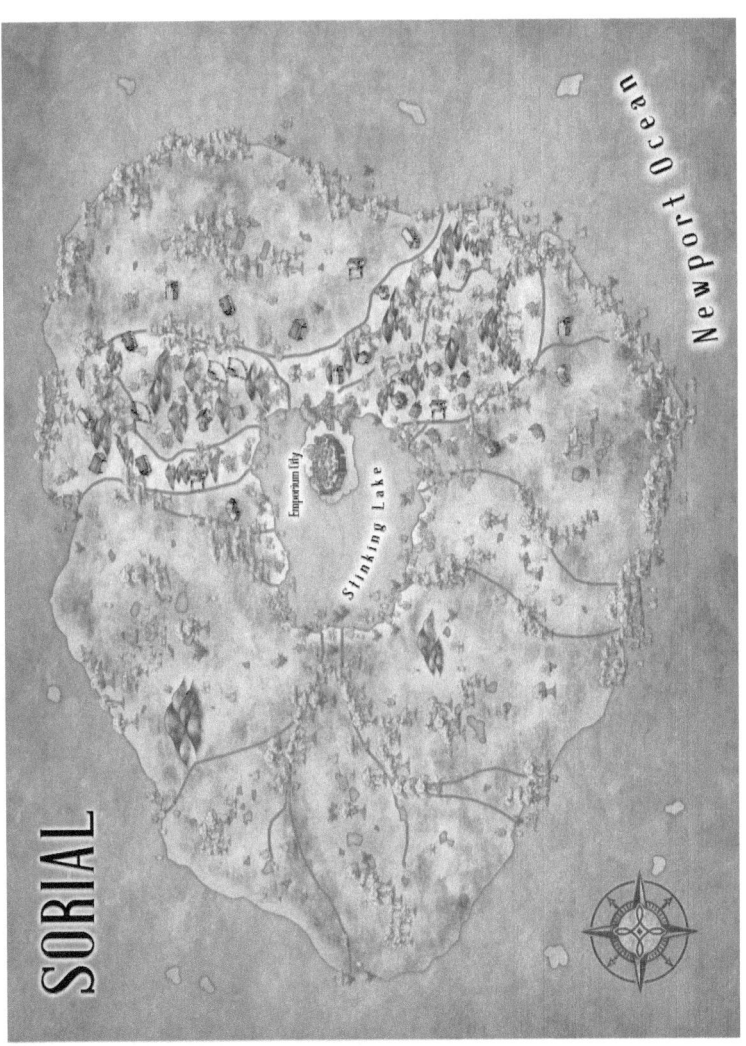

SORIAL

Newport Ocean

Emporium Isly

Stinking Lake

VERES

Naameth Sea

Naal Caarwyn — Headwaters of Caarwyn Fall

Taljesin Mountains

Blain River

Melai

Anderson Mine

Anderson Gaming Complex

River River

Eleri

Griffin Mine

Sharron Mine

Sharron River

THE SEVEN WORDS SERIES
LIST OF CHARACTERS

FROM: THE SORCERER'S BANE

TRAVIS ILLK—resident of Amathea; hired by Sigmund to kidnap Rayne

SIGMUND OF BAINARD—ancient evil being; Wren's owner

PONCE—Sigmund's myrmidon; a rubiate

REGINALD CLOUSON—master manipulator; places wire in kidnapped Rayne

RAYNE KIERKENGAARD—Crown Prince Rayne Nathan Samuel Kierkengaard of Corylus and the Ochen system; son of Theodor and Rowena; kidnapped by Sigmund and given the name Wren

THEODOR KIERGENGAARD—King of Corylus and the Ochen system; enemy of Sigmund; father of Rayne

MORROW—daughter and only child of Sigmund; executed by Theodor for murdering King Samuel, Theodor's father

SAMUEL KIERKENGAARD—King of Corylus and the Ochen system; Theodor's father; murdered by Morrow

VAN CORONUS—leader of a group of highly-skilled assassins; owner of the compound where Wren grows up

ROWENA KRAFTSMUNN KIERKENGAARD—Queen of Corylus and the Ochen system; originally from Nemora; mother of Rayne

MARTHA—Rayne's nurse

ANNE PARSON—Coronus' slave and healer; originally from Veres; friend of Wren/Rayne

THORVIN KRAFTSMUNN—Coronus' trainer; master swordsman

WARREN—tutor to nobility; kidnapped and enslaved by Coronus

BRIAN, DONALD, MARCIE—people Wren meets on the way to Coronus' compound

LEN FERNHARDT—ferryman

ALAN (AL)—Coronus' cook

RUFUS, CAINE, LOGAN—assassins-in-training at Coronus' compound

WALTER—A guard at Coronus' Compound

MITCHEL—Coronus's Stable Master

LORD WILLIAM ANDERSEN—powerful Sorial merchant; head of Merchants Guild

JASON ANDERSEN—Lord Willliam's son

BISHOP JONATHAN HEDRICK—head of the church of Corylus; Bishop of Westvale

SHAW RADINAJAN—monk from Arisima; friend to Light Bringer

ELSIE—church cook; friend of Theodor and Rowena

YOUMUND—fighter/warrior hired by Sigmund

SIR HECTOR—target of Wren's first contract

COLE WRIGHT, TYSON WRIGHT—brothers; residents of Highreach

SION—Cole's and Tyson's dog

ROGER—a guard at Coronus' compound

NATHAN—first Kierkengaard king

LADY LILITH—best friend of Morrow; friend of Sigmund

ROLAND—friend of Lady Lilith

CAPTAIN ELLIS—young captain of palace guard

STEVIE KASPER—twin to Sashi Kasper; friend of Rayne

SASHI KASPER—twin to Stevie; friend of Rayne

CAPTAIN ANTON FONTAINE—captain of palace guard

PRIVATE RICHARD MATHESON—palace guard

SERGEANT PETERSON—palace guard cook

LIAM, ABBY WRIGHT—parents of Cole and Tyson
BOONE (LIGHTENING BOONE)—Rayne' dog
ANDREW—Rayne's page
NOAH REESE—palace guard
BRAYDEN KRAFTSMUNN—Rayne's cousin
LADY ELAINE—member of court; friend of Brayden
LANDON WESTON—son of Duke Weston; friend of Brayden
WESLEY HARTSON—son of Sidney Hartson, Earl of Sidmore; friend of Brayden
SIR TYLER OF BAINARD—friend of Brayden
SHALIMAR—Rayne's horse
RUTHIE—kitchen maid

FROM: THE LIGHT ARISES:

RECLAMATION COMMITTEE MEMBERS:

FROM CORYLUS—Ria, Weston, Dunn
FROM SORIAL—Eliot, Jareth, Sterling
FROM ARISIMA—Sanje, Abhay, Deven
FROM NEMORA—Blossom, Powell, Wynne
FROM AMATHEA—Travis, Amalie, Dante

CORPORAL JOB PARKER—palace guard from Nemora

ON SORIAL AND VERES

LOUVAIN ANDERSEN—nephew of Lord William
LEXI (LADY ALEXIANNDRA) ERLAND—Duchess of Veres and daughter of Duke Justus Erland
DUKE JUSTUS ERLAND—Duke of Veres and father to Lexi; friend of King Theodor and Queen Rowena; wife

Tressa (deceased)

ETHAN—rebel; Lexi's second in command

SILAS—rebel; works closely with Lexi and Ethan

CAI—rebel from Mistal

SEREN—rebel healer; servant to Duke Erland

JESPER—Seren's deceased husband; part of Duke Erland's personal guard

LUCIUS—man servant to Duke Erland

YURI—works at Andersen Family Gaming Complex preparing slaves to fight in the ring

SHIN—guard at Andersen Family Gaming Complex

KYLE—rebel spy

BRAN & ALICK—boys from the village of Rheems

TAL—takes care of stock for Lexi and the rebels

ZACHARY—Tal's son

ALEC—rebel spy at Andersen Mining Complex

KEMP—rebel spy at Andersen Mining Complex

ALRICK—Sigmund's servant

EMMA—young lady Stevie befriends in the mine

ELDER JIRO—Third Elder of Caarwyn Rill; twin brother to Shin

FIRST ELDEST TEGAN—First Eldest of Caarwyn Rill

ELDER OWAIN—Fourth Elder of Caarywn Rill

ELDER AFON—Fifth Elder of Caarwyn Rill

ELDER POWELL—Second Elder of Caarwyn Rill

ARI—ancient guardian of the Words of the One to Veres

LUCAS—boy from Caarwyn Rill

GAWAIN, FREEMAN, ROBYN—rebel leaders of Mistal

LLOYD—resident of Mistal; owner of ancient sword

DALLIN, AIKEN—mercenaries from Corylus

GILES—friend of Lady Blossom; half-brother to Brayden

FROM: THE DECEIT OF DARKNESS

ON AMATHEA

JED (JEDIDIAH)—Travis' partner who runs orphanage
BETHIE (ANNABETH)—young orphan girl
MICAH, LOTAN, ARON—older orphan boys
MR. SLOCOM—overseer at Fox Hollow Farm
NOAM—temporary help at Fox Hollow Farm
MARTHA—cook at Fox Hollow Farm
MR. PAHLAVI—owner of Fox Hollow Farm
ISAAC—temporary help at Fox Hollow Farm; friendly, mute, slow
JAKE, JORAH—Mr. Pahlavi's sons
ELI & ABIGAIL ELLK—Travis' brother and sister in law
BROTHER ANTHONY—Cashel monk
FATHER NICO—head of Cashel monks
FATHER EMERITUS XAVIER—oldest of Cashel monks
MERYN—ancient guardian of the Words of the One to Amathea
GRAYSON—leader of a band of Tri-zone residents who offer protection to the Light Bringer
HEINRICH—Sigmund's associate; ancient evil; also known as the Lord Master Mage
MISTRESS BOYLE—owner of The Plowshare Inn

ON GLACIERIA

YAMA—portal warden
MIZU—Official of Khalon tribe; son of Akira
AKIRA—chieftain of Khalon tribe
CALAIS (PRIMAL WARRIOR)—Cleatus' twin brother; demon possessed warrior

ZENTARO—Akira's great nephew
TETSUYA—spiritual leader of the Michi tribe
HARUKI—Tetsuya's son
HANA—Tetsuya's wife
CLEATUS—ancient guardian of the Words of the One to Glacieria; twin to Calais

ON NEMORA

Alton—servant of King Theodor

FROM: THE LIGHT UNBOUND

ON CORYLUS

MILO—Sigmund's new secretary
JEFFREY DANTON—Theodor's chief advisor
CHARLOTTE—a healer at the palace
BISHOP NEWSON—Bishop Hendrick's replacement

ON NEMORA

DUCHESS CAILYN WOODFIELD—Rayne's aunt; Rowena's sister; Brayden's mother
DUKE MILES WOODFIELD—Rayne's uncle; Brayden's father
AQUILA—a demonic hunter
SIMON—tavern owner
KRIZIA—a demonic hunter, associate of Aquila
MARIUS—a possessed hunter, associate of Aquila
MITE—child-like ancient
EMERSON—leader, Camp of the Forgotten
GRETEL—Emerson's wife

BODIE—resident, Camp of the Forgotten
HUGH—resident, Camp of the Forgotten
KIEFER—deaf child, Camp of the Forgotten
FALLON—Kindred, elder
DARCY—Kindred
NEAL—Kindred champion
SLONE—Kindred warrior
ELSPETH—Kindred healer
EAN—Kindred healer
ENYA—Kindred
KEIRA—Kindred
NECI—Kindred, Fallon's wife
NAARAH—ancient guardian

ON GLACIERIA

DAICHI—Khalon warrior; believer
HOSHIKO—female Kahlon warrior; believer

ON SORIAL

CORALEA—widowed believer; Ponce's lady friend
PASTOR ZEB—Pastor to the remnant
TINDRA—ancient guardian

ON ARISIMA

KAYDIN—innkeeper
BEHNAM—religious leader; Shaw's mentor
NAIL—pirate captain
BADR—ancient guardian
TEREV—ancient tree

SEVEN WORLDS OF THE OCHEN SYSTEM

AMATHEA:
Farming world; magic deficit

ARISIMA:
Desert world; magic saturated

CORYLUS:
Royal world; home of Kierkengaard family line; magic saturated

GALCIERIA:
Ice world; magic saturated

NEMORA:
Woodland world; home of Kraftsmunn family line; healing sun, two moons: Rem and Ledia; most magic saturated planet

SORIAL:
Merchant world; two suns: Xanthe and Ortrun; magic deficit

VERES:
Mining world; source of veredium; magic deficit

1

𝔫

My beloved servant who was lost and found will be tested. Though light is shrouded and severed spirit wandering, he will find rest in my truth, and I will be his shelter in the tempest. For the darkness that claims victory is already defeated. I will guide his steps by the least of lights until the three are found and the cup of wrath is full. Then the true heart will be known by the bond I have made and the broken made whole once again.

Disquiet gnawed at Thorvin's nerve endings as he nodded good-bye to Anne and turned to open the heavy wooden door. From the time he was a child, Prince Rayne had been proficient at getting himself into trouble and Thorvin wondered what kind of mess his young charge could have gotten into in the last five minutes.

Despite his churning stomach, the sound of voices coming through the door soothed Thorvin's tension and he expected to find Rayne already enjoying the benefits of a nice warm bath. Something Thorvin himself could use after spending the last few days riding in a dog sled and skipping from Glacieria to Corylus then Nemora. But even his premonition of danger had not prepared Thorvin for the image of Rayne, not leisurely bathing, but crumpled on the cold slate floor of the storage room, still as death.

The hairs on his arms rose and a shiver traced up his spine as phantom words whispered like an evil wind through the room. *Fulfill the vow ... anything ... come out now.*

No! The internal scream barreled through Thorvin's mind, knocking every other thought aside. Rayne was so still, too still, and his skin looked the color of putty. Numb, Thorvin knelt and checked for air movement at Rayne's nose and a pulse at his neck. What he found sent his already churning stomach into a well of despair, no breath and a barely existent pulse.

"Anne." It came out as a breathy whisper. Looking up, Thorvin noticed the three dressers huddled against the far wall. "We need to get Anne!" he shouted. "Now!"

Not getting a response from the men, Thorvin was about to shout again, when a dark-cloaked stranger slammed the door open and pushed him out of the way. "Move you fool. I have the antidote."

Pulling the cork from a vial containing a swirling brown liquid, the stranger poured the contents into Rayne's mouth before Thorvin could even think to protest.

But then the stranger's focus shifted to the ceiling.

Is he praying? Thorvin's eyes traced the man's gaze up to the shadow-drenched ceiling but he saw nothing. Then Rayne's chest moved as he sucked in a breath. He took in several deep breaths and his eyes fluttered open. Whatever the stranger had poured into Rayne's mouth must have taken effect. His eyes still focused on the shadows above, the man grunted something then turned his attention back to Rayne.

Thorvin's stomach rose, the acid climbing. He swallowed hard, forcing it back down. *It's going to be alright. Rayne's going to be alright!*

"Can you see me?" the man asked Rayne.

Thorvin, kneeling behind the stranger waited in silence, praying, while the dressers, still huddled against the far wall, all began to whisper about such terrifying happenings.

After a moment's hesitation, Rayne smiled. "Yes. I see you perfectly."

"How does it feel? Any discomfort?"

"Quite fine. Yes, yes, I feel marvelous." Rayne sat up and

flexed his arms, his eyes focused on the motion as he pulled in his fingers, made a fist and then released. He smiled at the stranger. "Very nice. Well worth the wait."

The two conversed in low whispers for a few minutes while Thorvin looked on without a word, still shaken by the events, until Rayne said, "Help me up."

Thorvin leaned in to help, but confused by the apparent relationship between Rayne and the stranger, watched unsure of what had just happened, as the stranger rose and helped Rayne to his feet.

Once he was standing, Rayne's nose wrinkled, and his mouth turned down at the corners. "By the seven, I stink, don't I? Where are those dressers and that bath? It had better ..." His eyes lit on Thorvin. "Get up man."

The prince turned to examine his reflection in a standing mirror and grimaced as Thorvin climbed to his feet. Flicking his attention to Thorvin's reflection in the mirror, Rayne said, "Yes, well, I'll not be needing your services for now, Lord Kraftsmunn. Go and get yourself cleaned up. I'm sure you, too, need a bath. There must be some servants about to help you. We both stink of sweat and ... what is that other stench? Oh, yes, *dog*. Disgusting. You are dismissed."

"What?" Thorvin's breath huffed out with the word, confusion and alarm battling in him. He took a step back and shook his head. "Rayne? Talk to me boy. What's wrong with you? You like dogs. And ... and ... you're *dismissing* me? You've *never* dismissed anyone."

Flicking his attention to the stranger, Thorvin groaned as his head began to pound. Everything felt wrong. Rayne felt wrong. Thorvin was certain whatever was happening, the stranger was behind it. "I don't trust this man, Sire. You were barely breathing; he appears out of nowhere and everything's fine? By the seven, it's all just a little too convenient. How do we know he wasn't the one behind the attack? Who is he? How did he even know you needed an antidote unless he knew you were poisoned?"

Thorvin's eyes blazed and his hand went to his sword.

Rayne turned back from the mirror and raised his hands in a calming gesture.

"Yes. Yes. You are right to question what happened. Calm yourself, Thorvin, I can explain. This gentleman did not poison me. He is the Lord Master Mage sent by the Interplanetary Council to help the king and queen. He's the reason I'm here now and not a prisoner of some bounty seeker."

Rayne glanced at the Lord Master Mage and inclined his head before turning his attention back to Thorvin. "We met as I was entering the castle and spoke briefly. He explained who he was and what he had done. As we were speaking, I began sipping a drink I had been handed in the hallway, oblivious to its poisonous nature. I don't remember anything else until I found myself lying on the floor with the master mage kneeling over me. I am grateful for his immediate action. If he hadn't realized what was happening and acted so quickly, I would be dead.

"I suppose my words and behavior seem strange to you at the moment. The poison has left me rather fuzzy. But if the Lord Master Mage had not been here, I'd be dead, not jumbled."

Thorvin, still struggling to come to terms with the bizarre circumstances, stood, his fists clenched, trying to make sense of Rayne's explanation. In that moment, the door opened and Brayden sauntered into the room. After giving Thorvin a dismissive look, he walked up to Rayne. "Your Highness. Am I correct in assuming all is well?"

A sly smile spread across Rayne's face, lifting the hair on the back of Thorvin's neck. "*Cousin*, I can see that you are eager to meet our … new friend. I, too, am quite excited to see the Lord Master Mage's vindication."

Rayne stumbled as he stepped away from the mirror and the master mage grabbed his elbow, guiding him unsteadily toward the door.

"Stop right there," Thorvin grunted, stepping in front of Rayne and holding his palms out to stop him. "Wait, just wait a minute. Rayne, what are you talking about? What new friend?" Thorvin turned and paced, grinding the heels of his hands into his temples. "You were just *poisoned!* Yet you act as if nothing happened. This is crazy. You can barely walk. You're

not yourself. You need to sit for a bit to be sure you're alright."
He shook his head and stepped in front of Rayne again. "You react to being poisoned as if it happened every day. You dismiss me like I'm nothing. And now you want to go traipsing off with this Nemorian serpent and a total stranger? No, Sire; I won't allow it!"

"Won't *allow*? *You* won't *allow me*!" Rayne emphasized each word, his voice soft and dangerous. "Lord Kraftsmunn, though you committed yourself to protecting me, and have done an admirable job under the difficult circumstances we faced, things have changed. I'm home now. All is well. Our relationship can no longer be what it was. I am the Crown Prince after all; it's time I began behaving like one.

"And as for traipsing off with my cousin, well, I know what we believed in the past. We thought he was an enemy. We were wrong. The Lord Master Mage explained how Brayden had been coerced against his will from the time he was a child. Sigmund was the driving force behind everything, not just the harm done to me and my parents, but the manipulation and harm done to my cousin.

"Now that Brayden is free of Sigmund's influence, I want to give my cousin a chance to redeem himself and work to build a new relationship with him, the kind we should have enjoyed since we were children. Do you understand?"

"No, Sire." Thorvin shook his head, still standing between Rayne and the door. "Begging your pardon, Your Highness, I don't understand. And I don't think you should go anywhere either. You're talking strange. Maybe this mage saved your life, but I'm not convinced. Things don't add up." Thorvin rubbed his chin, anxiety sharpening his tone. "I've got a bad feeling—a really bad feeling. You need help we can trust. Let me get Anne. We can trust her, and she can help."

"I do not …"

"Careful, my lord," the Master Mage stepped to Rayne's side, his eyes boring into the prince's.

"Yes. Yes, of course." Rayne waved as if in annoyance. Clearing his throat, he turned back to Thorvin. "Lord Kraftsmunn, you will stop this nonsense immediately. This man just saved my life. Now he has requested I accompany him for a short walk to meet with someone who can testify to Brayden's innocence. I'm willing to do that. Giving him a few minutes of my time for such an important task is the least I can do to show my appreciation. Don't you agree? If you must insist on pursuing this matter, we'll continue this discussion later. But for now, go, get yourself a bath, get ready for the party, and stop being so suspicious."

Somewhat mollified, Thorvin huffed a breath out his nose. "I would still like to have Anne check you out before you go anywhere. And we need to find out who poisoned you and why."

"My dear Thorvin." Rayne released an exaggerated sigh. "I'm confident the Lord Master Mage is already on top of the situation. It's only a matter of time before he discovers the culprit who sought to harm me. Rest assured, I am now quite safe." Turning to the cowed dressers, Rayne said, "I will return shortly. I expect my bath to be ready and appropriate clothing choices set out. And now, once again, Lord Kraftsmunn, please excuse me."

Thorvin stood as if frozen, trying to understand the events of the last few minutes as Rayne, Brayden, and the master mage walked out the door. Then, with a shake of his head and a murmured exclamation of frustration, he followed.

When he exited the castle, Rayne, Brayden, and the master mage were already cutting across the wooded area toward the door in the wall he and Rayne had come through earlier. He waited on the landing until they were through, sprinted across the grounds, then slipped through himself.

Once Thorvin was beyond the wall, he scouted for the three. At first, he thought he had lost them. But then, looking to his far right beyond a stand of hemlocks, he caught sight of them crossing a stream and walking into a wooded area. Keeping his distance, he followed them to a small run-down cottage. As Thorvin watched, Brayden entered the cottage, leaving Rayne and the mage outside. After a few minutes, Rayne entered the cottage with the mage following a short while later.

By the seven. What's going on? Thorvin considered sneaking up to the run-down hut. But while he was debating, Giles and Blossom approached, spiking his curiosity even higher. When they followed the others inside, Thorvin moved in for a closer look. He was about to sneak around the back of the shack to see if he could find a window to listen through, but Blossom practically fell out the door and ran from the tiny cottage back toward the castle grounds. *Is she crying?*

Thorvin was even more mystified. *What is that boy up to?* Everything that happened since they arrived at Castle Inverness had been beyond strange and Thorvin struggled to process his conflicting thoughts.

Okay. Think. What just happened? Someone poisoned Rayne. He almost died. That much is clear. But then that Lord Master Mage showed up. Thorvin gritted his teeth. *At just the right moment, with just the right antidote?* Thorvin grunted. *Then Rayne revives as if nothing happened? Rayne and Brayden are friends? No! This is all wrong.*

Thorvin was still mulling the situation in his mind when Rayne, Giles, Brayden, and the mage left the cabin. Their quiet murmurs were punctuated with laughter as they headed up the path toward the castle, following in Blossom's footsteps.

Thorvin considered confronting them but decided to follow instead and see what else would happen. As he moved away from the old cottage, a rather frail-looking, elderly man leaning heavily on a staff, came out.

For a second, Thorvin thought to intercept the old man to see what he could learn from him, ask him what was going on and why Rayne was meeting with him. But as Rayne and the others were disappearing in the direction of the castle and the old man began hobbling away in the opposite direction, Thorvin decided to follow the prince instead. He continued moving toward the castle, shaking his head at a sleeping guard he passed.

Once Rayne returned to the dressers with Brayden, Giles, and the mage, and it looked as though he would be busy there for a while, Thorvin decided to find Anne and Shaw to see if they could shed light on Rayne's strange behavior.

Snagging a page, he asked where he might find Shaw and Anne Radinajan.

"I believe they are with King Theodor and Queen Rowena in the royal suite," the boy said. Thorvin headed to the suite. The castle was a maze of wings, corridors, and rooms, but memory served Thorvin well and he found his way without getting lost.

2

Thorvin broke into a sweat as he traversed the hallways of Castle Inverness. Would Theodor and Rowena even receive him after the way he had left Westvale with Rayne? He hoped the change in his old friends' attitude toward their son extended to him as well. He hadn't needed to worry. Theodor and Rowena greeted him with open warmth and thanked him for watching over Rayne during his recent travels.

It felt good to reunite with Shaw, Anne, and Lexi, and to be welcomed into the company of his old friends, Theodor and Rowena. After his experience with Rayne, Thorvin breathed a sigh of relief to find his friends acting and talking normal.

"So, is Rayne with the dressers now?" Theodor asked.

"Yes," Thorvin said, stretching out the word, hesitant about what to say.

"What?" Theodor asked. "Is there a problem?"

"I'm not sure." Thorvin shook his head, the corners of his lips curling downward. "When we arrived at the castle with the dressers, I left Rayne for a few minutes."

"Yes." Anne smiled. "We spoke briefly outside the room where Rayne was dressing."

"After you left me, I went in. I expected to find Rayne enjoying a bath, or at least getting ready to bathe." Thorvin pushed up on his feet and began pacing as he relived the moments after entering the dressing room. "When I walked in …" He paused, caught up again in the memory. "When I walked in, Rayne was lying unconscious on the floor."

A weight of silence fell across the room, then Theodor jumped to his feet, alert and primed as though ready to fight an unseen foe.

"When I close my eyes, I can still see it." Thorvin met Theodor's eyes. "Rayne, just lying there. Crumpled on the floor. So still—too still." Thorvin began pacing again, his steps rushed and agitated, as he recounted what had occurred in the storage room.

"I felt as if I had stepped into someone's nightmare. Well, with my gut squawking loud and clear, when Rayne, Brayden, and the Lord Master Mage headed out to meet this witness they said could clear Brayden's name, I followed."

As Thorvin finished recounting the details of what had transpired at the cottage, he groaned and lowered his face into his hands. Pulling in another gulp of air, he raised his eyes to Theodor's

"Now I don't know what you might think, but the Rayne I know would never treat anyone like he treated me. It's not in him. And the Rayne I know is not the type of person to enjoy the company of someone like Brayden." Thorvin snorted through his nose. "Wouldn't happen."

Thorvin turned to the queen. "Rowena, do you think you could do that questing thing and make sure Rayne isn't being controlled or something?" Thorvin was past thinking about proper addresses. At this point, Rowena was just Rayne's mother and Thorvin's old friend.

"Other than the strange behavior you spoke of, Thor, did you notice anything wrong with him after he recovered?" Rowena asked. "You say you think he was poisoned. If that was the case, there should have been some physical after effects."

"I don't know, maybe it wasn't poison. Maybe it was some

kind of magic. But that master mage said he had the antidote. Doesn't that mean poison?"

"Not necessarily. But whatever it was, after Rayne came to, he seemed physically fine?" Rowena asked, looking at Anne.

"Yes. A little unstable on his feet at first, but other than that, fine."

"Anne, would you please accompany me to the dressing room. Thor's story is very disturbing; I want to personally check to make sure Rayne is alright."

"Of course, Your Majesty."

"The two of you are not going alone," Theodor said in a voice like veridium. "If Sigmund is behind this, I won't have you facing him unaided. I'm going with you and we'll bring a contingent of soldiers. Besides if something has happened to Rayne, if my child has yet again been harmed, I want to know."

"You're not going without me." Lexi shot up and walked toward the door, chin jutting out at a stubborn angle.

"Or without me," Shaw added.

A few minutes later, the group crossed the lawn to the kitchen entrance, climbed the heavy granite steps up to the entry, and proceeded down the hallway toward the small storage room that was doubling as Rayne's dressing room.

Theodor's eyebrows descended into a frown. "Why would Cailyn and Miles assign Rayne a room down here? He should have been given the suite next to ours, not be isolated in the servant's wing near the kitchen."

Thorvin nodded as they approached a pair of guards. "That's what I thought. But something's changed. There were no guards here before."

"Soldier, how long have you been here?" Theodor asked the older of the two men stationed at either side of the door.

Bowing, the guard said, "We were summoned by the Lord Master Mage to watch this door about a half an hour ago, Your Majesty. He said there was a threat against the prince's life and we were to keep everyone out."

"I'm quite sure that order does not pertain to us." Theodor bristled, eyeing the guards with mistrust. "Announce us."

"No, wait," Rowena said, a look of concentration creasing a line between her eyes. "Thorvin's right, something's wrong. My sense tendrils aren't picking up Rayne. In fact, they can't even penetrate that room. It's as if something is blocking me. Be careful Theodor. I can't identify it, but the energy here is heavy with power."

"Yes, my love," Theodor said.

Theodor met Thorvin's eyes then Rowena's and they nodded, as if reading each other's thoughts.

Turning his focus to the guards who had accompanied them, Theodor said, "Wait out here, but stay alert and be ready." He turned back to the men stationed at the door. "Now, announce us."

The guard gave a quick rap, and called in a loud voice, "Open in the name of King Theodor and Queen Rowena."

A moment later, a very subdued Alton opened the door a crack. His eyes grew large when he saw Theodor and Rowena and opening the door wide, he bowed. Leaving the dozen guards who had accompanied them in the hallway, Theodor strode in followed by Rowena, Thorvin, Anne, Shaw, and Lexi.

Brayden sat in one corner of the room in a straight-backed chair while Giles lounged on a short couch with the council's mage. The two looked up from a small game board set on the couch between them. Rayne, with his back to the door as he surveyed his reflection in a large mirror, was surrounded by three dressers who were straightening folds and fluffing ruffles.

Thorvin noticed with a grimace that Rayne was dressed in fancy, white, knee length knickers, a white shirt with lacy flounces billowing over his hands. Over the shirt he wore a buttoned, embroidered vest of a shiny silver material with a matching thigh length jacket of the same material. He wore silver buckle shoes over white stockings. His black hair had been pulled into a short tail high on the back of his head and tied with a matching silver ribbon.

Thorvin swallowed a heavy lump of fear. *Rayne would never wear something so ridiculous.*

3

A sly smile spread across the prince's face as he turned and snared Rowena's eyes. In that instant, Rowena understood. Though she had heard Thorvin's words and felt the heavy magic lingering in the hallway, she had walked into the room expecting to find Rayne, troubled and maybe confused, but still the sweet boy she knew. Taken off guard by the awful truth now facing her in the guise of her son, she hesitated for a fraction of a second before pulling the magic-laden energy of Nemora into herself in an extremity of fear and need. But her moment of hesitation came at a steep cost. Heart pounding, she watched her son smile while the powerful being within him attacked, sending a massive energy spike into her chest. Staggering, Rowena grabbed at Theodor's jacket, unable to draw breath, her legs giving out at the force of the spike.

"No," she gasped, groaning. She collapsed to the floor, staring up at Rayne as she fell.

Everyone froze as the scene unfolded in slow motion to the queen's gaze. Theodor fell to his knees next to her, crying out, "Rowena, Rowena! Talk to me! What's wrong?"

But though the queen was aware of her husband's cry, she

was unable to respond. She stared out of glassy eyes, powerless to move or speak, trapped inside her head with the truth of what she had just seen. Never before had she felt such a need to speak, to move; and yet, never before had she been so helpless.

Aware of the dark, gloating presence invading her mind, Rowena struggled to regain control of her body. Sigmund's distinctive brand of darkness now permeated her being. The spike was impossibly strong, too strong to resist. It was Sigmund's evil she sensed within Rayne's body, not the beloved sweet savor she had longed to touch again. Sigmund's abhorrent spirit coiled within Rayne, rolling off her son's body in waves of darkness only Rowena could see.

Where's Rayne? Her spirit screamed at the demonic presence. *What have you done with my son?*

At first, the image of Rayne just smirked at her. A quick wink, then he fell to his knees next to Theodor, an expression of profound grief twisting his features. He cried out in an anguished voice, "Mother? Mother? What's wrong?" He shifted to scan those standing frozen around him. "Somebody? Somebody do something. Please, somebody help her."

Feeling no trace of her son's spirit, Rowena collapsed into herself. Grieving in unbelieving horror, she did the only thing she could do to protect her spirit from the demon now tunneling into her mind. Rowena retreated into her innermost self, throwing up walls of protection and praying to the One for her son and herself.

As Theodor fell to his knees next to Rowena, muttering unintelligible words, Anne watched, a rising sense of alarm sparking warning signals through her. She never imagined she would see the strong ruler so overcome. She lost herself in shock. But with an internal snarl breaking the spell that held her frozen, Anne dropped to the floor next to the king, her training kicking in. Shaw stepped in behind her, resting his hands on her shoulders, supporting her.

C. S. WACHTER

Though Rowena's pulse was strong, she was unresponsive, staring into space, her eyes empty. Theodor's pleas for her to say something produced no discernable response. Noting the queen's condition, Anne's first reaction was to send in a sense tendril, but she recoiled instantly when she was confronted by an alien presence of immense power.

She looked over at Rayne, kneeling beside his father, his expression twisted with sorrow. But despite the appearance of grief, Anne sucked in a breath. Thorvin was right. Rayne wasn't himself; something in his expression seemed fixed and false.

But Rayne would have to wait. It was Rowena who needed her help right now. *What do I do? This is really bad. I've never seen its like.*

Even with Anne's years of experience, Rowena's condition was beyond her. Then a memory surfaced. She and Rayne had faced something similar when they healed Lexi's father. *Yes. This is what Duke Erland was like. The power here is stronger, darker, and yet, the same.*

"Rayne," she said. He didn't respond. "Rayne!" she called again, louder.

He looked up at her. The eyes that a moment ago had been filled with grief, were now cold and hard. "Why address me so informally, healer? Am I not highness to you?"

Anne's mouth dropped into a circle of disbelief. Her thoughts collided with the reality facing her. *Rayne? No! He's definitely not himself! Later ... I'll deal with him later.* Swallowing the exploding fear that threatened to undo her, Anne said, "Your Highness, please, I need your help. I think your mother has fallen prey to a spike, like the one Sigmund placed in Lexi's father. Remember what we did for Duke Erland? We can do the same thing here. You send a sense tendril into her and I'll follow with my healing sense. But beware, there is something there, another presence."

Rayne stared at Anne for a moment, his face an emotionless mask, before he rose and walked away. "I can't do that. You can't ask me to do that now. I'm still weak from the poison. There must be someone else who can help you."

Theodor looked up to Rayne, tears forming watery pools

in his eyes. "Please, Son, this is your mother. You have to help her."

Rayne's eyes swiveled to Theodor and, for only the briefest instant, Anne saw something that chilled her to the bone. An unmistakable look of cold disdain flitted across Rayne's features. Then it was gone, concern again reflected in those familiar jewel-like orbs as Rayne knelt beside Theodor. "Father, I'm so sorry. I want to help; I really do. If I were stronger now, I would help her in a heartbeat. You understand, don't you. Please forgive me."

Anne sucked in a breath as something sparked in Rayne. His demeanor changed as a sliver of anger surfaced and his eyes glinted like cold stones.

"Perhaps my weakness is for the best." Rayne pushed up to stand over his father. "It does seem fitting that, given your lack of trust in me these last few months, *Father*, I should be unable to help Mother now. After all, you mistrusted me; even accused me of stealing from you. What makes you think you can trust me now?

"Perhaps when I'm stronger and I've once again gained your confidence we can attempt this thing the healer suggests. For now, Father, you should call your guards. I think it best you and Mother return to Westvale immediately. There she can receive the care she will need."

Anne stared at Rayne, a mix of shock and dismay curdling in her stomach.

Rayne's face darkened as he caught Anne's gaze. "Would *you* judge *me*? What about my feelings? Perhaps facing death yet again has left me feeling somewhat less than gracious. Please, go back to Westvale. Take the queen with you. I've a feeling she will be needing bed rest for quite some time."

His eyes drew to narrow slits as he focused on Theodor. "Oh, and Father, when I return to Westvale we will discuss my status as Royal Heir. I am certain you will want to care for Mother personally, therefore, a reorganization of power will be in order. I'm sure you understand."

Lexi's heart thudded to a panicked rhythm in her chest, but there was no feeling. It was numb, detached, as if some inhuman hand had just reached in and cut off all circulation to the organ. Where moments earlier, joy had filled her in anticipation of seeing Rayne again, now dread flooded her soul. She had watched in disbelief as Rowena collapsed, Theodor following in her wake. Then Rayne's voice was speaking, but the words were incomprehensible. The Rayne she knew, the heart of her heart, would never treat his parents in this callous manner. She trembled as a chill washed over her.

"Rayne?" she murmured. She was drowning in a sea of confusion and wasn't even sure herself if she was asking a question or trying to decide if the man in front of her was Rayne or someone else.

Turning to her, Rayne smiled. Her heart melted at the familiar expression. "Ah, yes, the lovely Lady Alexianndra of Veres. How marvelous. Please, my dear, stay for my party. I have an inordinate desire to show you off this evening. You're ... quite lovely."

"Rayne?" Lexi questioned again, struggling to breath around the burning lump in her chest. "What's wrong with you? Why are you talking like this?"

Drawing himself up, Rayne scanned those around him then spoke. His voice quiet but intense. "You think this isn't me?" His eyes flicked back to Lexi. "You think I've changed? But you're wrong. You're all wrong." He started pacing. "What did you think? That I would survive all I've gone through, suffer all I've suffered, have no life of my own and just go on being a good little servant, obeying without question, without anger?

"Well, let me enlighten you. I've learned things and I've changed. This is the new me now! The Rayne who thinks about what he wants. The prince who has great plans for Ochen." He rounded on his friends, taking time to meet each one's eyes. "Don't look at me as if I just crawled out from under a rock.

For once, show *me* some grace and patience. Don't you think I deserve some?"

Then, turning back to his reflection and straightening a fold in his lacy jabot, Rayne smiled at Brayden. "Tonight's entertainment should prove to be most diverting, Cousin. I am anxiously awaiting Jason's promised birthday surprise. And, of course, I'm quite excited about your gift."

Brayden glanced once at Theodor and Rowena, but then with his trademark, wolfish smirk answered, "Oh yes, *Cousin*. Jason took care to follow your instructions regarding the amusements for this evening. Everything is in place just as you requested. And, I've gotten word that the Interplanetary Council members have all arrived. Unfortunately, only six of the nine judges from the Interplanetary Court have come. You might want to discuss the situation with those who scorned your invitation."

Thorvin rose and after sending a searing glare at Rayne's back, went to the door and waved in several guards to carry Queen Rowena back to their suite. Theodor followed, stumbling like one caught in a dream. After a quick glance at Rayne, Anne averted her gaze and strode out the door behind Thorvin without a word.

Shaw turned to Rayne. "Will you be returning to Westvale tomorrow? Jonathan, Anne, and I are studying the scrolls, Your Highness. May I assume you will be joining us?"

For a moment, Rayne stared at Shaw's reflection in the mirror. "Not at this time. Though, I will want to examine the … originals … soon."

Shaking his head, Shaw also left the room.

Lexi still stood, unmoving, watching silently as Rayne continued to converse with Brayden about their plans for the evening while ignoring her.

"Jason assures me he has brought some superb fighters with him for tonight's entertainment." Brayden rubbed his hands together. "Two are favorites of several of the councilmen and the third is a newcomer with potential. He's survived his first two fights quite nicely. And, of course, Jason has procured several females. He promised to offer you first pick since it's your birthday."

"Who are you?" Lexi asked, as pain shredded her resolve and tears threatened to flow. "I don't even know you."

Rayne rolled his eyes at Brayden and sighed. "I have no choice, Brayden, I must tell her the truth." Gazing at Lexi through the mirror, Rayne said, "I'm sorry if I've hurt you, Lexi. Truly I am. I can't tell anyone else about this yet, but … well … I can't keep any secrets from you." He turned from the mirror, walked up to Lexi, and reached out to put an arm around her shoulders. She took a step back, a shiver running up her spine as she avoided the gesture.

Rayne dropped his arm but stepped in close, too close. Lexi could feel his warm breath on her cheek as he spoke in a confidential whisper. "I'm going to tell you something important. But I must ask that you keep this between us. Please discuss this with no one." He licked his lips, and again a shiver ran through Lexi. "The Lord Master Mage has asked for my help to uncover corruption in the Interplanetary Council. Although he assures me Sigmund is gone, he believes that another like him is controlling certain key figures. That is why we have invited the council members to the party and why I am behaving in this despicable manner. Though it is breaking my heart, I can't help my mother until I've tricked the traitor into revealing himself. Trust me, Lexi, please. I promise I'll prove myself to you once I've discovered Sigmund's colleague. Will you trust me? Of all people, it is your trust I desire the most."

He stepped back, giving her space, holding out his arms in an invitation, smiling.

After a moment's hesitation, Lexi stepped into the embrace. Though her heart didn't thud with its normal response to Rayne's touch, Rayne's familiar warm arms were a balm to her warring emotions. Looking up into his gem-like eyes she said, "I will trust you. But I will not stay for this sham of a party tonight. Do what you need to do. Then, please come back to me with no more deception."

"Always, my love, always." Rayne kissed her. At first, she stiffened, her mind revolting against something she couldn't identify. Ignoring the internal alarm, she gave herself over to the pleasure of Rayne's lips questing against her own.

After a moment, he pulled back. "You'd better go, my love. Otherwise, I might end up missing my own party." He winked at her and a shy smile worked its way across her face. *It's going to be okay. Rayne's just playing a role and soon it will be over.* "I'll see you back on Corylus."

After Lexi left, the pretender prince turned to Brayden and Heinrich and chuckled. "Well, that was more fun than I thought it would be. Did you see the way she looked at me? I think she loves me. That was almost as amusing as our time with the prince." He turned his attention to Giles. "Before I forget, you had better set a perimeter of guards around that cottage. We wouldn't want to lose our prize, would we?"

4

Lexi drifted in a cocoon of silence as did Anne, Shaw, and Thorvin as they entered the skipping portal for Corylus later that evening. Theodor and Rowena had already made their way onto Corylus, carried through the large shipping portal in a small coach pulled by four matched bay horses and escorted by the contingent of palace guards who had accompanied them from Westvale.

"I can't understand how Rayne could say the things he said, especially to his parents. I know what they did hurt him, but it's not like him to be cruel." Anne's brow scrunched, and her steps seemed weighted as they slowly walked the short distance from the Corylus Portal Station to the Great Square before the Westvale Palace. "I understand that he's angry, but he didn't even try to help Rowena or seem happy to see any of us. Not even Lexi." She shook her head. "And he's never treated me like a servant before."

"Well, a lot did happen on Glacieria," Thorvin grumbled.

Though Lexi had remained silent, her need to defend Rayne drew out a quiet response as they reached the square. "Maybe he has a reason for acting the way he is, and we just don't know it. We shouldn't jump to conclusions and judge him without knowing all the facts. He's right, you know; it's time we showed him a little grace. He's been pushed and pulled so much for so long. Anyone would start to respond to the stress. We need to give him a little time, that's all."

They stopped in the middle of the Great Square, as if unwilling to part. Lexi stared with unseeing eyes at the milling crowd bustling around them. The sun, a bright shiny ball in a perfect blue sky above, reminded Lexi of days on the farm at the orphanage. She bit her lip, wondering if she should tell the others what Rayne told her. She sighed. He asked that she speak to no one. So, at least for now, Lexi said nothing. But if Rayne wasn't acting like himself when he returned to Westvale, she would tell their friends everything she knew, though it wasn't a lot.

"I'm going to the barracks to get some rest," Thorvin mumbled. "We should get together soon and discuss what happened. Shaw, would Bishop Hedrick allow us to meet at the church house like we did before?"

"Once I explain the situation," Shaw said, "I'm sure he'll want to join us. We should also spread the word to Rayne's other friends and have them come as well."

"Don't you think we might be over-reacting?" Lexi asked.

"Absolutely not!" Anne's voice rose with unusual vehemence. "If something's wrong with Rayne, and I believe that's the case, we need to know. The more people putting their heads together, thinking about the problem, the better."

Shaw and Thorvin nodded, but Lexi said, "We should wait until Rayne returns to see if he's still not acting like himself before we start calling meetings."

"I think Anne's right," Shaw said. "If Rayne returns to Westvale and he's back to his normal self, we'll just laugh at ourselves for jumping to conclusions. But if there is something wrong with him, the sooner we address it, the better it will be for everyone."

Agreeing to meet soon, they parted company.

ᴖ

Something in Theodor had broken when Rowena collapsed. Thorvin had seen it. And now he watched, tension tying his stomach in knots, as his old friend struggled to find balance between his duties as king and his concern for his beloved wife. It was like the king was walking a slippery tightrope and with every step, he seemed to find it harder to cope. Holding audiences, his mind would drift. After the first day, Thorvin agreed to stay by Theodor's side, allegedly as his bodyguard. In fact, he was there to help keep the king focused and functioning.

A few days later, Theodor asked Thorvin to take a more active role, and, within hours, Thorvin found himself sitting alongside the king as his new counselor and spokesperson. If Danton, Theodor's chief advisor, had any qualms about the appointment, he kept them to himself. But, from time to time, Thorvin would catch a grimace of disgust on the man's face. Over the next week, the fog that surrounded Theodor grew thicker, his attention repeatedly diverted from his duties as king to concern over Rowena's unchanging condition.

Thorvin took on more duties, attending meetings with Captain Fontaine and Captain Ellis, representatives of the army, Danton, and Theodor's other counselors, as well as anyone else he needed to meet with to cover for Theodor's diminishing mental and physical state.

Though experts came and went from the palace, there was no change in Rowena's condition. Anne and the other healers took turns sitting with her. When Thorvin convinced the king to carry on with his duties, he would comply for a few minutes, but then dismiss those around him and wander back up to the Queen's Chambers.

This morning, almost two weeks after their return from Nemora, Theodor hadn't shown up to hear a report from one of his informants. Thorvin sat with Danton in the small conference room, representing the absent monarch yet again. After working closely with Danton, Thorvin had come to appreciate the man's wisdom and honesty. He confided in the advisor, even to the point of confessing his concern for Rayne. With fuller understanding of the situation, Danton expressed his willingness to help Thorvin in any way he could.

"Please do not hesitate to speak plainly before Lord Kraftsmunn," Danton said as the informant moved in front of the raised dais, eyeing Thorvin and Danton, seated on either side of the empty throne. "He has King Theodor's utmost confidence."

Thorvin grumbled under his breath, *Theodor, where are you? Your people need to report to you, not someone they don't know and don't trust.*

Squinting at Thorvin, suspicion evident in her manner, the tall, large-boned woman from Arisima released a huff of exasperation. "If you vouch for him, Counselor Danton, I guess that'll do."

Clearing her throat, she lowered the hood that had kept her angular face in shadow, exposing iron gray hair in a multitude of braids framing her face. "The last time I was here I updated His Majesty about a developing cult that we've been watching closely. I'm sure you remember our concern over how much its grown the last couple years. Well, things have gotten worse. It continues to attract more members and it's gotten even more active. They call themselves the Vagrants of the Scroll and preach that Arisima's source of power is some ancient scroll. They attack the tenets of the monks who worship the One, saying he's nothing but a myth.

"Until recently, we'd see one, maybe two at a time, hanging around in the cities. They kept to themselves. They're easy to spot, wear robes like the native monks but of a muddy, dark red color. They also always stink because, apparently, bathing is frowned upon.

"Anyway, in the last six months, they've become dangerous. They're banding together now, traveling in large companies. They take what they want and if anyone stands up to them, they are badly beaten or killed. At least one of these bands has moved from small attacks on individuals to full-scale attacks on our religious communities. Several monasteries have been assaulted and the residents killed. The pirates—filthy opportunists—are taking advantage of the increased violence. Kidnappings and disappearances are on the rise and so is the slave trade.

"The king has worked with us these last few years, sending more soldiers to rein in the pirates and put an end to their attacks and their slave trade. Things were improving, until now. I came to meet with King Theodor because we need help. Our local militia and the troops the king already sent are doing their best to quell the rising violence, but they're stretched thin. Well ..." She released a weighty sigh. "That's it."

Lexi sat at her dressing table, her mind drifting as she ran a comb through her hair. Almost two weeks had passed since Rayne's birthday, and he still hadn't returned from Nemora. The situation seemed to be held in a kind of suspension with everyone holding their collective breath, waiting to see what he would do when he arrived. *It's all so hard. I need to cry and yet ...* A curious numbness claimed her spirit and she clung desperately to the last words Rayne had spoken before they parted.

Lexi released an anguished sigh; she had promised Anne she would stop in and sit with her at Rowena's bedside today and she endeavored to prepare herself for the draining task. Rowena's disorder reminded Lexi too much of her father's condition after Sigmund spiked him. She wrestled with a growing conviction that the same thing had been done to Rowena. Yet, she couldn't accept the awful suspicion that hovered, unmoving, from the edge of her mind. The only people in the room when Rowena walked in were Rayne, Brayden, the Lord Master Mage, and Theodor's dressers. Common sense dictated she dismiss the dressers, and the Lord Master Mage had come as a representative from the Interplanetary Council. Even though he had the ability to place a spike, why would he? That left Brayden and Rayne. And if Brayden was unable to harness the energy needed to produce magic, as the mage had testified, the only person who could have spiked Rowena was Rayne. That relentless conclusion was ravaging her spirit and turning her nights into an ongoing battle between lying awake tossing, and nightmares.

Lexi sat frozen, staring at her reflection. *Get up! Move!* But she lacked the energy; every action seemed to drain her already depleted reserves even further. Finally, knowing Anne was waiting, she forced herself to rise, dress, and walk down the hallway to the Queen's Chambers, which had now become Rowena's sick room.

Since the day Theodor and Rowena married, they shared his larger suite, so the queen's quarters had remained empty. Until now. Seeing Rowena lying on the over-sized bed, a slight, still form that looked almost child-like, sent a wave of foreboding through Lexi.

As Lexi walked up to her, Anne reached out a hand to take Lexi's and asked, "How are you doing?"

"I'm not sure." Lexi chewed her lower lip then allowed a grimace to surface, distorting her features. "I still don't know what to think." She pulled over a chair to sit next to Anne. "Did that all really happen on Nemora, or am I trapped in some on-going nightmare?"

"I'm glad you came," Anne said. "We need to talk, if you feel up to it."

Lexi sighed. "No, I don't feel up to it. But you're right, we need to talk. Maybe talking will help me see things more clearly."

"Good." Anne's quiet yet strong presence grounded Lexi. "We were all there; we all saw Rayne—how he talked, what he said, and how he acted. Though he didn't behave like we expected, it was Rayne in that room. We can agree on that, right?"

"Oh, Anne." Lexi moaned. "I know that. It was real. But something felt *wrong* about him. I mean, he was Rayne, but he didn't *feel* like Rayne. But that doesn't make any sense. I can't explain what I don't understand myself."

Lexi considered the implications of the One's words; that she would know the truth of Rayne's heart. Though her arms had welcomed his embrace back on Nemora, he had felt cold, alien. But she wasn't ready to share this with Anne, choosing instead to cling to Rayne's words of explanation. That he was playing a part and would soon return to Westvale, once again the man she had come to love. But, with a groan, Lexi admitted to herself that she no longer had the strength to carry the burden of his words alone.

"After you left the room, Anne, he confided in me. He asked me to keep what he said to myself. But ... I need to talk to someone." Lexi swiped at the tears now trickling down her cheeks as she faced Anne. "Rayne told me he was *pretending.* That's why he was acting so strange. He's working with the Lord Master Mage. Someone is trying to take control of the Interplanetary Council and Rayne's helping to find out who. He said I need to trust him and everything will be okay when he comes back to Westvale.

"But, Anne, I just can't let go of the impression that Rayne did something to Rowena. Why would he do that? He wouldn't do that to his mother. As I know him, I know he wouldn't. Oh, Anne, I'm so confused. I don't know what to believe."

Lexi broke down. Anne rose and gently wrapped her arms around the sobbing girl. "Shhhh, I know," Anne soothed. "I know."

After a few minutes, Lexi calmed, and Anne said, "I understand why you're so confused. If Rayne is helping the master mage, that could explain his behavior. And yet, if something else is going on he may need our help to fight it. One thing I know for sure, Rayne was not behaving like the young man we know and love, no matter what he says. Unfortunately, the person most qualified to deal with this if magic is involved, is the person lying on the bed in front of us right now, incapable of doing anything.

"I'm loath to admit it, but as a healer I'm at a loss; I don't know what to do. Shaw says he suspects something, but he wants to talk it over with Bishop Hedrick before he talks to me about it. In the meantime, are you willing to set the problem of what to do about Rayne aside long enough to help me care for Rowena? I think she's suffering from the same malady your father suffered from before Rayne and I helped him. Without Rayne's strength, I can't duplicate what we did on Veres. I asked for help from the Lord Master Mage, but he hasn't responded. In the meantime, I need to know how you cared for your father, so we can do the same for Rowena. Will you help me?"

Shifting her focus to Rowena, Lexi swallowed her fear. The queen's condition was too much like her father's after Sigmund placed the spike within him. Lexi didn't want to help, didn't want the reminder of what she and her father had suffered. She just wanted to go home and be left alone to nurse her own pain. But her heart was touched by Rowena's condition and she couldn't leave her like that.

"I'll help you," she said in a hesitant whisper.

5

Two days after Lexi had spoken to Anne an official messenger arrived from the Interplanetary Council. Thorvin and Danton received the man in the name of the king.

"You mean to tell us that *His Royal Highness* actually petitioned the Interplanetary Council to assign Lord Woodfield as regent? In place of his father?" Thorvin swallowed his outrage as he glanced at Danton whose face had gone pale.

"That is what I said," the man replied, his back as stiff as a board. "Crown Prince Rayne and Lord Woodfield of Nemora petitioned the Interplanetary Council to assign a regent for Corylus. His Royal Highness claimed King Theodor has been incapacitated ever since an inexplicable malady struck down Her Majesty while they were visiting family on Nemora.

"Lord Woodfield, as he had formerly been proposed as Adopted Heir Apparent, was the logical choice. Once His Majesty recovers or the prince reaches his eighteenth birthday the position will be terminated. The council was quite impressed by the wisdom of the two young men seeking their guidance.

"I was sent to inform you that both will return to Corylus after a brief stop on Sorial."

After hearing the news, Thorvin sent word to the core group of friends to gather and discuss the situation at sunset in the dining room of the church house.

By the time the first stars were brightening in a velvety, dark blue sky, Captain Fontaine, Andrew, Travis, Shaw, Anne, Noah and Sashi, Stevie, and their parents, Kori and Mace, had joined Thorvin, Lexi, Bishop Hedrick, and Elsie around the large tables in the dining room where they had met with Rayne months before. Having come to appreciate Counselor Danton's wisdom and care for the royal family, Thorvin also invited him to the meeting.

As Thorvin rose from his seat and cleared his throat, Captain Fontaine pushed to his feet and said, "Excuse me, Thorvin. Before you begin, I have some disturbing news to share." He paused, coughed into his hand, and shuffled his feet. "Early this morning, two fishermen found the body of Lady Blossom of Derren on the beach near the cliffs. The evidence points to her having been attacked by a wild animal. Although it appears that she had attempted to defend herself … she …" he shook his head.

Sorrow etching lines on his rough features, Travis asked, "Are you sure it was Lady Blossom?"

"I am sorry, but yes," Captain Fontaine said. "This afternoon, after your Reclamation Committee had dispersed, I asked Deven, one of the delegates from Arisima, if he would identify the body; he confirmed that the victim was, indeed, Lady Blossom. I know Lady Blossom will be missed. She should never have been out on that beach by herself after sunset."

"How do you know she was by herself?" Thorvin asked, remembering the look on Blossom's face when she ran from the cottage on Nemora.

"When we investigated the area, we found no other footprints except Lady Blossom's, ours, and the two fishermen's, but there were large animal tracks all around her body. They were like no tracks I had seen before, so I'm hoping it doesn't rain while I wait for a local hunter to return home. I'm trusting that with his experience, he will be able to identify them."

Still, something about Blossom dying at this time wouldn't settle for Thorvin. He suspected there might be more to the story, but he didn't know what. Leaving his misgivings behind, Thorvin started the meeting.

"Thank you all for coming and for being discreet. I called you here because you are close friends of Prince Rayne's and I can trust you."

Indicating Danton and Lexi, he continued. "We have two new acquaintances here tonight. You're probably all familiar with Counselor Danton. He's a friend of the royal family and has a sharp mind. And this is Lady Alexianndra. We met her on Veres and she has become very special to all of us, especially Prince Rayne." Thorvin pulled in a deep breath and let it out with a huff.

"By now I'm sure you've heard the reports coming from Nemora. That Brayden Woodfield has been named regent at Rayne's request." He shook his head and ground his teeth. "This is a disturbing turn of events. Especially on the heels of what happened on Nemora."

Thorvin paused again and drummed his fingers against his thighs. Letting out a sharp breath through clenched teeth, he said, "Something happened to Rayne at Castle Inverness. I know it and you know it. He was fine when we skipped in from Glacieria, but the prince we left on Nemora that evening wasn't the same prince I had arrived with only a short while earlier. What it all means, I don't know. But whatever's happening, this whole regent business is part of it.

"We need to figure out what happened and what we can do about it. Right now. Once Brayden and Rayne return, we could be charged with treason for openly discussing His Royal Highness' bizarre behavior.

"Over the last few days, I've met with Shaw and Jonathan to discuss the situation. Jonathan has a theory."

Nodding to Bishop Hedrick, Thorvin sat down. Rising, Jonathan looked around the tables, his blue eyes peeking over his glasses, and cleared his throat. "What I am about to say may anger or disturb some of you. At this point it is nothing more than a theory. But after discussing the alteration in

Rayne's personality with Thorvin, Shaw, and Anne, who know the prince well and witnessed the change, I believe my theory has validity.

"As many of you already know, Shaw, Anne, Prince Rayne, and I had come to the conclusion that Sigmund is, in fact, a demon who has possessed a human body. The question I must ask is, what if this demon, or one like him, decided to leave the body he's possessed in favor of taking the body of our prince?

"Think about it. Possessing the Crown Prince would be a very shrewd political move. What better way could there be for a demon to gain access to great power, not only here on Corylus but throughout all Ochen, than to render the king and queen ineffective and take over the prince's body?"

Bishop Hedrick waited as several people spoke out at once. After they quieted, as he was about to continue, Lexi spoke up. "No. You're wrong." She turned to Anne. "I'm sorry, I can't be a part of this."

Lexi chewed her lower lip as she debated what to say. She took a deep breath, closed her eyes, and decided. Opening her eyes, she scanned the faces around her. "On Nemora, after Anne, Shaw, and Thorvin left with the king and queen, Rayne spoke to me. He told me there is a reason why he is behaving as he is. I won't tell you the details because he asked me to keep what he said confidential. He asked me to trust him, and I do."

She dropped her eyes to her twining fingers before looking up again. "When I spoke to Anne earlier, I agreed with her. Rayne's behavior was different. But now, after thinking it over, I've decided I was wrong to agree."

"Lexi," Thorvin said, his voice softer than normal. "Whatever he said after we left doesn't change the fact that he wasn't himself after he was poisoned; he didn't act like himself, and he didn't talk like himself. Even you admitted he felt wrong. We need to face the facts. His current behavior is the opposite of normal. And, if he's not himself, who is he?"

"But what if Lexi's right and you're wrong?" Sashi said

tapping a finger on the table. "I mean, you only talked with him briefly. Maybe something was affecting him just then, like this thing he told Lexi about, and now he's back to his normal self. Aren't we jumping to conclusions with all this talk of demons and possession and stuff? Nemora's moons, shouldn't we give him the benefit of the doubt?"

"You make a good point, Sashi," Anne said. "But we also have to consider what happened to Queen Rowena. The minute she came into Rayne's presence, she was struck down. What happened to her?"

"It's a spike." Lexi's words came unbidden, soft and painful. "I recognize the effects. A horrible use of magic energy. It's what Sigmund did to my father. He lived like that, trapped, unable to do anything for himself, for years. Until Rayne and Anne destroyed the spike and healed him. Now, without Rayne's help, Queen Rowena remains trapped in her mind just like my father.

"But Sigmund wasn't in that room in Inverness, was he?" Lexi continued, her mind rebelling against the words pouring from her mouth. "Rayne was. And you're right, Thorvin, if Rayne was able, nothing could have stopped him from helping his mother." Lexi pulled in a faltering breath. "But I have to believe he chose to not help her then with good reason. When he returns to Westvale, he will explain everything and do what he can for his mother. Until then, I'm going to trust him. So, once again, I can't be part of this group. If you will excuse me, I'm going back to the palace."

ᚾ

After Lexi rose and made her way from the room, Thorvin said, "How do the rest of you feel? Should we continue, or would you all rather we wait until after Rayne returns?"

"I don't know about anyone else," Kori said. "But I'd like to hear the rest of what you have to say. If you're right about this whole thing, it's best we know what we're dealing with. But if Prince Rayne returns and is his old self, we can forget this meeting ever happened."

"Well said." Bishop Hendrick nodded his agreement. "Why don't you resume your story, Thorvin."

Taking a deep breath, Thorvin set aside the doubts brought on by Lexi's words and continued. "The strange behavior we saw at Castle Inverness must be connected to Rayne supporting Brayden's bid for regent. Lexi may be confused, but she was right about one thing, Rayne would never harm his mother. And he would never petition the Interplanetary Council to have his father set aside in favor of Brayden. He just wouldn't do those things.

"Regardless of what he told Lexi, I'm convinced the person who did these things is not the Prince Rayne we know. He's a pretender who now has immense power and is capable of doing terrible things, including harming Her Majesty without hesitation. We need to figure out a way to stop this pretender and get our true prince back."

"There's another thing we must also consider," Bishop Hedrick said. "*If* my theory is correct, Rayne's spirit would be trapped in that body, held prisoner by the demon. If that is the case, this thing is most likely tormenting him. That would be especially true if Sigmund is behind this change, knowing how much he hates the prince. And the real Rayne could be trying to expel the invader from his body. I would like to do some research to determine if there might be a way to help the prince drive out the demon."

"I agree with Jonathan," Shaw said. "Something has changed our friend. And *if* that something is a demon, it's inherently evil and now controlling one of the most powerful people in Ochen. Whether Rayne's spirit still resides in his body with that thing or not, we have no way of knowing. But we do know that the pretender is strong and cunning and has already taken steps to change the very structure of rule here on Corylus.

"Think about this. Within a very brief time, the king and queen have been attacked and their rule weakened. The prince has yielded the king's power to Brayden and has assured that the Interplanetary Council will not interfere with whatever happens here on Corylus. If Jonathan's right, and a demon has taken over the prince's body, this is a political nightmare."

"If Rayne is still not himself when he returns to Westvale, we will have to do something." Thorvin's fist struck the table. "We must stop this pretender from grabbing any more power. Like Shaw said, if Rayne is possessed, this demon did not take him on a whim. No, this thing knew taking control of the Crown Prince of Ochen was the best way to gain unquestioned political power. This whole thing was planned and set in place with an interplanetary goal in mind."

"Perhaps I have allowed myself to jump to an unwarranted conclusion." Shaw said. "What if Lexi's right and we're making baseless wild assumptions? Before we start talking about taking action, we should assess the situation when Rayne returns, see if he's still behaving strangely."

"The prince is due to return to Westvale soon," Bishop Hedrick said. "I propose we all move forward as if nothing untoward has happened, so this person, royal pretender or true prince, will not be aware that we suspect anything. The only way to be effective is to stay within the circle of those close to the prince. If we remain quietly present so we draw no special attention to ourselves, we can be in positions to observe and learn all we can. It is only by this proximity that we can be effective no matter what the outcome. We must focus on finding out the truth as soon as possible."

When Bishop Hedrick stopped speaking, silence ruled in the dining room for a long time. Then Andrew spoke up in a small voice. "I'll try my best, Your Eminence. I'll do whatever I can to help Prince Rayne."

"And to that, I think we can all agree," Shaw said. "We will all strive to do our best and pray to do what we can to help our friend."

"Yes," Jonathan added. "Let us all commit to keeping Rayne in our prayers."

"And pray for the system of Ochen, itself," Captain Fontaine added. "I've got a bad feeling about this. I fear we'll all be shaken by what's coming."

6

"Three weeks!" Sigmund roared as he flung a half full glass of wine across the room to smash against the hungry flames flickering in the large stone fireplace in the great room of Lord William's country house.

"He's just one feeble old man. How did he even get away? That pathetic old body couldn't get far without help."

Pacing across a thick, gray and red carpet, the pretender continued, snarling. "How has he managed to elude your men for this long, Brayden? Are your people that inept that one helpless boy trapped in a frail, diseased body can outwit them?"

"They have scoured the entire area around Castle Inverness and the city of Inverness, itself. It's like he was swallowed up with no trace left behind." Brayden gulped down a full glass of honeyed sherry.

Frustration twisted Sigmund's stomach as a niggling fear lodged in his chest. He couldn't lose the boy to his enemy again. His pride would not allow that.

Lord William motioned for a young, scantily-clad, slave girl in a costume of sheer red silk to pour another drink for the angered pretender and said in a soothing voice, "And that is why you've come to me, my lord. I have the perfect hunter for the job."

"No!" Sigmund snarled. "That's why I've come to Sorial. You just happen to live here. I have come here to retrieve my own hunter. One such as I am, who will be able to sniff out that rebellious snot of a prince once and for all. When he's returned to me, I will remind him of his place as my property and use him to locate those loathsome scrolls. With all seven in my possession, I will be able to finally destroy them and that repulsive prophecy once and for all. Then I will be the ruling power here and all will bow to me and the truth I plant in their feeble brains."

Lord William's slave trembled as she handed the prince another glass of wine. He smiled down at her, catching her eyes, knowing she feared him even as she was attracted to the handsome body he possessed. The power to do with her as he wished created a warm sensation in the pit of his stomach. But venting his anger on William's slaves would do nothing to drown the dark anger rising within him, and he waved her away. "Your slave has heard more than is healthy, William. You should cut out her tongue."

He paused, frowned as he considered, then said, "Oh, wait, I tried to silence a disobedient slave once before by removing his ability to speak and that didn't work out well. You'll have to kill her."

Shaking even more, the girl ran from the room back toward the kitchen. "Look what you've done now," Lord William whined. "I liked her, she was so pretty and submissive. Now I'll have to replace her."

"I'll reimburse you," Sigmund said. "We're on Sorial after all, humanity is cheap here, just like I planned. You have no right to complain, William; my favors have set you up like a king here, and soon we'll have Veres under our control once again. Unless, of course, you want to give it all up and volunteer to head up the search for my missing prize."

"No, my lord. I'm not complaining. You have my complete loyalty."

"Loyalty, hah!" Sigmund said, the darkness at his core a

churning mass of sour hatred directed at everything human. "Your loyalty is meaningless, you stupid swine. Unless I destroy those noxious scrolls, everything is meaningless." Sigmund downed his wine and growled. He flung the now empty glass to shatter against its predecessor in the fireplace and paced once again.

"Calm yourself, Sigmund." Heinrich spoke up from his seat next to the hissing fire. "We've only temporarily misplaced that servant of our enemy. He can't evade us for long, and once we've retrieved him you can vent your frustration on him rather than William's wine glasses and slaves." He gave Sigmund a knowing look. "And ... admit it my old friend, you have enjoyed using his body. Even the little slave girl who just ran away was drawn to you before you scared her off. Perhaps you can convince William you were joking and bring her back to Westvale with us. She is, after all, a rather pretty little thing."

Sigmund pursed his lips for a moment but then curved them into a smile. "Once again, Heinrich, you have made an astute observation. This body does suit me. I just wish Coronus hadn't been so ready with his whipping rod, or Ponce with his knife. I am covered with these unsightly scars. My last body was pristine and scar free. In some ways, I do miss it. But you're right, I am enjoying the youthful vigor of this body."

"Even more to the point, you are pleased with having taken it from the boy who irritated you for so long, the slave responsible for the destruction of your well-kept body when our master punished you for not having proper control of him."

Sigmund ground his teeth at the reminder of his chastisement. "It's a shame he isn't still in here with me. It would please me to no end to taunt that obstinate spirit, force him to participate in my most loathsome actions until he finally came to enjoy them with me. Even as an assassin, he hated spilling blood. His need to protect others was his downfall. I doubt that's changed. Though what he can do to protect anyone in the body he now inhabits is beyond me."

Heinrich rose to fill his glass from the bottle of wine. "Aquila will be here soon. You need only set him on the scent and he will return soon with your prey. Then you can torment the young prince to your heart's delight."

"Just so long as he lasts until I destroy those obnoxious scrolls," Sigmund said, mollified.

"And if he survives," Brayden asked, "what do you plan to do with him then?"

A look of disgust passed across Giles's face. "What brother? Why would you even ask that?"

"Because I want him."

"Haven't you done enough yet?"

"Ho!" Brayden crowed. "It looks like my little bastard brother is developing a conscious."

"No. I don't regret what I've done. I've been paid well. It's just that I know when enough is enough. You, dear *legal* brother, have no concept of restraint."

"And that's why I love him so much," Sigmund said, moving behind Brayden and running his fingers through the young man's hair. "But, Brayden, you must remember. I promised our master that if there's anything left of the boy in the old man when I'm done, he will receive the final remains to adorn his throne room on the Wasted Continent. A slap in the face of our enemy. Of course, once our plans are established and I no longer need this body for political gain, I might move on. I'm sure our master would appreciate the gift of a whole Light Bringer."

"Ah yes, my lord, a most gratifying gift." Brayden inclined his head to Sigmund.

"William, William," Sigmund drew out the name, fixing his pale eyes on the overweight human and contemplating how pig-like the human vermin was. He vowed that one day he would make delicious bacon from the self-absorbed swine. But first things first. "We should discuss business. Brayden and I have already approached the Interplanetary Council with the petition to once again declare Veres a subservient moon to Sorial. With the support I've put in place over the last ten years, the petition will pass with no objections. In return for our work on your behalf, I'll need something from you."

"What?" William asked, hesitation and fear mixing in his small, hazel eyes.

Waving his finger back and forth, the handsome young prince smiled with a knowing grin. "Not yet. I know you'd prefer something quick and easy, but I'll let you know when and what in my own good time."

Brayden let out a snort and stood up, staggering and blinking, then righted himself. "I'm bored! Let's do something exciting. I despise boredom. I require amusement."

Sigmund looked at Heinrich and rolled his eyes. "And what is it you would like to do now, Regent Woodfield?"

Brayden's eyes lit up. "Let's go to one of the gaming complexes and watch a death match or two. That always puts me in a good mood, especially if my fighter wins."

Irritation ignited Sigmund's ire. "You're forgetting one thing, Veres is still blocking its skipping line. We can't go there now."

"Not a problem." William spoke up, his tiny eyes bright and eager. "We set up a temporary gaming ring not far from here. It's not as large or luxurious as our complexes on Veres, but it's very nice if I do say so myself. It's in the lower level of my nephew's house. And Van Coronus has been doing an excellent job snatching potential fighters—he's brought us some very promising stock."

Sigmund released a sigh. "I suppose it will do for some nominal entertainment, but those fights can be so numbingly tedious if the slaves are not talented or well-trained. Now, that Thorvin was a genius at training fighters. Too bad the man is so loyal. Such a waste."

Brayden looked at Sigmund, running his eyes from head to toes. "You now possess the body of a superb fighter trained by Lord Kraftsmunn. Have you tried swinging a sword to see if you have any of his moves?"

"Absolutely not," Sigmund huffed, a shudder running through him. "I would not demean myself in that way. But now that you mention it, I do miss orchestrating the young prince's kills; he was so adept at spilling blood."

Rubbing his chin and smirking as he thought, Sigmund pondered out loud, "Now that you've pointed out the obvious, you've sparked the beginning of a very interesting idea. When our plans have come to fruition and I claim my new host, before we present the failed Light Bringer to our master, let's get him in the ring once or twice and see for ourselves whether he's still the fighter he was before we broke him. If there's any talent left, we might even gain the admiration of our colleagues."

Hunger filled Brayden's eyes at the suggestion. But Sigmund dismissed the tempting fantasy. "Enough daydreaming for now; perhaps we can revisit the idea later. Come, let us take William up on his offer and check out his new sporting ring. It will help us pass the time while we await Aquila."

The games proved to be relatively entertaining and bloody enough to satisfy even Brayden. William had started out sullen and irritated at being required to accompany his guests, but by the beginning of the second match—and after consuming multiple drinks—he became more civil. When Jason showed up during that fight, supplementing the entertainment with his dry wit and more drinks, William finally loosened up, competing with Brayden for the title of most blood-thirsty, entertaining Sigmund and Heinrich for the rest of the evening. They were given the best seats in the house—comfortable, rounded, over-stuffed chairs at a ring-side table where gourmet food was served in abundance and drinks came on a regular basis.

It was almost first sunrise when they returned to Lord William's estate. Stable hands ran to take their horses, and when they climbed the stairs to the back entry to the house, a slave greeted Lord William with the news that a guest had arrived seeking to speak with the prince.

"Where is he waiting?" the false prince asked.

"In the great room, Your Highness."

"Excellent. Heinrich, Brayden, join me. William, thank you for an entertaining evening; you and Giles are dismissed."

7

The man, if he could be called such, sat in front of a roaring fire, drumming thick, dark gray claws against the arm of his chair, an area of shredded leather attesting to their keen edges. At over eight feet tall, and broad enough to dwarf the oversized chair in which he sat, he was impressive. Long gray-black hair covered his head, falling over his shoulders like a ragged shawl. Deep-set, dark eyes caught the light from the fire, reflecting it like luminous pale green moons behind his shaggy hair. The bottom half of his face was more wolf than man, and when he smiled, Sigmund caught sight of his large, sharp canine teeth.

"Good fortune to you and welcome, Aquila," Sigmund purred as he walked in and motioned for Brayden to bring drinks for Aquila, Heinrich, and himself. "I hope your business in Corylus was successful?"

"No challenge." A rumble sounded deep in the man thing's throat. "She was easy prey."

After Brayden delivered the drinks and took a seat across the room near the door, the thing spoke again. "You called?"

Sigmund stared at the fellow demon with cold eyes, assessing, before he spoke. "I have a slightly different task for you this time. I want you to hunt someone special. But the trick is, I need him brought back to me alive."

"Newcomer?"

Sigmund sighed. "Yes."

"Newcomers are for sport, not to keep as pets." Aquila's eyes flashed, and he curled his lip. "What is your purpose in this?"

"You would question me?" Sigmund asked, a sharp edge to his words. He had grown tired of the hunter's attitude long ago.

"No, I will not question. Our master gave my contract to you and so I serve you." The crackling and popping of the fire filled the silence for a few minutes before Aquila spoke again. "Newcomers are fragile. They are too easily damaged."

"Yes, yes," Sigmund said. He would have to placate Aquila in order to achieve his goal. "Unfortunately, this particular human has eluded my Nemorian hunters and I must rely on you. There is no other hunter like you in all of Ochen, great Aquila. I need him brought to me in Westvale as soon as possible. And I need him alive, unharmed if possible. I know this will be a humiliating assignment for you. The prey is quite old and even more fragile than most newcomers. But I also know how capable you are."

"You cloak this dishonorable request in praise of my talents?" Aquila spat, his disgust blatant. "I find it distasteful that you would task me with bringing this runaway newcomer back to you undamaged. You think me unaware of what you and Heinrich have done, but news like this travels quickly among the colleagues. You have lost the spirit bound to the body you now occupy, the spirit chosen of our enemy, and now you need me to cover your mistake. I will not forget the duty you are forcing on me. Does our master know of this?"

Sigmund rose and began pacing. His breath came in sharp huffs as he fought to contain his dark anger. "Our master does not need to be bothered with such inconsequential details. Will you obey me in this or would you prefer I report your lack of respect to him?"

Aquila took his time, swirling the sweet amber liquid he had been served around in the fine crystal goblet that looked like a child's plaything in his huge hand, watching the liquid catch the light of the fire.

"I will obey you," he growled, finally.

"Of course you will," Sigmund said, contemplating how he could punish the hunter later for his lack of respect.

"Is he still on Nemora?"

"I have watchers at the station in Inverness. He could not possibly have left Nemora."

"And yet this servant of the One has troubled you much already. It is rumored he was the reason our master disciplined you."

With a hiss of hatred, the pretender spat out, "You are never to mention our enemy's name in my presence!" With an effort of will, Sigmund caged his raging desire to inflict pain. "Yes, he has been protected and strengthened. The body in which he is trapped is extremely old for a human. I thought that it would hold my prey like a prison so I could control him easily. But the spirit of the boy is strong, and special to our enemy. You may think this is an easy task I have put before you, but it is not. You must be on your guard and handle everything carefully. If our enemy suspects you mean to harm his chosen, you will be in danger."

"I will do this," the hunter said. "Now it sounds more like a worthy challenge. I will return this runaway to you."

Without another word, Aquila rose. Despite his size, he left the house on soundless feet. When he was gone, Sigmund said, "What do you think, Heinrich? Can Aquila do this?"

"Unless you were to seek the boy yourself, Sigmund, you could leave this hunt in no better hands. Or should I say paws?" Heinrich grinned, prompting Sigmund to laugh.

Heinrich continued. "If the boy's spirit can be tracked, Aquila will find him. Your bigger concern should be, will Aquila hand him over to you readily or demand a reward first?"

"Yes. Aquila will ask to be released from his bondage to me. But if he can bring me the old man unharmed and with the spirit still safely imprisoned within, it's worth it to me. I would rather lose Aquila's services than lose the chance to destroy the scrolls."

With a sigh, Sigmund sat back down. "This would be so much easier if I could just destroy the scrolls one at a time. But I've tried that in the past. I burned the original scroll to Corylus along with all the copies I could find there during the Hundred Years War. I never expected to see that odious thing again.

"When that idiot prince found it, I suspected what needed to be done. But it wasn't until you and I studied those ancient texts that I was certain. To destroy the scrolls, all seven must be incinerated by dark fire simultaneously. Only then can we be rid of them and escape the prophecy. I long for that moment when I see them go up in smoke, destroy the remnants of that abominable Kierkengaard family line, and put an end to our enemy's machinations."

"Then, having thwarted those *precious* prophecies, we can take our leisure dismantling whatever is left of the political and religious structure of Ochen, opening the system and its delicious humanity to all colleagues to use as we see fit," Heinrich said, lifting his glass to the pretender in salute.

"What about me?" Brayden asked. "You promised I would rule Ochen. You broke your promise. I'm human, will you destroy me as well?"

Sigmund chuckled. "Oh, Brayden, you are so precious. I've never before met a human like you. For now, be patient. When the time is right, I'll make arrangements for you to host one of us in your body. With your bloodlust and selfish nature, you'll enjoy the bonding and we will be able to assure you remain young and healthy forever. You'll join us in our victory, I promise. You'll not be disappointed. All your wishes will come true … when the time is right."

"You'd better remember. You promised."

"Oh yes. I promised."

Within the hour Aquila was paying to skip to Nemora. He breathed deeply as he strolled to the portal, enjoying the smells of Emporium City. When this job was over, and he was free of Sigmund, he looked forward to taking advantage of the delights

Sorial had to offer without needing to hide his face. He didn't begrudge Sigmund; his plan was a good one. And if he succeeded, all Ochen would be like Sorial. Darkness would grow strong and overcome any remaining light. All the human vermin across the planetary system would be reduced to slave status and Sigmund's colleagues would be free to live here and use them without fear of reprisal from the enemy. Yes, Aquila would help Sigmund; but before he returned that servant of the enemy, Aquila would claim his own freedom. Drawing in another deep breath, Aquila promised himself he would return soon; and he would not return empty handed.

It was late evening when Aquila arrived on Nemora. He headed toward his favorite tavern in Inverness where he hoped to meet up with a couple associates who would be useful in the hunt. Sigmund had been right. As the only spirit hunter left in the Ochen system, Aquila was uniquely qualified for this assignment. And with his partners to assist, he was confident he would be skipping to Corylus with Sigmund's quarry within a few days.

At least this job might prove more of a challenge than the last job Sigmund assigned him. That had been beneath him. The woman in Westvale had been so stupid. One silly love note claiming to be from Sigmund's newcomer friend Brayden had brought her running to that empty beach in the middle of the night. The girl had been hopelessly in love. Too easy. Killing without the hunt preceding it was just a waste of time. It was the hunt Aquila enjoyed; it was the thrill he lived for.

And Nemora was such a great place to hunt! Heavy magic saturation increased all Aquila's powers and heightened his senses. He pulled the cowl of his cloak farther down over his face as he entered the Black Wolfe Tavern. The owner was an old friend, but it didn't do to scare his customers. Simon could get touchy if his customers were jittery. Aquila moved with care to a table in the dark corner at the back of the common room. A few minutes later Simon came over. "Are you here fer food and drink or just business?"

"A little of both," Aquila rumbled.

"Some roast and trimmings and a mug of ale?"

"The best of what you've got, Simon. Have you seen Krizia or Marius yet tonight?"

"Not yet, sir. But I 'spect they'll be in soon enough."

"Bring the food and ale and send Krizia and Marius back as soon as they come in."

"Yes, sir."

Aquila was enjoying his second ale and finishing his meal when Krizia arrived. Aquila liked working with Krizia, she was smart and talented, and because she appeared human, blended in well. She was tall and willowy, and though she looked fragile, she was strong and wicked. Long, dark red hair framed a heart-shaped, pixie-like face with large blue eyes. She looked like a dream, but Aquila knew she could hunt and fight like a nightmare. She wore her scanty outfit well on a toned body most newcomer men drooled over.

She slid in across from Aquila and waved to Simon for a drink. "I hear you got a job for us."

"A special hunt."

"The one that's been causing talk amongst the colleagues?" she asked, interest burning in her crystalline eyes. Aquila was about to respond when a dark shape slipped into the chair next to Krizia's.

Sliding the shadow hood back from his head, Marius revealed short, blonde hair. He was human, but a possessed human. The demon within had taken his body nearly forty years ago, even adopting its human name. As was the habit among the colleagues, he used his arts to keep his human host young, holding his age in the early twenties. He was handsome with dark chocolate eyes and a closely-trimmed beard. The host spirit had welcomed the demon and appreciated its ability to keep him strong, healthy, and attractive. Aquila studied Krizia and Marius with appreciation. As a couple, they were handsome and always acceptable to the newcomers, mingling among them in places Aquila couldn't go.

Once Marius had gotten a drink and ordered some food, Krizia broached the subject of the hunt again. "So, Aquila, is it true? Are we hunting the severed spirit of the chosen Light Bringer? Rumors are swirling among the colleagues that Heinrich finally achieved his goal of severing a protected human. Sigmund must be delighted at possessing such a politically powerful body."

"We are not concerned with rumors," Aquila rumbled. "What you need to know is this: As you suspect, Krizia, Sigmund has ordered me to find the broken one. When we locate him, we are to capture him and deliver him to Sigmund in Westvale, unharmed; or at least as healthy as possible. The real complication to this job is the care we will need to take with the old body in which he is imprisoned. It will require careful handling. Any questions?"

Marius shrugged and the two shook their heads.

"Then gather whatever supplies you will need and meet me at the stream behind Castle Inverness at daybreak. That's the last known location of the old man and where we will pick up his trail. It's rained since he left, but that will not be a problem for us."

8

Numb and beyond himself, Rayne huddled at the bottom of the rocky incline he had tumbled down last night. In the rain and darkness, he lost his footing when the muddy ground gave out beneath him and slipped down to land partly in the stream at the bottom. Now he shivered, wet and cold from the night chill. The ankle he had twisted in his fall throbbed in time with his heart beat. And he cried.

All that had gone before, all he survived, hadn't prepared him for the despair now flooding him. The faith and determination that sustained him when he left the cottage behind five days ago were gone; washed away in the rain of the last three days, forsaken somewhere in the trackless wilderness surrounding him. Lost, alone, and numb, he refused to pray. He had trusted the One and look where it had gotten him. Maybe he should have given in to Sigmund years ago. Maybe if he had, he would at least still be himself. But deep down, Rayne knew; that too was just an illusion. Whatever he would have become, that person would not have been him anymore than this old man body was him now.

Sometime during the last five days, he lost himself; physically, emotionally, mentally, and spiritually. Rayne was nothing more than a shadow. He stopped crying, spent, beyond tears, and allowed the mind-numbing nothingness to claim him once again. He was reduced to the reality that he had been nothing more than a disposable pawn in a game of Kings and Swords between Sigmund and the One. If he wasn't so past feeling, he would laugh at the absurdity of it all.

Since he had fallen, he hadn't moved more than what was necessary to drag himself out of the flowing water. Even now, hours later, he lay on his back wondering if he should try to sit up, or look for his staff, or even just turn over to his side and drink. *I'm thirsty*. He was thirsty and starving. He was going to die. Did it really matter if he died from thirst or hunger or ultimately sickness and old age? At least thirst would be quickest.

Then a word wormed its way into his consciousness. It was just one little niggling word ... *why?* He stuffed it back down, screaming inside his head. *Shut up and let me die already!*

That spark of indomitable will the One had given him just wouldn't quit. It flickered even in the old man body.

When Rayne was certain he had smothered the spark, it started up again ... *trust*. Just like it had refused to die every time he worked to snuff it out over the last few days, just like it had refused to die when Sigmund sought to extinguish it when Rayne was a child. This time he did laugh, an aborted rough hack, as he tried to sit up. After struggling for a couple minutes, he managed to prop himself up against the trunk of a large willow tree with roots flung out into the stream.

"I'm done." He spoke into the hushed wilderness surrounding him. "I won't be your pawn anymore." He felt better for having said the words aloud. Though they came out with little force, he took pleasure in the sound and the acknowledgment of his true feelings.

"What was the purpose anyway?" His voice grew stronger as he gave vent to his frustration.

Having started, the words now came as if of their own volition. "I'm going to die here you know. This body is sick. And starving. So what was it all for? Why? Why did you even call me? All I've ever gotten from this was Sigmund's and Ponce's loathsome attention and Brayden's animosity. And now, here I sit, too weak to stand.

"And even if I could walk, where would I go? I'm starving; I have no idea where I am. So tell me, O great One, why?

"No!" Rayne shook his head, wispy white hair fluttering as anger flamed within him. "Don't bother! I don't want to hear it; I don't care. Because in the end, Sigmund won anyway! Do you hear me? Sigmund's won! SIGMUND WON!"

"Who's Sigmund?" a childlike voice asked from Rayne's right, startling him.

Though Rayne looked to the spot where he was sure the voice had originated, he saw no one. But he heard a giggle, like the sound a child would make when playing a delightful game. Then the voice came again, this time from Rayne's left. "Silly, silly Sigmund. Sigmund sounds silly."

The voice got silent and though Rayne listened, he could not hear any sound of movement in the brush around him, just the singing of birds overhead, the rustling of leaves in the trees as they flew, and the continuous babbling of the stream near his feet.

Then from right behind him, Rayne heard a whisper. "Are you Sigmund?"

"No!" Rayne blurted out as he tried to turn and catch a glimpse of the speaker. But this time he hadn't moved; he sat a few feet behind Rayne, knees pulled up to his chest.

He was slight, a small child with lavender-blue hair cut in shaggy layers around his head. Two long braids, tied with leather thongs dyed orange to match his over-sized jacket, framed his face and fell to well below his shoulders. He had deep-set eyes of storm-cloud gray and a tiny upturned nose set over full, almost feminine lips. In fact, Rayne wasn't sure if he was a he or a she.

They stared at each other, the exceedingly old man and the impishly young boy, without saying a word for several minutes, studying each other in the dawn light.

Rayne spoke first. "I thought I was alone."

The little boy just sat and smiled for a moment before saying, "Never alone, no, no. You are never alone. I am here. Who are you?"

"Ray …" Rayne started to say. But then he stopped. He didn't know who he was, not anymore. "Ray …" he started again.

The little imp broke in and said in a sing-song voice, "Ray-ray! I like that. Reminds me of the sun. Sun, sun, sun. I'm Mite, Ray-ray."

Then standing and making a dramatic bow, Mite's manner turned serious. "Good fortune to you and welcome traveler, Ray-ray. Are you lost? You look lost."

Rayne couldn't help but smile. "Are you a girl or a boy?" he asked, and then wondered why he had asked such an embarrassing question.

Standing very straight and rising on his toes, Mite said, "I am a boy! Can't you tell, Ray-ray? Why would you even think Mite is a girl? No girl, no girl."

"Yes, Mite. I can see now that you are a boy. Please excuse my ignorance but you are a very pretty little boy." Rayne tried to soothe the child's ruffled feathers.

"Boys aren't pretty. We are handsome. I am a handsome boy. And so is Ray-ray."

Rayne's smile died. "No, Mite. I'm not a handsome boy. I'm a very wrinkly, very sick old man."

"Have it your way, Ray-ray. I see what I see." Mite jumped up and scooted up the incline to the path and vanished.

"Mite!" Rayne called, suddenly afraid that Mite would leave him and he would be alone again.

But then Mite's head reappeared at the top of the slope and he scrambled down toward Rayne, half sliding and half running, with Rayne's staff in his hand. He slid to a stop inches from the stream. "Ray-ray will need his staff if he wants to come and eat with Mite."

"Is your home far?"

Mite laughed, pure joy. "Mite's home is far, far. Ray-ray and Mite go to Camp of the Forgotten. It is not far. Come, Ray-ray. You need to eat."

Mite held the staff out for Rayne to grab. Once he had a firm grip, Mite took his other hand and helped to pull him upright. The strength in the little boy's grasp was startling, and the moment they touched, a spark of something ageless filtered through Rayne.

As Rayne put weight on the injured ankle though, his leg gave out. If he hadn't been bracing himself with the staff, he would have fallen.

"Ray-ray is hurt?" Mite's eyes clouded and a sad expression flitted across his face. "Sit, sit. Let Mite look at your hurt."

Rayne hissed as he lowered his body to the ground. Mite held his elbow, helping him to control his descent. Rayne pulled the bottom hem of his garment up to his bony knee, exposing a thin, white leg, and groaned when he saw the swollen and discolored ankle.

Mite reached out, cupped his hands around Rayne's ankle, and closed his deep gray eyes, his face scrunched in what Rayne assumed was deep concentration. A minute later, Mite's eyes popped open. "It will hurt, but it is not broken. Mite will help Ray-ray to walk."

Rayne watched with interest as Mite pulled a battered old pack from behind a rock. Opening the pack, he began tossing out crumpled garments, moldy bread, two dried and wrinkled apples, and an empty water bag. When he got to the bottom of the pack, he pulled out a jar and several rags.

"Ray-ray sit still. Mite fix you up quick-quick."

With dexterity and a practiced hand that seemed incongruous in one so young, Mite rubbed salve into Rayne's swollen joint, then tore the material into strips and wrapped the cloth tightly around the ankle. Rayne released a sigh of relief as heat from whatever Mite had rubbed into the joint eased his pain.

"Sit Ray-ray. Sit." Mite said. Leaving his pack with everything from it still strewn on the ground around Rayne, he grabbed the water bag and scurried to the stream where he filled it with icy cold water.

Mite darted back to stand in front of Rayne, holding out the water and staring at him until he took the bag and had a good long drink. When Rayne thought he was done, Mite pushed the bag back up to his mouth. "More. More. Ray-ray needs water. Needs water to heal."

With a sigh, Rayne lifted the bag again and took another long drink. "Okay?" he asked as he handed the bag back. Mite smiled large and nodded before taking a long drink himself.

Rayne felt better once he had enough water in him. The little scamp was right. Rayne was certain the water coursing through him was, in some way, speeding his healing. He grunted with the realization that it probably was; Nemora was known for its healing energies. With the realization, the acute pain of another loss impaled Rayne. He couldn't sense the magic around him. This body was not sensitive to the energy. He'd never thought much about it before, but his mother's bloodline had given him the ability to sense and even, given training, use magic. Just one more thing he had lost. Rayne felt the deadness inside growing again.

"No, no, no." Rayne heard Mite mumbling to himself. "We must not stay here long. Ray-ray needs to walk. Need hope, need help. Mite must get Ray-ray to Camp of the Forgotten now. No time, no time."

"Who are you?" Rayne asked, beginning to wonder about the person of Mite. Was he a child, or was he something more? Rayne remembered his mother speaking of ancient beings that resided in the heavy magic of Nemora, and Rayne's own experiences with the ancient guardians of the scrolls was evidence that such beings existed.

"I told Ray-ray, I am Mite."

"And how old is Mite?"

Mite pouted at Rayne and refused to answer. Finally, he said, "Mite is what Mite is. Mite does not know his age. Mite's age does not matter. Does Ray-ray want Mite to be his friend or not? Need to know, need to know now or Mite can't help."

Anger and suspicion budded like a corrupt flower from the darkness within Rayne, intense and undeniable. Rayne sputtered, his voice harsh and low. "You're my friend, Mite? Really? I think the truth is you're working for my enemies and leading me into a trap. How do I know I can trust you?"

Mite jumped up and started hopping from foot to foot and mumbling to himself. "Trust, trust, no trust ... can't help if no trust. Mite can't help ... Ray-ray thinks Mite of darkness.

Hurts feelings. Tell him? Tell him now? Yes, yes, yes ... ancient bond, ancient trust."

Mite stopped mumbling and looked at Rayne with deep, wise eyes. Rayne was pierced by the reality of how incredibly young he was compared to Mite. He was just a human youth trapped in an old human body, but he was looking into the eyes of an exceedingly ancient being trapped in the body of a child. Or maybe not trapped, maybe that was just what Mite was.

Rayne knew at that moment, if he held Mite's gaze, allowed Mite to plumb the depths of his spirit, this young-old creature would know him in some profound way. Rayne looked away. He was too scared and unsure to trust this stranger, would not allow himself to trust anyone.

But I need help. Okay. Okay! Just for now. Only until I can travel on my own again.

Mite shifted position to look Rayne in the eye. "Ray-ray talks of trust. Ray-ray does not trust Mite. But Ray-ray is running out of time. He must decide, must decide now before it's too late. Newcomers are coming, many newcomers, searching. They are searching for Ray-ray."

Covering his face with his hands, Rayne moaned. His need to protect himself, to trust no one, prevented him from even looking at Mite. He still refused to call out to the One; would not allow himself that crutch. Fear of betrayal hovered like a hungry vulture.

No! I can't do it. Won't trust anyone except myself. Mite can just go to this camp without me. I can take care of myself and if I can't, I'll just die. So be it.

Anger driven by fear boiled to the surface and Rayne lashed out. "How would you know people are searching for me unless you're working with them? Who asked you to help me anyway? I didn't ask you, did I? Leave me alone. Go away, Mite. I don't need you. I don't want your help! Just GO! GO!"

Mite jumped up and down first on one foot and then on the other in an attempt to harness a boundless energy that coursed through him. He knew he was supposed to help this stubborn, stupid newcomer, but the newcomer didn't trust him, didn't like him. What was he to do?

He started to gather his belongings and stuff them back into his pack when the newcomer yelled again, "I said Go! I don't need you."

But then the newcomer was crying. So sad, so sad. The child inside the old man was so sad. Mite did the only thing he could think to do. Releasing a portion of his frustration with a grunt, he sat down next to the stupid newcomer and, scooting close, wrapped his arms around the old man with the child inside, and began to sing.

He sang a song of praise to the Creator-Father in the old tongue. Mite sang low and quiet, knowing the others were near now, newcomer hunters, searching. But he knew Ray-ray—silly, stubborn newcomer—couldn't move now. Mite started to sing another song, a song of hiding and protection. He could feel the life in the being he held, so fragile. It reminded Mite of the time he had held a dying baby bird, so broken, so brittle.

You were right, Creator-Father. Mite prayed while he continued to hum his song of protection. *He is so lost. Almost all used up. You were right. You always are. Please help Mite to be patient with the stupid newcomer.*

Know, my servant Mite, the warm voice of the One spoke into the spirit of Mite, *he too is a bearer of light.*

How can that be? He is newcomer.

Oh, my servant Mite. Have you forgotten the prophecies? The warm voice spoke with humor.

This one is your chosen vessel of light? But he is so young; he is stupid and stubborn.

And have you never done anything stupid? Have you never been stubborn? This weak human will spread the light of truth, the light of my Son, to all of Ochen. Or have you forgotten, my servant Mite, that I love to pull down the strongholds of the enemy with weak vessels.

The sounds of loud voices, and unwary feet snapping twigs and smashing dried leaves, broke into Mite's consciousness. *The hunters come.*

They will not see or hear what I have covered, my servant Mite. Be at peace. But beware the other hunters. Those of darkness who will come to seek my servant. He has no strength to resist them now; he is lost and broken. Take care of him, Mite. Be patient with him. He has suffered much, and he needs your help to find the guardians. Show him grace, Mite, because he is too afraid to trust yet. It will come in time and then he will grow in faith and trust until the courage to be my strong arm is birthed in him.

Mite began to sing the words of protection again as the sounds of the hunters surrounded him and his charge. He kept his arms around Rayne, who had fallen into a deep slumber, and trusted the Creator-Father's protection.

𝕸

Two hours later, Rayne woke to find Mite still sitting with his small arms wrapped around him, gently humming. When Rayne stirred, Mite said, "Ray-ray is up now. Time to go, time to go to the Camp of the Forgotten."

Rayne blinked and looked around, disoriented. "Where are we?"

"Not far from camp. Come, friend Ray-ray. We must go, must go now."

Rayne picked up the staff and started to pull himself upright before he remembered his damaged ankle. But when he gingerly put some weight on the leg, the ankle held strong. It was sore, but he could walk.

After Mite hoisted his pack onto his back, he came alongside Rayne and pulled Rayne's arm over his shoulders. He looked up and smiled. "Mite help Ray-ray. Ray-ray pretty helpless without Mite."

Thinking back to what he said before he ... *fell asleep?* Rayne didn't remember falling asleep. But then, he just woke so he must have been sleeping. As he thought back to that point, the words he had carelessly flung at Mite echoed through him. "I'm sorry, Mite. I know you're trying to help me. I shouldn't have yelled at you."

"That is right," Mite said, scrunching up his face. "Ray-ray should never yell at Mite when Mite is helping him. Mite is good friend to Ray-ray."

Rayne walked in a shuffling gait, clutching the staff in his right hand while Mite added support on his left. More than an hour passed and still they walked. Growing tired, Rayne asked, "Is the camp far now?"

"Not far, not far. Does Ray-ray need to rest?"

"Not if the camp is near."

9

Rayne and Mite topped a rise. The trees thinned, and the collection of huts Mite referred to as the Camp of the Forgotten spread out below like a patchwork quilt. From his vantage point, Rayne counted close to one hundred huts. They took him back to the days he had travelled to Coronus's compound with Ponce, reminding him of Ponce's little house on wheels, his peddler's wagon. These houses didn't have wheels, and although some were no bigger than Ponce's wagon, most varied in size and shape. They were set in a circle around a large central tent attached to the front of a sizeable stone building.

Though a large number of the huts looked to be well built, with straight walls, others leaned in various directions as if ready to collapse. They created a kaleidoscope of color scattered across the clearing. When Rayne got closer, he realized the diverse colors were a result of the building materials used. Each dwelling was made of what looked to be scraps of anything from stained wood, to painted sheets of veredium, to animal skins or even oiled cloth. The people who gathered here had built their homes of anything they could find.

Tucked between the houses were tents of various colors,

shapes, and sizes. At the far end of the camp sat a Khalon tent of superior construction that looked out of place next to the other miss-matched dwellings.

"Welcome, Mite, good to see you again," a man called out as he hurried past Rayne and Mite. "Good fortune to you and welcome traveler," he said to Rayne, looking back over his shoulder as long strides propelled him down the hill toward the camp.

When they got closer, numerous people heading toward the large central tent called out greetings to Mite. A tall, lanky man with long gray hair pulled back into a thin tail and dark eyes encased in laugh lines waited as Mite and Rayne approached. "And what have you brought us this time, Mite?"

"Good fortune, Em-em! Another lost one. Mite found another lost one."

A short, plump woman with hair the color of old, dark wood, walked over to stand next to the man and said with a friendly laugh, "Yes, so we can see Mite."

Watching the people streaming into the central tent, Rayne couldn't help but notice they were, like their homes, of varied shape, color, and size, and they were dressed in clothing that looked as if it had been patched together from a clothier's scrap bin. There were children, too. Running into the tent with happy screams and squeals. In fact, there seemed to be too many children compared to the number of adults Rayne was seeing and he wondered what the Camp of the Forgotten was, exactly.

"Come," the tall, thin man said. "We are about to share the midday meal. Please, join us."

Still leaning on Mite and his staff, Rayne shuffled into the large tent where close to three hundred people were lined up along the wall. The line began near a couple old, wooden tables set up as a serving area. Five people stood behind the serving tables, holding large spoons, ready to dish up the food steaming in pots set before them. The scent of warm bread called to Rayne's hollow stomach like an irresistible force. If he could, he would let go of Mite, drop his staff, dash to the serving tables, and begin stuffing mounds of food into his mouth with his bare hands. His stomach clenched, and Rayne groaned as his mouth watered in response.

As the gray-haired man entered the tent, all eyes turned to him. The noisy din grew silent in expectation. Raising his hands above his head, he said, "My friends, let us thank the One for the food we are about to eat."

Every head in the room bowed, including the children who stood still and quiet. Bowing his head as well, the man prayed, "We come together as your people, O most bountiful Provider. We join with one another to find joy in sustenance for body and soul. Thank you for every gift you have given, for all good things come from your generous hands, blessed One." The man looked up with a smile. "Let us eat, friends."

The noise level spiked again as the people conversed while they waited to stand before the servers. Moving to the end of the line, Mite must have noticed Rayne's weakness because he whispered something to the man who had prayed. He looked at Rayne and nodded.

Rayne tried to protest as Mite pulled him out of the line, but Mite said, "Mite knows. Ray-ray is weak from not eating for many days. Ray-ray needs to eat special food. Emerson is getting something for you. Sit. Sit. Emerson will bring good food for Ray-ray."

Mite helped Rayne to an empty seat at the end of one of ten long tables that looked to be able to seat fifty people each. Within minutes, Emerson strode toward them followed by the short round woman.

Emerson set a plate in front of Rayne. "I'm sorry I didn't notice your hunger sooner. We try to be sensitive to the needs of visitors, but I guess my mind was on other things when you arrived with Mite. Please eat."

Though there wasn't a large amount of food on the plate, Rayne's mouth watered at the sight of applesauce, a mashed vegetable, and a small portion of light colored meat cut into tiny pieces.

With a compassionate smile lighting her wide face, the woman placed a tall pottery mug of water next to the plate. The food was simple, no fancy sauces or seasonings, but it was fresh. Rayne moaned as the first spoon of applesauce slid down his throat. It was hard, but Rayne forced himself to eat slowly, chewing each bite and savoring the textures and flavors.

"You can have more later," Emerson said. "But you need to start slow if you haven't eaten in a while."

Emerson, the round lady, and Mite all walked back to the food line and returned a short while later with plates of their own. Soon they were joined by several other people and talked quietly among themselves, allowing Rayne some uninterrupted time to concentrate on eating. After Rayne had eaten about half the food on his plate, he knew he needed to stop.

Emerson's gaze flicked to Rayne with an appraising look. "Now that you have taken the edge off your hunger, stranger, why don't we talk a bit. My name's Emerson, but most people just call me Em, and the lovely lady sitting to my right is my wife, Gretel. What's your name?"

Before Rayne could speak up, Mite said, "Ray-ray. His name's Ray-ray. Mite found him lost, lost, lost."

"Yes, Mite, I can see that," Emerson said. "Why don't you let the man answer for himself now Mite."

Emerson's attention focused back on Rayne. "Ray-ray, huh? That's an unusual name. Where are you from, *Ray-ray*?"

Rayne hesitated and wrinkled his already wrinkly brow even more in concentration while Emerson watched him closely. Rayne was uncertain how to answer the man. What could he say? He was no longer Prince Rayne, so he couldn't say Corylus; but then, he had no idea of the old man's history or where he was from. Maybe someone here already knew the old man.

"Is there a problem?" Emerson asked, raising his eyebrows. "Some reason you don't want to share where you're from? You don't have to share if you don't want to. You're welcome to keep your secret, unless it puts anyone already here in danger."

Relief filtered through Rayne. "I don't have to tell you where I'm from? You'll let me stay even if I don't?"

By this time, everyone else at the table had eaten and left, except for two younger men who moved over to sit with Emerson, Gretel, Mite, and Rayne.

"Introduce us to Mite's newest friend, Emerson," the taller of the two men said.

"His name's Ray-ray," Emerson said. "Ray-ray, this is Bodie." The shorter of the two young men inclined his head. It was covered in very short, prickly, strawberry blonde hair and his eyes reminded Rayne of Lexi and Anne, brown with golden flecks. "And this young trouble maker is Hugh," Emerson continued, indicating the taller man who had asked for the introduction. He reminded Rayne of a young Thorvin. He was a big man, maybe in his early thirties, with large shoulders, a narrow waist, shaggy dark hair worn shoulder length, and deep gray eyes. After looking him over, Rayne was certain he either was a warrior or had been in the not too distant past.

Rayne nodded at the two. "Pleased to meet you."

"So, what brings you to our little corner of Nemora?" Hugh asked.

"Mite found me wandering and lost. He brought me here."

"You a native?"

When Rayne hesitated, Emerson spoke up, "You know our rules, Hugh. Nobody needs to share if they don't feel comfortable doing so. I never pushed you when you first got here. I expect you to show the same consideration. I'm sure Ray-ray will share when he's ready."

Hugh ducked his head toward Emerson. "Yeah, Em, I know you're right. I'm just a little on edge after those soldiers came through here yesterday looking around and disrupting everything." His eyes drifted back to Rayne, suspicion written in the tilt of his head. "Searching for some old man, causing a disturbance and scaring the kids with their talk of a missing slave."

"I understand Hugh," Emerson said. "That was alarming, especially following on the heels of the troubling news coming out of Inverness. I wonder if the two are connected?"

"What news from Inverness?" Rayne asked. Then he added, "How far are we from Inverness here?"

"You really are lost." Hugh shook his head.

"We're far enough from Inverness to have been forgotten," Emerson said. "But not far enough for them to completely leave us alone."

Confusion surfaced on Rayne's face and Emerson added, "We're about two-days ride or four-days walk from the capital." Emerson took a sip of coffee and settled into his seat facing Rayne. "Almost a hundred years ago, the Nemorian royalty decided to clean up the city of Inverness by rounding up the homeless and sending them away. They sent soldiers to gather together those who were too poor or broken to take care of themselves and brought them here. They gave them this land and said, this is yours as long as you take care of yourselves and don't bother anyone. Those first people built the beginnings of this camp and some of us living here are their descendants.

"Over time, if the homeless population in Inverness began to increase, soldiers would again round up all the poor and broken people who had nowhere to go and bring them here.

"Then, about forty years ago, a severe illness spread through the city. It came quickly and went just as fast, but many lives were lost. After the time of sickness passed, the city had many abandoned orphans with no one to care for them. Not knowing what else to do, the Kraftsmunns sent the orphans here as well.

"Ever since then, outcasts and orphans seem to find their way here. We now call ourselves the forgotten because nobody wants to remember we're here. But we do reach out to abandoned children in and around Inverness. And Mite travels the area looking for lost or poor people who need help.

"Most of those living here now have come on their own. Like you, they were looking for a place where they could feel welcome even if they had nothing and a background they didn't want to talk about.

"So, like I said, we're far enough from Inverness to be forgotten. But when there are problems in the capital, the soldiers tend to harass us. We're a nest for unrest and rebellion, they say. But they normally just stay on their horses, give us a hard time, yell for a bit, then move on.

"Yesterday was different. The soldiers didn't just yell and leave. They gathered everyone together and searched every tent and dwelling, throwing belongings around and dumping out the food that had been made for the evening meal. After examining all our old men, they gathered up the little boys and looked at their eyes. Like Hugh said, everyone was frightened and concerned. We were afraid they might take the children from us. They said they had orders to search for a little boy with amethyst eyes, that he was an escaped slave belonging to the Crown Prince of Ochen. Can you imagine that? Even more upsetting was the news that His Royal Highness was lifting the ban on slavery here on Nemora." Emerson looked away, disgust turning down the corners of his mouth. "So, tell me, what's gonna happen the next time, if he succeeds in legalizing slavery here? Will the soldiers come and take any orphan children they want?"

"Does he really think the Interplanetary Council is going to let him get away with that?" Hugh spat out, his face a mottled red. "He may be the Royal Prince of Ochen, but he still answers to the council."

Rayne sat for a long time staring into space as the conversation ebbed and flowed around him. He knew this search was a message directed at him. Sigmund and Brayden were counting on him hearing this news and reacting to it. Only he knew the significance of little slave boys with amethyst eyes. But what could he do? Was the threat to legalize slavery on Nemora a trap, or was Sigmund actually looking to change the very laws and political structure that formed the Interplanetary Confederation? Was he the real force behind what had happened on Veres just like he had manipulated things on Glacieria?

Rayne ground his teeth. *This isn't my problem. I'm not a pawn in that game anymore. I'm no longer a prince; I have no political power; I'm not the Light Bringer. I'm just some worthless old man who's going to die soon.*

Pushing upright, Rayne grabbed his staff, left the table, and walked back out to the sunshine of a blue-tinged autumn afternoon. Mite followed, silently watching as Rayne stood off to the side of the tent and avoided thinking. Rayne cast his gaze down at Mite who looked up with large, sad, gray eyes.

"It has nothing to do with me," Rayne whispered.

10

ท

The next couple weeks Rayne spent most of his time alone, allowing a spiritual malaise and inactivity to plunge him deep into a fog of self-pity. It seemed appropriate, he thought. Nobody at the camp asked him questions about who he was or why he was there. After the first week, Emerson told him that even at his age he was expected to do more than sit around and let others serve him.

"If you don't work," Emerson said, "you don't eat."

Rayne looked around at the jobs people were doing but couldn't find any he thought practical because of his physical limitations. Until the day Mite took him by the hand and led him to the small building used as a school. Rayne fumed and complained as Mite sat him down, putting him in a position where he was forced to interact with the children.

"Ray-Ray's job," Mite said, "Ray-ray must read to the little ones. After midday meal, every day." That first day, Rayne had glowered at Mite who looked back at him with deeply serious eyes. "Ray-ray must care again," was all Mite said before disappearing out the door.

After the first week of reading duty, Rayne was surprised

to realize he enjoyed being around the children. They sat quietly, most of the time, and looked up at him with wide eyes as he read stories from a collection of books the camp had acquired over the years. One little boy always climbed up into Rayne's lap and watched him intently as he read. When Rayne questioned the teacher about him, she told him that the boy, whose name was Kiefer, couldn't hear, so he needed to watch people's lips to know what they were saying.

"Has he always been like this?" Rayne asked, his heart breaking for the little boy who was different.

"As far as we know. From the time Kiefer first came to the camp he has not been able to hear. We think he must have been born that way."

Slowly, as the days passed, Rayne began to care again. It surfaced in little ways. He read to the children more than he was required to read. Then he started helping the older children with their school work. When his hip wasn't bothering him too much, he helped in the kitchen. He scrounged up an old Kings and Swords game and taught Kiefer to play. Rayne used the game as a starting point for teaching Kiefer the sign language Warren had taught him when he was a child.

Kiefer looked up into Rayne's face with total trust one afternoon as he worked to make the hand signs just the way Rayne made them. Rayne figured he was probably the same age as Bethie back on Amathea.

If only things were different. He looked into Kiefer's large dark eyes and, for the first time in weeks, Rayne prayed. *Can you forgive me for being so obstinate? I know you brought me to this point for a reason. Help me to trust you again.*

Kiefer was a quick learner, picking up many of the hand signs with ease, impressing Rayne. They made a game of talking to each other across the noisy dining tent and soon all the other children were asking to learn the signs as well. They challenged each other to see who could go longest without speaking.

Emerson thought the game was a wonderful way to encourage the children to learn to work together, and once Rayne finally convinced the man to call him Ray instead of Ray-ray, Rayne taught him the sign for thank you. Soon everyone caught on and began calling him Ray. Everyone that is, except Mite who still insisted on calling him Ray-ray.

Rayne had been at the camp more than a month when he realized he was at ease. He had settled in as part of the community and enjoyed working with the children. It reminded him of the peace he had experienced while working at the farm on Amathea. He wouldn't say he was happy—he had lost so much that he could never recover—but he found a level of contentment despite his circumstances. He began to consider telling Mite who he really was. Asking if Mite would help him look for the Words to Nemora. If he reclaimed the scroll, perhaps he could get someone to deliver it to Bishop Hedrick in Westvale.

It didn't take Rayne long to realize Mite was an ancient. Not the same kind as the guardians of the scrolls, but Mite had a way about him that reminded Rayne of the guardians. As Rayne watched Mite head out on guard duty with Bodie and Hugh, he knew the others relied on Mite because he possessed the ability to manipulate the heavy magic of Nemora even if they couldn't feel it. Everyone at the camp knew Mite was special. If anyone could help Rayne locate the hidden scroll, it would be Mite.

Guard duty was a new thing. Everyone in camp had voted to institute regular, nightly rounds to protect the children after the incident with the soldiers. The orphan's quarters were moved to the dining tent so they would be in the most protected spot, the center of camp.

Rayne took to spending much of his free time reading. One evening he found a manuscript that spiked his interest, causing him to stay up well past his usual bed time. Though the old man body required a lot more sleep than his young body had, what he was reading caught his attention so completely, he sat in the dining tent reading until his eyes were too blurry to read any longer. It was a study based on prophecies of the Light Bringer, telling about how the guardians of the scrolls had been chosen.

Closing the book, Rayne rubbed his gritty eyes, grabbed the book and his staff, and headed toward his assigned quarters for some badly-needed sleep. The night was clear, the air crisp with the tang of early autumn. As he crossed the camp, his gaze drifted up to Nemora's twin moons. Both were waxing toward full and at this time of the month, they tracked close to each other, bathing everything in a ghostly, silvery-blue light.

After standing for a few minutes, slowly inhaling and releasing the refreshing nighttime air, Rayne started toward his tent. With a sharp intake of breath, he stumbled to a halt. A disruption in the ever-present flow of energy around him thrummed through his body. *What was that?* He had been numb to the prevailing Nemorian energy since he had been broken. Whatever was affecting the magic now had to be potent for him to sense it.

He remained frozen for a few seconds, letting the energy flow over him, feeling it pulse through him. He puffed out an exclamation of fear. "Mite!" *No, he's on guard duty with Hugh and Brodie. Em! Must warn Em.*

As he hurried forward in a shuffling gait, Rayne lifted a prayer to the One. *I know I have no right to ask anything of you Father One, but the people here all trust you. Whatever is happening, please help us.*

Dread, like an irresistible flood, swamped his spirit, sending his heart into a wild rhythm ... *the children! They're in danger!*

He turned back toward the dining tent then stopped in his tracks. *I can't help them like this. Stupid, worthless body!* Reversing direction yet again, he struck out toward Em's house. He moved with speed if not grace, grateful for the bright light of the moons. By the time he got to Em's door, his breath was coming in sharp gasps and he coughed as he knocked.

"I'm here," Em grumbled, opening the door just as Rayne was preparing to pound on it again.

"Is something …"

"The children!" Rayne shouted at Em. "Can't you feel that? Something's wrong. It's disturbing the energy flow and it's after the children."

Gretel had come up behind Em and instantly the two were out the door and running toward the dining tent yelling an alarm. While Em ran straight for the dining tent, Gretel veered off toward the alarm bell. She sprinted up the steps to the plat-form and began ringing the bell, sending its piercing clangor through the nighttime air.

Rayne stumbled along behind Em, his breath a shrill wheeze—until he saw the stranger. Even with his limited senses, he knew this creature was the cause of the disturbance he felt.

Mite, Bodie, and Hugh sprinted through the camp, sliding to a stop in front of the stranger who held up a paw-like hand, stopping the three. Em ran up next to them then froze. "Our children, our children are gone." His voice was harsh with fear and anger. "What have you done with our children?"

"The young newcomers are fine for now," the huge man, covered with a heavy cloak, rumbled from deep inside his cowl. "I seek a simple exchange. Tomorrow morning you will bring me the one I am hunting, the protected one, the broken. In exchange, I will return your young ones, unharmed. I know he is here; I have tasted him on the air.

"Though my enemy has placed a covering of protection over him, blinding my sight, I will not be fooled. Tomorrow morning, when the sun rises he must reveal himself to us or we will kill the young ones. I will be waiting where the path meets the stream. If you value your young ones, do not make me wait long."

With a quick flick of his wrist, the man was gone. Mite began hopping from foot to foot and moaning. "No, no, no. This is bad, bad, very bad. Mite was supposed to protect. What should Mite do? This is bad."

"What do they want?" Em said. "We know nothing about a protected one."

More people came streaming from their houses and tents, and as the stranger's words spread, people began shouting.

"Who is he?" They asked, talking over each other, voices growing louder. "Why did he take our children? What does he want? Does anybody know what he's talking about? Does anybody know who this protected one is?"

Fear fueled more fear and they began accusing each other of knowing something and not confessing, and their dread stoked their anger.

"Settle down, everyone," Hugh shouted, waving his hands in a placating gesture. "We don't even know who this man is talking about." Turning to Emerson, he said, "What was it he said? Tasted? … Covering of protection? … Sensing a spirit? What do these things mean? Who is he and why did he take our children? He didn't say anything about making them slaves or working for that prince. This is something different. What should we do Em?"

Rayne stood silent, fighting an internal battle against his decision to distance himself from the need of the children— Kiefer's need. It was useless. He shook his head and grimaced. *It doesn't matter. This body. My own body. It doesn't matter. I can't change what I am.* No longer able to justify his silence, Rayne spoke. "It's me they want." He said it so softly, only Mite heard.

"No, no," Mite said. "Ray-ray must not do this thing. It is not time. Do not, do not do this thing young Light Bringer. We will find another way. There must be another way."

11

An unnerving silence descended at Mite's words, like the stillness before a storm. Rayne spoke up, his voice strong enough for everyone to hear. "It's me they want. I'm the broken. The lost and broken they are hunting. I'll go."

"No!" Mite shouted, hopping from leg to leg in a frenzied manner. "If you go, they will give you to Sigmund. The scrolls will not be found! The light will not come to Ochen!"

Rayne stared at Mite, anger burning the back of his throat. "How long?" he asked, his voice cold. "How long have you known who I am, Mite?"

"Enough!" Em shouted. "I won't know how to help the children if I don't know what that man was talking about. Ray, Mite, Gretel, Bodie, Hugh, to the dining tent. Everyone else, go to your homes for now. Petition the One for the children. I will call you as soon as I have figured out what's happening and what we need to do to help the children."

With a look that brooked no disobedience, Emerson turned and led the way to the dining tent. He waved everyone to seats around the table next to the door, then lit several lanterns placing them on the table.

Still standing, Emerson glared at those seated, his gaze landing, finally, on Rayne. "Okay, Ray, you seem to know something about this. Explain to me why our children have been taken."

Rayne closed his eyes for a moment, trying to decide what to say, how to explain things that defied explanation. Ultimately, he knew he had to tell the truth; nothing else would do in this situation. But he was unsure how to get Em and the others to believe him and not try to lock him up as a crazy person.

Rayne met Emerson's gaze. "I'm going to tell you a story, a true story that will sound insane. I mean, it happened to me, and I still can't believe it's real."

He paused and pulled in a deep breath before letting it hiss through his lips. "Okay. Here is the truth and the reason that man took the children. I am ... oh, this isn't going to work. I can't even say it without thinking I'm crazy."

His eyes fixed on the table, Mite said, "Just say it young Light Bringer. Ray-ray must tell the truth now. It is the only way to save the children and save you too, only way."

"You knew, didn't you? You knew all along?" Rayne stared at Mite, anger once again digging at the residual darkness coiled deep within him. "You knew who I was from the beginning, didn't you?"

"Mite knew Ray-ray from the beginning. The Creator-Father told Mite. He said the young Light Bringer needed help, needed time. But now there is no time. Time is gone."

Scanning the faces all focused on him, Rayne lifted a prayer to the One for help and guidance even though he knew he didn't deserve it. "You were told the Crown Prince of Ochen was looking for a little boy, an escaped slave with amethyst eyes. That was a message for me. He wants me to know he's looking for me. You see, that Prince Rayne is a pretender; he's not the real prince. I know, because I'm the real Prince Rayne, Light Bringer of the One, and the person the kidnappers want."

"You're talking nonsense." Emerson waved his hands in dismissal.

"Yeah," Hugh added, his features twisted as if he had eaten something sour. "Everyone knows the prince is a youth. He just celebrated his seventeenth birthday in Inverness. What are you trying to pull? If you try something stupid and those children get hurt, I'll ..."

"I'm not lying," Rayne said with all the force he could muster. "I'm not trying to *pull* something. And if you don't listen to me now, those children *will* die in the morning.

"I am the prophesied Light Bringer, the thirtieth generation in the line of King Nathan, son of King Theodor and Queen Rowena. I've studied the Words of the One to Corylus and reclaimed four of the seven Words of the One to Ochen. But the demons couldn't abide what I was doing. Sigmund, their leader, feared what I might yet accomplish."

"There is a prophecy. 'In the fullness of time the Light Bringer will arise. The lost will be found and he will bring to light my seven words hidden on the seven worlds and I will guide his steps. Sing for joy my people, the broken will be restored; the lost will be found. When the broken is restored and the lost is reclaimed, he will bind the living darkness. Know my people, the fullness of time has arrived; the time is now. Arise my Light Bringer.'

"That man asked for the broken one. I am the broken one." Rayne paused, laboring to still the anguish that threatened to undo him. "Sigmund shattered me by driving my spirit from my body into this old body. I don't even know who the old man is—was. But Sigmund needs me, the real me, my spirit imprisoned in this body, to reclaim the remaining three scrolls so he can destroy them.

"I'm the reason this is happening. I have to face that man at sunrise so he'll free the children. He must have been sent to retrieve me. I escaped from Sigmund right after he did this to me and he wants me back."

"The One will cover you and protect you, Ray-ray." Mite said. "You are his Light Bringer."

"No," Rayne groaned. "You don't understand. I turned my back on him. Told him I refused to be his pawn any longer. I'm getting what I deserve because I turned away from the

One. How can I expect him to save me from Sigmund when I haven't even prayed in weeks? After what I did, I can't just call on him now. I would be treating him like a servant, like I was just using him when I needed him. He's not the servant, I am. A disobedient and stubborn servant. I deserve the punishment I get. But I promise you this, I will not help Sigmund to find the last three scrolls. I will find a way to stop him even if I'm no longer the Light Bringer."

Mite jumped up and started his hopping routine again. "Wrong, wrong, wrong. Ray-ray is wrong. The Creator-Father still loves Ray-ray. He never stopped loving Ray-ray even when Ray-ray was so angry and sad. He is covering you still. Call him, Ray-ray, he will hear you. But you need to be ready; you need to decide to call. Otherwise all is lost. You must trust again."

"I'm not sure I can, Mite, it hurts too much to trust. How can I get back to what I was before? I'm broken, don't you understand. I'm not me and yet I am me. I can't deal with that. I just want to be me again, whole. I want my life back again, my friends, my parents, my dog, my normal life."

"Ray-ray must decide. Which is more important to him; having what he wants or serving the Creator-Father? Ray-ray must know who he will serve, himself or the One."

Mite's words rang in Rayne's head. *Ray-ray must know who he will serve, himself or the One.*

Whom will I serve? Myself or the One? The One who loved me even when I allowed the darkness to nest within me? The One who sent the Son to pay the penalty for all the lives I took for Sigmund and Coronus? The One who calls me his beloved, fills me with his warmth and strength, and never leaves me alone!

Are you here? Have you been here all along? Are you here with me now, even now?

For the first time since he had been broken, Rayne felt the warmth of the One. It was gentle and comforting. *I have made you and I have never left you. You are my beloved Light Bringer. Are you ready to let go of your anger and trust me?*

Can I trust the One? Do I trust the One? Deep down, under all the anger and fear, did he still trust even when he denied it and the darkness coiling within him screamed its defiance?

It's so hard, my Lord, but I will try. I want to let go of the anger and trust you. Please help me.

My beloved child, will you seek rest in my truth?

I will try always to rest in your truth, my Lord.

Light filled the room and the voice spoke. *Though light is shrouded and severed spirit wandering, he will find rest in my truth and I will be his shelter in the tempest. Know my beloved Light Bringer, I am your shelter. Reveal yourself to the dark ones and trust that they cannot touch you, for I am your strong shield. Be very courageous and trust.*

With tears streaming down his cheeks, Rayne looked up to see the others staring at him; Mite with a smile of contentment, Em, Gretel, Bodie, and Hugh as if he were some strange creature dropped into their midst. And he realized in many ways he was. He was no longer the young prince, but he wasn't the old man either. He was something different. But now he would embrace that difference. The One loved him and that was enough. It was time he stopped feeling sorry for himself and trusted the One to give him the strength to be courageous and trust.

"Mite. We need to leave now. It will take time for me to get to the place where the path meets the stream."

"What just happened?" Hugh asked.

"The broken has trusted again, again, again." Mite said, and he began to dance around the table.

"Mite," Emerson scowled "Sit down!" Emerson looked back and forth between Ray and Mite as if trying to decide whom to address, the crazy old man or the bouncy sprite. He focused on Ray and breathed in through his nose then released the air in a huff. "You're not crazy, are you? You really are *the* Prince Rayne, Crown Prince of Ochen, and you really are the One's prophesied Light Bringer, all trapped in someone else's body?"

Rayne gave a slight nod.

Looking around the table Emerson continued. "You all heard it too, right? That voice? It spoke with such power and yet it was gentle at the same time. That just really happened, and we are sitting across the table from ... this is insane!"

"This is real." Rayne spoke with a weight of quiet calm.

"This is the reality of what has been going on while people have been living their normal lives, unaware of the actions of beings like Sigmund and this creature who has taken the children. We don't have time for you all to come to an understanding of what's happening, because the children's lives are in danger. Trust me now. Sigmund took my body for himself so he could defeat the prophecies, but also so he would have the power to change the political structure of Ochen, and he's already changing things.

"But he needs my spirit too. Without all of me he cannot find the remaining scrolls. If not, he wouldn't have sent these others to hunt me and bring me back. He knows I'm weak now. That's why he chose this body to be my prison. But he made a fatal mistake. He forgot that the One loves to use those who are weak to defeat the schemes of his enemies.

"You must trust me now. At daybreak, I'll reveal myself, but I'll keep my distance until the children are safe. Mite, Em, Gretel, Hugh, Bodie, I'm trusting the children to you. Once they're safe, I'll give myself to Sigmund's hunters."

Mite shook his head, blue braids swinging. "No, no, no, Ray-ray will not face hunters alone. Mite will stand with Ray-ray. It is his calling. You may be Light Bringer, but Mite is of light as well. It is my purpose. Mite will stand with the Light Bringer."

Rayne plunged the depths of the earnest gray eyes and nodded. He looked long and invited Mite to know the depth of him, finally opening his spirit to the spirit of the diminutive ancient. After a moment, Mite shook himself as if coming up out of water and with a knowing smile, bowed his head to Rayne.

"I thank you, Light Bringer."

"Okay," Rayne said. "Mite, you will stand with me. Em, Gretel, Hugh, and Bodie, you get the children."

12

Worry overriding caution, Rayne pushed the boundaries of his physical limitations. Tripping over a black knot of root, he reached out for Mite's shoulder as his staff twisted. The slight ancient slipped under Rayne's arm like a crutch, keeping him from hitting the ground on his knees. Try though he would to keep his frustration in check, it surfaced from time to time as his frequent need to stop and rest slowed their progress.

As he struggled, Rayne came to understand another truth. His wounded pride was the true source of his bitter rejection of the One. He wasn't the strong, gifted young warrior any longer. And that stung. He couldn't fight his own battle this time, couldn't even walk to it without help. And that fact was ripping a gaping hole in his pride. His words came back to haunt him: 'The One loves to use those who are weak to defeat the schemes of his enemies.'

I have tried to run from you, broken and angry because my pride was wounded. I thought I was strong. Even now, I struggle with pride when I have nothing left to take pride in. Except you. You never left me even when I was screaming defiance at you. I tried so hard to be strong in myself when you were always standing next to me, willing me to understand that you alone are my true strength.

The truth is I needed you, still need you. The only difference now is that I know true strength doesn't come from my abilities or my pride or my identity, or even that rebellious spark you placed in me to defy Sigmund. True strength is found resting in you, my Creator-Father, my shelter in the tempest.

Even in the darkness, you were there, holding me when I was so weak. And I know you're here now with Kiefer and the other children, sheltering them. Thank you for being patient with me all the time it took for me to realize this. I know I'll fall again—you know how weak I really am—so I will trust you for then, too.

They approached the designated spot with time to spare. Splitting up, Emerson, Gretel, Bodie, and Hugh continued toward the stream while Rayne and Mite climbed to an open spot that overlooked the path. When they reached the clearing, they waited in the predawn gloaming as a light fog spread its misty, pale blanket outward from the gurgling water. Rayne stood like a statue, eyes fixed on the point where the path crossed the stream, both hands wrapped around the staff, while Mite shifted silently from foot to foot, muttering under his breath. "Ray-ray okay?" he asked after a bit.

"You know my name isn't Ray-ray."

"Mite is not my name either, Ray-ray. Our names do not define us; they are still being written. You are Ray-ray to Mite and you will remain Ray-ray until the lost is found." Mite spoke into the growing dawn, his voice quiet and serious.

They stood without moving for another few minutes. As the sun crested the horizon to send rays skimming through the trees, and birds sent tentative notes into the cool morning air, the hunter called.

"Broken one, show yourself; I know you are here. I sense your undone spirit." His voice thundered through the woods, echoing, sending flocks of birds winging into the morning air.

Stepping back, deeper into the shadows, Rayne shouted, "Release the children to my friends first."

The mountain of a man turned and waved to someone behind him. A few minutes later, the children walked out onto the path. Their hands were tied, and they were tethered along the length of one long rope. A beautiful young woman with deep red hair that caught the early morning sun, held the end of the rope looped around her hand and led them up to the path, while a tall, young blonde man walked behind. Both the man and woman had bows, the woman's slung over her shoulder, freeing her hands to hold the rope. The man held his with an arrow already nocked.

"You see them now," the large man rumbled. "Come, broken one, reveal yourself. It is time to return to your master."

"Release the children first."

A harsh laugh burst from the lips of the hunter. "Strong words, broken one, but you have nothing to bargain with." He turned back to the woman and nodded. She dropped the end of the rope and with a swift motion pulled a knife. She grinned, shifted behind the first child in the line, Kiefer, and pressed the sharp point into the side of his neck.

"No!" Rayne shouted. "Stop."

The woman froze, a thin stream of red droplets dribbled down Kiefer's throat.

The man shouted, "Then reveal yourself now."

Rayne stepped out of the shadows into a beam of sunlight angling through the trees. He stood balanced on spread legs, holding the staff for support.

"Here I am. Now, please ... let the children go. You see what I am, I cannot fight you or flee from you. I can barely stand on my own. Please let them go now. You have what you came for."

The hunter stared at Rayne for several minutes, sniffing the air. "I see you now, undone spirit." He turned back and waved to the woman. She sheathed her knife and motioned for the children to move up the path toward where Emerson, Gretel, Hugh, and Bodie were waiting, calling the children toward them. The man with the nocked arrow took aim at Rayne, holding him with the promise of a well-placed arrow if he tried to move.

Emerson and the others gathered the children to them. With Gretel in the lead and Hugh and Bodie flanking, they started the children, still bound, up the path. Em looked up to Rayne and saluted him before he followed the disappearing children.

Rayne sensed Mite slip back into the surrounding woods as the woman and the big man strode toward him while the man with the bow kept his arrow ready. As they approached, Rayne understood; neither was human. There was something about both that spoke of demon, and Rayne swallowed his revulsion as they came within a few feet of him.

The large man threw back his cowl and Rayne couldn't stop himself from stepping back. The inhuman face of the man-thing sent needles of fear skittering up his spine. It was like a cross between a man and a wolf and reminded Rayne of the hunters he had run from at Sigmund's years ago.

"So, this is it?" the woman sneered. "What we've been chasing these last weeks? This scrawny, weak, pathetic new-comer?"

Discernment showing in his deep, golden eyes and the tilt of his head, the wolf-man answered, "Yes, Krizia, but don't be deceived. He may be trapped in that weak outer prison, but the spirit inside is not weak. My fur is set on edge from the savor of the One surrounding him. We must handle him with extreme care. Do not try to touch him."

He took a step closer, studying Rayne. "I am Aquila, a spirit hunter. I see you within that shell and now understand why Sigmund imprisoned you in this form. Yet, even trapped as you are, Krizia and I cannot touch you without harm." He turned back to the man with the bow and yelled, "Marius, we need your human."

The young man relaxed his bow and after replacing the arrow, slung the bow over his shoulder and bounded up the slope.

"Untouchable?" he asked Aquila as he eyed Rayne.

"Yes," the wolf-man replied, still studying Rayne. "And something more. Something powerful. This undone spirit is well protected. Tell me boy, is it true? Are you the child proph-esied to bring light to Ochen?"

Before Rayne could respond, he heard Mite laugh then

speak in a voice of power so unlike his normal voice, Rayne blinked in disbelief.

"Undone, undone, but Light Bringer still. Sigmund's bane he has been; Sigmund's bane he remains. Know, creatures of darkness, when light is united, judgement is near. For you are lost to this world. Run while you can."

The three hunters spun in diverse directions as if each had heard the voice from a different spot. Aquila turned back to Rayne and growled as golden light began seeping from within the old body, highlighting Rayne with a corona of energy. Fine, gossamer webs of blue light appeared, mingling with the golden light like two dancers moving in perfect harmony to an unheard melody.

"Curse Sigmund, and that fool Heinrich with him," Aquila snarled.

"Told you, told you." Mite's normal sing-song voice filled the air, echoing from every direction at once. "You would not hear and now your end is near. I love to rhyme when the Creator-Father says it's time." Child-like laughter rang through the woods.

"What is that?" Krizia said as she turned in circles, her eyes scanning the underbrush.

Warmth, soft and feather-like, flickered through Rayne and the swirling lights continued to build and brighten around him. The voice of the One spoke, filling the woods with its echo. "You have overstepped your bounds, Spirit Hunter. You have hunted my chosen and been judged; now you must forfeit your very existence here. Be gone."

Aquila's eyes went wide, and he shouted to Marius and Krizia, "Run. Sigmund has condemned us! Run!"

Then Mite was in front of Rayne, wrapping thin arms around Rayne's legs, supporting him. They stood together, untouched, in a calm sphere of gold and blue light as a violent storm broke around them with unimaginable fury. At a gentle prompting of the One, Rayne closed his eyes. *It is not for you to witness the true fury of the tempest that brings my judgment.*

The preternatural fury didn't last long, mere seconds by Rayne's reckoning. Then silence descended. The beautiful sense of completeness and love that surrounded Rayne in the cocoon of light was too intense to release and he rested in the moment, his eyes closed, breathing lightly.

The change came in increments, a gentle release of the warmth, the awareness of the bird song, the everyday feel of sunlight on skin where beams filtering through the trees touched his arm, the soft caress of the morning breeze. He sobbed at the loss as, once again, he felt the constraints of his old body cut off the final residual remnants of otherworldly warmth and peace.

When Rayne opened his eyes, he saw Mite sitting on a rock in front of him, staring. "Ray-ray is indeed beloved. Never before has Mite seen the Creator-Father dismiss with such fury and protect with such warmth."

With both hands wrapped around the staff like a pair of hoary twigs, Rayne picked his way to a rock near Mite and lowered his old man body down. He couldn't speak; everything was still shimmering with afterimages of the One's judgement, so he just sat, breathing.

"The hunters are gone, gone from Ochen. Gone from this realm," Mite whispered.

Rayne and Mite sat in silence for a long time before Mite's ever-present need to release energy prompted him to jump up and start hopping from foot to foot. "Ray-ray ready to go now?"

Rayne laughed at Mite's antics. "We need to find the Words of the One to Nemora, Mite. I think it is time I left the Camp of the Forgotten."

"Yes, yes, yes!" Mite shouted as he executed a quick jig. "Time, time, time. It is time to go; the Light Bringer has been summoned."

He reached out a hand toward Rayne. Still chuckling, Rayne grabbed his staff in one hand and reached to take Mite's hand with the other. Pulling himself up, he asked Mite, "Do you know the way?"

"Mite knows the way. Has always known the way, just waiting for Ray-ray to ask."

Rayne's eyes roamed the area and he took a deep breath

of the fresh morning air. "Then let's return to the camp and make sure the children are alright. We can gather the supplies we need and leave tomorrow morning, if that is okay with you Sir Mite."

"Sir Mite? Sir Mite! I like that. Sir Mite, Sir Mite, Sir Mite."

By the time they got back to the camp, Rayne had come to regret his impulse to call Mite, Sir Mite. The little ancient was still repeating the name in a kind of made-up song when they came over the hill and walked into the camp.

Within minutes, the two found themselves surrounded. Everyone seemed to want to ask questions at the same time. Rayne felt someone take his hand and gazing down he saw Kiefer looking up at him with tear-filled eyes.

"I thought I lost you," the little boy signed.

With a chuckle Rayne signed back, "I am not so easy to lose."

Lunch turned into a major celebration, and though Rayne tried to keep Em and the others from spreading the story of who he really was, it didn't take long for everyone to start treating him with a level of respect that created a rift between him and the people of the camp.

They seemed uncomfortable in his presence now and even though he insisted he be treated the same as before, he realized it was good that he and Mite were leaving. He was no longer just the lost old man. His identity was now that of the true Crown Prince of Ochen and the One's Light Bringer who had been imprisoned in the old man body. His continued presence in the camp not only put the people there at risk, it created an awkward situation.

Early the next morning, while everyone slept, Rayne and Mite left.

13

Craftsmen scurried around the Great Square erecting a tall platform draped with banners exhibiting both the Kierkengaard and the Woodfield crests while His Royal Highness, the Lord Master Mage, Brayden, Giles, and several others who had accompanied them from Sorial spent the day sequestered in the prince's suite. Later that evening, His Royal Highness, sent out an official notice: *Tomorrow, at noon, all citizens of Westvale are commanded to congregate in the Great Square for a public statement.*

The next day, at precisely noon, His Royal Highness began his address. He affirmed the news that Queen Rowena was suffering from disabling illness, then went on to announce that King Theodor, in his grief, had become so distraught, he was no longer capable of ruling.

"It is with profound sorrow that I share the news of Queen Rowena's illness and King Theodor's resulting incapacitation." His Royal Highness' voice trembled, and he stopped speaking for a minute, his head bowed. With a deep breath, he raised his eyes and scanned the crowd. "Ever since Queen Rowena—my ... mother—suffered a full collapse from an unknown malady while we were on Nemora, my father has been in shock and unable to discharge his duties as king." He paused and wiped several tears from his eyes with a lacy handkerchief before continuing.

"I am sure you all share my grief at the loss of both King Theodor and Queen Rowena. My sorrow knows no bounds and I am grateful for my cousin Brayden's innocence coming to light in time for him to be my strong support in this time of grief."

After pausing and turning his back to the crowd for several minutes to compose himself, the pretender turned to face the stunned gathering again.

"While on Nemora, I petitioned the Interplanetary Council to name a regent. Accepting the situation and my proposal, the council made the decision to name my cousin, Lord Brayden Woodfield of Nemora to the position. He was my parent's choice for Adopted Heir Apparent and is well versed in the intricacies of political rule. I am too young and inexperienced to pick up my father's mantle. So, until such time as either King Theodor or Queen Rowena recover sufficiently to resume rule, or I am better prepared to rule, I join you in bowing to our new regent, His Highness, Regent Brayden Woodfield."

As His Royal Highness moved back and Brayden came forward, a hush descended on the square.

Brayden lifted his nose, his eyes scanning the crowd, his aristocratic face a mask of cold disdain. "My fellow citizens, I greet you all in the name of King Theodor. As your new regent, it falls to me to address you regarding our current situation. In that capacity, I will, at this time tomorrow, make my first official address here in the Great Square. Every citizen of Westvale is required to attend; any who disobey this official command, will be arrested. That is all."

Regent Woodfield turned his back on the crowd and His Royal Highness stepped forward again.

"As a representative of the Interplanetary Council, I am pleased to announce the council has voted unanimously to accept Sorial's petition to reduce Veres' status from that of an independent sovereign planet to the position of a satellite, a vassal, of Sorial.

"A military action, initiated by the Interplanetary Council and sanctioned by both Regent Woodfield and me, took place two days ago at the Verenian portals on Sorial. This engagement succeeded in returning control of the skipping line to the proper authorities on Sorial.

"Travel to Veres will remain restricted. We hope by this action to avoid any future influence of off-world rabble rousers. Without the pressure of those negative elements, we believe the Verenians will come to a peaceful resolution with the Sorial Mining Guild.

"You will be pleased to hear that the cost of veredium will, once again, be controlled by the Mining Guild instead of fluctuating wildly the way it has been since the off-world trouble makers ousted the guild. We are confident this official change will be beneficial to all."

His Royal Highness inclined his head to the people, turned on his heel, and, with the regent following, left the platform.

After several minutes of confused silence, the crowd began to disperse. People spoke in hushed whispers as they filtered from the square, giving a wide berth to the skeleton of the rising scaffold. Like a river flowing to either side of a rocky outcropping, they parted and then merged once again beyond the ominous structure.

Lexi wiped tears from her cheeks as she listened to the news from Nemora. Veres was no longer an independent, sovereign planet. Her people were, once again, subject to the control of the powerful Sorial merchants. She swallowed her shock and moved forward, a mechanical doll on stiff legs, numb, certain that if she allowed herself to feel, her heart, like a stressed gem, would shatter. After climbing the grand staircase to the second level of the palace, she turned into the family wing, continuing to move forward, outwardly calm. Inside, she held all in stasis. Pulling in a deep, shuddering breath, Lexi knocked on the door to Rowena's suite and walked in. Anne was sitting next to the large bed, reading aloud to the slight form of the queen. Lexi's throat constricted at the sight. The still, silent figure reminded her so much of her father; and now she had just found out she couldn't return to Veres to see him.

When Lexi entered, Anne stood and opened her arms. "I just heard. I'm so sorry."

Without hesitation, the dam within Lexi broke and tears flowed as she ran into Anne's comforting arms. After allowing her pain to flow freely for a few minutes, Lexi pulled back and said, "I'm sorry Anne; I know you and Shaw were planning to skip to Veres to see if you could find your family. It looks as though we will both have to wait.

"It's hard though, I need to talk to my father so badly, it hurts. The last time I saw him, he was still so weak, and now I don't know when I'll see him again. And it scares me, not knowing what's happening on Veres. Is he even okay? How could Rayne have done the things he did on Veres and now turn around and do this? It makes no sense."

Anne cupped Lexi's damp chin. "You know how. Whatever is controlling Rayne isn't him. We need to find a way to free him from this thing using him."

Hurt and confusion swirled in Lexi and she nodded. "Maybe you are right, Anne. Maybe something is controlling Rayne. But I'm not ready to give up on him yet."

Lexi had been so intent on Anne and her pain that she hadn't seen King Theodor sitting in a dark corner, watching his wife resting on the bed, his eyes staring, unfocused. Letting go of Anne, Lexi ran to the king. "Your Majesty, you can stop this. You can convince the Interplanetary Council that you don't need a regent. You can tell them how wrong they are about Veres. Oh, Your Majesty, please hear me. We need you now."

King Theodor raised bleary eyes to Lexi for a moment, wrinkles of sorrow furrowing his face. "No, my child. I am sorry. It's too late. I've been declared incompetent. You must take your petition to Regent Woodfield now." Theodor looked down to his folded hands. "My son knows what he's doing. I must trust him now. I didn't before, and it was a disaster. Rayne and Brayden are right, their willingness to take on the mantle of rule will free me to watch over my wife."

Lexi glanced over at Anne, fear spiking in her at the king's statement. Anne's mouth bent down in anger. "His Royal Highness and the Lord Master Mage visited His Majesty earlier. I don't know what was said, no one was permitted in the room while they spoke. But ever since that conversation, His Majesty has been like this."

"Oh, no." Lexi moaned. "I have to go. I almost forgot. Rayne invited me to a small dinner party this evening. He even mentioned sending a special tailor from Sorial to my rooms with several outfits he deemed suitable for the occasion. Perhaps I'll find out the truth of what's happening if I attend. But Anne, I'm scared. What if Rayne is still not himself? What if Bishop Hedrick is right? What do I do?"

"You're going to go to that party and pretend whatever happens doesn't upset you. You're going to be strong for Rayne and try to learn anything you can about why he is behaving in this way."

Anne stepped up to Lexi, reached out to grasp her upper arms, and caught her eyes. "I know you, Lexi, you're strong; you can do this. Keep reminding yourself that you're doing it to help Rayne. We can't help him if we don't know what's really happening. All we have at this point is suppositions and maybes. Perhaps this party will prove to be the opportunity we've been waiting for. You may be our only hope of finding out the truth."

Lexi pulled in a deep breath and allowed it to hiss out through her teeth as she recognized the truth of Anne's words. Chewing her lower lip, she nodded. "You're right Anne. I can't run away from this. I have to be strong for everyone, Rayne, my father, our friends. You're meeting at the church house again tonight, aren't you?"

Anne nodded.

"Would you ask everyone to pray for me, please?"

"We will keep you in our prayers. You have my word."

The Pretender Prince, Brayden, Heinrich, Giles, and Jason

Andersen sat in the rooms Brayden had confiscated and redecorated to his own garish tastes when Rayne left for Veres months ago. The pretender reclaimed them the morning after they arrived in Westvale, moving Brayden back to his old quarters. At first, Brayden objected, pointing out that as regent, he was entitled to the larger suite. But one cold look from His Royal Highness convinced the regent to accept the situation. Milo, Sigmund's newest assistant, had also come, and was now busy working on writing missives to Sigmund's agents on the other worlds.

"So, did the announcements go over well?" Jason asked Brayden as the new regent sniffed at his glass of honeyed sherry.

"Bunch of stupid idiots, those commoners," Brayden mumbled. "I don't understand why we have to court their favor. They're just sheep and we can herd them any way we want with the proper show of force."

"You mean like on Veres?" Sigmund asked. "No, it will take some effort to create the proper atmosphere of fear and obedience that we need to move forward with the next step in our plans. Our master is already on the move, spreading darkness on all seven worlds. Our work with the scroll worshippers is right on schedule and going well. Soon we will finally be able to disband that annoying Interplanetary Council, and then, my dear regent, we will have our sheep ready for sacrificing. We will be gods to them, and they will all serve us as slaves. Once Corylus and Nemora fall, the others will follow without a whimper."

The pretender turned his focus to the Lord Master Mage. "I have to hand it to you, Heinrich, your plans to take Ochen without full-blown war were brilliant. Political intrigue, religious control, and small conflicts are proving to be so much more effective than outright war. Although since that idiot prince visited Glacieria we are having some difficulties reinstituting scroll worship there. But once we have them under control again, we will end up with the total population of the seven in the palm of our hands. Our master will be pleased."

Heinrich lifted his glass to the pretender and inclined his

head. "You are forgetting one little fact though, my friend. That *idiot prince* is still on the loose. We of the living darkness will not be safe until the scrolls are eliminated and the spirit of the boy is dead or bound at our master's feet."

Sigmund growled. "Don't you think I know that? Aquila should have returned weeks ago. I would send another hunter, but Aquila was uniquely qualified. That annoying boy has eluded even him. I must think of another way to acquire him."

Sigmund thought for a while as the other occupants of the room remained silent. He ground his teeth. Though his plans were progressing as expected, he had one problem; without its natural spirit to sustain it, the prince's body was weakening. Slowly, and unnoticed by his co-conspiritors, but weakening none the less. Not a true threat at the moment, but something Sigmund couldn't just ignore. *I can't wait any longer ... I need that boy now, before Heinrich learns what is happening and challenges me. What to do?* Finally, Sigmund stirred. "I have an idea. Instead of trying to track him down, what if we lure him in with a trap?"

"What kind of trap?" Brayden asked, leaning forward.

"What does he care about?" Sigmund asked.

"The girl," Jason said. "I understand that while he was on Veres the two grew quite close. I think he loves her."

"Enough to sacrifice himself for her?" Heinrich asked.

"Of course," A sly smile surfaced on Sigmund's handsome young face. "Our young friend has a thing about sacrificing himself for others and if he would do it for a stranger, he will do it without question for the one he loves."

He closed his eyes, thinking again. *Now I've got you.* "Tonight, at dinner, I will convince our diminutive Lady Alexianndra of Veres that I am still her lover. I was hoping to have a little fun with her, but this might prove to be even more entertaining."

"After what you just did to Veres," Giles said. "I think you will have to work hard to get her to believe you."

"Oh, I don't know," Sigmund purred. "I can be quite charming when I want to be."

"A wager," Jason said, his eyes flashing. "Let's all predict how long it will take our prince to earn back the lady's love.

Will he earn it tonight? Tomorrow night? A week from now? And how do we determine his success? Will she bed him or just kiss him? Come now, place your bets. But this is too delicious for just monetary bets. What shall we wager?"

Allowing himself to relax into the conversation, Sigmund said, "My design is to get her to accompany me back to Nemora and then lure the prince out with a threat to her life. I propose we wager on how long it will take for me to convince the lady to accompany me to Nemora. And the prize for the winner will be what, my friends? What shall we wager on my success?"

"Wait," Brayden said. "How can we be sure you won't cheat and use a weave to lure her to Nemora. No, you have to do this just by charming her, no magic. If fact, you shouldn't even be allowed to wager. You'll cheat just to win."

"I give you my word; I won't use magic."

Heinrich, Jason, Brayden, and Giles all snorted in disbelief, then laughed at their common response to Sigmund's statement.

"Delight me, gentlemen with your creativity. What would you propose?" the prince asked.

"Once you pervert the religion on Corylus, you're planning to tear down the cathedral and erect a colossal gaming complex next to the palace. That's correct, isn't it?" Heinrich asked.

"Yes."

"Whoever wins the wager will have his own private box ringside for which he will never be charged."

"Hear, hear!" Jason crowed. "I like that, Heinrich. What say you gentlemen, shall we agree on the prize?"

Sigmund nodded. "I agree. A private box for the winner of the wager. Pick your timeframes. I must warn you, however, I am impatient. If the lady is too reticent, I might just resort to a little unorthodox persuasion after all."

14

Lexi wrinkled her nose at the clothing Mathias, the new tailor from Sorial, presented to her. Though many of the young ladies who had attended the crown prince's recent parties on Nemora and Sorial, and followed the prince back to Westvale, swooned over his designs, calling them stunning and unique, Lexi found Mathias's dresses either too garish or too skimpy. After several confrontations, Lexi achieved an acceptable compromise when the man agreed to alter one of his simpler gowns to allow her a proper degree of modesty and taste. Now, she chewed her lip as she stood like a wooden statue while his assistants fitted the gown to her body.

Closing her eyes, she strove to remain still as, once again, she thought back to the day Rayne changed. He had been standing, just like she was now, and Theodor's dressers were altering the clothing he had chosen. She chewed her lip, her mind wrestling to reconcile what her eyes saw with what she felt. Her thoughts wandered, and she imagined what it would be like to have Rayne act normal this evening. She visualized him dressed in a fashionable outfit similar to the one Giles and Blossom had picked for him on Amathea, her hand on his arm.

She had relaxed into the border of hazy consciousness, barely maintaining her balance when her skin prickled, and a gentle warmth pervaded her. As if in a waking dream, she saw a fragile old man and a child standing in the calm center of a violent storm. The image was distinct, clear, and undeniable. The voice of the One spoke to her. *You will know the truth in him.*

Lexi's eyes popped open. *Did I just hear the voice of the One? Was that a dream?* She wanted to be alone to think about what just happened, but Mathias's assistants were still hovering. They had taken the pinned dress from her and were sitting next to each other on the floor, each working on a small section of the gown, talking in quiet whispers while Mathias preened in the mirror.

Finally, Mathias and his helpers left her room, but before she had a moment to herself, three ladies' maids arrived.

"His Royal Highness sent us. We're to help you get ready for his special dinner."

After helping Lexi bathe and dress, the three divided her hair into a multitude of braids, which they wove into a series of loops draping down onto her shoulders. As they were putting the final touches on her hair, she was summoned to the small family dining room for Rayne's private affair.

Rayne had told Lexi it would be a small dinner party. Indeed, only a few of his closest associates were in attendance; Brayden, Giles, the Lord Master Mage from the Interplanetary Council, and to Lexi's disgust, Jason Andersen. His Royal Highness had also invited Lady Elaine and two other ladies Lexi knew only in passing. Lexi was surprised to find Rayne waiting for her at the door. He greeted her with a broad, open smile and her heart beat faster as he seated her next to him at the table.

He was attentive and personable, and even got her to laugh a couple times. Lexi let her guard drop a notch and gave herself permission to enjoy the company and the evening. When the conversation turned to the situation with Veres, Rayne faced Lexi, his brows drawn together in concern. Lexi couldn't miss the remorse reflected in his eyes when he said, "I am quite sorry. The council gave me no choice but to agree with their decision. Though I argued for the independence of Veres, it was to no avail." He sighed and shook his head. "And now, to make matters worse, I'm expected to act as the spokesperson for the council. But all is not lost. I hope to gain ground on my next trip to Nemora, a trip I plan to make soon."

"Rayne, do you think it might be possible for me to get permission to travel to Veres to see my father. I haven't seen him since we left Veres and I long to talk to him. I'm sure he would be delighted to see you again too and thank you for what you did. Perhaps, if your schedule permits, we could travel there together." Lexi looked into the deep amethyst orbs she had missed over the last several weeks as the thumping beat of her heart echoed in her ears.

A dazzling smile brightened Rayne's face, the smile Lexi remembered with affection from Veres. Her heart thumped even faster. She was right. Her friends misunderstood. Rayne had just been pretending, playing a role. He was okay now; everything was okay now.

Rayne leaned in a little closer. His lips brushed hers, soft as butterfly wings, and with that touch, something sparked through Lexi. Revulsion for the man before her churned her stomach, turning it acidic and foul. Her heart screamed *wrong* to her mind. She began to pull away, but words Anne had spoken to her earlier blared through her mind with force. 'Bishop Hendrik advised we remain in our positions and not let on what we suspect. It is the only way we can find out the truth.'

Lexi steeled herself to play along. She had already decided on a way to test Rayne; a plan she had avoided until now, but one she could no longer avoid. With her heart deflating like an empty wineskin, she resolved to search out the truth of the man before her.

Pulling in a deep breath, she placed her hand on Rayne's chest, her fingers brushing his jacket, and looked into his—way too alluring—eyes. She smiled what she hoped was an inviting smile. "Please, Rayne, I know if *you* asked, you could arrange for us to visit my father. I would be so appreciative. It would mean so much to my father to thank you in person for helping him rescue Lloyd when he fell into that well on the way to Eleri." Lexi walked her fingers up Rayne's chest and lowered her lashes. "Lloyd's always been such a clumsy little boy but he's special to my father. I know it would mean the world to him."

"Perhaps we could arrange a visit," the prince purred as he shifted even closer to Lexi and claimed her lips with a full kiss.

She leaned into the kiss, giving and taking, running her hand up Rayne's arm onto his shoulder. *I'll play along whoever or whatever you are. But I'll not let you fool me again. You are not my Rayne. Rayne would know. Lloyd was the old man who gave him the ancient sword in Mistal* Though her test had revealed the truth, a part of her died at Rayne's words.

He began to ease his right arm around her back, pulling her into him, increasing the intimacy, obviously confident his advances wouldn't be repelled.

Once more. Just once more. I must be certain. "You do remember how much my father appreciated your help then, don't you?"

"Yes," the pretender murmured then kissed her again. His lips shifted from her mouth pressing little kisses, soft and demanding, down to her throat. "We rescued Lloyd ... clumsy little boy ... how could I forget?"

"Yes, my love," Lexi murmured as she gently pushed the pretender away before his lips could continue their descent. "When we get to Veres, I'm sure my father and you can enjoy remembering how you lowered yourself into that well and my father pulled you and that little boy to safety. He'll probably want to throw a party in your honor since we didn't have any time for that before we left."

The thing that was Rayne began to draw Lexi closer once again, but she kept her hand on his chest, creating a distance between them.

"Well, my love," Lexi licked her lips. "Do you think we could visit Veres?"

The pretender ran a fingertip in a swirling pattern up her bare arm and fingered a loose tendril of hair before slipping under the material at her shoulder. "I am sorry, my dear. But I don't see that as a possibility at the current time. But, since I am planning to meet with the council when I return to Nemora, why don't you accompany me and plead your case in person?"

With an effort of will, Lexi stifled the shiver that threatened to reveal her true feelings. "Let me think about that ... for just a bit ... please." Slipping out from the encircling arm she rose. "I am feeling unwell." Her eyes scanned the group seated around the table, noting other couples embracing, before meeting the mage's cold silver eyes. *Stay strong.* "If you will all please excuse me, it's been a very full day."

She turned back to the pretender and, leaning in, kissed him on the lips. Then, with a curtsy, walked from the room, head held high. She kept her composure until the door to her room closed behind her. As the latch clicked, Lexi bent over with her hands on her knees and fought the urge to be sick. "Oh, blessed One, what am I going to do?"

Andrew stumbled his way down the pathway between the royal palace and the cathedral, clutching Boone's leash with a white-knuckled grasp in one hand and a bundle of his belongings in the other as he sniffed back tears that threatened to fall. He glanced over his shoulder to make sure none of the guards were watching. So much had changed in the last day that Andrew no longer knew if up was still up and down was still down. Now he sought the only comfort he could be sure of, Elsie's kitchen.

"Please," he pleaded with the kind-hearted cook. "You have to let me bring Boone inside. If His Royal Highness finds out I've got her, I don't know what he'll do. Please."

"My dear, dear boy, what happened?"

Andrew shook his head, unable to say any more without releasing the tears that clung to the lashes of his eyes.

Elsie shook her head. "Come on. Bring her in here."

"It'll just be for a little while, until I can find her a new home. I don't know what else to do." He knelt next to Boone and wrapped his hands in the fur on her neck. After sniffling a few times, he asked, "Are we meeting tonight?"

At Elsie's nod, Andrew breathed a sigh of relief. "Good. Maybe someone will be willing to take Boone and keep her safe."

Andrew put his bundle on the table and Elsie looked at it, her eyebrows climbing her forehead as her eyes widened. "What do you have there, young man?"

Andrew wiped his nose with his sleeve and started to cry again.

Elsie looked down at the boy, the lines on her face deepening with sorrow. She moved to him and wrapped her arms around his shaking shoulders. "Hush, hush, dear boy. It'll all be okay. You just go ahead and cry it out now, then you can tell us all what happened. Everyone will be here in another hour. For now, you just have a good cry and I'll get you something to eat."

As Elsie hugged the sobbing form to her, the action brought to mind all the times she had done this for Rayne when he was just a little thing. But if the rumors floating around since the prince's return had any basis in reality, Jonathan's suspicions might just be true. The prince was not Rayne. He may be *His Royal Highness,* as he had commanded everyone to address him, but he was no Prince Rayne.

Andrew finally fell into a fitful sleep with his head on one of the long tables in the dining room and Boone curled up at his feet. After Elsie explained the situation, Jonathan readily agreed to allow Boone to stay as long as needed. But once Andrew woke, Jonathan asked that he try to find a more permanent solution soon. The church house was too close to the palace and a barking dog there would raise questions.

15

Andrew sat at one of the tables in the church house, his mind miles away as he scratched behind Boone's ears absentmindedly. He looked up from time to time as friends trickled into the room. They came in ones or twos, so they didn't draw attention. Rumors were spreading that the new Royal Highness had already demanded several people on Nemora be brought before the Interplanetary Court for speaking out against him and, like Thorvin had predicted, meeting this way was risky.

Elsie left small candles lit in the kitchen, the front foyer, and the side entryway. Everyone knew to slip into one of the three doorways without knocking and creep down the shadow strewn hallways to the dining room.

Kori and Mace were first to arrive, followed a short time later by Stevie. Sashi and Noah ducked in through the kitchen entrance. Travis arrived next with Deven from the Reclamation Committee, who had joined the group recently. Thorvin ghosted in with Captain Fontaine on his heels. They were beginning to question if Danton, Anne, and Shaw were going to make it, when Shaw and Anne arrived, followed by Danton.

Bishop Hedrick opened the meeting with prayer, specifically asking for protection and guidance for Lexi this evening. Andrew focused on Boone, patting her head and shuffling his feet at the curious stares aimed in his direction. Jonathan caught Andrew's eye, and with a kind wink, announced that everyone needed to hear Andrew's story before they got into the purpose of their meeting.

Andrew looked up at the friendly faces around the table and, with a deep breath, began his tale. "I got the summons to return to the palace yesterday and got back after the announcements in the square this afternoon. I hurried to the prince's suite with Boone. I hadn't been in his rooms since Brayden took them and everything was different. It was a mess. I started to try and organize the clothing that was all over the floor, but then Boone growled and ran into the sitting room.

"She was really upset, barking and snarling. I ran after her thinking someone was there who shouldn't be, like before when Sigmund did that thing to me. But when I ran in, I couldn't believe what I was seeing. She was snapping and growling at Rayne. Lord Brayden, his brother, Giles, and two other men I didn't know, were laughing. And then the prince ... the prince, he—oh, I can't even say it—he kicked her!

"Rayne kicked Boone!" Andrew dropped his gaze to the table, still trying to come to terms with what he had seen. "I couldn't believe what I was seeing. Rayne kicking Boone? No!" Andrew's hair bounced wildly as he looked up and shook his head. "He wouldn't do that. Rayne loves Boone and she loves him." Andrew sniffed and ran his hand under his dripping nose. "Boone let out a yelp and then lay still for a minute before she got back up and started barking again. Then the prince was yelling, "leash that animal." He was so angry, not like himself at all. If I didn't see him standing right in front of me, I would never have thought the person screaming at me was Prince Rayne.

"I got a leash on Boone and got her to settle. By that time, the prince's friends were all sitting around, still laughing and making comments about a boy and his dog and why his dog hated him. I didn't understand most of what they said, but the prince, he got really red in the face. Then, with his voice all soft and scary, he said, 'Destroy that flea infested piece of boar bait. Drown it or smack it on the head, or slice it open, I don't care. But don't come back until you've gotten rid of it.'"

Andrew's voice cracked as tears tracked down his cheeks to drip off his chin. "What's happening? Why did Boone try to attack Rayne? Does this have something to do with what you talked about before? Boone's smart; she knows the truth. Boone loves Rayne, but she hates this person. And Rayne would never hurt Boone. It just wouldn't happen. Now I'm supposed to get rid of Boone. I can't do it; I just can't do it. I've got to find a safe place for her."

"We'll figure something out," Thorvin said, his voice calm and reassuring. "Neither you nor Boone is going anywhere near the palace until we figure out what's going on."

"I don't think it's a good idea for Andrew or Boone to stay here," Jonathan said. "We're too close to the palace. If Boone starts barking, people will be suspicious. They know we don't allow dogs in here."

"They can come stay with us," Kori Kasper said. "We've got room for Andrew, and Boone can sleep in the shop. Andrew, would you like that? Would you like to stay with Stevie and Sashi?"

"Are you sure, Mrs. Kasper? I don't want to make any trouble for anyone. I don't want to go home, in case the prince sends someone after us. But it would be nice if Boone and I could stay together. I could help in your shop too, you know, earn my keep."

"That sounds like a good idea." Kori smiled. "I can teach you some basics and you can help with simple jobs. With Mace gone to Nemora the next few weeks, I would enjoy your company. And I would feel safer with Boone around too."

"Hey, what about us?" Stevie asked. "Don't Sashi and I count?"

"Nemora's moons, Stevie," Sashi gave her brother a disgusted look.

"Oh!" Stevie said after a moment, his eyes widening as the light of understanding dawned in them. "Yeah! We're busy a lot lately too and mom could sure use the help."

"That's right," Sashi said. "And with Boone sleeping in the shop, we won't have to worry that anyone might try to break in. We'll be safer with Boone there, right Stevie?"

Stevie nodded.

Jonathan smiled and nodded a thank you to Kori. Then he turned to Thorvin. "Were your friends from Nemora able to tell you anything?"

"Nothing really important." Thorvin released a huff of air. "But remember how I told you that after Rayne was poisoned and the mage gave him the antidote, they went to that rundown cottage? Remember how I said I saw an old man leave the cottage after they left?

"Well, I find it kind of interesting that our new regent has left standing orders for units of soldiers near Inverness to hunt for an old man, a *particular* old man. In fact, the man who used to live in that cottage.

"I don't know if this is the same old man I saw, but it does seem peculiar, especially since Blossom died under suspicious circumstances. Something happened in there, and the only people who know what, are the prince, his pet mage, Brayden, and Giles ... and the now-missing old man that the soldiers are hunting.

"I'm beginning to wonder if there is more to the old man than I originally thought and if I shouldn't skip back to Nemora and do a little looking around myself."

"It does seem as though there might be some connection," Shaw said.

Clearing his throat, Captain Fontaine said, "But now is not a good time for you to leave. We need to have at least one person here with authority and it can't be me. I've been reassigned to Centerville. And I'm not the only one. Captain Ellis has been reassigned to Easton. We're both due to leave in three days. Captain Ellis and I, along with several other senior officers of the guard, are being replaced by people the new regent is bringing in from Nemora.

"And remember those soldiers who came from Nemora right before you left with Prince Rayne? Well, they've all been promoted. Corporal Job Parker? Well, now he's *Lieutenant* Job Parker. Every one of those Nemorian recruits has jumped two or three ranks overnight by order of the regent.

"I know you would like to see if you could find that old man on Nemora and try to solve the mystery surrounding what happened there, but I don't think this is the time for you to leave Westvale. We need a voice of reason here at the capital who won't bow down to these new officers. You're the only one I trust my men to. Good men like our friend Corporal Noah Reese, here, might just find themselves being forced to obey orders that go against their moral convictions."

"I don't know if I can do anything, Anton. You know I'm not officially part of the guard. My position is only that of a civilian instructor." Thorvin grimaced as he rubbed his hands over his prickly chin.

"The men respect you," Captain Fontaine said. "If we start to have real problems here—and with the way things are going now, I'd be surprised if we didn't—the men will look to you for guidance. You see it coming, too, don't you, Thorvin? Gallows being erected in the Great Square?

"We've got trouble staring us right in the face and that idiot reassigns Ellis and me to new posts away from Westvale and promotes his friends from Nemora. Not one of them is a worthy soldier, Thorvin. You've worked with them. Tell me I'm wrong. Go ahead and tell me. You can't.

"And nobody knows anything about the incoming officers. They won't even arrive until the day we're leaving. The whole thing smells, and the problem is right at the top. You know it, and I know it. That pretender prince and his sidekick regent are going to tear Corylus apart and maybe even the whole system. Someone has to stop them before it's too late."

Everyone got quiet and Andrew pulled Boone to him, as Captain Fontaine's words faded into silence. Then the captain filled the void. "You understand, Thorvin? What I'm saying? If things continue to deteriorate and we can't fix the prince, we will have to …

"Stop right there," Thorvin growled. "Do you have any idea what you're suggesting? This is insanity! It's treason! And we're not there yet."

"Remember." The captain's voice turned low and intense. "You're the one who said this person is not the real prince. If he's truly a pretender, then think about what I'm suggesting. Over the years, I've watched the political maneuvering King Theodor accomplished with those nobles from the Interplanetary Council. I've seen the games they play. King Theodor was a genius at those political games, but we no longer have King Theodor in power. He's been pushed out by the very people he worked with on the council.

"Are you even aware who our prince and regent plan to execute on that new gallows in just a few days' time? Of course, you couldn't know. The information has been kept to official channels. One member of the Interplanetary Council and three judges from the Interplanetary Court, all charged with treason against the Ochen system. Do you know why they're being executed here on Corylus instead of on Nemora? Because His Royal Highness petitioned the council to grant him jurisdiction over the execution of interplanetary traitors. Jurisdiction over interplanetary anything is just opening the door to disbanding the Interplanetary Council—and those idiots agreed.

"From what I could find out by cashing in a few favors, the only crime these prisoners committed was to question the decision to make Veres a possession of Sorial.

"I have to leave in just a few days." Captain Fontaine shook his head, looking as if he had swallowed something sour. "I know it sounds insane but watch over the next few months and then tell me what's insane. Allowing our whole planetary system to be destroyed or deposing and imprisoning the impostor who's fostering that destruction, and his co-conspirators with him."

Danton cleared his throat. "I am quite fearful you might be right. I would suggest speaking to His Majesty in the morning, however, that will be impossible. I, too, have some unsettling news. Soon after the prince and regent made their pronouncements, I saw His Majesty. He was quite upset by what he had heard and was on his way to speak with the new regent and the prince. I spoke briefly with him in passing but was most gratified to see him behaving as was his want before the *incident*, and I harbored hope that he would confront the two and straighten out this whole disorder.

"Less than a half-hour after we parted, I received a summons to meet with Regent Woodfield in the small audience chamber." He squeezed his eyes shut, the wrinkles around them deepening, then opened them and sighed. "Well, to keep a long tale short, I was told King Theodor is now confined to the Queen's Chambers with Her Majesty."

Andrew bit back an exclamation of alarm as the old counselor looked down, chewed the tips of his thin mustache, and watched his fingers twine and untwine. Voices rose in shock and protest until Thorvin stood. "Settle down and let him finish."

With a nod of gratitude to Thorvin, Danton continued. "As you can imagine, I was quite shocked at the news. Upon questioning the regent, I was informed that the king had, just moments earlier, suffered a complete breakdown and was now under the personal care of the Lord Master Mage. And—for his own protection—would now be confined with the queen … under guard. Before I could ask anything more, I was summarily dismissed. As I was leaving, the regent also commanded I deliver a message to you, Lord Kraftsmunn. I'm sorry, Thorvin, but your presence is no longer required at the palace."

Andrew's hands shook as he wrapped them deep into Boone's fur.

The whole meeting had been like some impossible nightmare for Anne and as she and Shaw were returning to their quarters she debated whether to visit Lexi yet tonight. Though Anne still worked with the healers in the palace, Bishop Hedrick arranged for them to live in a small cottage on the church grounds. It made sense to have them close since they were, once again, meeting with Jonathan most mornings to study the scrolls.

"I don't even know what to think anymore," Shaw said as they walked into their cottage. "Like Andrew, I no longer know up from down. Our world has been turned on its head. That the king and queen would be kept virtual prisoners is outrageous enough, but that Anton would even mention something so traitorous as removing the prince, is an indication of just how bad things have gotten. And he's right, this is just beginning. Even Councilor Danton agreed with him."

Anne responded, her voice soft as conflicting thoughts circled in her mind. "No, I disagree. I don't think this is just beginning. I think what is happening now is the result of years of planning and preparation. And I think you know that too, so does Jonathan. Deep down, we know, or at least suspect this, but no one wants to admit the truth."

Shaw's eyes widened as he turned back to where Anne was standing in the bedroom door. "What truth?"

"The truth that Sigmund is using Rayne's ... body for his own purposes."

"Do you think he ..." Shaw shuddered.

"I don't know what else to think, Shaw. But if I'm honest with myself, it makes the most sense. It's like Jonathan said weeks ago. Rayne is possessed by something evil and that evil thing is Sigmund."

Anne breathed in a sob at the last statement, an emptiness growing in her spirit. This was the truth no one wanted to admit, the truth everyone had danced around for the last two months. This was the truth Danton's and Anton's words were forcing them to admit. Prince Rayne was in fact dead and Sigmund was using his body to take control of Ochen.

Anne didn't go to see Lexi. She didn't have the heart to face her with what she needed to tell her friend. *Tomorrow. I'll tell her tomorrow. Not now. Tomorrow.* Anne slipped under the covers of her bed next to Shaw, her heart ripped by the pain of what she had finally voiced aloud.

16

𝕳

Anne and Shaw met with Jonathan the next morning at the time they normally set aside for studying the scrolls. But today, instead of studying, Shaw wanted to discuss Anne's fear. What would they do if the Rayne they all loved, the Light Bringer they all believed in, was, in fact, dead?

Thorvin showed up unannounced. Elsie had sent plenty of food to the library study, so Jonathan invited him to join them for breakfast. No one had much of an appetite, though. They just sat picking at the bones of what they would do if Rayne was really, irretrievably gone.

After poking at his cold food for over an hour, Jonathan got up and began pacing, mumbling under his breath, until a nudge in his spirit exposed a truth he had overlooked. With a huff, he straightened his shoulders and pushed his glasses up his nose. He released a mild chuckle of disbelief. "I can't believe I didn't see this before. We have been so preoccupied with what's happening politically, we have missed the most important point. Who is really in control here? Sigmund or the One?"

He paused and looked at Shaw and Anne sitting next to

each other on a short leather couch, holding hands, and Thorvin sitting in a wing back chair in front of the dark fireplace. "We must trust that whatever has occurred, the One knows about it and is still in control, regardless of what we see. Thorvin, what were those words of prophecy Tetsuya told you when you were on Glacieria?"

Thorvin thought for a minute. "Something about the beloved servant being lost and found. I don't remember most of it, but it ended with something like a true heart, a bond, and something broken will be made whole once again."

"Oh, Thorvin, think!" Jonathan said, excitement stirring within him as his hands waved in the air. "If this prophecy refers to the Light Bringer, our own Prince Rayne, then there is hope, because it ends in hope, *the broken will be made whole once again*! Did anyone else hear this prophecy?"

"Not that I know. If it's that important, why don't we send someone to Glacieria to ask for the complete prophecy?"

"Who?" Jonathan asked.

"I'll go," Shaw said in a quiet voice.

"What?" Shock widened Anne's golden eyes.

"Why not?" Shaw asked. "I'm not exactly a person of interest in all this. I could skip to Glacieria unnoticed and be back in no time. Besides, I would like to meet this Tetsuya and learn a bit more about how the prophecies were preserved on Glacieria. Thorvin, not to be impertinant, but you're no scholar. You didn't think to memorize the prophecy, and there were probably other important things you missed."

"Yes," Jonathan said, Shaw's words making sense to him. "Before we lose all hope, we need to hold onto that which is to be found in the prophecies. The One is worthy of trust and he gave us the prophecies. Because we can trust him, we can trust the prophecies. There is hope!"

"I see what you're saying." Anne nodded. "We've been so focused on our circumstances that we've forgotten to look past them and trust the One. Shaw, what did that first prophecy say again?"

"That the Light Bringer will bring light to Ochen and seal the living darkness ... and that he will appear when he is sixteen."

Shaw said. "But that doesn't help us now. It says nothing past Rayne's sixteenth year."

Jonathan waved his hands as if chasing flies. "Yes! Yes! But the second prophecy, the one brought to us by the Reclamation Committee says more. It says the lost will be found and he will bring to light my seven Words hidden on the seven worlds. It talks of joy and how the broken will be restored; the lost will be found. And only then does he bind the living darkness.

"Think of how much the Light Bringer is supposed to do that Rayne hasn't done yet. He *must* return to us. It's the only way for him to fulfill the prophecies. Don't you see? He hasn't yet recovered the seven scrolls and he hasn't bound the living darkness. And if he is the lost, he will be found again. If he is the broken, he will be restored. The One's prophecies are always true. Shaw, if you're willing, I think we need you to go and speak with Tetsuya so we can see how that prophecy fits with what we already know."

Shaw looked at Anne. "I won't go if you don't agree with this, Anne. But I think Jonathan is right. We need to know what that other prophecy says in its entirety."

"I will agree, but only if you take someone with you," Anne said in her quiet, firm way. "I don't like the idea of you traveling alone. I would go, but I don't feel comfortable leaving Queen Rowena. And now with King Theodor confined and that questionable Lord Master Mage in charge of their healing …" She shook her head, concentration creasing her brow. "I can't go. There's something off about that mage. He's part of Rayne's and Brayden's inner circle. I don't trust him."

"Ask the twins," Thorvin said. "I can't go right now; you heard what Anton said last night. I won't leave Westvale until I've found out more about what's happened to King Theodor. But the twins might enjoy getting off world if Kori can spare them."

"Good idea. I'll ask them," Shaw said. "And if they can't come with me, I'll ask Noah."

"The church will cover your expenses," Jonathan said. "It's the least we can do. And that is all I can do for the moment, my friends." He stood and stretched, arching his back slightly and kneading the lower muscles along his spine. "Getting old is frustrating." He shook out his arms. "I get stiff when I sit for so long. But I must leave you now. I have another meeting. It's getting so I can't turn around without hearing more disturbing news concerning this cult that's been on the rise these last few years."

He focused on Thorvin. "If we'd had time last night, I would have brought it up at our meeting. Thorvin, have you heard much about the group calling themselves the Scroll Worshippers of Corylus?"

"Just bits," Thorvin said, still sitting across from Anne and Shaw. "Some radical religious reformers from what I've heard. They were having some problems with a similar group on Glacieria as well. I thought they were just a small, fringe movement."

Jonathan sighed, shaking his head. "However they might have started, they are growing into a major problem now. Their numbers seem to increase by the day and I got word the other day that they burned a church in Centerville. Anyway, I'm meeting with a local man who says he has information about a splinter group growing here in Westvale." He laughed ruefully. "I know the One has his hand on things, I just wish he would give us a little insight into what he wants us to do under the current circumstances. Speaking of which, don't forget to be in the Great Square at noon. I don't think it would be wise to miss the new regent's speech."

Thorvin, Shaw, and Anne walked down the first couple steps of the King's Library out into the bright, hot sunshine of a midsummer day. Stifling heat and humidity rose in waves from the Great Square, drawing beads of sweat onto Anne's upper lip. With the square packed and people already jostling each other, they decided to remain on the upper steps where they would have a good view of Regent Woodfield. Glancing out in the direction of the Cameron Sea, Anne squinted at a dark line on the horizon and prayed the promise of a late day storm would bring a cooler night.

Regent Woodfield, wearing a storm-cloud gray outfit trimmed with silver, looked puffed up with self-satisfaction as he stepped up to a podium and raised his hands for silence. "Loyal citizens of Westvale, I am proud to announce that with the completion of the new gallows here in the Great Square, we are ready to take on the responsibility of executing those criminals found guilty of treason against Ochen. This heavy duty has been accorded us by a unanimous vote of the Interplanetary Council. The first executions will take place tomorrow morning at sunrise. The condemned prisoners His Royal Highness and I brought from Nemora have been tried and found guilty of serious acts of treachery against the Ochen system. It is our duty to see justice served."

The exact nature of the crimes of which they were accused was not announced and no mention was made of them questioning the council's decision that now condemned Veres to a position of servitude.

"Westvale has been chosen for this task for it is one requiring both dignity and resolve. Thus, all citizens of Westvale will report here tomorrow morning at dawn to act as witnesses to the righteous executions of these traitors."

Anne's fists clenched, her nails cutting into her palms as she listened to Brayden's lies. Just the evening before, Captain Fontaine had said that the prince *himself* petitioned the council for the right to oversee the executions of people deemed interplanetary traitors. It wasn't a command from the council. *It's like Captain Fontaine said, a first step on the part of His Royal Highness to shift power from the Interplanetary Council.*

The whole thing turned Anne's stomach as she tried to stuff down her anger at the young man standing to Regent Woodfield's right. She no longer harbored any doubts. *That young man may look like Rayne but he's nothing more than a demon in sheep's clothing.* Her stomach dropped another notch as a disturbingly sly smile hovered around the handsome lips. She wondered what could be going through the demon's mind now.

Not long after they were dismissed, Shaw headed down to

the craftsman quarter to see if Stevie and Sashi would consider skipping to the ice planet with him. Anne walked toward the palace to sit with Queen Rowena. She knew Lexi would come to the Queen's Chambers to talk with her as she did every day, and Anne worked to quell the anger that had surfaced during the regent's address.

As she approached Queen Rowena's chambers, misgivings assailed her again. Two guards she didn't recognize flanked the door. Danton's words from yesterday came to mind. *They're here to keep the king from leaving. He's a prisoner.* Her eyes lighted on Charlotte, the healer she had come to relieve. *Charlotte's supposed to be sitting with Rowena.*

"Charlotte? What are you doing out here? Her Majesty shouldn't be left alone," Anne said as she walked up to the healer, her gaze focused on the guards.

"It's okay, Anne, King Theodor's in there. The crown prince and regent too. They came to visit the king and queen. Took me by surprise they did—just walked in—all unexpected like. Well, they dismissed me, told me I was off duty, but I didn't want to leave until you got here." She smiled. "Oh Anne, isn't it wonderful? Prince Rayne visiting his parents and bringing Regent Woodfield with him. Who would have thought the two would reconcile? Why, it's just the thing their majesties need, a visit from their son and nephew." She paused, her eyes clouding. "But … something isn't sitting right with me. I can't explain it, but I just have this strange feeling …"

17

ท

Sigmund fidgeted with several large rings he wore as he stood at Brayden's right shoulder on the platform while the regent addressed the milling, irritating crowd. Sigmund despised the part he had set for himself in these proceedings, taking on the role of a politically-concerned and relevant crown prince. But he was committed to playing the part for the time being, or at least until he had dismantled enough of the political, economic, and especially, religious structures of the Ochen system, to allow his servants to take over the process of destruction and domination.

Every piece he had worked to place in positions of power over the years was now being moved in concert with his own actions. Thrilled by his successes, he anticipated future accomplishments to move forward just as readily as his plans all came to fruition within his calculated time frame. His current distaste for dealing with the rabble was a small sacrifice to pay for the harvest he soon would be enjoying.

While Brayden was wrapping up his address, Sigmund took time to confront the true source of his disquiet. Once again, his inner self felt a twinge of foreboding at his inability to locate and hold on to the Light Bringer. As that repugnant idea filtered into his mind, a more pleasant inspiration rose to displace it. He chuckled. He may not yet have the Light Bringer under his control, but he did have Theodor and Rowena. Perhaps he would feel better if he amused himself in playing with the two royals he did have in his power.

As they left the platform, the pretender turned to Brayden. "Do you have any plans at the moment, my young friend?"

"No." Brayden hesitated. He had grown cautious about angering the power that possessed his cousin's body.

"Good. If you have no other plans, I think it is time you and I visited my *parents*. Daddy wasn't very happy yesterday when we confined him, and I think a visit is in order. Don't you agree, Cousin?"

Masking his irritation at needing to abandon the entertainment he had been looking forward to this morning, Brayden agreed to join Sigmund. He knew the old sorcerer well enough to realize the time spent with Theodor and Rowena would prove entertaining. Dismissing their guards, the two sauntered through the palace to the Queen's Chambers.

It had been simple enough to chase the healer from the queen's rooms. One haughty command from the crown prince had sent the old biddy scrambling for the door while the pretender and his regent laughed at her retreat.

"What are you thinking?" Brayden asked Sigmund when they were alone with the king and queen. Sigmund walked over to King Theodor and crouched in front of him, looking into his blankly staring eyes.

"That tincture Heinrich gave him yesterday is working better than I had hoped," he said as he tilted his head to look more closely into the eyes of the shattered monarch. "I knew taking down Rowena would affect Theodor, and it almost worked. But his reaction to my speech yesterday proved we needed something more to keep the old goat down. That was another brilliant stroke of Heinrich's. Take charge of the fool's care. And now that he's stuck in here with the witch, we don't have to worry that he'll try to interfere."

Pushing upright, he barked, "Hello Daddy! Do you see me? Can you tell who is talking to you, you piece of garbage? No. You are now even less aware than that precious wife of yours, or even that bothersome son. Don't I look good wearing his body?"

After staring for a moment, Theodor lifted dead eyes to Sigmund. "Rayne?"

"Oh, how delightful," Sigmund crowed, clapping his hands. "This is so much more invigorating than I had imagined. So, there is still some awareness in there my old friend." Chuckling, Sigmund pulled a chair up next to Theodor's and sitting, crossed his legs and leaned into the king, wrapping an arm over his shoulders.

"Come now, you must remember all the fun we had partying while Morrow and I poisoned your father. She really liked you, you know. Now look at you, you pathetic excuse for a man. Your kingdom torn from you. Your wife in my power. My power! Held in that death-like state by my spike. My power! My spike!"

Laughing, Sigmund rose to stand in front of Theodor, then turned in a circle.

"Look at me, Theo, don't I look young and handsome clothed in your son's body. Oh, yes. You see the truth now, don't you? I have taken your only son from you and broken him in two. I stand here in his body while he tries to run from me in that wretched old body in which I trapped him."

Theodor looked up, confusion wrinkling his pale brow. But as the words began to penetrate, a look of horror crossed his face.

"Yes," Sigmund purred, amusement warming his icy core as he watched Theodor's reaction. "Now you begin to understand. Remember. I promised. A child for a child. And when I finally locate that old man, I'll bring him here. Then you'll see first-hand what your lack of care for your own son has wrought. Morrow was taken from me against my will. But you and the boy's *loving* mother willingly delivered your son to me."

Sigmund walked over to Brayden, and grabbing him by the arm, dragged him in front of Rowena while Theodor watched, weak hands clawing at the arms of his chair.

"Greetings, Mommy dearest," Sigmund crooned. "You know you are being held by a spike, don't you? Master mage that you are, of course you do. And I know you heard every word I spoke to your dear, beloved, yet you can't even move a muscle in response. How frustrating it must be."

Sigmund grabbed the back of Brayden's neck forcing him into a position where his face was inches from Rowena's.

"Here. Take a good look at the traitor you sacrificed your son for. You know now that's exactly what happened don't you, Mommy dearest?"

Letting go of Brayden, who backed away rubbing his neck, Sigmund laughed in glee, enjoying his power over the couple. "I'd love to be in your head so I could listen in to your thoughts at this moment. What does it feel like to be the mother who never believed her own son's words, preferring instead to embrace my pawn? He took much pleasure in turning you against your son over the years. Do you take pride in your motherhood? I do. I was behind it all."

"Stop." Theodor's dry whisper floated across the room as he tried to rise from his chair. "Leave her alone."

"Don't even try it, old man!" Sigmund hissed. He sat next to Rowena, leaned in, placed a hand on each cheek, and looked into her eyes.

"Do you even realize what I can do to your beloved wife with my spike in her? If you don't behave yourself, take Heinrich's tincture and keep your mouth shut, I'll cause her spirit so much pain, tears will flow from her dead eyes. I can do that! In fact, I would find immense pleasure in the exercise.

"No, you pathetic excuse for a king. You will bend to my will. I have too much at stake to risk your interference. But I know your love for this woman. You will not allow her to suffer for your disobedience. You will sit back down and behave yourself. I'll tell you when I need you to do something. Until then, you will remember your place."

𝖛

What's going on here?" Anne demanded as she walked in to see the prince holding Queen Rowena's face in a tight grasp while he glared at a scowling King Theodor.

Seeing the anger on Theodor's face, Anne moved toward him. "Your Majesty! What can I do for you?"

As she approached, Theodor's eyes clouded over, and he turned from her.

"Your Majesty?" Anne asked, leaning down, fear constricting her heart.

Standing, she turned to the pretender. It was so hard to look at Rayne. To see the amethyst eyes and black hair, his fine nose and firm chin, intensely aware of every inch of his body, the body she had tended so often over the years, and yet know that he was no longer there.

She wanted to yell at Sigmund, demand that he tell her where her beloved brother was now. It took every ounce of will power to refrain from screaming her frustration as the teenager standing before her looked at her with haughty eyes and said, "Who gave you permission to enter here, woman?"

Anne sucked in a breath, stuffed down her anger, and bowed. "I am sorry if I have intruded. It is my time to sit with Her Majesty and I didn't think you would take it amiss if I entered. Are you staying long?"

With a dismissive flick of his wrist, the prince said, "No, the regent and I were leaving. You may attend to my parents. I'm certain you have been informed that the king is to remain here, sharing the queen's suite until further notice. Do you understand?"

Anne kept her eyes focused on the floor as she nodded and curtsied. With her hand half-hidden in the folds of her skirt, she signed, *I do not understand.*

The pretender's eyes narrowed with suspicion, but he said, "Good. Make the other healers who sit with the queen aware that they will be caring for my father under the supervision of the Lord Master Mage. The men stationed outside this door have orders not to let the king leave. I wouldn't want him wandering about and possibly hurting himself."

Casting a glance at Brayden, the pretender waved. "Come along, *Cousin.*"

Once the door closed behind the prince and the regent, Anne dropped heavily into a deep chair, broke down, and allowed her tears to flow unchecked. She was startled when she felt a hand on her shoulder and looked up to see King Theodor standing over her, tears streaming down his face as well. He didn't say a word, just stood by her side while Anne cried. Once she settled, he returned to his chair and again sat staring with unseeing eyes.

The next morning dawned gray. Sporadic heavy rain fell. Anne thought the sky must be crying. The citizens of Westvale assembled in the Great Square, silent and anxious. Despite the number of people, they were all so quiet the rain could be heard spattering on the ground and running down the sides of buildings and streets. Neither the crown prince nor the regent made an appearance at the execution. One of the new officers from Nemora took charge. After the bodies were taken back to the dungeon under the palace, the people were dismissed. They moved with slow steps down the streets and alleys, murmuring. The murmuring turned into muttering and began to grow in volume. Confusion and anger grew thick in the humid air.

Voices surrounded Anne, rising in complaints and fragments of conversations. "Not for the best." "Take it before the council." "Thought the crown prince was different, thought he cared." "What's wrong with King Theodor and Queen Rowena?" "Why don't they do something?" "Maybe those scroll worshippers are right." "Things are really getting bad here."

When they were back at their cottage, Anne helped Shaw finish gathering the supplies he was taking with him to Glacieria. Stevie and Sashi showed up soon after and Anne hugged them both before giving Shaw a long heartfelt hug and kiss goodbye.

"I should be back in about two weeks," Shaw said. "Jonathan

told me to remind you that if you need anything, he and Elsie are at your service. And Thorvin said he'll make it a point to check on you at least once a day while I'm gone."

"I'll miss you, my love," Anne said. They hugged once again, then Shaw turned to follow Stevie and Sashi who were already walking toward the portal station. They had decided it would be best if Anne didn't go to the station with Shaw, but she stood in their doorway, her heart like a heavy lump in her chest, watching until he was lost to sight.

18

Mite caught another fish. It was the third he had caught since he and Rayne stopped near the chuckling little stream they had followed for the last day and a half. In a secluded hollow next to the stream, the moss grew thick and soft, and the graceful green branches of several large willows created a sheltered spot for Rayne to rest. Mite gathered kindling and several small logs so Rayne could build a fire while Mite fished. By the time the sun was disappearing behind the trees, and the smaller of Nemora's moons, Rem, a radiant silver disc, could be seen rising, the fire had reduced to hot, smoldering coals.

After catching the fish, Mite dug up a couple tubers from the other side of the stream and now, after wrapping them in large leaves, he buried them in the hot coals. When the tubers had been cooking for almost an hour, Mite erected two tripods of sticks and, after skewering the fish on another stick, set them to cooking over the fire.

Rayne had fallen asleep again. The old body could only do so much before it tired and needed rest. Mite looked over at the sleeping man and shook his head. They had been walking for three days now, but because of their slow pace and frequent rest stops, it would take another three days to reach their destination. If Mite was traveling alone, he would have continued without stopping and arrived at the Blessed Hollow by the coming morning.

As the tubers and fish cooked and Rayne slept, Mite hopped from foot to foot while trying to figure out a way to get Rayne to move faster. He knew there were still newcomer hunters roaming the forest; he had seen their signs and feared for Rayne's safety. And yet, Rayne struggled to keep up a pace his body just couldn't sustain. He was getting weaker. Mite could see that each day, his movements came with more difficulty.

⚘

"You're worried," Rayne said, startling Mite.

"Oh. Mite did not know Ray-ray awake."

"You're worried," Rayne repeated. "I'm moving too slow and if things don't change the soldiers looking for me are going to find us."

"No. No. Mite just thought it would be nice if the scroll wasn't so far, so far, that's all."

Rayne shifted to look at Mite. "You're a terrible liar, Mite. I wish I could just send you for the scroll. I'm too slow."

"Mite knows Ray-ray is trying hard. It will be okay, okay. Mite and Ray-ray will be fine. The Creator-Father will keep us safe, he will, he will."

Mite met Rayne's eyes. "Ray-ray will eat now?" Mite asked. "Fish should be done. Good fish, yes, yes, yes."

"No, I'm not hungry. You go ahead and eat without me, Mite."

"No!" Rayne caught Mite staring and knew he was worried. "Ray-ray must eat. He will not be strong enough to reclaim scroll if he doesn't eat. Ray-ray ate little, little this morning. Ray-ray must eat now. Fish is good; make Ray-ray strong. Then Ray-ray will move fast, fast, fast."

Rayne sighed. "I know, Mite. But I'm not hungry. I can't

make this body hungry, just like I can't make this body stronger, or younger, or faster."

"Ray-ray must eat anyway." Mite proceeded to put together a plate for Rayne with one of the fish and a tuber and handed the plate to Rayne. "Please eat, Ray-ray."

At first Rayne just picked at the food with no desire to eat, but as he forced himself to keep eating, he succeeded in finishing everything Mite had given him. Exhaustion had become a constant companion and the ache in his back and hip wore on him without relief. When he thought about the daunting task of finding the three remaining scrolls and returning to Westvale with them, his heart sank.

Rayne had been asleep for a couple hours when Mite heard the voices. At first, he was afraid the soldiers had found them, but soon his fears were laid to rest as he recognized several of the voices. The people approaching were friends. And even more than that, they could help. In the faint light of Rem, just as Ledia, the large purple moon, was rising and casting her blue light, Mite could see the several figures shifting through the bands of light and shadow created by the large, leafy trees and the two moons. They were Kindred, another ancient race who avoided newcomers. He moved with silent stealth into the deeper shadows, away from Rayne, allowing the Kindred to come close, while he prayed to the Creator-Father to soften their hearts.

Eight Kindred, speaking in their own tongue with hushed whispers approached the camp. Mite listened to their quiet conversation, disturbed by what he heard. The Kindred were worried. Over the last year, Mite, himself, had begun noticing pockets of heavy dark magic in his travels. They would appear randomly and then dissipate so he had not been too concerned. But what he hadn't known was that these pockets of darkness were appearing in Neth Forest. And that was reason for worry. For in the heart of Neth was the Source, and if darkness overtook the Source, all magic in Ochen would cease.

The Kindred stopped talking and with noiseless steps, crept into the mossy area where Rayne was sleeping. They had smelled the embers of the fire from a distance and now surrounded the sleeping newcomer with caution. Mite could have just called out and asked the Kindred for help, but he wanted them to decide to help Rayne on their own, rather than risk asking for help.

Kindred were unpredictable, they could be difficult and standoffish if they chose to be. In the past, Mite had learned the hard way, they were always more cooperative if they came to the decision to help of their own volition. Especially when newcomers were involved.

Kindred were often mistaken for newcomers, but Mite knew the differences. Natives of the magic saturated world of Nemora, Kindred were more spirit than material. They looked human, but when caught in certain light, they would appear almost ethereal, vanishing as the light passed through them. This allowed them to easily avoid contact with newcomers whom they found to be clumsy and stupid and altogether too solid. And though some newcomers were born with the ability to manipulate magic energies, Kindred were magic energy itself in a personal being.

But one thing Kindred and newcomers had in common was worship of the One. He was the Creator-Father to the Kindred just as he was to Mite. And it was this common link Mite was counting on now. Mite prayed that the Kindred would sense Rayne's special nature as the Creator-Father's Light Bringer and offer their help even though he was a newcomer.

Rayne stirred in his sleep, perhaps sensing the Kindred moving silently around him. Mite was just about to speak up so the Kindred would not startle and vanish, leaving Mite and Rayne without help, when a Kindred Mite didn't recognize spoke up in the common language.

"Ho, Fallon, what's a niggling newcomer doing in these woods? I thought we made things too worrying for them to be coming back here now. Last time I saw a newcomer here we had him running fearful of the wraiths of the forest. Looks like we're going to have to teach them to fear the spirits of Neth Forest again."

Fallon, whom Mite knew as a leader of the Kindred, stood still, silent, as if listening to the nighttime sounds of the forest. After a few minutes, while the other Kindred spread out, looking around Mite's and Rayne's camp, checking their supplies, and nibbling on the remains of the last fish, Fallon said, "More's the problem, Slone, that the meddlesome little sprite from Rockhall has found his way this far south again to be intruding on our territory.

"Mite, I know thou art here. Show thyself and explain why thou hast brought this newcomer with thee."

Mite bounced from foot to foot trying to decide how to approach Fallon with Rayne's need, when another of the Kindred Mite recognized as Elspeth, a healer, spoke. "Ho, Fallon, this newcomer is in sore need of succor."

"What's the disorder, Elspeth?" Fallon asked. A split second later, Fallon flashed like a streak of lightning to where Mite was hiding and stood over the little ancient, eyes filled with fire. "Mite, Mite lost thy light, lost thy way on this bright, bright night. Mite, Mite, be contrite, broke the rules thou annoying sprite. Thou knowest best that's not right, to bring a newcomer under Ledia's blue light. Under the moons he'll have to pay, him to stay in the shadows of Neth at night."

Mite crept out from the gloom beneath one of the willow trees and bowed deeply to Fallon. "Your pardon, my Lord Fallon."

"Enough playing around, Fallon. Mite, tis good to see thee again," Elspeth said. "Fallon, leave the sprite alone. Come, look at this newcomer. Thou needest to see this."

"Please," Mite said, scooting next to Rayne who was now mumbling in his sleep. "Please, there is no harm in him. I meant no harm bringing him here. We must get to the Blessed Hollow. Please forgive me, the decision to come into Neth Forest was not made lightly but in true need."

"Be still," Fallon said, then moved next to Elspeth who was kneeling beside Rayne with another Kindred Mite didn't recognize. Mite could feel Fallon reach with searching tendrils of his innate magical energy into Rayne and was relieved as he sensed how Fallon was searching out the truth of Rayne with gentle care. But even as Fallon paused, his eyes wide with wonder, Rayne startled awake.

At Rayne's movement, Slone and another Kindred, the largest of the six, both leaped into positions on either side of Fallon, weapons drawn, ready to defend their leader if the newcomer posed a threat.

But Rayne didn't move again, he lay still, blinking in the moonlight. "Mite?"

"Mite's here, Ray-ray. We are among friends, they are Kindred." Mite hoped he was right and the Kindred would accept Rayne as a friend.

Fallon lowered himself to his knees next to the healer. "Elspeth, what dost thou read?"

"He's very weak," Elspeth answered. "It saddens my heart to see such evil. Someone has broken the spirit within from its natural moorings and fixed it to this body which is far too weak for the powerful spirit it now holds. The body is dying and unless we help it without delay we will lose both body and spirit.

"But even more, Fallon," Elspeth whispered, her voice filled with awe. "Dost thou not see the truth of him? He is chosen, Fallon. We must bring him into the heart of Neth. Ean and I wouldst try to save this newcomer who is chosen by the Creator-Father. Ledia's blue light shines on the shadows of Neth tonight and I know it is trespass to allow a newcomer within when Ledia is full. But Fallon, if we do not bring him now, he will die. We cannot let that happen. This one must be saved. The light of the Creator-Father shines within him even now."

Fallon looked closely at Rayne who stared with widened eyes into the deep dark eyes of the Kindred.

"Newcomer," Fallon said. "To come into Neth when Ledia's blue light shines full as it does tonight is forbidden to newcomers. The light is powerful and it changes them. If thou dost come with us now and if thou dost live, thou wilt never be the same again. But my healers, Elspeth and Ean, tell me thou wilt die if we do not bring thee now. It is thy choice. Wouldst thou live even as the light transforms thee?"

With each passing day, the old-man body enshrouding Rayne had grown weaker. His spirit mourned the truth that, as he was now, he could no longer fulfill the One's prophecies. Rayne had no idea what change the blue light of Ledia may have on him if he went deeper into Neth Forest. He had survived so much already. But, he was determined to face the change if it gave the body in which Sigmund imprisoned him enough life to bring the prophecies to fruition. And he trusted that the One was still with him and working to bring about his will through these strangers. "I will trust the One and go deeper into Neth."

"Thank you, thank you, thank you, O worthy Kindred," Mite crowed as he hopped around the camp gathering up Rayne's and his belongings.

Rayne pulled his staff to him and struggled to rise. Elspeth and Ean came to either side of him and Ean said, "Be at peace newcomer, rest for now. We will help thee journey. Thou wilt not have to walk. Just give Darcy, Enya, and Keira some time and thou wilt see what they devise."

As Darcy, Enya, and Keira worked on their project, Slone and the large Kindred stood guard, while Ean, Elspeth, and Fallon sat by Rayne. Once Mite had gathered Rayne's and his few belongings, he came and sat next to Rayne. With a small grin, Fallon inclined his head to Mite and said, "Good fortune to thee and welcome Mite of Rockhall."

"You rhymed me!" Mite complained, a hurt look unfurling across his impish features.

Fallon laughed. "I believe thou dids't earn that ridiculous bit of verbiage the last time thou wast in Neth, old friend. Not that thou hasn't already merited it this time. And studying the situation," Fallon sent a pointed look in Rayne's direction, "I must ask, how does an old soul like Mite come to be roaming in such company as this? I sense this is a tale worth time before the hearth."

"You honor me, Fallon," Mite inclined his head at the Kindred lord. "The tale is indeed a long one and worth the telling. But I fear ..."

"Fallon," the large Kindred called in a soft voice.

"What, Neal?"

"Newcomers approach. Twenty, perhaps more. They haven't yet entered our borders, but they roam close. Mayhap this one understands why they journey at this hour of the night." Neal pointed at Rayne.

Fallon gave Mite a hard look and then turned to Rayne. "Is thou the reason these creatures skirt our border?"

"I am." Rayne swallowed hard and averted his eyes wondering what the Kindred might do knowing he was hunted. "They hunt me. They would return me to the evil who broke me." Rayne shifted his gaze to meet Fallon's eyes. "If they succeed, the prophecy he seeks to destroy will fail and darkness will cover all Ochen."

"Darcy?" Fallon asked into the blue shadows.

"We are ready, my lord," Darcy responded in a hushed whisper.

Fallon looked from Mite to Rayne. "Then let us make haste. But I would impartial hear more of this when we are at my hearth. Come!"

Rayne floundered as he was suddenly lifted by Ean and Elspeth into a kind of sling that was hanging from two sturdy branches. Slone, Darcy, Enya, and Keria each hoisted the end of a branch over a shoulder. Before he could even think to protest, the whole group was ghosting through the forest as if they were nothing but wind passing between the boles of countless large, dark trees. From time to time, Rayne imagined he was being carried by the wind as the Kindred seemed to vanish from sight, only to reappear once again farther on. Fallon was leading with Mite right behind him and the large warrior, Neal, drifted in and out of the shadows behind everyone else.

Rayne struggled to stay awake as the harness swung in rhythm with the four bearers as they sprinted hour after hour, never seeming to weary with their task. At times, there would be breaks in the trees and without warning, Rayne would feel a surge of energy as the blue light coming from the moon, Ledia, warmed him and whispered into his spirit. He tried to grasp what was happening, but though he felt something changing in his spirit, the old-man body prevented him from hearing what was whispered.

It reminded him of the Sun Sparrow light, something of a like nature, yet without the physical manifestation. But he could not be sure of anything. He wondered about his own body. Did the Sun Sparrow light reside in his body or was it somehow still within him? Or, had Sigmund's presence destroyed the light? He questioned if he would ever be whole again, if he would ever be able to feel the joy of the light flowing through him again. Any change brought about from being in Neth now didn't scare him, it felt natural, right, just like the Sun Sparrow light. What scared him was the possibility he would never be whole again. But the One's pervading presence warmed his spirit and he rested in that warmth. As the rhythm of the runners and the peace of the One lulled him, Rayne dreamed.

He was himself, whole and complete; and he held the blue light of Ledia as well as the golden light of the Sun Sparrows within him. Standing before him was the Son, just as he had seen him with Lexi. The Son smiled at Rayne and he felt unutterable joy. As the exultation intensified, an upsurge of light flowed within and around him, blue and gold streamers whirled as if dancing, before dissolving into a muted, pale yellow glow. Then the Son spoke. *What do you see, Light Bringer?*

Rayne looked and saw a man, wounded and suffering beyond anything Rayne could imagine. The man was in a strange place and the people were speaking a language Rayne had never heard before. Then the man died.

Rayne's heart broke, shattered and torn at the man's death, and when Rayne turned to look at the Son again, he knew it was the Son he had seen die.

Again, the Son spoke to Rayne. *What do you see, Light Bringer?*

Rayne looked yet again. The man who had died, the Son,

was once more, alive. He glowed with a radiance so intense that Rayne could not look into the light, but lowered his gaze.

The seed cannot bring forth life unless it is first buried in the ground. Beloved Light Bringer, your time of sacrifice has not yet come. You will understand when the cup is full and the time of judgement is nigh. Know that, even then, I will be with you. Do you trust me Light Bringer?

I trust you. Rayne breathed out.

And then in his dream, Rayne saw that he was no longer whole. He was, once again broken, his body gone, and his spirit trapped in the prison of the old man. The Son stood before Rayne and looked into the old-man eyes with eyes of compassion and asked, *do you trust me even now, Light Bringer?*

Understanding flashed through Rayne; a weight of knowledge crushed him. If the will of the One was that Rayne stay broken, never be whole again, he would still need to trust. With that awareness, Rayne looked into the eyes of love. *Even now I trust you. You are the true source of light and life.*

Beloved Light Bringer, do not lose hope. Be very courageous and know I will never leave you or forsake you. Trust the Kindred. They need to hear your words and they will bring you strength to fulfill the prophecy. Hold to the truth you carry in your heart. Remember the prophecy. Where darkness seeks to grow, shine my light.

19

Rayne woke to morning light shining through the branches of a great tree with immense blue leaves beyond an open window. A fresh, woodsy-scented breeze caused the large leaves to whisper and ruffled small white curtains at the window. Children's voices drifted to Rayne, singing in a language he didn't know. He tried to push upright and his hands sank into a soft mattress. *I'm in a bed? How? When?*

"Awake, awake, finally awake," Mite crooned from where he sat on a short wooden stool near the open window. He popped up and coming to the side of the bed said, "How does Ray-ray feel?"

Rayne shifted again and smiled at the absence of pain in the movement. "Good, Mite, I feel good. When did we get here? Last night? The last thing I remember is being carried in that sling. And where is here anyway?"

"Ray-ray and Mite did not arrive here last night. Ray-ray has slept for three days. Ean and Elspeth watched over you. They worked hard to make Ray-ray better. We are in the heart of Neth, the home of the kindred. Newcomers have not been allowed here in a long, long time. More than one-hundred years. But Ean and Elspeth wouldn't take no for an answer. Told Fallon to bring you here. They did, they did.

"Is Ray-ray hungry? Elspeth said you would be hungry when you woke. That would bring Mite joy, if Ray-ray is hungry."

Rayne thought for a moment and then his eyes lit up. "You know, Mite, I am hungry, hungrier than I've been in a long time. Do you think you could get me something to eat?"

"No need for that," Elspeth said from the open doorway, her voice deep and melodic, as she walked in carrying a tray of food. She was short and, though not heavy, seemed well-fed. Her silver-streaked, chestnut brown hair was pulled into a soft bun on the top of her head. Though her skin was wrinkle-free and smooth, when Rayne looked into her deep brown eyes, he was aware of a depth of age.

"I had sensed thy awakening and have already brought thee something to eat."

Rayne's mouth began to water as he smelled fresh baked bread. Not only was there a still-steaming chunk of warm, brown bread, but there was honey, a variety of fresh fruit, and a large mug of water.

Ean walked in behind Elspeth holding a pottery cup. "But before thou eatest," he said, "thou must drink this healing tea."

Ean, tall, thin with dark brown hair falling over his narrow shoulders, and a rather long nose, smiled as he handed Rayne the cup. Rayne smelled the tea; it had a strange aroma and he looked up at Ean, suspicion churning his stomach as he remembered the cup he had taken without question at Castle Inverness.

"What's in this?"

"Never thou mindest," Elspeth said, as she bustled around and put the breakfast tray down on a small table she had moved to the side of Rayne's bed. "Thou just drink it up young man. Tis full of good things to help make thee strong."

"Thou must listen to her," Ean said, his smile etching laugh lines around his deep-set brown eyes. "We spent much time gathering and preparing the ingredients for this tea. Now, please drink."

Rayne took a small sip and waited. When nothing happened, he decided the tea was probably okay and didn't taste bad, so he drank the whole cup while Ean and Elspeth stood over him nodding their affirmation of his obedience. After Ean took the empty cup, Elspeth spread some honey on a piece of bread and handed it to Rayne. "Now thou mayest eat. The tea will settle with the food."

Soon after eating, Rayne grew drowsy again and slept. So began a series of days of eating, sleeping, and growing stronger. Rayne lost any sense of time until, finally, the day came that Elspeth gave permission for him to go outside. Through the days that Rayne mostly slept, there were times he would wake to find Mite sitting, watching. But mostly, Rayne was left alone. Mite explained how he kept busy helping the kindred. He spent much of his time with Fallon, Sloan, and Neal patrolling the borders of Neth.

Ean and Elspeth refused to discuss anything of a serious nature with Rayne, saying he needed to concentrate on resting and healing. He understood the body they were trying to strengthen was very frail and the two healers were using their skill to get it to the point where it would serve Rayne for at least the next couple months before, once again, succumbing to the effects of illness and old age.

With Ean on one side, and Elspeth on the other, Rayne walked out onto a covered porch that overlooked a large, sparkling lake. Everything around him was so blue-green and fresh he drew to a stop, standing still and staring at the beauty. Green deciduous trees of giant proportions were covered with dark blue moss that grew so thick in places that it hung like furry blankets of deep blue. The color reminded Rayne of blueberries and Al's tarts.

Giant evergreens bordered the far edge of the lake, reflecting shades of green and blue in the crystal-clear water. Gentle breezes on the air carried the scent of growing things and of deep, ancient woodland life. Looking out at the lake and the forest beyond, a quiet, peaceful harmony blanketed Rayne and he spoke in a soft murmur. "Mite tells me we are in the Heart of Neth Forest."

"Yes, it is our home," Ean answered. "A place few new-comers have seen."

"It's beautiful," Rayne whispered, afraid to break the spell surrounding them. Closing his eyes and breathing in the rarefied air, Rayne was unexpectedly mindful of the magic encompassing him.

"I can feel it." He thrilled to the sensation, eyes squeezed shut. "I can feel the energy around us. I have not felt this since Sigmund trapped me in this body."

"It is the healing." Elspeth's voice was soft and filled with compassion. "Thy spirit is so resilient; it has pulled healing to itself to strengthen the energy within. Not only has the body in which thee currently dwells been strengthened, thy spirit has as well. So now thou wilt be more aware of the magic around thee even though this body isn't tuned to it."

She paused and smiled at Rayne. "Thou are indeed greatly gifted. Though thou hast been broken from thy natural body by this Sigmund thou hast mentioned, thy spirit still carries within it the light of the Creator-Father. I would hear more of this Sigmund, but now is not the time. Come, sit. We have talked enough."

Elspeth led Rayne to a wooden settee with padded covers. Once he was comfortable, she took a soft green woven throw from the back of the settee and covered his legs. A young Kindred girl came out with a tray holding a cup of the tea Rayne had been drinking daily and some small cookies. Ean brought a table to the side of the settee and nodded to the girl who placed the tray on the table within Rayne's reach. Sitting on the tray with the tea and cookies was a small silver bell.

"If thou needest anything," Ean said, "just ring the bell and someone will come out to help thee. For now, try to relax and allow the magic of Neth to enfold thee."

When Elspeth, Ean, and the girl left, Rayne thought back to the dream he had when he was being carried into the depths of Neth. He closed his eyes and watched again the scenes of the Son's death and rebirth, and he remembered the words the Son spoke to him.

The seed cannot bring forth life unless it is first buried in the ground.

Beloved Light Bringer, your time of sacrifice has not yet come. You will understand when the cup is full, and the time of judgement is nigh. Know that even then I will be with you. Do you trust me Light Bringer?

He had answered yes. And in this place of quiet peace, he prayed for the strength to answer yes again, if the One asked again. The cavity of grief he hollowed out in his heart after Sigmund and Heinrich had broken him had been filled by the incredible peace of the Son. The Son had known suffering intimately and yet smiled at Rayne in loving acceptance.

The One helped Rayne grow so much in these last months, that he found it hard to even recognize who he had been when he first donned the mantle of Light Bringer the day he and Thorvin staged the exhibition in Westvale. And though he couldn't feel the presence of the Sun Sparrow light, he knew it still resided deep within him. Just as now he knew the light of Ledia was a part of him. The One had created him to bring his light to Ochen and Rayne understood at this moment, that the One was forming him into the vessel he was meant to be. Rayne wanted to serve the One, wanted his answer to always be *yes,* but he still feared losing himself completely. For now, though, he would rest in the peace he was given, and move forward one step at a time.

Other memories ghosted through Rayne's mind and he let them wash over him. The words Jiro had spoken in Caarwyn Rill, when Rayne wished he had died instead of Shin, echoed through him.

Do not diminish Shin's sacrifice. Do not say you should have died; that makes Shin's death meaningless. Live fully as the One's Light Bringer, serve him and his people as you are meant to do. In this way you honor Shin's gift and you honor Shin's life as well.

Anne's words spoken on the way to Caarwyn Rill joined in. *Rayne, breathe deeply and enjoy the journey, the destination will come in its own good time. But don't discount the wisdom gained along the way.*

Rayne knew the One had sent him on an extraordinary journey; a voyage of mountains and valleys, heights of joy and swamps of pain. And though he could not control the circumstances, he could choose to live each day honoring the One with hope and trust, breathing deeply of the glorious gifts of light and life.

The fact that he was now trapped in this feeble old body, and no longer had his strength or youth, didn't change the fact that the One was in control. And when, at the One's chosen time, he faced the destination, he would again trust the One to give him the courage and strength to say *yes*.

20

Rayne sat on the porch a long time, picking through memories, thinking. He was startled and delighted when Mite's voice pierced his reverie, ready for the little sprite to lighten his mood.

"Hello, Mite!" Rayne called.

"Ray-ray!" Mite bounded out the door onto the porch. "Ean says Ray-ray is doing a good job at getting better. He said if you feel up to it, tomorrow we can go for a walk together. Ray-ray must see more of Neth, must walk in the Heart, must, must."

Rayne laughed as Mite started the familiar routine of dancing from foot to foot. "I would like that. I feel ready to walk some."

"Tomorrow," Ean said, as he walked up behind Rayne, his ever-present smile evident. "Tomorrow thou shalt walk some. If thou dost well with that, then the next day thou canst do more."

"When will I be able to go to the Blessed Hollow?"

Ean's smile broadened. "The Blessed Hollow isn't far. It is very close; in fact, it is the Heart of the Heart. I think thou wilt be able to go soon, as long as thou keepest improving and Elspeth gives her permission. She is very protective of those whom she has worked to heal."

The next morning, dressed in a new robe of deep midnight blue and a matching cloak, Rayne walked through the Heart alongside Mite. The Heart of Neth was like no village Rayne had seen before. When he and Mite walked out the front door of the House of Healing, Rayne thought he was imagining a vision of blue and green light as random shafts of Nemora's blue-tinged sunlight filtered through a high, dense canopy of the largest and oldest trees Rayne had ever seen. He couldn't even imagine the age of most of the forest giants surrounding the Heart. They made the giants on Caarwyn look young. As the trees had grown upward, their branches had interwoven making it difficult to tell where one tree ended and another began, creating a leafy roof over the entire area. Many of the giant trees were of a variety unknown to Rayne, with large blue leaves more than five times the size of his hands. No shafts of light penetrated where those trees grew and beneath them the shade was deep blue to the ground below.

There were a few traditional dwellings in the Heart of Neth. The House of Healing, where Rayne had been staying since he and Mite arrived, had stone walls and a slate roof. But most of the residents lived in small, vine-swathed, stone cottages, with thatched or sod roofs covered in the dense blueberry-colored moss. There were no streets, just paths that wound willy-nilly around the cottages which seemed to be tucked amongst the boles of the huge trees in a random fashion. Some were even built right around large trees, with stone walls tied into the tree trunks and doors cut through the trees themselves.

There were flowers everywhere. Most bloomed on small, mossy plants in shades of white and pink, but where the sun shone through the canopy, larger varieties grew. Daisy-like flowers in yellow and gold grew in medium-height clumps; cups and bells, with long wispy stems, in chocolatey maroon and shades of lavender grew as high as Rayne's waist.

Under the deep shade of the blue-leaved trees, mushrooms grew in profusion; mushrooms of all sizes and colors, from tiny little white ones to huge blue giants as big around as large serving platters. Though most were white, green, or blue, Rayne's eye caught on some that were white at the base with bright red caps that rose into sharp peaks.

Though the kindred kept their distance, going about their business avoiding contact with the sprite and the newcomer, some drifted by and greeted them in the common language with the standard cross-world greeting, "Good fortune to thee and welcome traveler." And though they didn't see any children, Mite and Rayne heard their voices in the distance. They had been walking slowly for about a half hour with frequent stops to admire a particular tree or house, when Fallon came up and greeted them.

"Come, walk with me a smidgeon, Mite, newcomer." Fallon waved them down a winding path. After walking for a bit and chatting about the architecture of the dwellings, Fallon said, "I see thou hast grown stronger, newcomer. We have yet to meet at my hearth and discuss what it is that hast brought thee here to Neth. Elspeth tells me thou art well enough to join me at dinner this eventide. Wouldst thou, newcomer?"

"My name is Rayne. I would be happy if you would call me by my name rather than newcomer. Or you can call me Ray as Mite does."

"I thank thee, Rayne. It has been a long time since I have spoken with a newcomer. It is rare that newcomers have reason to be in Neth, most especially when Ledia and Rem are at their fullest. Thou art an anomaly, but a welcome one."

"Hasn't Mite told you why we're here?" Rayne asked, surprised that Mite hadn't talked to Fallon at length, explaining why they had come and where they were heading.

"Mite has said naught, except to ask me to wait and talk directly with thee. He tells me thou hast a curious story, and that it is not his to tell."

"I wouldn't have been upset if he told you what he knows."

"And yet, his choice was to wait." Fallon stopped and pointed up another path. "I must part with thee here. I have business to attend to. I look forward to sharing my hearth with

173

thee later. I will ask Elspeth to help thee to my home at the proper time."

"And thou," Fallon added, looking at Mite. "Thou art welcome as well."

Rayne leaned on his staff as he watched Fallon move up another path with a rapid stride. Mite looked at Rayne with a critical eye. "Ray-ray is tired, tired. We will go back to the House of Healing. Yes, yes, yes."

With a weary sigh, Rayne nodded. He had walked farther then he thought he could. He still needed his staff for balance, but he felt stronger and, for the first time since inhabiting the old body, moved with a degree of confidence.

It had grown dark by the time Mite showed up at the House of Healing and even later by the time Elspeth came to lead Rayne and Mite to Fallon's house. After his morning walk, Rayne rested the remainder of the day so he would have energy for his meeting with Fallon. He was unsure how much of his story to tell, or what Fallon might ask, but he wouldn't try to skirt the truth if Fallon asked him direct questions.

As they came down the front steps of the House of Healing, Rayne was keenly aware of the silvered light of the early moon, Rem, filtering through the breaks in the canopy, sparkling in the air around them. Though Rem's energy wasn't strong like Ledia's, Rayne still felt a subtle energy infusing him and the silver light gleamed with an uncanny brightness under the trees.

Elspeth led them the short distance to Fallon's house. Saying good-bye at the door, she wished them a pleasant evening.

Mite knocked on the cherry red, heavy wooden door. Within seconds a woman with flowing black hair and dark eyes opened it and greeted them with a large smile.

"Good fortune to thee and welcome, Mite. Newcomer. I am Fallon's wife, Neci. Come, please, thou art welcome here in our home. There is room at the hearth to eat and to talk."

Neci slipped past Rayne and Mite in the small foyer. As they followed her down a narrow hallway toward the back of the house, Rayne understood why Mite warned him to not mention anything if he noticed the Kindred fading from sight in certain light. Neci appeared translucent in the faintly lit hall. Mite had said it was normal. To the Kindred themselves, it was considered a gift that the Creator-Father had made them unique in this way, and they were quite proud that they were less physically dense than other races. By using their innate ability to harness the magical energy of Nemora, the Kindred were able to manipulate the physical world as easily as more substantial races, if not more easily. And it would be impolite for a newcomer to mention their translucency.

If not for the tendency to fade that Rayne had just witnessed, he would have thought the Kindred were human like himself, and he hoped to learn more about them without being too discourteous.

Neci was very like Fallon, both looked to be in their late thirties with dark, chestnut brown hair and deep brown eyes. Their skin would be considered pale for a human and on closer examination, a slight tinge of blue could be seen.

Neci showed her guests into the hearth room where a lively fire was crackling and popping in a fireplace built of round, white stones that took up one entire wall. The whole room was bright and inviting with white and yellow walls. Sitting in front of the fireplace was a grouping of brown leather chairs and a settee and on the other side of the room was a finely crafted wood table. Rayne admired the patterned wood. The top of the table was the color of dark coffee with a pattern which looked like swirls of cream run through it. The chairs looked too fragile to sit on and were made of the same beautifully patterned wood. When Rayne ran his hand over the top of the table it was as smooth as glass except where a border had been worked around the edge in a deep bronze color. As Rayne was admiring the table, Fallon walked in and greeted Mite and Rayne.

"Welcome. I am pleased to have thee at my hearth. Neci will bring the repast shortly; wouldst thou desire something to drink while we await?"

"Water," Rayne said. "If you have water, I would drink that."

"Ray-ray must drink Fallon's ale, must try." Mite prompted. "It is kindred ale, not newcomer ale. No, no, not newcomer ale. Ray-ray must try."

"Okay. But just one mug and after that water."

Fallon nodded. "I will be but a moment. Please, be seated."

Cautious about sitting on the fragile looking chairs set around the table, Rayne moved to the area in front of the hearth and awkwardly lowered himself into one of the stuffed leather chairs. Mite followed his lead and sat in the matching chair across from Rayne. Fallon returned a couple minutes later carrying a tray with a blue pottery pitcher and four matching mugs. After placing the tray on the table, he filled the mugs from the pitcher and brought two over to Rayne and Mite.

As soon as Mite held the mug, he sighed and took a long, deep drink. He lowered the mug, and with another sigh, said, "Fallon makes proper ale, yes, yes. Like we used to make before the newcomers came. Kindred keep the old, old ways they learned from the elders before the old ones went away."

Mite's reaction peaked Rayne's curiosity and he took a tentative taste of the incredibly thick, dark brew. And nearly choked. Not only was it much stronger than the ale Rayne was used to, it had a bite, as if it had been infused with something sharp, biting, and spicy. It was definitely not for the faint of heart or weak of stomach. Rayne determined he would take his time and nurse the brew, slowly sipping through the meal, drinking just enough to be polite. But after a few more sips, he found himself enjoying the combination of rich ale and spicy aftertaste.

While Neci brought in several trays of food, Fallon convinced Rayne of the strength of his chairs and helped him to sit at the table.

The mainstay of the meal was mushrooms. They started with a course of cold mushrooms stuffed with a bread and nut mix, followed by a creamy mushroom soup. The main course was a layered dish with mushrooms, onions and cheese that made Rayne wish for his old body so he could enjoy more of the tasty fare. A salad of wild greens, sliced mushrooms, and nuts drizzled with a tangy dressing followed.

Fallon helped Neci clear the table. A few minutes later, they returned from the kitchen. Neci carried a tray of dessert dishes and a mushroom custard tart while Fallon followed with a tray holding four mugs of cream-colored coffee. The tart was sweet and tasty and slightly spicy. Rayne had never imagined he could enjoy mushrooms in so many ways. And, though Rayne rarely sweetened his coffee any longer, the rich, sweet coffee was just the right accompaniment for the mushroom tart.

21

Fallon was a perfect host, keeping the conversation to light matters until after the meal. But once the last dishes were cleared and the four had moved to the leather chairs and settee, nursing mugs of the sweet coffee, Fallon said, "Mite, I would speak with the newcomer. If thou hast something to say, fine. But please do not answer for Rayne. I would that he speak for himself."

"Mite will behave. Allow Ray-ray to speak to Fallon." Mite kicked off his shoes and pulled his feet up onto the chair, curling up as if he was planning to sleep. Once again, he looked like nothing more than a small child sitting in a grownup's chair.

Fallon watched Mite for a minute, then rose and added a log to the fire before turning his attention to Rayne.

"Mite hast informed me thy story is long and extraordinary and I would not be so rude as to ask it all. However, the protection of Neth is my first concern, and so I must ask what hast brought thee here?"

Rayne had been thinking about what he should tell Fallon for days now. Yet, when faced with Fallon's question, he still was unsure what to say. Where should he begin and how much should he tell the Kindred?

"Like Mite, Kindred worship the Creator-Father, right?" Rayne asked.

"Yes, this is so," Fallon replied.

"We newcomers worship him too, but to us he is known as the One. My family is a very old family by newcomer standards and prophecies from the One were written many centuries ago about a descendent of King Nathan who would bring light to all Ochen and bind the living darkness that we know as Sigmund. Are you familiar with any of the newcomer prophecies?"

Fallon's brow wrinkled in concentration. "The Kindred have kept our traditions and avoided contact with newcomers. We have prophecies of our own, but I am not familiar with any newcomer prophecies."

Rayne nodded. "The first newcomer prophecy mentioning the Light Bringer goes like this. In the thirtieth generation, the Light Bringer will come from the blessed line. In his sixteenth year, he will cling to the One and he will grow in wisdom and strength to fulfill his destiny and seal the living darkness. He will bring light to the people of the worlds of Ochen.

"A little over a year ago, I found out that I was the youth mentioned in the prophecy, the One's Light Bringer.

"Then, a little over three-months ago, I was betrayed. My enemies forced my spirit from my own body by bringing it to the point of death and claiming a promise I had foolishly made. They then forced my spirit into this old body, taking both my body and the power of my royal heritage for themselves.

"I have no idea what they've done since then with the power my name has given them, and I pray for those I've left behind. But I'm constrained to fulfill the One's prophecies, to find the Words of the One to all seven worlds of Ochen. It's only by finding and bringing the scrolls together that I can fulfill the prophecy, defeat my enemies, and bring the true light of the One to Ochen.

"Before Sigmund trapped me in this body, I had already reclaimed the scrolls to Corylus, Veres, Amathea, and Glacieria.

The scrolls' guardians recognized me as the Light Bringer of the One. That's how it works, the guardians will only reveal themselves to the true Light Bringer. That's why Sigmund needs me, why those men are hunting me.

"Sigmund wants to collect the remaining scrolls himself before they can be used against him and the only way he can do that is by using me. He can't destroy them individually, so, at least for now, I know those already in Westvale are safe. He won't chance doing anything to them until he has the remaining three.

"Mite brought me to Neth so I could find the Words of the One to Nemora. We're seeking the guardian who lives in the Blessed Hollow. I don't wish to cause you any problems or harm, I wish only to reclaim the scroll and then move on to either Arisima or Sorial to reclaim the next scroll.

"As I'm sure Ean and Elspeth have told you, I don't have much time. This body, my prison, is dying. But I refuse to give up." Rayne shook his head, his mouth set in a line of firm determination. "I will fulfill the prophecies and destroy Sigmund even if it's with my last breath. Will you help me?"

Fallon looked to Neci, then turned to Mite. "Mite of Rockhall, what can you add to the words we have just heard?"

"Mite knows the heart of the Light Bringer. It is strong and courageous and full of care for all living things. And he is much loved of the One. Chosen and loved. Mite was called by the One to care for his Light Bringer. But sorrow of sorrows, the Light Bringer is dying. Mite cries inside. Mite will not leave Ray-ray's side, not leave, never leave the One's true Light Bringer. No, not until the end. And Mite will hope. The One has spoken words of hope.

"Ray-ray must not forget the second prophecy, the prophecy of promise. Ray-ray needs to remember to trust, he does, he does. The lost will be found. The broken restored. So the Creator-Father has spoken and so it shall be. Yes, yes, yes.

"Ray-ray is broken and lost. But now he has Mite. He will not stay broken and lost. And Ray-ray *will* bind the living darkness. It is written.

"Kindred worship the One who is the Creator-Father.

Kindred must help the One's Light Bringer. If the prophecy fails, even the Kindred will be taken by the darkness. Fallon has seen the dark magic growing. Fallon knows this to be true. All will be lost, lost, lost with none to mourn. Friend Fallon, if the young newcomer trapped here refuses to yield to the living darkness, how can we not help him?"

The crackling and snapping of the fire was the only sound in the room for many minutes after Mite spoke. Rayne felt a stirring of magical energy and understood Fallon and Neci were struggling with the truth they had just heard, sending waves of energy across the room. And as he watched them, he was aware of a flickering in their forms as they communicated in their own language.

Finally, Fallon spoke in the common tongue. "These are heavy matters thou hast brought before the hearth of Wife Neci and Fallon. I do not have the authority to speak for the Kindred, yet I know thy time is precious. The darkness grows even in Neth."

Turning to face his wife, Fallon asked, "What say thee, Wife Neci?"

"As the young-old one spoke, I heard the truth in his words. Truth of the Creator-Father. And when friend Mite spoke, my heart was stirred with a penetrating fear, a fear I know thou dost share my husband. Mite has spoken of darkness coming if the Light Bringer fails. I too, have seen the darkness in Neth. Trees are dying, animals changing, and each new moon, Rem's and Ledia's light shine less brightly. Husband Fallon, thou hast witnessed this too. Thou must speak for the Kindred now. We do not have the time needed to call an assembly. Thou must speak with the authority of thy office."

"Wife Neci, I have not this authority. To take newcomers into the Blessed Hollow is prohibited unless the assembly votes and agrees. Thou knowest this Wife Neci. I can do nothing except call an assembly."

"And yet to wait, is to choose, Husband Fallon. Look to the fruit of what thou wouldst choose," Neci's gaze rested on Fallon, her eyes brimming with compassion.

Fallon looked down as he wove his fingers together,

turning his hands palms up like a basket. "It would seem the fate of all Ochen has been placed in these uncertain hands."

He pulled in a long breath and released it with a sigh. "Although we do not acknowledge the newcomer prophecies, Kindred elders have spoken of a time to come when our ancient enemy would strive to rise again and seek to plunge all Ochen into fear and darkness and slavery. It is written:

In deceit and darkness, the evil ascends. Binding true light, it welcomes the night. The chosen arises, the bound, the broken.

From newcomer chosen a choice will arise. Follow the light or be bound by the night. To slavery and fear away from true sight.

Kindred shall cling to the truth of the Son. The broken, unbroken, unbound he shall be. Bind now the darkness, the broken restored.

The seven shall rise, the truth be made whole. The light comes to life when by will of the One, united in might are the word and the sword.

They sat unmoving and listened to the crackling of the fire as the words of the prophecy worked into the minds of Rayne, Mite, Fallon, and Neci.

After a bit, Fallon continued. "This is the only place in our holy writings where the Creator-Father is identified as the One. And, as the prophecy tells, our enemy will seek to take Ochen quietly by deception and lies so no one will understand the danger until it is too late. The Kindred will be called to see the truth through the lies and to choose between darkness and light. A Light Bringer chosen by the Creator-Father will arise from among the newcomers and seek help from the Kindred."

Fallon pressed up to stand and paced to the flickering remains of the fire, staring into the glowing embers. He turned back, eyes locked on Rayne's. "I had hoped this trial would not come in my lifetime. Yet here thou sittest before me, claiming the title of the servant prophesied to bind the darkness and bring the light. And here I stand, responsible for the safety of the Kindred."

"What art thou saying, Husband Fallon?"

"I know thou hast felt the truth of his words, Wife Neci. I too have sensed the truth in him. But how can I trust even my senses when the prophecy warns us of deception and lies.

How can I be sure this strange newcomer before us is truly from the Creator-Father and not deceiving us even now?"

"No, no, no." Mite hopped up and proceeded to bounce from foot to foot. "Lord Fallon knows Mite. Known Mite for long, long time. Mite has heard the voice of the Creator-Father. Ray-ray is a servant of the One. Truth, truth, no lie. The One came in power to protect Ray-ray when the enemy came to take him. No No! No!" Mite was getting more upset than Rayne had ever seen him.

"Mite," Rayne said quietly.

Mite turned to Rayne, his face a mask of sorrow. "Oh, Ray-ray, Mite has failed. Has not brought help for Ray-ray."

"Mite," Rayne said again, his voice even and calm. "It's okay, Mite. Fallon is right; his first responsibility is to his people. I know from experience how deceptive the enemy can be. But there is a way to prove what I say is true."

Turning to Fallon, Rayne asked, "Fallon, you would trust a word from the One, wouldn't you?"

Fallon thought for a moment, then nodded. "If I could be certain I was hearing the voice of the Creator-Father himself."

"If it is the will of the One that the Kindred should lead us to the Blessed Hollow, then he will make it so."

Rayne looked from Fallon to Neci, then focused on Mite. "Come, Mite, Neci, Fallon, join with me in prayer to the source of all truth, the One, the Creator-Father."

Rayne closed his eyes, energy shifting the air around him. He sensed Fallon, Neci, and Mite praying. He sought his center of calm peace and called out to the One. The response was swift and certain, warmth filled the room.

Fallon and Neci of the Kindred, you have pleased me. You have called on the source of all light. Know that my beloved Light Bringer speaks words of truth. Do not fear to take him to the Blessed Hollow. My guardian will receive him with joy.

Rayne blinked his eyes open to see Mite jumping from foot to foot, his face reflecting the joy in his heart. And Rayne loved him, loved the pure heart of Mite. Looking around, Rayne saw that both Fallon and Neci remained still, eyes closed, but glowing with an inner peace.

"That was the voice of the Creator-Father," Fallon whispered. "There can be no doubt. I will speak with the authority of my office."

"And as I know thee and know thy heart," Neci said. "I will stand with thee in choosing to take Mite and Rayne to the Blessed Hollow."

Fallon met Rayne's gaze. "Thou dost shame me with thy strong faith. To be so young and yet to face such trials with courage and conviction stirs the very spirit within me. Wife Neci has spoken and I will bind with her. When Elspeth gives leave for thee to travel, we will go to the Blessed Hollow."

22

ᚼ

The next day was spent in preparation to leave the following morning. Elspeth gave her permission for Rayne to travel. But once the permission was given and preparations begun, when Elspeth found out Rayne and Mite didn't plan to return to the Heart, she began to huff and moan that she should never have agreed to allow Rayne to go. She and Ean refused to leave his side for the entire day and Elspeth kept repeating all her instructions to both Rayne and Mite.

"Now, thou must remember, the dose must be taken every morning. If thou wast to start missing doses, the effectiveness would be compromised." Elspeth fussed as she handed Rayne two bottles of the potion she and Ean had made to strengthen him for the next few weeks.

"Mite, thou irresponsible sprite, thou watch over our young servant of the Creator-Father. Keep him well fed, be certain he drinks plenty of water, make sure he rests, don't let him get a chill, and make certain he takes his dose every morning."

Ean wasn't much better, pushing Rayne to drink several cups of the healing tea throughout the day. By evening, both Elspeth and Ean would look at Rayne and start to cry.

"Thank you for caring," Rayne said, trying to comfort the two distraught healers. "You have done so much for me. I would be dead by now if not for you two."

That produced another round of tears. Mite, complaining he could stand the two no longer, headed out for one final border patrol with Fallon, Neal, and Sloan.

Elspeth and Ean spent the night in Rayne's room using the excuse he might need something and their little silver bell had disappeared.

As Rayne was beginning to drift off, Elspeth came to stand over him. "I am so sorry, young one, that I was not able to do more for thee. If I could, I would return thee to thy own body, where thou dost belong. That would require more than the healing I can do. But know this, Ean and I will keep thee in our prayers daily."

She started to sniffle. "I am saddened that we will most likely not meet again in this life. It still sorrows me that, unless something changes, thou wilt not survive past the next couple months. Thou dost not deserve such an end and if I ever set eyes upon that Sigmund person, I'll give him a piece of my mind."

Rayne chuckled at Elspeth's words. She and Ean were such gentle souls, he hoped and prayed she would never come into Sigmund's presence. Elspeth made her way back to the chair where she had been sleeping, and soon Rayne heard her even breathing. Within minutes, he also was breathing deeply in sleep.

The next morning dawned gray and rainy. Elspeth and Ean insisted Rayne eat a full breakfast and bundle up well so he wouldn't catch a chill in the wet weather. Once Elspeth made sure he had taken his dose, he was ready to leave. Rayne and Mite walked out the front door of the House of Healing to find not just Fallon, but Neal, Slone, Darcy, Enya, and Keira waiting for them with the sling contraption they had used to carry Rayne into Neth.

"This will be the swiftest way to travel," Fallon said when Rayne questioned him.

The turn of events thrilled Mite. "Yes, yes, we will move fast, fast, fast now. This is good Ray-ray."

With Fallon helping, Rayne, once again, positioned himself in the sling seat. Slone, Darcy, Enya, and Keira hoisted the branches and they were off. As when they had brought Rayne to the Heart, Fallon and Mite ran ahead, while the warrior Neal brought up the rear.

Rayne was stronger after Elspeth's and Ean's care and it was hard for him to let go of his pride and allow others to carry him. Before, he had been too weak and sick to care. Now, he struggled with frustration at needing help. But he knew Fallon and Mite were right. There was no way he could sustain the kind of ground-covering speed Slone, Darcy, Enya, and Keira were providing. Plus, when the time came for him to meet the guardian, he would be stronger. Being carried allowed Rayne to conserve his strength for when it would be needed. Like before, the Kindred and Mite seemed to have boundless energy as they ran hour after hour. When it was nearing midday, Fallon called a stop for rest and food.

Neal had volunteered to carry Rayne's staff and as he approached, he was swinging it in practiced figure eights.

"Agreeable weapon," he said to Rayne as he handed him the staff. Those were the first words the Kindred had spoken to him.

"If one has the strength to wield it," Rayne replied.

"Wast thou a warrior before?" Neal asked. Rayne appreciated Neal's attempt to be friendly, knowing the Kindred warrior rarely talked and didn't like newcomers.

"Somewhat."

"What weapons?"

"Mostly the long sword, but I did train in a variety of other weapons. I had a very good teacher and he helped me develop a unique fighting style that combined various techniques."

As dried meat, apples, and water were passed around for everyone, Rayne and Neal continued to talk about weapons; what made a particular weapon superior, the pros and cons of various fighting styles, unique maneuvers and when to use them. Even Fallon was surprised by how Rayne could get the usually taciturn Neal to carry on a conversation.

Rayne had also warmed to the subject. "The most amazing

weapon I ever wielded was the King's Sword. Just holding it, power coursed through me and I sensed a feeling of kinship. I felt invincible. It spoke to my spirit and guided my actions, raised my speed and accuracy to a whole other level," Rayne said, remembering the day back at Coronus's compound when he had fought with the King's Sword. "It was just a shame the only time I got to use it was to kill men who were ... not enemies, just pawns of my adversary." Rayne paused.

Neal looked at Rayne with wonder. "Is it not true that no one except the king of Ochen is capable of activating the King's Sword? How then was it possible that thou didst do this thing? There is indeed more to thy story than we know. I would have thee at my hearth to tell it someday."

Rayne flashed a bittersweet smile. "That is a long, long story. A story for another time. If I live, I promise to come back and tell you the whole of it." He paused, then added. "Yeah, if I somehow live through this trial, I promise to come back and visit you, and Elspeth and Ean. If at that time, I'm still welcome in the Heart of Neth and if I could bring a couple friends, I'd like to spend time in the Heart, sitting with the Kindred, and telling you the whole story."

The afternoon went by in the same manner as the morning, with one slight change. Fallon and Mite took the rear position, following the others, while Neal took the lead. Rayne wondered how they found their way through the trackless forest. It all seemed the same, towering old giant trees with a canopy that let in little light. The rain from the morning had turned into a misty drizzle and everything was shadowed and gray. Even though it was early autumn on Nemora, Rayne was grateful for the heavier clothing and the woolen blanket Elspeth had insisted he bring. The old body always seemed to be cold.

They slowed their pace to a gentle jog in the late afternoon. Rayne was amazed at the endurance of both the Kindred and Mite. They didn't stop to set camp until the disappearing light led them to know the sun was setting. The sky was still gray through the gaps in the trees, but Fallon predicted tomorrow would be a sunny day. And tomorrow morning they would reach the Blessed Hollow.

As Rayne was finishing Enya's meal of cooked grain laced with mushrooms and wild onions, Mite surprised him with a mug of Ean's and Elspeth's healing tea.

"Ray-ray must drink it all, all, all." Mite hopped his foot to foot dance and watched until Rayne finished the whole mug.

"How did you get this?" Rayne asked between sips of the warm brew.

"Ean. Ean gave me some. Said it will help Ray-ray. Mite will give Ray-ray one cup a day until it is all gone, gone. And then, Elspeth gave Mite more and said the same things Ean said. So now Mite has twice as much tea. Mite will give Ray-ray one cup every day, just like his dose, to help Ray-ray be strong and find the scrolls and return to Westvale. Yes? Yes, yes, yes!"

"You're a good friend Mite. Thank you."

Mite started singing his Sir Mite song and skipped into the woods to stand guard. The little sprite had more energy than anyone else Rayne knew. Even the Kindred were sitting quietly around the fire, beginning to doze, while Mite still had energy to burn.

Rayne turned to Fallon and asked, "What is Mite? I mean, what kind of creature is he? He isn't Kindred, nor is he like the guardians of the scrolls. And he certainly isn't newcomer."

Fallon leaned back with a sigh and laced his hands behind his head. "Now that is a good question. We don't know exactly. As far as we know, we have never met another like Mite. He is sole, only. When the Kindred came, Mite was already here. As thou seest him now, so he was then. A kind, childlike creature of great energy and compassion. We know he is smiled upon by the Creator-Father and much beloved by many. Other than that, thou wouldst know as much as we."

Rayne snuggled into his blanket and sought sleep but with dozing and resting so much during the day, sleep eluded him. He thought of Mite and thanked the One for giving him the gift of such a special friend. As he lay there praying for his friends and wondering how they were and what they were doing, Fallon's words from two evenings ago circled in his mind, "*It would seem the fate of all Ochen has been placed in these uncertain hands.*"

Though Fallon had been speaking of himself and the decision he faced, Rayne had taken the words to heart. They applied to him just as much as they applied to Fallon. For the first time since Rayne had learned the truth of his calling as Light Bringer, he was coming to fully understand the implications if he failed. He had known from the beginning that he was to bring the One's light and he found joy in sharing what the One had given him. Rayne knew he was called to bind Sigmund, needed to bind the living darkness, whatever exactly that meant. But he had not fully thought through what would happen to Ochen if Sigmund succeeded and darkness ruled in the land.

The idea of Sigmund in control sent his stomach into flips. What he had experienced as a child could be the fate of other children, raised to darkness and Sigmund's will. It would affect every man, woman, and child throughout the Ochen system.

The immensity of the task dropped into him with a boulder-like weight at Fallon's words. The mention of a rising darkness and its desire to take all Ochen not by force, but by guile and deception triggered an explosion of fear in Rayne. It brought back the feeling of intense cold and the premonition of coming darkness he had experienced months ago in Westvale, before the exhibition match with Thorvin.

He trusted the One, trusted in his strength. But Rayne knew that Sigmund was now using Rayne's own body to advance his agenda of deception and darkness. Remembering Shaw's words about Sigmund's master, he began to think in terms of turning a powerful darkness back on itself and saving the entire system. This was beyond him, the fate of Ochen had truly been placed in weak and uncertain hands.

This truth drove him into a depth of prayer. Only in the One would he find the strength to even consider facing this rising darkness. Only the One could bind the darkness that was more than just Sigmund. And Rayne finally understood, the living darkness was more than just one demon, it was a wave of dark creatures like Sigmund and Heinrich and the hunters Sigmund had sent after Rayne. And it was a wave of slavery and terror if their plans succeeded. All living creatures on all the seven worlds of Ochen would become part of a living darkness.

And only the One could release the light and bind the living darkness. Only the One could save Ochen and drive back the wave of darkness that was now threatening all who lived on the seven in ignorance of the danger that was quietly threatening. And the One had chosen as his prophesied Light Bringer, a broken youth trapped in a fragile, dying body.

The lost will be found and the broken made whole.

Rayne knew he was lost and broken. But he also knew the One was never lost, or taken by surprise, or overwhelmed by darkness. The will of the One would always, *always* be worked out in his good time. Rayne rested in the truth he knew, and trusting the One's words, fell into a deeply peaceful sleep knowing he was never alone.

Early the next morning, after they had eaten and travelled the remaining distance to the edge of the Blessed Hollow, Fallon and the other Kindred left Rayne and Mite.

Rayne's eyes widened in surprise when Neal hugged him gently and the large warrior said, "I found pleasure in discussing weapons with thee. I pray thou wilt find strength to return and I will await our continued conversation, Light Bringer of the One."

Slone came forward and took Rayne's hand and arm in a sturdy grasp in the Kindred tradition. "I be sorry I called thee niggling afore I even knew thee. When I first laid eyes on thee, I was all set to drive this stupid, feeble, sleeping newcomer from Neth. I be glad Ean and Elspeth stopped me. May the Creator-Father guide and guard thy steps, Light Bringer."

Darcy, Enya, and Keira all gave Rayne gentle hugs but didn't say anything.

Then Fallon came forward. "Thou hast changed me, young Light Bringer. I thank thee for helping me to see the path set before the Kindred now when the darkness seeks to blind us. It is not a path of ignorance any longer; now we too will work to defy the darkness and seek the light of the Creator-Father.

May he guard thee and guide thy steps, and may thou find the promise in the prophecy come to be for thee."

Fallon reached into a deep pocket of his oversized jacket and pulled out a small leather bag. "Take this; may it help thee on thy journey. Do not open it until thou hast left the Blessed Hollow."

He hugged Rayne and with a quick nod to Mite, waved. Then, along with his fellow Kindred, he vanished like smoke into the shadows of the forest.

After the Kindred left, Mite promised to set up a camp and have food ready for Rayne when he returned. Leaving Mite to his task, the Light Bringer entered the Blessed Hollow to find the guardian of the scroll.

23

ᚾ

Shaw, Stevie and Sashi dressed in heavy clothing after being warned by Thorvin that Glacieria was indeed as cold as everyone said, even though it was now late spring there. Though the Westvale Portal Station was as noisy, crowded, and busy as ever, the area in front of the portal to Glacieria was empty when they arrived. They had a few minutes to wait before the skipping line was scheduled to switch direction, so they were standing near the portal talking amongst themselves when two-dozen men, wrapped in heavy, hooded, fur-lined cloaks of a deep muddy red color marched over. When the light came on signaling the line was open, the men shoved past Shaw, Stevie, and Sashi, entering the portal as a group.

"So rude," Sashi mumbled as she set her hands on her hips while the three waited their turn to enter the portal.

Stepping out onto Glacieria, an icy wind barreled into Shaw. He pulled his heavy cloak tighter as he walked behind Stevie and Sashi, following in the footsteps of the cloaked men along a shoveled path. Shaw had expected to see a portal warden as soon as they skipped, but no one was around.

"Look," Stevie said, pointing to a spot near the path. At

first, Shaw could see nothing. The sun in a clear lavender sky reflected off the pink-tinged snow with blinding intensity. He couldn't believe Stevie had seen anything. But once Shaw shielded his eyes and squinted, he saw the spot Stevie was pointing out. Droplets of blood.

"That's not the only thing," Sashi whispered. "Did you notice how well armed those men up ahead are?"

Shaw's heart skipped a beat and he was grateful Thorvin had insisted he bring Stevie and Sashi with him. He would not have noticed the blood and, even now, he couldn't see the weapons Sashi mentioned.

A couple minutes later they trailed the men into a snow-covered building that Shaw assumed was the portal station. He hadn't given much thought to what Glacieria would be like when he volunteered to come look for Tetsuya, but what he saw in the station was the last thing he would have expected. It looked as if a battle had just been fought there. Bodies were scattered along the hall and in the large central room. The fire was out, and everything felt oddly cold.

The men in front of them payed no attention to the bodies. They walked right through the room and out a back entrance without stopping. With the door open, Shaw and the twins heard shouting and weapons clashing, but when the door closed behind the men, the sounds were silenced.

Sashi ran down the hallway, opened the door a crack, and peeked out. "There's fighting going on out here. What do you want to do Shaw?"

But the question lost all meaning, as Sashi suddenly back-tracked up the hallway. Several men bounded in the door in front of her, pulling it shut and locking it behind them.

The men looked exhausted and a few were injured. A middle-aged, heavy-set man who looked to be in charge, glanced at Sashi then stared at Shaw and Stevie. The thin line of his mouth turned down at the corners and he said, "Who are you? Off-worlders? Why have you come here now? Do you not know Glacieria is at war with herself?"

The men, more than a dozen of them, moved about the main room, finding places to sit and lowering packs to the floor. A couple uninjured men helped those who couldn't walk to places where they could lie down. Another man scrambled to the fireplace and built a fire while two more began checking the bodies and moving the dead outside the far entrance.

One of the soldiers, a slight, skinny man, looked at Shaw with dark, piercing eyes and said in a cold voice, "We should kill these strangers, Daichi. They must have come with the scroll worshipers."

Shaw started, his mouth dropping open. The fighter he had thought was a young man was a girl, and she looked just as deadly as any of the men she was with.

"Hoshiko, no." The big man, Daichi, whom Shaw supposed must be the leader of the group spoke. "To kill without reason diminishes us as warriors. Please, leave this to me and go help the wounded."

Daichi looked at Shaw a moment longer and then looked at Stevie and Sashi. Turning back to Shaw, he asked, "Off worlder, who are you, and why have you come to Glacieria?"

"My name is Shaw Radinajan and my friends are Stevie and Sashi Kasper. We've come from Corylus in search of friends. What happened here? Not long ago other friends of ours were here and things were peaceful when they left."

"I am Daichi of the Khalon tribe. For what friends have you come? What tribe?"

"We are seeking Tetsuya and Jiro of the Michi."

"I know these men you name. If you are followers of the One as are they, you cannot be with the scroll worshipers who have come to stir up war between brothers on Glacieria."

"I thought that after Prince Rayne spoke here, the tribes were willing to at least listen to the Michi," Shaw said. "My friends said when they left Glacieria, the One had touched the hearts of many of the Wataru and Khalon, opening their minds to the truths the Michi had preserved, and helping them to understand that the power of the scroll was a lie."

"Your friends spoke the truth. I myself, and my fellow soldiers, are all members of the Khalon tribe. We bowed to the One after the Light Bringer spoke to us, as did many of our tribe and of the Wataru."

"Soon after the Light Bringer left though, groups of scroll worshipers began skipping onto Glacieria, like the one that just arrived. The first group to come brought with them a new scroll they claim is the true scroll of Glacieria. They stirred up those who were unsure. Now brother takes up arms against brother. The scroll worshipers say that any who refuse to bow to the scroll must be killed."

"This is terrible," Shaw said, rubbing his hand on the back of his neck. "How many of these scroll worshipers have come to your world?"

"We do not know," Daichi said. "After the Light Bringer touched our hearts, large numbers of Khalon and Wataru stayed many days in the Meeting Bowl to listen and learn from the teachers of the Michi.

"My cousin, Mizu introduced me to your friends, Jiro and Tetsuya, and I spent much time with them. But we became too engrossed in our studies and made the mistake of leaving our portal unguarded. The scroll worshipers arrived and began to sow discord among the people. By the time we understood what was happening, innumerable off-world scroll worshippers had come through the skipping line and the fighting had already begun.

"My clansmen and I are part of a group sent to retake the portal and prevent more enemies from coming through.

"A couple hours ago, we were separated from our clansmen during a skirmish. When we realized we would not be able to rejoin our people, we decided to continue toward the portal knowing they would join us here as soon as they could. Approaching the station building, we ran into a large group of off-worlders. Once they saw us, we had no choice but to fight our way through to the station and lock ourselves in. We do not have the strength of numbers to fight the scroll worshippers. We will go out and join the fight when more of our people arrive."

Hoshiko moved to stand by Daichi. "Let me sneak out Daichi. I will kill the scroll worshipers from the shadows."

"No, Hoshiko. I do not want to lose you. But there is a task I need you to do. Run to the portal, switch it, and lock it.

That will stop others from skipping onto Glacieria. When our people arrive, and the fighting begins again, we will then go out and fight alongside them. For now, remember our reason for coming here was to lock the portal."

Hoshiko, looking angry and fierce, turned and sprinted down the hallway toward the path to the portal.

"You must excuse Hoshiko," Daichi said. "She is angry and hurting and desires nothing more than to fight and kill. Her brother was one of the first to die at the hands of the scroll worshipers. He refused to bow to the scroll when they paraded it through their village, claiming he would worship the One alone.

"She feels much guilt that she was not with her brother. Hoshiko was with those of us who desired to remain at the Meeting Bowl after the Light Bringer left, so we could continue studying with the Michi. But since she heard the story of what happened to her brother, her heart has cried out for vengeance. This is not a good time for any off-worlders on Glacieria. You must turn around and return to Corylus."

"But we came here to find Jiro or Tetsuya," Shaw said. "Things have changed on Corylus and we have been sent to learn the words of the prophecy that Tetsuya told our friend Thorvin. We cannot leave until we learn what that prophecy says in its entirety. It is vital we accomplish what we came to do. Can you help us?"

Daichi looked at Shaw, indecision battling resolve across his broad face. Finally, he said, "Remain here when we go out to fight. Once we defeat the scroll worshipers, I will speak to my superior about taking you to the Meeting Bowl."

Hoshiko came ghosting in. "It is done."

With stealth and grace, she moved back to the outer door, cracking it open a sliver to listen, but she returned immediately with fire in her eyes. "They are here Daichi. We must go out and fight."

Leaving the wounded behind, Daichi led his people out the back door.

Sashi paced nervously until a moan from one of the wounded men drew her to his side. "This is crazy," she said.

"If I don't do something, I'm going to go nuts. Stevie, help me." Sashi saw to the needs of the three wounded men, while Stevie stoked the fire, and Shaw drew up his hood and prayed.

Less than a half-hour later, Daichi was back in the station with Hoshiko.

"I have spoken with my superior about your need to find your friends," Daichi said. "He has given permission for me to take you to the Meeting Bowl. Hoshiko has asked to join us and I am grateful for her offer of help. But we must leave immediately. Word of our taking control of the portal will reach the ears of the scroll worshipers and if they come with strength to retake it, they will block the path to us."

Hoshiko took the lead as they headed out from the station. Stevie and Sashi, swords drawn, positioned themselves before and after Shaw. Daichi brought up the rear. They wasted no time, but moved with speed, jogging through the icy cold air, down a path cut through the snow. The sun cast everything in a pinkish glow, and the snow-coated fir trees they passed looked like tall lumps of fluffy pink wool growing out of the ground. As they ran, Shaw appreciated the heat of the spring sun warming his back in spite of the biting cold. After they had run for a little over an hour, they passed through the remains of what must have been a large campsite.

Minutes later, Daichi whispered, "We are close to the new Khalon camp. Please stay right behind Hoshiko so the guards do not mistake you for enemies."

With Stevie's toes knocking into Hoshiko's heels, they approached the Khalon camp. Several guards surrounded them but once they recognized Hoshiko and Daichi, they moved off to continue patrolling. Not a word was said.

Daichi led them into a sheltered glen housing a surprisingly sizeable camp. He moved with confidence to a large tent and motioned for them to follow him inside. Shaw, Sashi, and Stevie were all impressed at the level of warmth and comfort the tent offered. Shaw, desert dweller that he was, directed his steps to the fire pit at the center of the tent and removed his gloves, holding his hands out to the heat of the crackling fire.

"Please excuse my lack of hospitality," Daichi said. "Under

normal circumstances, my wife and children would be here to greet you and offer you a warm drink. But these are not normal times. My family is back at our home village. I pray they are safe. I chose to come with the warriors who volunteered to close the portal to off-worlders and protect it from those already here."

After telling his guests to take off their heavy cloaks and settle in front of the fire, Daichi and Hoshiko disappeared through a door at the back of the tent for several minutes. They reappeared with trays. Hoshiko carried a tray holding a large loaf of rough brown bread while Daichi carried a tray holding a large pitcher and several mugs.

Once everyone had a cup of icy water and some bread, Daichi said, "We must wait here until morning to traverse Roaring Mountain. Since the scroll worshipers have come, the path through the mountain has become dangerous. A darkness possesses the heavy magic of the Burning Cavern and has been growing farther out through the tunnels, day by day. To attempt the passage at night is to seek death. I have arranged for a meal here and we can talk while we eat. But then we should sleep as we must leave very early so we can enter to the mountain at daybreak. That is the safest time to move through the tunnels and cross the cavern."

"Is that Burning Cavern the place where Rayne fought the beast?" Sashi asked.

Hoshiko looked up at Sashi, interest burning in her dark eyes, as Daichi answered, "Yes. The Light Bringer defeated the Primal Warrior in the Burning Cavern. After that, the cavern lost much of its heaviness. But now, it is worse than ever. No one travels through there unless they are with others and it is day."

"You know the Light Bringer?" Hoshiko asked Sashi.

"We are all friends of Prince Rayne," Sashi said. "We traveled with him to Veres but weren't able to be with him when he came here. We were all supposed to get together again on Nemora, but things changed, and now ... I don't know what's going to happen."

"When he spoke to the tribes about the truth of the One,

my heart burned within me," Hoshiko said, thumping her fist over her heart. "I do not understand those who would bow down to worship a lifeless scroll. There is no power or truth there, only the power of fear and the rule of deception."

"Ah, Hoshiko," Daichi said. "Well said. The ability to control through fear and deception is a powerful tool."

"And our enemies seek to use it to its fullest potential," Shaw added.

"Yes." Daichi nodded. "It sounds as if you speak from experience."

"At least we have not experienced such a thing as brother fighting against brother," Shaw said. "How did this manage to turn bloody so quickly?"

"I told you what happened to Hoshiko's brother. So has it been in each village the scroll worshipers have visited. Those who bow down are enlisted to fight or serve in other ways, those who do not bow down are killed. Some villages were turned completely, the people believing they have returned to the true worship they were already practicing these past ten years. Other villages packed up everything and have moved close to the Meeting Bowl or onto Michi lands.

"The first villages to be visited by the scroll worshippers, like Hoshiko's village, fared the worst because they did not realize the danger. Many of those who have lost loved ones now fight out of anger. We are a strong people with much honor given to those who are accomplished warriors. Skirmishes between tribes have always been a way of life for us, it is our nature. But never before have we fought within our tribes. This is an evil thing that is being done to Glacieria."

"Shaw," Sashi said, her voice low and intense. "Do you think Sigmund is behind this too?"

Shaw grimaced, nodding. "I believe Sigmund and his servants of darkness are the driving force behind this cult. When Rayne defeated Sigmund's inhuman warrior and taught the truth about the scroll and the One to these people, he created a situation where the demons' hold on Glacieria was threatened. They must have responded by sending large numbers of scroll worshipers, forcing a choice on the tribes before the people were ready to stand strong on their faith in the One. And now with Rayne taken from us, we have no one who can rally the people the way he did."

"What do you mean?" Hoshiko's voice was as icy as the air outside their tent. "How was the Light Bringer taken?"

"We have sent requests to Prince Rayne for help," Daichi said. "We understood that he is ruling now in Westvale and although he has not yet responded, we held out hope he would return to us soon."

"Oh, this is bad!" Sashi moaned.

"What has happened?" Daichi looked from Shaw to Sashi.

Shaw squinted in thought then breathed out a huff through pursed lips. "I don't even know what to tell you because we don't know for certain what's really happened. All I can say for sure is that Prince Rayne ... well ... he's *changed*. He no longer seems like himself and that's why it is important we speak with Tetsuya about the prophecy. We fear the prince has come under Sigmund's control and we're trying to find a way to reverse the situation. So, you see, you can't expect any help from Westvale."

"If even the Light Bringer is not safe from our enemies," Hoshiko said, raising her chin. "What chance do we have?"

"Do not despair." Shaw looked up, meeting the girl's deep eyes. "Even without the Light Bringer, we have the One. The Light Bringer is like a sign pointing to the One. He is not the power, the One himself is the true power. If Rayne were here, he would be the first to remind us of that fact. We need to seek the One; his power, his wisdom, his guidance. Rayne has given us that much, that truth. Now we need to act with faith in that truth."

"Your words are wise, Shaw," Daichi said. "But without the Light Bringer to rally behind, I fear our people may be lost."

"Then let us pray that is not the case." Conviction hardened Shaw's voice.

The discussion continued through the meal, but soon after, everyone settled in to sleep. Tomorrow would start early and looked to be a very long day. As everyone else breathed evenly in sleep, Shaw thought about Anne and his friends back in Westvale, now facing something even larger than they had realized. And he prayed. He prayed for Anne, for his friends, for the king and queen, but most especially he prayed for Rayne.

24

꿔

As promised, Daichi woke everyone long before sunrise to assure they would reach the mountain tunnel by daybreak. After grabbing a quick cold meal of day-old bread and dried fruit, they packed their few things, lit two lanterns, and headed up the path cut in the snow. On their way, they passed several guards coming off duty. Daichi expressed his relief when he heard there had been no skirmishes during the night and that the guards had seen no signs of scroll worshipers.

After walking a couple miles, they met a group of volunteers coming from the Meeting Bowl. "The darkness surrounding the Burning Cavern is bad," a grizzled older soldier reported to Daichi with a shake of his head as the rest of his band continued plodding past Shaw and his companions. "Never seen nothing like it. The tunnel through the mountain is saturated with heavy magic. It's so bad, even I felt it and I'm not one to sense that. We made the mistake of pushing through the mountain at night and the light from our torches was so muted by that eerie darkness, that it only carried for a foot or two."

"Did everyone make it through alright?" Daichi asked.

The man growled. "We used rope to tie ourselves together and still we lost two people to the darkness around the Burning Cavern. If I were you, I'd take the pass. Forget going through the tunnel." The man's eyes went wide. "I won't go through there again. I don't care how long it takes to go around. Never again. Those voices … that feeling of evil … nope … not me. Not again." The man continued to mumble and shake his head as he walked away.

"Are Jiro and Tetsuya still at the Meeting Bowl?" Shaw called after the retreating man, his throat tightening.

"When we left," the man said over his shoulder without stopping, "they were both still teaching. I don't think they planned to leave anytime soon. Tetsuya was waiting for word from his tribal leaders about whether they had sighted any scroll worshipers on Michi lands though. That might change things."

The volunteer moved out of earshot and Shaw asked Daichi, "How much longer would it take to travel to the Meeting Bowl if we took the mountain pass rather than the tunnel?"

"It would take us a least a week longer, maybe even two weeks at this time of year."

"We don't have the time for that," Shaw said as his hope of avoiding the Burning Cavern evaporated. "We have to take the tunnel."

"That is good," Daichi said. "I do not wish to be gone from my duties for so long. But we will have to take precautions."

As they approached the mountain, the warmth from the ground beneath their feet crawled up Shaw's legs, just like Thorvin had described. Heavy cloud cover added to the early morning darkness, thick and foreboding. Just as they reached the entrance to the tunnel, the sky brightened over their heads, revealing the surrounding landscape in shades of gray. The tunnel entrance itself looked like a living thing. Tendrils of living shadows, like questing fingers of night, defied the early morning light.

Daichi hissed at the sight. "They were right. The darkness is indeed worse. We must hurry."

C. S. WACHTER

Hoshiko dropped her pack to the ground and pulled out a rope, handing the end to Daichi.

He tied the rope onto his belt and handing it to Shaw to do the same. Shaw complied. Sashi and Stevie repeated the action after him and then Stevie handed the other end to Hoshiko who tied it to her belt as well.

While the others were tying the rope, Daichi checked the level of fuel in each of the lanterns and, pulling a skin of additional fuel from his pack, filled both. Shaking the fuel skin, he nodded at the sound of remaining oil before returning the skin to his pack. He re-lit both lanterns, passing one back to Hoshiko at the end of the line and keeping the second himself.

The rope was tied to keep them close together with just enough slack between to allow them to walk comfortably. When all was ready, Daichi met each individual's eyes. "Is everyone ready?"

"Wait," Shaw said. "We need to pray first. Before we go into the darkness, we must seek the One's protection."

They bowed their heads as Shaw prayed for guidance and protection. When he finished praying, Daichi led the way into the tunnel entrance. Immediately, the light from the lanterns dimmed as if something translucent was growing around their glass sides, blocking most of the light.

"Nemora's moons," Sashi whispered. "The very air here seems too heavy to breathe."

"Keep talking," Daichi said. "I have been told people hear voices that try to lure them deeper into the darkness. We must be sure we talk to each other and do not allow anyone to remain silent for too long. Perhaps while we are proceeding through the tunnel, you can teach us more about the One and his prophecies, Shaw. And ask us questions, make us answer back."

The first hour went by without incident but as they approached the Burning Cavern, the darkness thickened and swirled with an evil malice that seeped into Shaw's spirit. Stevie got quiet and though Shaw asked him a direct question, he didn't respond.

"Stevie?" Sashi said, concern for her brother in her voice.

"Don't you hear her?" Stevie suddenly asked. "It's Emma. She's here. Can't you hear? She's calling me. She's in trouble and needs me. I have to go!"

He tried to untie the rope but because he was in the middle of the line all he succeeded in doing was yanking Sashi and Hoshiko closer to him. Unable to undo the rope, Stevie began unbuckling his belt, mumbling under his breath about how he needed to help Emma.

"Stevie," Sashi turned to him and grabbed his face. "Look at me Stevie. Emma isn't here; she's back in Westvale. Listen to me. Stevie! It's a trick of the darkness. Stevie!"

Sashi's words seemed to get through and Stevie went still. "I ... I'm sorry," he mumbled. "It, it seemed so ... real."

Stevie had pulled everyone to a stop when he thought he heard Emma calling. Now, immobile in the heavy air, no one seemed capable of even taking a step. The darkness sucked the will from them, and they were mesmerized by the surrounding, gray nothingness.

Daichi shook his head and mumbled about cobwebs in his brain. Grunting with the effort, he shouted, "Don't stand still. We have to keep moving. Move! We're almost to the Burning Cavern."

Shaw began praying aloud, petitioning the One for his help and power to keep moving.

The close sides of the tunnel gave way to the open expanse known as the Burning Cavern, the place where Rayne had fought the Primal Warrior—where the magic saturation was thickest and most powerful. The air was alive with purpose, as if cognizant of their presence. It sapped energy from them as they entered the cavern. Voices whispered.

Daichi hurried everyone forward across the cavern, stumbling through the sandy circle at the center, calling out to Hoshiko at the end of the line. "Hoshiko, talk to me. Can you hear me? Are you okay?"

Breathing hard, the young warrior huffed a reply. "I am fine. Don't stop; keep moving."

Even in the dense darkness now filling the Burning Cavern, the muted wavering glow from the crevice of the molten river of rock far below drew Shaw's eyes. The glow cast shimmering blood stains on the gloom surrounding them as they passed close to the edge of the crevice. With Daichi's lantern swinging wildly as he ran, they found the entrance to the far tunnel and left the Burning Cavern behind.

Although the air still thrummed with magic energy in the tunnel beyond, some of the knot in Shaw's stomach unclenched as they moved away from the Burning Cavern. They still had a five-hour hike before they would emerge from the far side of the mountain, but the worst of the heavy magic was now behind them.

Daichi wouldn't let them rest. He continued to press for as much speed as they could marshal. The twins and Hoshiko were jogging as if they could run without stopping for several hours yet. *Probably thinking how much they want out of this darkness.* Shaw was finding it harder to keep the pace. Then, he heard the laughter.

It was all around him, rippling through the dark air. Everyone was dragged to a stop as Shaw pulled up and tried to turn back toward the Burning Cavern. He was battered by the surrounding laughter and the voices calling him back toward the cavern.

Come back, servant of our enemy. We know you seek your Light Bringer. You will not find him where you are looking. Come back to us. We know where the broken one cries. We know. Come back to the cavern before it is too late. He's dying. Come back and you can save him.

The laughter rose in volume, forcing Shaw to cover his ears yet still he heard the voices in his head.

He's dying. All hope is gone. He's dying now. Come back. All is lost; all is lost. Can't you hear him crying? Come back. He's calling for you.

Shaw, like Stevie before him, tried to work the rope from where it was wrapped around his belt, but before he could do anything, Daichi shouted for everyone to run. With Sashi and Daichi pulling him along and Stevie and Hoshiko pushing from behind, Shaw was forced to move forward.

"Let me go, you fools. Don't you hear them. The voices. They know where Rayne is. Please, let me go. We can find him, help him." He cried and fought to pull away from the others, but they forced him forward until the voices stopped.

With Shaw breathing hard, but back to his senses, Daichi began jogging again and they put the miles behind them. With no breaks they walked and jogged until they came to a lighter area of the tunnel where the darkness still hadn't spread.

Shaw pulled up, huffing and sweating. "Please, could we rest for a bit."

Daichi grimaced but then relented. "Yes, Shaw. We could all use a break. But only for a few minutes."

Sitting in the now normal darkness with the lit lanterns giving enough light to see each other easily, Shaw glanced around the group sheepishly and said, "I'm sorry. Stevie was right. The voices seemed so real. They told me that they knew where Rayne was and that he's dying. They promised to take me to him."

"They were lying," Hoshiko said. "The voices in the darkness never speak truth. If you had gone back, you would not have found your friend, you would have found your death."

Shaw swallowed back his fear as he looked at those around him, uncertainty churning in his gut. "But what if it's true? What if I could have found out something?"

"No." Sashi shook her head, her shoulder-length red hair bouncing. "Hoshiko's right. It was nothing more than a lie. The best way to help Rayne is to keep moving forward and get the prophecy. That's the truth."

Shaw nodded, but he lowered his eyes to stare, unseeing, at his hands cupped in his lap.

After a brief rest, Daichi checked the fuel levels in the lanterns once again. He added a bit more fuel to each, then they moved on. When, nearly two hours later, they saw the light of the tunnel entrance in the distance they all put on a burst of speed to get out of the stifling heat and dark energy of the tunnel, and into the open air.

Though the sky was still cloudy, the light nearly blinded everyone as they stumbled out onto a path cut into the side of the mountain, overlooking a vast plain dotted with clumps of fir trees. Patches of windswept grasses showed through where snow had begun melting in the intermittent warmth of spring.

"I don't know about anyone else," Sashi said. "But I don't care how much longer it takes to go around. I'm not going back through that tunnel again."

Though Shaw shared her thought, he didn't say a word.

They undid the rope, unwrapping it from each belt, and then Hoshiko wound it up and replaced it in her pack. Daichi said that everyone should wait near the entrance to the tunnel and that he would be back shortly. He strode up the trail to their right with quick steps.

"Daichi has gone to get horses." Hoshiko explained. "When he returns, we will need to take the trail west, toward the Meeting Bowl. He will not be long." She pulled a canteen from her pack and passed it around. "We should drink while we are waiting."

The breeze, though cold and raw under the heavy clouds, felt good to the travelers after the closeness of the tunnels as they stood looking out over the rolling plain.

"Are they always so warm?" Sashi asked Hoshiko.

"What?"

"The tunnels," Sashi said. "Are the tunnels always so warm and close?"

"Yes," the girl warrior said, her voice soft. "But I have never felt such heavy air before. That must be from the growing darkness. When I came through the mountain the other day, only in the Burning Cavern was the air so heavy."

While they were talking, Daichi returned pulling five horses after him. "Come, friends, the Meeting Bowl is only a couple hours away now. We need to move with speed and caution if we wish to avoid scroll worshipers. If we hurry, we can enjoy the comforts of a warm meal and shelter before it grows dark. At this season of year, we would usually be enjoying lengthening days of spring, but the darkness now seems to claim more of the day than normal."

Crossing the plain, they kept a steady, but not grueling, pace that ate up the miles without undue strain on the shaggy little Glacierian horses. After they had been riding almost two hours, they caught sight of a large group of people heading toward them. Unsure if they were scroll worshippers, Daichi led the friends in a short detour around a copse of fir trees to avoid notice. Everyone breathed a sigh of relief when they finally arrived at the Meeting Bowl without incident.

25

ᴜ

Though most of the tents that had filled the bowl when Thorvin and Rayne were there were now gone, there was still a smattering of varied tents representing all three tribes. And as they made their way among the tents, Shaw saw a familiar face. "Jiro," he called, relieved to see the large Michi at last.

Jiro looked up and around. When his eyes lit on Shaw, Stevie, and Sashi, a huge grin split his face and he ran to greet them. "Good fortune to you and welcome my friends," he shouted as Sashi leaped from her horse to be taken up in a bone crushing hug. Shaw and Stevie dismounted, and Jiro hugged each in turn.

Jiro waved to Daichi and Hoshiko. "Greetings Daichi. You and your young friend are welcome to join us. I will call for someone to come take your horses."

"Thank you for the welcome," Daichi said. "But Hoshiko and I have family here we would like to see before we return to the portal." He inclined his head to Shaw and the twins. "It has been an honor to help friends of the Light Bringer. If it is the will of the One, perhaps we shall meet again."

Hoshiko dismounted and taking the reins from Shaw,

Stevie and Sashi, said, "It has been an honor. I will keep you and the Light Bringer in my prayers. Farewell."

Daichi and Hoshiko walked away as Jiro, still wearing a huge smile, turned back to Shaw, Stevie and Sashi. "Come, we will go to Akira's tent. She will want to meet you and we have much to talk about."

Jiro ushered the friends toward a large tent. When they entered, several people who had been sitting cross-legged by the central cook fire looked up. One, a slight man with deep gray eyes rose. "Jiro, have you managed to find off-worlders wandering lost on Glacieria at a time like this?"

"Father Tetsuya, I would like to introduce three friends from Corylus. These are Shaw Radinajan, Sashi Kasper, and her brother Stevie Kasper. They are all friends of the Light Bringer."

Tetsuya bowed. "Please come sit around the fire so we may talk in comfort."

The two other men who had been talking with Tetsuya rose and excused themselves, saying they would arrange to have food and drink sent for the travelers.

When they were all settled, another huge smile spread across Jiro's face. "I told you he would come Tetsuya. I knew my friend Prince Rayne would not ignore our call for help. Is he following behind you? Is he on his way?"

Shaw looked at Stevie and Sashi before meeting Jiro's hope-filled eyes. "Jiro, Rayne isn't coming."

"But the darkness is rising." Jiro's smile wilted behind a cloud of confusion. "We ... we need the Light Bringer ... to push back the darkness and expose the lies of the scroll worshipers. Why ... why wouldn't he come?"

"Jiro." Shaw swallowed around the burning lump in his throat. "Something's happened to Rayne. We don't understand it or even know for sure what *it* is. But Rayne's not himself. That's why we came, to learn the words of the prophecy Tetsuya told Thorvin. We hoped the prophecy can help us figure out why Rayne's acting the way he is."

"What do you mean ... when you say the Light Bringer is not himself?" Jiro asked, his words slow and measured.

"We can't be certain, but Bishop Hedrick thinks Rayne might be possessed. And, it looks as though Sigmund is behind this. The things Rayne is saying, what he's doing, his very temperament, is in complete opposition to the person we know. He has done unspeakable things which would have sickened him in the past. He's taking more political power and has even been involved with Sorial reclaiming Veres, something Rayne would never do."

Jiro looked at Shaw, the whites of his dark eyes showing. "Veres is taken again?"

"That's what we've been told. And according to the news from Nemora, Rayne was one of the people responsible for the Interplanetary Council reissuing the proclamation declaring Veres a satellite of Sorial."

"You are right," Jiro said, shaking his head. "My friend, Prince Rayne, did not believe in slavery and fought to free Veres. He would not do this thing. Veres is under attack and so are we here on Glacieria. And the Light Bringer himself is under attack. But if he is no longer the Light Bringer, if he is indeed another spirit inside, where is the spirit of our friend?"

"Perhaps I can help answer that," Tetsuya said. "You came seeking the words of the prophecy. You were right to seek these words. *My beloved servant who was lost and found, will be tested. Though light is shrouded and severed spirit wandering, he will find rest in my truth, and I will be his shelter in the tempest. For the darkness that claims victory is already defeated. I will guide his steps by the least of lights until the three are found and the cup of wrath is full. Then the true heart will be known by the bond I have made and the broken made whole once again.*

"Since I spoke with your friend Thorvin, I have given much thought to the meaning of these words. Though there is much I still do not understand. From what you have just told us, I think I might understand more than I did before.

"Shaw, you have spent your life studying the truths of the One. Is this not so?"

"I have spent my life in studying all that we have preserved on Arisima about the Words of the One. That is why my community sent me to help the Light Bringer when we knew his time of unveiling was drawing near."

"Very good. Then you will understand. Follow. Each line has specific meaning. The first line ties into prior prophecy. It speaks of being lost and found. When I spoke to Thorvin about this we wondered if the words had already been fulfilled in Rayne's past or if they might refer to something yet to come. I suspect they signify both."

"Yes," Shaw said, drawing out the word as his mind picked through the prophecies he already knew. "That makes sense."

Two young girls came into the tent from one of the back entrances carrying trays of fresh bread and tea. They placed a short table next to Tetsuya and another next to Jiro and set the trays there. Once they left, Tetsuya continued.

"Let's look at the next line, or maybe just the next few words." Tetsuya quoted again. "'Though light is shrouded and severed spirit wandering.' I think this line is a good description of what is happening now. Isn't the light being shrouded? The young Light Bringer's spirit is absent and his body is in possession of his enemies. If he is lost to himself again, is he not wandering?

"But though it seems as if the enemy is succeeding in his quest to extinguish the light, think about what the next words say. 'He will find rest in my truth, and I will be his shelter in the tempest. For the darkness that claims victory is already defeated.' Are these not words of great hope? The One is protecting his Light Bringer even now. And the enemy who believes himself to be winning is, in fact, already defeated. These are surely words of great hope!"

"Nemora's moons," Sashi whispered. "That makes sense. Even if things seem to be out of control to us, the One is still really calling the shots. That's what Bishop Hedrick said the other day. And even before that, Rayne said Sigmund thoroughly underestimated the power of the One. Sigmund still thinks he's winning, but he doesn't see where it's all heading."

"Yeah," Stevie said. "But in the meantime, Rayne's gone or trapped or whatever, Veres is taken again, and darkness is growing on Glacieria. And we don't even know what else might be happening on the other worlds. How are we going to survive until the One decides it's time to put a stop to Sigmund and his followers?"

"But at least we know Rayne is being protected wherever he is," Sashi said.

"That's good news, right?" Stevie asked, looking at Tetsuya.

"Yes, young man. That is indeed good news. For the prophecy ends with the broken being made whole once again. The One will not leave his Light Bringer broken. The lines I still cannot fathom are: 'I will guide his steps by the least of lights until the three are found and the cup of wrath is full. Then the true heart will be known by the bond I have made.'"

"Well, I don't know anything about a *least of lights*, or three things that need to be found," Sashi said. "But I do know about the true heart. That's got to be Lexi. Remember what the One told her about always knowing the truth in Rayne and the joining of their hearts?"

"Yes, Sashi," Shaw said, allowing a trickle of hope to filter through him. "I think you're right about that. Somehow when Lexi and Rayne are brought together again, he will be made whole. And I think I might know what the three are. We already have four of seven scrolls. Wherever Rayne is, whatever he is now, I'm certain he's still seeking the other scrolls. If I understand this part correctly, he and Lexi will be brought together once he has reclaimed those final three scrolls."

They looked around at each other. "There is hope!" Shaw's face brightened as that truth found root in his spirit.

"Of course," Tetsuya said. "With the One there is always hope."

26

Leaving Mite settling into his nest, Rayne clutched his staff and moved forward. Even though walking was still painful, he was grateful to Elspeth and Ean for the ability to keep putting one foot in front of the other. He had not gone very far before he began to sense an increased level of energy and heavy magic saturation; he was entering the Heart of the Heart, the magical center of Neth, the Blessed Hollow.

The leaf-carpeted ground sloped downward into the hollow so gradually, Rayne had little difficulty descending into the Heart. As Fallon predicted, the morning dawned clear, and though Rayne couldn't see the sky, the air was already warm beneath the canopy of densely woven branches.

Between Ean's and Elspeth's healing potion, the tea Mite insisted Rayne continue drinking, and the powerful energy surrounding him, the old-man body moved with an ease Rayne had not experienced since his imprisonment.

He wondered again about the true owner, the spirit of the old man that belonged in the body he possessed. It was so strange to think of himself as a possessor, a thing like Sigmund. Because in one sense that was what Rayne had become, taking over someone else's body. While he walked, he tried once again to discern if the spirit of the old man was still with him. As before, there was nothing and Rayne wondered what Sigmund had done to the old man. Did he also inhabit a body not his own or was he floating somewhere like Rayne had before his spirit was sent into this body? Or was he dead? Was Rayne's spirit the only thing keeping the old body alive?

He continued pondering the fate of the old man as he shuffled through the shadow-drenched forest when a familiar chiming startled him. The guardian of the scroll was near.

Rayne walked for another half hour. The chiming continued, but it never grew louder or came closer. Approaching a crystal-clear stream gurgling over a rocky bed, lit by streamers of sunlight filtering through the trees, Rayne decided to sit and wait, hoping the guardian might come to him if he remained still. As the water gurgled at his feet, a demanding thirst grew in him. Maneuvering to lean over the stream, he scooped up several handfuls of the sparkling liquid. His teeth ached at the touch of the icy water.

After drinking, a feeling of lethargy overcame Rayne and, finding a mossy area near the bank of the stream, he lay down and fell into a deep, dreamless sleep. On waking, he blinked his eyes open on an expanse of pale blue sky framed by green and purple. He hadn't slept long; it was still morning. But when he moved to rise, Rayne saw that he was covered with flowers.

Dozens of flowers had been placed over and around him as he slept, flowers of various colors and shapes. The fragrance coming from them was strong and sweet but not sickeningly so. Movement drew his eyes and looking up toward the stream Rayne saw the guardian. She reminded him of Ari, but with subtle differences. Although both were old beyond reckoning, Ari had the appearance of a mature woman. The being sitting across the stream from Rayne now, looked childlike.

The ancient girl sat unmoving, watching Rayne. Not wanting to startle her, Rayne slowly levered himself up into a sitting position and waited a few moments before saying softly, "Good fortune to you. Are you the one who left me all the beautiful flowers?"

The girl rose with a graceful motion, and though she was tall, she was not as tall as any of the other ancients Rayne had already met. She reminded him of a young willow, thin and pliant. She laughed—a sweet tinkling sound. Without thinking Rayne chuckled in response and the girl giggled, a soft high-pitched vibration of the air. She said something in the chiming language and Rayne looked at her in confusion, hoping she knew the common language. She must have seen his confusion because she skipped across the stream and coming up to him, said in halting speech, "Good fortune to you and welcome traveler."

She laughed again and Rayne smiled. She was wearing a gown like the one Ari had worn, but where Ari had been all golden with a green and yellow gown, this ancient was pale with eyes the color of Rayne's own eyes and hair of midnight just like his had been. Her gown was a delicate, flowing vision of purples and blues that reflected the stream.

"My name is Rayne. What's your name?"

The girl-like ancient spun in a circle watching her gown bell out around her long legs and then stopped, facing Rayne again. "Naarah. My name's Naarah. And yes, I gifted you with the lovely flowers."

She paused and looked closely at Rayne wrinkling her nose. "You were supposed to be young and I was so looking forward to having someone to play with. But your vessel is old, at least for a newcomer. I thought we could play, but that stupid old body is far past playing. What happened to you Light Bringer?"

Without waiting for an answer, Naarah skipped back across the stream and then turned to face Rayne again. "Well, if you can't play with me, we might as well just go to the Source."

By the time Rayne maneuvered across the slippery stream bed and started up the incline on the other side, Naarah had disappeared into the deep shadows ahead. Rayne could hear her joyful chiming in the distance, so he followed the sound.

After trailing Naarah for nearly an hour, the trees surrounding Rayne were all the great blue-leaved giants. Their canopy of woven branches allowed only scant blue-tinged light through to the ground and the forest had taken on an air of twilight. Needing to rest, Rayne looked for a place to sit for a few minutes, hoping Naarah would not leave him.

He didn't need to worry. Within a couple minutes, Naarah peeked out at him from behind the gnarled trunk of one of the giants. When she saw that he had seen her, Naarah skipped out and sat down next to Rayne. Sitting, they were almost the same height. She looked over at him and pouted. "You never answered me. What happened to you Light Bringer?"

Rayne answered with a question of his own. "Aren't you a little young to be a guardian?"

Naarah harrumphed. "And how would you know anything, stupid newcomer? You are nothing more than a baby in there, and a rather stupid baby at that for choosing such a pathetic vessel. So if a stupid baby like you can be the Light Bringer, I can certainly be a guardian."

And for the first time, Naarah sat still and really looked at Rayne, her brow furrowed and her lips pursed. After a moment, she said, "Oh! I see now. You didn't choose this vessel. The darkness has done this to you. I am so sorry I called you stupid. My mother always said I spoke before I thought."

"I'm sorry I can't play with you," Rayne said, regret lancing through him. "I guess it's been lonely for you without friends or family."

"Not so lonely. I have made up many songs since I have been here and I sing all the time. I like singing and dancing. I have many friends who live among the trees and sometimes I sneak out of my hollow and watch the Kindred.

"They are fun to watch. They think because their energy is strong they see everything, but they never know I am there. Sometimes I trick them and sing, but they never find me even when they look very hard.

"Sometimes the Son, himself, comes and walks with me all through the hollow. Those are the best times. I couldn't leave the hollow for weeks now though, because I knew you were coming, and I had to be here when you arrived. But, now that you are here, the One will take me to be with my family and friends."

Naarah looked closely at Rayne again and asked, "Are you hungry, Light Bringer?"

"Not really. But I am a little thirsty."

"That is not a problem. We are close to the Source now and a water spring bubbles out next to the Source rock." Naarah jumped up and leaned down to Rayne offering her hand. "Come. I will help you the rest of the way."

As they walked, power thrummed in the energy-laden air, pimpling Rayne's skin. "This Source, is it the reason the magic energy is so abundant in Neth?"

"You have guessed correctly, Light Bringer. This is the fount of energy the One has created to fill all Nemora with magic energy. It is the only source like it in all Ochen. If you were whole, you would feel it infusing every part of your body with energy and comfort. It fills me with life and joy. And the closer I get to the Source, I cannot help but sing and dance. The darkness has broken you and this body you inhabit is not sensitive to the energies. But I can feel the strength in you. Your true self is connected to the power even now. But the body is heedless so there can be no fullness of life and delight."

"When I was on Glacieria, I felt heavy magic saturation, but it wasn't full of joy like this. It tried to deceive me into seeking its power instead of the power of the One."

The delight that had flowed from Naarah fled. Her lips turned down at the edges and her eyes grew serious. "Yes, that has happened in places. It is so sad that the darkness has taken a beautiful thing the One meant for good and turned it to evil. That is why you must bring the light, just as the One foretold. That is why I desired to be a guardian. I wanted to meet the servant the One chose to bring his light back to Ochen. You are not what I expected, though, but that is okay. I know you are just as the One meant you to be. Does not the prophecy say the chosen would be lost and broken. But take joy, there is the promise of wholeness once again as well."

Naarah dropped Rayne's hand and began to dance ahead

of him. She twirled several times, lifting her arms up to the canopy above before turning to look at Rayne again. "The Sentinel Path is before you, servant of the One. Follow the passage through the trees and at its end, you will find the Source and the spring. I will sing and dance here while I wait for you to return."

Looking past Naarah, Rayne saw two dozen of the blue-leaved trees spaced evenly like an honor guard, twelve to each side of a grassy passage glowing with hazy beams of blue sunlight. Their branches, woven together more then sixty feet above the ground, created an open weave of arched roof. A soft breeze stroked the air causing patterns of light and dark to waver and shift on the sward below.

Rayne moved forward into the passage with halting steps. A sense of holiness saturated the living tunnel and he felt as though he was entering the grand cathedral at Westvale. Awareness that the path he trod was hallowed ground blossomed within him and reverence for the very ground beneath his feet permeated his spirit. Using his staff, he grunted as he lowered himself to sit on a large, flat rock and removed his shoes. He levered back upright and, leaving his shoes on the path, continued to follow the sun-streaked passage forward toward the Source.

27

Emerging from beneath the last of the Sentinel trees, Rayne gasped as his senses were bombarded with sights and smells beyond anything he could have imagined. It was as though he had stepped into another realm of existence, into a pool of living air that bathed him in awareness. *Am I still on Nemora?* Light was clearer, brighter, and yet, at the same time, ethereal. A soft cool breeze caressed his face. *Or is it warm?* He couldn't be certain. And yet, it felt perfect. The magic here—*no, not magic—energy*—energy impregnated the air with power, vibrating and—*singing?* Yes, the air was singing. But he couldn't hear it with his ears. He felt it in his core. He was alive. Even the old man body thrummed to the power of the Source coursing through him.

A cliff face rose before him, a single great gray rock with blue veining soaring to a height of more than forty feet. Two of the giant blue-leaved trees flanked the precipice, towering above it. At about shoulder height, a horizontal crack split the rock creating a table-like shelf. The crevice narrowed as it wound around the side of the crag, climbing upward. Water flowed from the fissure, trailing the split and glistening as it splashed down, wetting the stone face. Droplets of the liquid danced in the air catching the light and blooming into colors beyond Rayne's comprehension, colors so intense he thought he would weep. His heart soared with the wonder of it all. Even trapped in the old-man body, he felt more alive than he had ever felt. Approaching through the soft, vibrant air, he saw the familiar satchel.

When he reached the cliff face, the hair on his neck and arms stood at attention in response to the energy flowing from it. Leaning his staff next to the ledge, he stood for a few minutes just breathing, allowing the experience to hold him. Then, using the rock for stability, he reached into the crack and pulled the sack to him.

Wondering if he would be able to unlock the seal while in the old man body, Rayne opened the satchel, unwrapped the scroll, and unrolled it with care. After a few minutes, he found the seal. Taking a deep breath, he held his age-spotted hand over it. With a soft snick, the seal sprang open and Rayne heard the words, *take and eat.*

He stilled, waiting for the pulse of power at the release of the seal to drum through him. But there was no pulse, just a subtle vibration at his core. A bittersweet smile hovering at the corners of his lips, he gently rerolled the scroll, rewrapped it, and placed it in the satchel.

Holding onto the rock for balance, he slung the bag over his shoulder and across his chest. Grabbing his staff, he turned toward the spring to get a drink before leaving the Source. A figure standing under the closest of the Sentinel trees drew his eyes.

Rayne stood frozen, mesmerized, watching the figure. The man smiled and Rayne recognized him. A light of softest white, like a living pearl, surrounded the Son.

"Know that you are much-loved faithful Light Bringer," the Son said, his voice falling on Rayne's ears like drops of dew and seeping into the very core of his being. "Though you have been sorely tried, your faith has been renewed. Go to Sorial. There you will find unexpected help. A remnant of my people are praying for light. Remind them. Speak to them my

Light Bringer. Tell them of my unfailing, deep, and steadfast love.

"Trust that you are never alone even in the darkest of times, for by my Spirit, my peace and strength are always within you. When the time comes, and you know what you must do, trust and be courageous. In my Words, you will find light and life."

Rayne couldn't speak, could only nod as the Son smiled at him once again. Then the Son waved Rayne toward the spring. "Drink of the Source Spring. It will sustain you for the task to come."

Then the Son was gone. Rayne was standing alone in the glade next to the Source, wondering why he hadn't asked any of the many questions that circled in his mind. Still feeling residual warmth, Rayne hobbled back to where the water splashed from the fissure, cupped the sparkling, crystal-clear liquid from the spring, and drank deeply. It was like drinking pure energy, light as gossamer, yet potent with vitality. With staff in hand, he walked back down the path beneath the Sentinel trees to where Naarah was waiting.

At the end of the pathway, Rayne stopped to put his shoes back on. Then he rose and stood for a time, watching Naarah play. She twirled and sang in her chiming language, full of joy and life, unaware of his presence. She moved through the patterns of light and darkness with abandon, and Rayne regretted he couldn't play with her. She must have sensed him watching, because she stopped mid-twirl and turned to face him. "You have been with the Son. Your face is shining. Come, it is time. I will take you to the edge of the Blessed Hollow."

As Naarah wrapped her thin arms around Rayne, he wondered if she would be strong enough to transport him the way Ari and Meryn had. But despite her smaller stature, Naarah brought him to the edge of the Blessed Hollow with ease. She started to skip away, but turned and ran back to Rayne, gave him a gentle hug, and whispered, "Remember the prophecies. When the One promises something, he keeps his promise. Always!"

Giggling, she turned from Rayne, skipping and singing.

When she passed into the shadows beneath the trees, she twirled once more in pure abandon, then faded from sight. Rayne watched the spot where she had vanished for a few minutes with a sad smile. Naarah's joy had been infectious. Now, sick at heart with the need to leave the Blessed Hollow and reclaim the remaining scrolls, Rayne turned away and made his way to where Mite was waiting.

As Rayne hobbled out of the Blessed Hollow, Mite ran toward him with joy shining on his face.

"Ray-ray walking strong. Saw the Son, saw the Son, didn't he? Mite is happy to see Ray-ray again. Has the scroll. This is good, good, good. Mite so happy. Now we can go back to the Camp of the Forgotten and get ready to leave Nemora."

Setting aside the longing and sadness that had filled him since Naarah disappeared, Rayne laughed at Mite's antics, until Mite mentioned leaving.

"You will come with me? When I leave Nemora?" Rayne asked, surprised that Mite would leave his home.

"Mite go with Ray-ray. Mite will stay with Ray-ray until all is done." Mite hopped from foot to foot. "The One has called Mite to this, and Mite will do this. Doesn't Ray-ray want Mite to be with him?"

"Yes, Ray-ray is happy to have Mite with him. I don't think I can do what needs to be done without you. Besides, if the One said you were called to do this, I don't think we have a choice. Just promise me one thing."

"What does Ray-ray want Mite to promise?"

"Promise me you won't sing the Sir Mite song anymore."

Mite began to dance around and sing Sir Mite, Sir Mite. But then he stopped and with a sly grin said, "I promise. I won't sing it again, unless Ray-ray tells me I can."

Rayne laughed. "Okay, I guess that's as good a promise as I can get. So, what did you make for us to eat while I was in the Blessed Hollow?"

Mite skipped to the camp fire. "Ray-ray is hungry! Yes, yes, yes. Mite has good food, good food for Ray-ray."

Rayne startled awake later that night, sweating and mumbling, scaring Mite. He dreamed of a ragged looking group of people, chained and being herded by guards wearing Andersen House uniforms. But the people were joyful and praised the One. He heard the voice of the One. *My people on Sorial are calling. Their time is short.*

When Rayne had come out from the Blessed Hollow with the scroll, he was even stronger than when he entered. Over the next days, he moved forward with purpose. But, as the days passed, and they got closer to Inverness, Rayne began to worry about their lack of funds.

"Mite, I don't have any money and I guess you don't either. How are we going to pay for food and lodging on Sorial? We can't even afford to skip off Nemora. What do you think, do you have any ideas?" Rayne approached the subject one night as he sipped the steaming cup of healing tea Mite had just handed him.

"No, no, money. Mite never needed money. Do not worry Ray-ray. The Creator-Father will take care of us. Trust. The One will make a way. He said you must go to Sorial. If you must, he will make it happen."

The evening before they arrived at Inverness, Rayne was reading in the Words of the One to Nemora when Fallon's words came back to him, "Take this; may it help thee on thy journey. Do not open it until thou hast left the Blessed Hollow."

"The pouch," Rayne murmured. "How could I forget."

Curious, he pulled the small leather bag from the recesses of a deep inner pocket of his cloak. Opening it, Rayne's eyes grew large as he discovered a small fortune in precious jewels, more than enough to pay for skips to Sorial, Arisima, and even Corylus two times over.

He thanked the One for Fallon's generosity. His amazing gift was such an unexpected blessing that it started Rayne thinking of other unexpected gifts he had received in the past year.

He thought of Boone and his mother's words about special gifts. Thoughts of his parents and friends, and what Sigmund might be doing, worried Rayne. Rather than letting his fears drag him down, however, he used them to inspire him to keep moving.

It's hard to keep going. I'm so tired of fighting, I could have easily stayed in the Blessed Hollow and forgotten the outside world. But I can't. I want so much to see my friends and family again. I need to save them from the darkness, and the only way to do that is to keep moving. That's why the One has given this body the physical strength to keep going. I won't waste his gift or Fallon's.

28

Three weeks after reclaiming the Words of the One to Nemora, Mite and Rayne approached the city of Inverness. Skirting Castle Inverness, they saw the cottage where Rayne had woke, trapped in the old man body. Tucked into a stand of fir and hardwood trees with a small stream running near, the place looked rundown and forgotten.

At first, Rayne wanted to stop and investigate. He thought he might be able to find out something about the old man whose body he inhabited, but Mite was opposed.

"No, no, no. Too many soldiers guard near the castle. Ray-ray must not do this thing. If Ray-ray goes too close, he might get caught. He will not find answers here now. Must go, must go."

Rayne followed with hesitant steps as Mite led him on a seemingly haphazard path. Mite would run ahead then return, pointing the way for Rayne to go to avoid the frequent patrols. Once they were past the castle, the number of guards decreased. Leaving Rayne in a secluded spot not far from the city gate closest to the portal station, Mite went into Inverness.

ↆ

With several of the jewels hidden on his person, Mite sought out a shop where he could trade the tiny treasures for sommes. Once he had cash, he would go to the portal station, determine the best time for them to make the skip to Sorial, purchase passes, then return for Rayne.

Though Mite's appearance was that of an innocent little child, his dealings with newcomers over the years had made him shrewd to the ways of men. When the first shopkeeper tried to give him much less for the gems than they were worth, he turned around and left the shop seeking to go to another. But the shopkeeper scurried out into the street, calling Mite back and promising a much fairer price.

Now, whistling with joy at his prompt success, Mite made his way to the portal station. It didn't take long for him to to notice the unusually large number of guards posted around the cathedral-like building. Sitting on one of the benches near the Sorial portal, he watched the guards' behavior for more than an hour. They ignored most travelers, but whenever an old man approached any portal, the guards would stop him, examine him closely and ask his business. Mite had no doubt they were looking for Rayne.

Their simple plan to skip to Sorial was now not so simple. Mite would have to think of a way to get Rayne past the guards. Putting on his most innocent face, Mite walked up to the soldier who seemed in charge of those guarding the Sorial portal. "What are you doing?"

The guard looked down and scowled. "What does it look like we're doing, little boy? We're guarding the portal."

"Why?" Mite asked in his most innocent little voice.

At first Mite thought the guard wasn't going to answer as he looked down at him, frustration evident in his expression, but then he said, "We're guarding the portal to prevent a dangerous criminal from skipping off Nemora."

"An old man?" Mite looked up at the guard, his eyes wide. He harnessed the surrounding energy and encouraged the man to speak openly.

The man's expression softened to one of open candor. "Yes, some sick old man. Sounds foolish to me. If this man is supposed to be so weak, he can't even walk without help, why assign so many guards to watch the portals? What a waste. The order didn't even come from Castle Inverness. It came from His Royal Highness, Prince Rayne. What right doe he have, coming onto Nemora and throwing orders around here?" The man shook his head. "For months we've been charged with watching for some old fool who's probably dead by now. We're tired of it. Who cares if some feeble old man skips? As far as I'm concerned, the old beggar could go wherever he wants. I couldn't care less what he does. I'm sick of this duty."

The guard gasped, confusion streamed across his features. Looking hard at Mite, he said, "You don't belong here boy. Go find your parents."

Mite skipped off, whistling to himself once again. Knowing the guards' attitudes about the duty they had been assigned to for so long now, Mite was certain he could convince them to look the other way when he and Rayne headed for the portal.

He stopped by the station master's window and purchased two passes for Sorial, scheduled to skip in the middle of the night. Less people around, meant less people Mite would have to influence when they made their move. Now he just needed to get back to Rayne. They would eat, then sleep until it was time to go.

Rem had already begun her downward journey and Ledia was at her zenith when Mite and Rayne approached the portal station. The streets were all but empty at that hour and the only activity in the station was at the Sorial portal.

Mite had already been singing his song of protection for a bit, ever since they entered Inverness. Now he pulled more energy and increased its power as he and Rayne crossed the main floor of the station to join the people waiting for the directional shift in the line to Sorial. They moved into the middle of the small group of travelers. Mite scanned the area to check for the positions of the guards and breathed a sigh of relief to see most of them huddled together watching four of their number playing a card game. One young guard, standing by himself, was staring at Rayne, his brow crinkled in thought.

"Stay here," Mite whispered to Rayne, then snaked his way over to the young man. Just as the guard started toward Rayne, Mite moved to stand in front of him.

"Sir," Mite said, reaching out to grab the guard's hand. "Sir, please, could you help me?"

Scowling, the man shifted his eyes from Rayne to Mite. "What's your problem?"

"I'm supposed to meet someone on Sorial, but I've never skipped before and I'm scared."

The guard looked up as the skipping line switched to outgoing and the waiting people began moving to the portal. He took a step toward the now moving travelers, but then looking down into Mite's wide eyes, sighed. "There's nothing to be scared of. You just walk into that opening like those other people are doing, and then it's all over."

With a quick glance, Mite discovered only two people were now between Rayne and the portal, he was almost there. The other soldiers were still involved in the card game, but the guard in front of Mite was, once again, staring at Rayne. With an oath, he released Mite's hand and started walking toward the portal. Mite lunged after him and grabbed his arm. "What do you mean, 'It's all over?'"

The guard snarled as he turned back, "Let go you annoying … clingy … sweet child. Of course I'll help you."

He knelt in front of Mite, gazed into the widened, gray eyes, a patient smile worming its way onto his face. "Would you feel better if I walked you up to the portal?"

Mite looked over in time see Rayne disappear through the portal. He grinned. "No, sir. I'll be fine now. Thank you for all your help."

He sprinted to the skipping line portal and with a shout of, "Excuse me!" cut in front of the next person and leaped into the opening.

Mite stumbled onto Sorial. Mumbling about how much he hated skipping, he scanned the area around him, looking for Rayne. Leaning on his staff, Rayne waited a short distance from the portal. Mite ran up to him, quite pleased with himself, and shouted, "We did it, we did it, Mite and Ray-ray are on Sorial." Pulling in a breath of air, he wrinkled his nose. "Eww, Sorial hot, hot. Sorial stink. Sorial really, really nasty."

Rayne laughed and shook his head. "It's always hot and smelly in Emporium City. Although it's not usually so dismal. Even with both suns up now, it seems darker than I remember, as if the sky was cloudy though there are no clouds to be seen. That's strange." Rayne looked up and around, his concern etching worry lines on his brow.

Shaking off his anxiety for the moment, he continued. "The city sits on an island surrounded by stinking water. Between that and the markets selling livestock, the odors here are strong and constant. Off the island, away from the lake, it doesn't smell. That's why the wealthy merchants do business in the city but live away from the lake."

"We won't stay on stinky island, will we, Ray-ray?"

Rayne shrugged and sighed. "We will for now. Until I know more about where I need to go to find the Words to Sorial, we'll have to stay here."

"How will Ray-ray know where to go?"

"I guess we'll just have to wait for guidance from the One. The few times I was off the island in the past are a little hazy for me. I really don't know much about Sorial at all, so I guess we'll have to be patient. In the meantime, we should find a place to stay. If I remember right, the inn we stayed at the last time was pretty awful, but I know there are better inns around.

"Oh wait. I remember now, the place where Giles and Blossom ..." Rayne stopped speaking, the pain of betrayal surfacing.

"What Ray-ray? Ray-ray okay?"

Rayne shook his head. "No, I'm not okay. Sometimes it's all just too hard." He shook his head again, dismissing the painful memory. "Going back to this inn won't be easy, but it'll be a good place to stay. Come on, Mite, it's this way."

Heading toward the inn, they passed through numerous markets. In one of the larger plazas several slave auctions were underway. Rayne struggled to keep moving. A few of the unfortunates they walked by were obviously meant for the fights and Rayne clenched his fists, wishing there was something he could do to end the sickening practice.

Keep moving forward. But he shivered. The premonition of coming darkness he had experienced so long ago in Westvale flooded through him. *Keep moving. Trust.* He repeated the words again and again, like a self-proclaimed mantra.

Though returning to the inn where Giles and Blossom had brought him when he skipped in from Veres was hard, Rayne knew it was a good, reputable place to stay. Keenly aware of how enticing a beautiful little boy like Mite could be in Emporium City, he elected to ignore his past so they could stay in a decent inn.

After paying ahead for a week's worth of nights, Rayne and Mite found their way up one flight of stairs and down a well-lit hallway to their room. Rayne would have liked the security of a higher floor, but more stairs would be too difficult for him.

The suite was painted a soft cream color. A small, round, blonde wood table with four matching chairs and a blue settee with two overstuffed chairs of the same material sat in front of a red stone fireplace in the sitting room.

In the bedroom sat two narrow beds with matching covers of the same material as the settee and overstuffed chairs, two small nightstands, and a larger stand with a sparkling-white, water basin and pitcher. The suite looked to be clean and comfortable. Mite enjoyed the several vases of herbs placed throughout to combat the ever-present odor of the city, running from one to another, sticking his nose in each bunch.

They decided to eat before getting some sleep and planned to head out and scan the market place in the cool of the evening. While they were waiting for the food to arrive, Rayne said, "Did you notice how gray everything seems, as though there is a haze between the suns and the ground?"

"Mite has not been on Sorial before, no, no. But light is strange, feels wrong to Mite. Wrong, wrong."

"Yeah. I wonder if the darkness Neci talked about is here. If any of the worlds would be ready for the coming darkness, Sorial would be the place."

Mite shivered, looking more serious than usual. "Yes, Rayray. Newcomers selling others like animals is very bad. This should not be. No, no, no."

As they were talking, a girl knocked. "I have your food, good sirs."

Mite opened the door. The young girl set a tray of food and drinks on the small table in the sitting room then bowed out. A stack of griddle cakes with a pot of honey, a pile of sausages, and a steaming crock of coffee set Rayne's stomach to growling.

Sitting opposite each other at the table, Rayne prayed a thanksgiving, and they dug into the meal. The food was good, especially after the camp fare of the past week, and Mite nodded his approval when Rayne ate almost as much as he did. Once they finished eating, Mite placed the tray outside the door, then curled up on one of the beds. Within minutes he was breathing evenly.

Unable to sleep, Rayne shunned his bed. The hazy, shadow-drenched look of the light on Sorial troubled him. *Do they notice? The people who live here? Have they noticed the change, or did it begin so slowly they were oblivious to what was happening? It's like the smoky fogs on Veres.*

Images from the slave auction they had passed blended with memories from his past to keep his mind racing, roiling his too-full stomach. Recollections of things he had done on Sorial in the past stirred and worked to weaken his resolve. It was as if the darkness in the air had wormed its way into his spirit and was now dredging up old pain and anger.

With an effort of will, Rayne tamped down flashbacks of meeting Sigmund, Heinrich, and Brayden here. Then he battled his feelings about Giles's and Blossom's betrayal. Just when he thought he could sleep, deeper memories of being on Sorial with Coronus ghosted through his mind. He pushed upright from the overstuffed chair in front of the dark fireplace, grabbed his staff, and began to pace.

Finally, he lowered himself down onto bony knees and prayed. Later, when he sought his bed, he fell into a comforting well of deep, restful sleep.

29

Ever since leaving the Blessed Hollow, Rayne had been strong enough to move with more speed and less support from the staff. Now, as he meandered through a series of stalls lit by the twin moons of Sorial, he held the staff lightly in his right hand for balance. He looked over the wares offered and wondered how much longer he would be stuck wandering the markets. They had been on Sorial for more than a week and Rayne still had no idea of what to do.

He and Mite had visited the teeming markets every evening, hoping to find direction or any clues as to where the scroll might be. Tonight, as usual, Mite ran ahead to explore the area, leaving Rayne to follow at his own speed. Scanning a group of stalls to his left, a familiar face came into focus. Old fear flooded through him and sent his heart into a panicked rhythm. It didn't matter that this body had no history with the person standing in front of a wine merchant's stand, haggling with the owner, the body responded in sympathy to Rayne's own reaction. He staggered to a halt, sweating, breathing hard, trembling.

Terror driving him, Rayne turned away from the face that had haunted some of his worst nightmares for years.

The voice of the One broke through Rayne's panic. *Speak to him.*

Rayne shook his head and continued shuffling away from the hated face.

Speak to him!

What? Rayne froze, shock spearing through him, sending his spirit reeling. *You want me to talk to Ponce? No, not Ponce. Anyone but him. You can't ask me to do this. It must be a miracle on your part that he hasn't seen me yet, and you want me to talk to him? He'll turn me over to Sigmund. I won't do it.*

Do you trust me?

Of course I do, you know I do.

If you trust me, you will talk to him.

But, my Lord, he is darkness itself to me. He haunts my nightmares. I'm not strong enough to do this thing you ask. Please don't ask this of me.

Rayne stumbled forward and fell onto one of the benches set along the main walkway. Terror threatened to undo him as he sat, sweating and shaking in the Sorial heat; old memories beat around him like raven wings, stirring up old darkness.

The One spoke gently into Rayne's spirit, dispelling the gloom. *This is hard for you my Light Bringer, I know. But I have made you strong. Know that I have chosen and called Marcus Ponce. He is no longer what he was.*

If he were physically able, Rayne would jump up and run from Emporium City, run from Sorial. He wanted to scream out to the One and remind him of how Ponce had abused him again and again when he was a child, poured darkness into his spirit. But the One already knew that. The One knew, and yet had still called Ponce.

The One spoke again. *What is the Light you bring? Is it not forgiveness through the Son?*

Yes. Rayne choked on the burning lump in his throat. *You chose to forgive and offer that forgiveness freely according to your own perfect purposes. But I'm not that strong. I can't do this thing you ask. Can't someone else talk to him for you?*

But I have called him. May I not choose forgiveness at my own discretion? Or would you seek to command me?

Anguish and pain clouded Rayne's mind.

And now I ask you, my beloved Light Bringer, to trust when, once again, the trust comes at a price. Will you talk to the man?

Rayne allowed memories to flood his mind as tears leaked from his eyes. He sat like that for a long while. Finally, with every instinct screaming no, Rayne said aloud, "Yes. Yes, my Lord." Then, crying out in his spirit, he added, *I have prayed that you would give me the strength to always answer yes to you. But what you ask of me now. How can I do this? I can't; you must help me. Only you can give me the strength I need to do as you ask. I will speak with him, but please, please don't ask me to forgive him. I can't do that.*

I will not ask more of you than what you can do. And what I ask, I will strengthen you to do. Talk to him.

Rayne rose from the bench and hobbled back to where he had seen Ponce, hoping the man had moved on by now and he wouldn't be forced to talk to the rubiate. But he knew the One would not have sent him unless Ponce was still there. As he got closer to the wine merchant's stall, Ponce looked up at him and startled in obvious recognition.

Of course he recognizes me. Rayne struggled to quell the quaking inside. *As Sigmund's trusted servant he would know all about what happened. Now he'll hand me over to Sigmund. Mighty One I'm trusting. Please help me. This is too hard.*

Ponce hurried over to stand in front of Rayne. "Grandfather, what are you doing on Sorial? You shouldn't be here; you should be home in Inverness, safe."

Rayne's throat seized and his jaw dropped open. Ponce took his elbow and helped him to sit on one of the benches lining the walkway, taking a seat next to him. "Why are you here, Grandfather?"

Unable to bear Ponce's touch, Rayne pulled his arm away from the man's hand. "Stop playing games with me. You know who I am."

"Of course I know who you are Grandfather. What's wrong? What's happened?" His eyes filled with suspicion. "Sigmund did something to you because I left him, didn't he? What has he done?"

Rayne struggled with the impossibility of what was sitting

right in front of him. It was Ponce, the rubiate who had abused and terrorized him for ten years. But although he was wearing one of his finely tailored suits, he spoke in a normal voice and he was well groomed. He seemed normal. Even his teeth were clean.

I have called him.

It was the hardest thing the One had asked him to do, but Rayne clamped a lid on his need to hate the little rat-faced man. "Has the One truly called you? Do you now believe?"

"Grandfather?" Ponce scanned the milling crowd, his eyes wide.

Ignoring the fear and doubt screaming within him, Rayne ground out, "Do you believe in the One?"

Ponce glanced around again, as if afraid someone was listening, but then answered, "Yes, Grandfather, you know I do. You know that's why I left Sigmund. What's wrong with you? You're not yourself."

Fighting every survival instinct he possessed, Rayne grunted a harsh laugh at the irony. "Yes. Congratulations. You've hit the target. I'm not myself." Shaking off the feeling that he was going insane, Rayne continued. "We must find the friend I'm traveling with. Then we need to go someplace quiet and talk."

His eyes scanning the market, Ponce whispered, "You're right. It's not good for us to talk like this here."

Mite must have been watching Rayne because as soon as they got up, he was right by Rayne's side. Rayne smiled down at the little sprite. "I need to talk with this person, so you have to stay with me now. Did you get enough time roaming?"

"Yes, yes. All ready to go now. Where to, where to?"

Ponce's eyes locked onto Mite for a moment before he shifted his gaze back to Rayne. "My place isn't far."

As he started forward, Rayne stepped in front of Ponce. He grabbed Ponce's arm and growled, "Will the boy be safe with you? Answer me. I must know before we go anywhere with you."

Ponce lowered his eyes to the ground. "Yes. He'll be safe. You, of all people, know how much I've changed. How I've lost the taste for blood. And since I've been here on Sorial, the One has changed me even more. I'll do the boy no harm."

"So you say," Rayne said harshly as rising suspicion nearly choked him. "But if I feel you're a threat to him in any way, I'll kill you. I may be weak, but not so weak I couldn't do it."

"Grandfather?" Ponce asked, hurt and confusion battled each other across his features.

Rayne turned and, without responding, waved for Ponce to lead the way. With one more hurt look, Ponce headed away from the bench with Rayne and Mite following. He led them back through the market and down several side streets until they came to a modest boarding house.

Ponce led them up to a small suite. Once again Rayne was taken by surprise. The rooms were clean, bright, and nicely furnished. The main room contained a round table set for four people surrounded by chairs in a golden-hued wood. A brown leather couch, two wingback chairs, two smaller tables, and a desk occupied the other side of the room. Ponce motioned for them to sit. Mite helped Rayne to one of the wingback chairs. Once he was settled Ponce took his staff and set it by the door.

"Would you like some tea or coffee? Something to drink?" Ponce asked.

Mite plopped down on the couch. "Water, water. Mite wants water."

Rayne gave him a warning look. "But taste it first to be certain it's pure."

After watching the exchange, Ponce asked, "Who is he Grandfather? You were never one to have patience with children. How is it you're traveling with one now? And why are you here on Sorial?"

"Get Mite his water and then sit down. I have a long story to tell you."

Ponce filled a pitcher with water, then brought it and three glasses over on a tray which he set on one of the small tables. Though Rayne refused to drink, Mite eagerly drank his water. Once Ponce had taken a glass for himself and was settled, Rayne took a deep breath, lifted a quiet prayer for guidance and strength, and, with a voice as cold as ice, began.

"I'm not your grandfather."

Seeing the protest forming on Ponce's face, Rayne held up a hand, shook his head, and continued. "I will try to explain this the best I can, but there's much I don't understand myself." He paused, grimacing, trying to gather scattered thoughts and quiet his misgivings.

"As I said, this is a long story. It'll take some time to tell. And, honestly, it will be hard to believe. And hard for me to share with you."

He stilled for a moment, staring at Ponce, his stomach churning like it wanted to empty upward. He shook his head. "In truth, your grandfather is most likely dead. I know, I know." He waved Ponce's protest aside. "This is his body. But Ponce ..." Rayne released a deep hissing breath through his teeth. "Oh, how do I even say this ... "

He stopped again, unsure how to proceed, then blurted out, "I'm not your grandfather but I know who you are because ... I'm Rayne Kierkengaard, Sigmund's slave boy Wren. Sigmund found a way to trap my spirit inside this body."

Ponce looked at Rayne, his eyes growing wide, but then anger drew his brows together. "You're lying."

"I'm telling the truth."

"No!" Ponce sat frozen. His eyes glazed for a moment, then blazed with anger. "If this is true ... If this is true ... then *you* did this. You hurt my grandfather in vengeance for what I did to you!"

"No! That's not what happened! And don't you dare accuse me of anything." Rayne shouted, his anger bubbling to the surface before he could keep it down. Taking a deep breath, he continued, his voice harsh. "If you don't remember, let me remind you. I am and have always been the victim in all this. I was the one kidnapped at six years old. Six years old! You weren't the one who had your memories and childhood stolen! You and Sigmund and Coronus did that to me! You were the one who abused me and planted darkness in me. And now, Sigmund's done this too."

"Sure, I hated you for what you did, what you are. I still do. Though I think the One may have something to say about that. Do you honestly think I would do this to myself? Really? Give up my body to live in this dying wreck of a body? Sigmund did it. But you already know this, don't you? You're working with him, looking for me. What game are you two playing now?" Rayne pulled in a gasping breath. "How could you let him to do this to your own grandfather? Unless this man really wasn't your grandfather."

Ponce sat back into his chair, his mouth hanging open. Then he said in a quiet voice, "No, I know nothing of this. I haven't seen Sigmund since that night at the palace. And yes, you are my grandfather ..." He studied Rayne for a moment. "It's true, isn't it? Of course it's true. Sigmund would do that. He took your body for himself, didn't he?"

When Rayne nodded, Ponce went on. "That makes sense. He would fantasize about possessing your body. But he wanted you trapped in it with him so he could make you suffer while he enjoyed using both your body and the power of your name to accomplish his goals. He always said he couldn't do it though, because you were protected by the One."

"That's why he couldn't just possess me the way he wanted. He couldn't even physically touch me without pain. This other demon, Heinrich, found a controllable way to bring me to the point of death—poison. But even before that, someone I trusted ... tricked me into making a promise that I would do anything she asked. The sad thing was, I didn't even mean it for her. But she convinced me to say it to her.

"Anyway, the poison brought me to the brink of death. The promise to do anything for the one who betrayed me was enacted, used to pull my spirit from my body when the bond between the two was weakened. Then it was like I was being pulled or pushed through the air, but I wasn't solid. After that I remember thinking I was back in my body and everything was going to be okay, but I was incredibly tired and fell asleep.

"I woke up in what must have been your grandfather's cottage and realized everything wasn't okay. I was trapped in somebody else's body. Brayden, his brother Giles—you must remember them—and Sigmund, paid me a visit. And Blossom, the young lady from the Reclamation Committee, was there too. But I think she regretted what she did, and I got the feeling Sigmund was going to kill her because of that.

"I learned that this friend of Sigmund's, the one with the plan, Heinrich, gave my body the antidote to the poison and then Sigmund slipped into my empty body bringing it back from the edge. It was an involved plan.

"Anyway, after they gloated about their genius and how they were going to use me—now trapped and helpless—to locate the remaining scrolls so Sigmund could destroy them, they left to go to my birthday party.

"That hurt. I mean, for as stupid as it sounds, it really hurt. It was going to be the first birthday party I got to go to since I was six. But you know all about that, don't you? Well, that was months ago and, I'm sorry, but your grandfather's body has run out of time. I've been told I have only a few weeks left before this body dies and me with it. So, I know I'll never get a birthday party. Silly, isn't it, that with all that's happened, the thing I complain about is so petty, just a birthday party."

Ponce looked up at Rayne, unshed tears reflecting the light. "No, it's not silly. You were just a child and we stole your life from you. And now, regardless of what you look like on the outside, inside you're still just that boy who never got the chance to be a child." Ponce rose and started pacing.

"I despise myself because of the pain I caused you. I can't even imagine what it was like for you as a child, not to mention the pain I must be causing you now just sitting in my presence, talking to me. How can you sit there and talk to me as if I hadn't abused you, instead of attacking me in anger?"

"Look at me," Rayne said sadly. "In spite of my earlier threat, how much harm do you think I could inflict with this body? From what Sigmund said, your grandfather was, what, one-hundred years old? And sick? This body is dying. Not a lot of strength or killing ability here. And no, I'm not that good a person. I still crave revenge. If I was sitting here now in my own body, you'd be feeling the edge of my sword.

"But I'm not here of own will. The only reason I'm here at all, is because the One told me I must talk to you. That's the only reason I spoke to you back in the market place. He told me he chose you and called you. As strange and unacceptable as it sounds, I think he means for you to help me.

"Since I walked away from your grandfather's cottage, I've recovered the Nemora scroll and now I'm here looking for the Sorial scroll. I have to admit, I need help; I have no idea where to even begin looking.

"Mite is a wonder," Rayne glanced over at the ancient who had curled up and fallen asleep on the couch. "If it wasn't for him, I never would have escaped Sigmund's hunters or gotten off Nemora. But I need help to find the Words of the One to Sorial. Neither Mite nor I know where to look. And Mite's magic is weaker away from Nemora. If you're now, indeed, a true believer in the One, please help me find the scroll before it's too late."

"May I ask you something?"

Rayne stared at Ponce, his face an emotionless mask, but then swallowed hard. "I guess."

"Is my grandfather in there with you?"

"I haven't felt him. No, I don't think so."

"And you are sure you're dying?"

"Yes."

"I'll help you get the Words to Sorial." Ponce sat with closed eyes for a few minutes. He blinked. "If Sigmund has your body, he's probably using your political position to advance his agenda. He won't waste time. He's waited for this kind of power for years. With you trapped and running, I'm sure he thinks he's untouchable. We must act now.

"The One worshipers on Sorial are suspicious and secretive. Several years ago, at Sigmund's request, the ruling merchants declared One worship illegal. The more powerful families, like the Andersens, sent their mercenaries to destroy the few remaining places of worship in Emporium City. Anyone now suspected of breaking the law and worshiping the One is rounded up and brought before the merchants' magistrates. If found guilty, they're sold as slaves either here or on Veres, with the profits lining the pockets of whatever family's men caught them.

"Some of the believers are ex-slaves who have either won their freedom or escaped. They live in fear of being taken again.

"I have been followed on several occasions. It took months of effort for me to connect with the remnant. And even then, I was tested before being invited to a gathering. If the merchants were to locate our meeting place, the remnant of One worshipers here in Emporium City would be wiped out."

Ponce paused and looked closely at Rayne. "But I know the truth of who you are, how Sigmund hates you for your identity as the One's Light Bringer. I will take you and your friend to meet with the believers tomorrow night and introduce you to our pastor. If anyone knows where the scroll is, it would be Pastor Zeb."

"Thank you," Rayne said. He poured himself a glass of water. Then sipping the cool liquid, met Ponce's eyes and frowned. "May I ask you something?"

"Of course, Sire."

"What happened to change you? I can see you're not what you were and I can't reconcile the person sitting before me now with the monster from my past. You still haunt my worst nightmares."

Ponce looked down at his hands as he twined his fingers in and out. "And for that, I am truly, truly sorry. I know the horrible things I did to you, and other innocents. I wish I could block them from my memory." Ponce shook his head and then rubbed his eyes with the heels of his hands. "I can't even begin to imagine what those memories are like for you. If it was at all possible, I would go back and change everything from the time you were first taken."

Ponce sniffed, wiped his nose with his sleeve, and took a deep drink of water. He released a puff of breath. "What changed me? You changed me. I could feel the strength in you that night I led you to the palace. When I looked into your eyes I saw something there I couldn't explain.

"Even before that night, though, with all the power at Sigmund's disposal, I knew you had something stronger. I hated you for that. You had something I could never have, or so I thought. The One forgive me, I hated you and that hate drove me to hurt you more and more."

Ponce shook his head, the edges of his mouth drawn downward in sorrow. "All those years Sigmund owned you, no matter what we did to break you, you were always so strong. I never saw Sigmund so frustrated as he would be around you.

"So, after I left you at the palace, I just walked away; back across the square, through the crowd that kept asking me if I knew where the prince was. I couldn't take it. I wanted to scream, 'I did it. I took the prince. Just kill me now and get it over with.'

"I began to feel the horror of what I'd done—was still doing. I struggled with the need to go back and get you, take you away with me, away from Sigmund and his plans for you. But I was afraid, weak, not like you. I didn't know then what was happening, but now I know; it was the One reaching into the very heart of me and convicting me of all the evil I had done. I ran to the portal station and bought a pass for Nemora. I left Corylus, Sigmund, the life I had known, and I left you. I never went back.

"I thought I was running away. But the One had other plans. At first, I returned home to Inverness, spent some time with my grandfather. He was angry with me for leaving Sigmund, but after we talked and I told him about what Sigmund had done to you, he came to understand what Sigmund really was. Grandfather had always thought he was a good man and a fine noble, worthy of our service, not some evil thing bent on bringing darkness to Ochen.

"Later, when I talked with Grandfather about the One and the strength he had given you to resist Sigmund, we started going to worship services at a little church outside Inverness. It was good. I was seeing everything differently. I began to hope the One might actually forgive even someone like me.

"But then, when I heard Sigmund had returned from the Shattered Continent and was looking for me, I left Inverness and came to Sorial to hide. Emporium City is a good place to hide. I was quite aware of Sigmund's obsession with revenge and knew he would search me out, but I thought if I wasn't on Nemora he would leave Grandfather alone. I guess it didn't matter where I hid, Sigmund found a way to hurt both of us.

"After arriving here, I tracked down any information I could about the small group of One worshipers still living in Emporium City. I heard rumors about an underground church. I sought them out and once they felt they could trust me, they welcomed me. The One had been working to soften my heart for a while and then, one day, he touched me with his love and forgiveness. I am a changed man. The One made me something different. He took away the darkness, helped me to turn from the rubiate life I had known.

"But if it wasn't for you and your strength, I would never have had the courage to leave Sigmund. So, although you will probably always hate me—and I can't fault you for that; if anyone has reason to hate me, it would be you—know you saved my life.

"I know what I was and all the evil I've done. That will always haunt me. But to feel the loving forgiveness of the One has become my strength and hope. I will help his chosen Light Bringer in any way I can."

30

Though the last few weeks had seen his plans moving forward on several worlds with enormous success, Sigmund strode toward the Nemora portal with frustration eating at his bowels, fueling a smoldering rage.

How dare that group of fools on the Interplanetary Council call me before them. Me! I'll make them pay for this affront!

He was making them pay, literally. The pretender to the crown was bringing a large entourage with him to Nemora and demanding the council foot the bill. In addition to Regent Woodfield, his constant companion, his Royal Highness was bringing the Lord Master Mage; Giles Woodfield; Lord William and Jason Andersen with their attendants and guards; several ladies from the court; Milo, his secretary; several dressers and attendants; as well as a full contingent of guards. One person he wasn't bringing was Lady Alexianndra of Veres and that fact stoked his anger.

Ignoring the captain's pleas to allow several soldiers to precede him into the portal, His Royal Highness, Prince Rayne, accompanied by the Master Mage, Regent Woodfield, Giles, Jason, and Milo all breezed through as the guards scrambled to follow.

Stepping out in Inverness, His Royal Highness noted with satisfaction that the portal station had been emptied as he had commanded. Marching through the echoing chamber, he demanded, "Where is my coach!"

As His Royal Highness exited the station, Duke Miles and Duchess Cailyn of Nemora attempted to greet him, but their words died on their lips as he brushed past them. Ignoring the duke and duchess, Sigmund and his companions strode to the largest of the three coaches waiting in front of the station. His Royal Highness came to a halt and stood tapping a toe and staring at the groom while the man hustled to open the door. After perching on the fine leather bench, he glared out the window while his companions followed his example, leaving the rest of the entourage to deal with Miles and Cailyn. Once they were settled, Brayden knocked on the roof and shouted, "Move!"

After that one word, the occupants lapsed into silence as the coach lurched with the movement of the horses and they traveled the short distance to Castle Inverness.

Three days earlier, after receiving the summons from the Interplanetary Council, His Royal Highness had ordered the removal of Duke Miles and Duchess Cailyn from the castle to their town house. He commanded their personal suite be stripped of all their belongings and redecorated with all haste and no expense spared, to accommodate him for the duration of his stay.

Even Heinrich knew better than to address Sigmund in his current mood. Right before leaving for the portal station in Westvale, he had gotten news from the Shattered Continent. Aquila was gone, banished from Ochen more than a month ago. Sigmund had flown into a rage that still smoldered. The silence persisted until the group was led to their commandeered suite and Heinrich had pressed a glass of honeyed sherry into the prince's hand.

"Gone!" he growled in frustration, throwing the glass against the grey rock fireplace and taking pleasure in the way the glass shattered.

"Aquila is gone! Even now, that boy is the bane of my

existence. I want him shattered like that glass, into little pieces. Why hasn't he been found and brought to me?"

"You know why," Heinrich said in a calm voice, sipping his sherry. "There is no power capable of banishing someone like Aquila except our enemy himself. He not only claimed the boy; he is now actively protecting him from those of our kind, our colleagues."

"Don't you think I know that!" Sigmund stormed, striding to Heinrich, grabbing his glass and shattering it, as well, against the gray stones.

"Why are you letting my cousin's absence upset you so, Sigmund. He is but one little inconvenience. Look at how well all your other plans are moving forward. Didn't we get news just yesterday that the number of scroll worshippers on Arisima has doubled in the past month? Your longed-for darkness is spreading on Arisima, Nemora, and Glacieria, as well as Sorial and Corylus. Just the other day, several fishermen brought word to the palace that a veil of darkness is moving across the Cameron Sea toward Westvale. Aren't these things more important than one missing prince with no power?"

Turning on his clueless protégé, Sigmund grimaced. "How can you still not understand after all this time? I suspect even Giles could answer that question for you." He stalked to Giles and looked down at the young man sitting complacently on a chaise lounge, with his legs up and crossed at the ankles. "Well, human, tell me why one little powerless prince is more important to me than the darkness spreading on Arisima or even Corylus."

Watching the irate demon with shuttered eyes, Giles said, "The reason you are so irritable is because nothing else matters if the Light Bringer is able to arise, reclaim all seven scrolls, and bring them together in some way that will bind you and all your colleagues before you can destroy the scrolls. I am unsure how, but apparently this binding will expel your kind from Ochen. Nasty business that. For you.

"And, to make matters worse, now with your enemy protecting Rayne from your colleagues, you are limited to hunting him by human means alone. A rather sad prospect as they have had no success thus far, even with Rayne imprisoned within a dying body. It would seem he has outwitted you at every turn. Have I hit the high points, my lord?"

Releasing his anger in a hiss, Sigmund whispered, "Exceedingly well. You have hit, the high points as you call them, exceedingly well. But if I were you, I would learn to show some respect. One might suspect you now regret your choice of sides."

"Oh, no, my lord. I just prefer to state the obvious, obviously."

"Relax, my old friend." Heinrich raised his palms in a placating gesture, attempting to defuse the anger sparking from Sigmund. "Brayden's right. You have moved forward with success on every other front, it is only a matter of time until you succeed here as well. And while we're on Nemora, we can encourage the soldiers to search with more diligence."

"I thought the girl had agreed to accompany you here. Wasn't she supposed to be the honey that drew the prince?" Jason asked.

Sigmund growled again, and Heinrich explained. "It would appear she changed her mind. Yesterday evening, she informed His Royal Highness she would only accompany him if she could bring that interfering healer, Anne, with her. Of course, that was not acceptable to our prince. Hence, we are here with a trap that lacks bait."

"Enough," Sigmund barked. "Someday I'll make that idiotic girl pay. And her father as well. I'll make slaves of them all and they will learn the price of defying me."

He paced before the fireplace for a few minutes before shouting, "All of you out. OUT! I have work to do and not one of you offers any help."

Sigmund grabbed Milo's arm as he tried to leave with the others. "Not you, you idiot! You will stay and do your job. And get a fire going! Now! This room is like ice."

Several hours later, Sigmund writhed at Milo's arrogant manner. He needed a Second, not just an administrator. He cursed Ponce again for deserting him. Where had that traitorous rubiate disappeared? When Sigmund found the little rat, he would make him pay for his desertion.

But Sigmund missed Ponce. The man was an excellent strategist and a genius at organization, and especially now at this stage of his plans, everything hinged on all his pieces moving in unison, something at which Ponce had excelled. Though Milo's abilities as a Second rivaled Ponce's, Sigmund missed Ponce's games. He had always taken pains to delight Sigmund with the quality and creativity of his dark and bloody play. Milo lacked vision. At least his skills at organization and business were acceptable, but Sigmund would have to train him in the art of imaginative play. With the day Sigmund was having, he longed for some diverting amusement. He fantasied about evenings with Ponce and the young prince. *Those were good times. Not like now.* He frowned, looking down at his scarred wrists. "Ahhh." He ground his teeth. "Must that whelp's rebellion always haunt me?"

The audacity of the Interplanetary Council in calling him to Inverness fueled his rage. His Royal Highness paused, frozen in thought for a few minutes, staring at nothing. A light blossomed in his amethyst eyes as he reached a decision. "Milo, summon Heinrich."

By the time the mage appeared, Sigmund's mood had lifted. His decision had brightened his outlook and now he sat on the chaise lounge Giles had occupied earlier sipping some wine and enjoying a blazing fire.

"Come join me in a glass." He waved Heinrich over.

With raised eyebrows, Heinrich approached. "Well you seem to have mellowed some."

"Pour a glass for the Lord Master Mage, Milo. When you've done that, go down into the city. Gather any current information you can from our spies."

Sigmund turned his attention back to his fellow demon. "I have a task for our colleagues. You do have certain contacts here on Nemora, don't you?" He sipped his wine as a rising contentment filled him. A smile curled his lips. "The time has arrived to destroy the Interplanetary Council. They have outlived their usefulness. Some restructuring is in order."

"Aren't you rushing things?" Heinrich asked as he received his glass from Milo who quietly bowed his way out.

"I detest that little man," Sigmund said after Milo left. "I will have to look for a replacement soon." He sighed and blew out a puff of air. "Back to what we were discussing. I see no need to wait any longer. It's time something lethal happened to the members of the council. Despite the execution of those who defied us regarding Veres, they have grown bold in their demands and think too highly of themselves. Their demise will also serve to remind our other associates where the real power lies."

Heinrich shook his head. "You just want satisfaction for them issuing orders for your appearance. Isn't it extreme and chancy to push our plans at this point?"

"Extreme or not, it's what I want. But it must appear natural. Can you make it happen, Heinrich?"

"Why use my people; why not use your own?"

Sigmund frowned. "A joint effort then? At least now with the darkness rising we have more of our kind at our disposal than in the past. A joint effort."

"If you think we'll succeed this early in the game, I'm willing to use one of my most highly trained colleagues in the undertaking. She is quite talented at mimicking natural death. Do you have someone she can work with who can get her near the council?"

"We will make it happen," Sigmund said.

"Aren't you at all concerned that our effort might be perceived as a direct attack against the Light Bringer if he is still here on Nemora?" Heinrich murmured. "That could bring the anger of our enemy down on us at a time when we're not ready to respond. Perhaps we should first find out where our missing prince is. To avoid any unforeseen incidents."

Sigmund nodded, thinking, tapping the side of his wine glass with a finger. "Send some colleagues out. But make sure they understand that if they locate the old man, they're not to approach him. Have them send word for human soldiers to come and seize our wayward prize.

"I don't want to spend too much time on this though." He thought a bit longer, then said, "I meet with the council tomorrow morning; regardless of whatever it is they want from me, I should have no problem manipulating them for the next few days. If we haven't gotten any response from your people by the time those fools begin to trouble me again, whether we have located the Light Bringer or not, I want those council members dead."

Heinrich inclined his head. "If you're prepared to step into the void created by the destruction of the Interplanetary Council, Your Royal Highness, I'll back you on this. What about the court though, don't you think they'll see themselves as more suited to step into the gap than a young, untried princeling?"

"Oh, so sad." Sigmund allowed a sly grin to spread across his handsome face. "It would seem the inexplicable malady that has taken the council has also spread to the court. They must all have been exposed to the terrible sickness at the same time. But, how marvelous, the ever-helpful young prince of Ochen will offer himself as a rightful, if humble, solution to the problem of who will rule in this crisis."

"I see. So, we have come this far, have we?"

Still smiling as he watched his wine circle around in his glass, Sigmund said, "It was inevitable, my old friend." Then he looked up at Heinrich. "Are you with me on this?"

"Of course. But before you move forward in your bid for more power, we should have the real prince in our possession."

Squeezing his eyes closed, Sigmund whispered, "Are you purposefully trying to ruin my good mood?"

"You know better. While you were busy, I sent out a call to some of my associates to report. I should be hearing something from those stationed here in Inverness by this evening."

"And what about our young friends?" Sigmund yawned. "What are Brayden, Giles, and Jason doing?"

"Once you dismissed them, Brayden claimed boredom and the three promptly skipped to Sorial for the rest of the day. I suspect they will be gone until sometime tomorrow. You know how Brayden hates being stuck on Nemora."

Milo slipped into the room and stood near the door staring at Sigmund.

"Well, what is it?" Sigmund asked, his voice a low snarl. "You have not been gone long enough to have even set foot in the city."

"Begging your pardon, Your Royal Highness. There is a person here seeking audience. He says he has news of prime importance to you."

"If some idiot is seeking an audience with the Royal Highness, inform him I am receiving no one," Sigmund said.

"No, Your Highness," Milo replied. "This man claims knowledge of your true identity. He requested a meeting with Sigmund of Bainard, currently known as Crown Prince Rayne. He was certain you would be interested in what he has to say. He was quite positive about knowing you."

Sigmund looked to Heinrich who shrugged.

"Well, I suppose we should find out who claims knowledge of my true identity and the nature of this important news he alleges would interest me. Show him up. Then continue with your assigned task."

The stranger was tall, blonde, and quite handsome, with the smooth movements of a hunter. He walked into the room with an easy grace and confidence.

Sigmund studied the man, certain he had not met him before, then spoke in a deceptively calm voice. "I don't know you. If you value your life at all, you'd better have a good reason for knowing my identity and seeking to come into my presence."

Walking over to the table, the stranger poured himself a glass of wine. "May I?" He motioned toward an empty chair.

"I'll give you marks for being brazen," Sigmund nodded once. "You may sit."

The man settled back into a deep chair and crossed his legs as if completely at ease. "My name is Marius. I was an associate of Aquila." He raised his eyebrows and paused a moment. "I was present when he was banished. Though I, myself, am only human once again, I acted as host to one of your colleagues until he was expelled along with Aquila."

Sigmund watched the man with lidded eyes, suspicion curling within him. "What exactly was your association with Aquila?"

"We hunted together, along with a female of your kind named, Krizia."

"And how did you manage to survive the expulsion? I didn't think that was possible."

A pained look flickered in Marius's eyes. "It wasn't easy. I think I survived because the colleague I hosted and I had a mutually agreeable, symbiotic relationship. I welcomed him to me and so was able to retain a certain degree of autonomy. When he was pulled from me, I almost died. But I am quite strong."

Sigmund looked at Heinrich, intrigued by this unusual human, then turned back to Marius. "Tell me; what happened?"

"We tracked our prey to the Camp of the Forgotten where we kidnapped their children to lure him out. After our target revealed himself, we released the children. Aquila and Krizia approached the old man hosting our prey, but realizing a strong protection around him, Aquila called for me to handle him. I had no sooner walked up to where they were standing, when Aquila shouted that we were in trouble.

"A great whirlwind sprang up around the old man and the young boy with him. While they stood protected in its center, we were flung from the area. I felt my possessor ripped from me and heard him scream. I woke up by the nearby stream. I don't know how I survived the whirlwind. It took me several days to regain my strength, drinking from the stream and eating fish. Once I felt strong enough, I walked to the Camp of the Forgotten, but the prey and the child were gone.

"Using skills I learned from Aquila, I began tracking the old man. I followed him to the edge of Neth Forest but could not enter there. I kept vigil near the border for over a month waiting for some sign of the one I hunted.

"In time, the old man and the boy finally emerged. I felt the presence of immense power with them and the old man was moving with more strength than before. I tracked them back to Inverness. Then, ten days ago, they skipped to Sorial.

"The young one is not a child as we had assumed. He used some kind of magic to trick the guards at the portal station which allowed the two to skip without being stopped.

"I followed them to Emporium City and have watched

them wandering around the markets as if looking for some-thing. I know where they are staying. Would you like me to capture the old man and return him to you now?"

"This is good news indeed," Sigmund crowed, rising to his feet. "I congratulate you Marius, you have done exceedingly well. Better than I could have hoped."

Sigmund moved in front of the fireplace and stood looking down into the flames, considering. "No. Do not seize the old man yet. I have a better idea. Continue tracking him. It would appear he has successfully reclaimed the scroll to Nemora and is now seeking the Sorial scroll. We will let our little Light Bringer continue working for us. Once he has the Sorial scroll, he'll skip to Arisima. Then he will return to West-vale. That's when we'll take him.

"Come to me at the palace in Westvale when he skips to Corylus. We will prepare a proper welcome for my wayward slave, one he won't expect. It would be almost worth giving him back his body just to see the expression on his face once he understands he's failed."

Meeting the hunter's gaze, Sigmund asked, "Would you be interested in participating in springing the trap, Marius? It would seem right to honor Aquila's memory in that way."

"That would please me, my lord. But we do need to discuss my remuneration."

"Of course. What do you think your services are worth?"

"I don't want to grow old and I miss the power hosting one of your kind gave me. I want a new possessor. But I reserve the right to choose whom that will be. My last arrange-ment was most … agreeable … and I would like to try to achieve the same with a new union. I'm aware you are highly connected and that is the reason I continued serving on this assignment. In addition, once the mission is complete, I believe ten million sommes should suffice for my services."

"You are indeed a greedy human," Sigmund smirked. "I like that. We have a deal. Return to Sorial and keep a good watch on our prize. Do not allow him to escape your observa-tion.

"Once the scrolls are destroyed and I have the spirit of the boy back in my possession, I will spread word among my kind of your involvement in the destruction of the enemy's chosen. Many of the colleagues will fight to partner with you then. I'll choose several of the most desirable from those who are willing, and you may have your pick."

Marius inclined his head. "Thank you my lord. I hope this will be the first of many collaborations." He tipped his wine glass toward Sigmund, then downed the last of the wine. "Well, if you gentlemen will excuse me, I must skip to Sorial. I look forward to meeting you soon on Corylus."

After Marius left, Heinrich walked over to a bag he had left on the floor near the door and pulled out a bottle of Amathea Gold.

He poured glasses for himself and Sigmund. "I brought this in the hope that we would have something to celebrate while here on Nemora. I think your day has taken a turn for the better my old friend and now is an appropriate time to enjoy a celebratory toast."

"Yes, yes indeed," Sigmund agreed. "I should not have been so hard on Brayden. He's right of course. Everything is moving according to plan and even ahead of schedule. All I have planted over the years is now blossoming with my efforts. Our colleagues have been successful at creating an atmosphere of unrest on five of the seven, no six, worlds. Veres no longer counts. They have done well not only tainting the energies on those worlds, but their efforts in the area of scroll worship are paying off. Only Amathea remains resistant, but that too will change."

Sigmund paused, sipping the sparkling beverage and nodding his appreciation to Heinrich.

"Our early efforts on Glacieria have proven worthwhile. Milo has informed me the humans are fighting brother against brother within the tribes now, a most desirable outcome.

"And the scroll worshippers on Arisima have intimidated the rest of the population. Soon that world will bow down to the scroll with the exception of a couple pockets of resistance where worship of our enemy remains. I think our little scroll collector will be in for quite a surprise when he skips onto Arisima."

"Within a few days now, we will rid ourselves of that both-ersome council and court. The end is in sight, my old friend. All Ochen will soon belong to the living darkness with no one left to save them." He sighed as contentment flowed through him like a warm wave. "What do you think, Heinrich? Is it too early to congratulate ourselves by seeking out some amusement on Sorial with our young friends? Sorial, what a delightful world. They fell to us without even knowing it. Even now they remain oblivious to the descending darkness and their own bondage."

31

꒐

Ponce invited Rayne and Mite to stay at his place, but Rayne refused. Just being in Ponce's presence required an effort of will that sapped Rayne's energy.

"You tell me the One has changed you and that may be so; he told me he's called you and he told me to talk to you. But sitting here, across from you ... I ... I can't do this." He lowered his face and rubbed his temples with the heels of his hands.

"I'm struggling with rage I can't act on and loathing for what you are and what you did to me. Even in this body, your grandfather's body, I still feel fear in your presence, a deep seated need for heightened vigilance. No Ponce, I'll accept the One has the ability to change you, but I don't trust you and I'll spend as little time in your presence as I can. Mite and I will return to our inn and meet you here tomorrow evening."

"If that is your wish, Sire." Ponce bowed his head. "I know you can never forgive me or trust me after what I did, but I will not betray you. I will not fail you. However, Lord William's men have been following me lately. They think I don't know, but they are foolishly obvious. Coronus is working for Lord William, has been for almost a year now, traveling, collecting men for the games. My source tells me he returned from a trip to Arisima two days ago. Whenever he's back on Sorial, I'm even more careful, leaving my rooms only when I must. Sigmund is offering a sizable reward for my return. Alive. Knowing Coronus, he'd be only to happy to collect. It'll be safer if we meet in a crowded public place.

"Be near the wine merchant's where you found me at this hour tomorrow. I'll stop and speak with him. When I leave his stall, follow at a distance. Once I'm certain we're not being followed, I'll lead you to the meeting place."

"Okay. But if you're lying, I will kill you." Rayne's voice was soft but clear.

The next evening, Rayne and Mite trailed Ponce through several markets. Ponce was right. The muscles between Rayne's shoulders twitched as he felt eyes watching him.

"What do you think?" he whispered to Mite. "Are you as aware of being watched as I am?"

"Ray-ray speaks true, he does, he does."

"Can you misdirect them like you did at the portal station?"

"Not sure. Guards on Nemora bored with meaningless task, Mite's power stronger near the Source. If newcomer following is focused, misdirect will not work."

Ponce slipped into a large market made up of dozens of stands situated under one roof. Rayne and Mite moved as quickly as Rayne could manage, striving to keep Ponce in sight. Under the metal roof, the air was even more oppressive than out in the open. Dark shadows that seemed alive with purpose lurked in every corner. Rayne's breathing grew heavy. Even without his physical senses alerting him, the heavy magic saturation in the crowded arcade was stifling.

Ponce led them across that market and along several alleyways into another covered square where he negotiated a series of twists and turns. Even with his new-found strength, Rayne was gasping and stumbling as he struggled to keep up with the rat-like little man.

Without warning, Ponce grabbed Rayne's wrist, yanked

down to his knees, and pulled him under a table. Mite scooted under next to him. Ponce looked out past them with a finger to his lips motioning for silence.

Rayne nearly cried out as pain shot through his knees and speared up into his back but seeing the man who had been following them stop and scan the area, he clamped a hand over his mouth and swallowed a muted whimper. Dressed in Andersen House colors, the man sprinted past their hiding place. Ponce settled back and whispered, "We'll give it a few minutes then sneak out."

After a short wait, they watched as the Andersen guard jogged back past them and vanished through the market entryway. Mite sprang out from under the table followed by Ponce. The two turned and helped Rayne up. He rubbed his knees and groaned while Mite retrieved his staff.

Scanning the area, Ponce said, "Okay, now we can go."

After losing their tail, Ponce moved at a slower pace that didn't tax Rayne. They continued in the direction they had been heading and soon crossed one of the many bridges over the mired and mucky water. The few times Rayne remembered leaving the island in the past, he didn't stay near the lake or its overpowering stench. Now, Ponce followed a path that took them down to the very edge of the water. They walked along the festering shoreline toward a group of buildings that looked like giant barns.

"What are they?" Rayne asked, keeping his voice low.

"They're warehouses," Ponce replied. "These are currently in use, but a short distance beyond these, we'll come to an area of older, crumbling ones that have been abandoned. We meet in one of those. Actually, to be technical, we meet under the building."

Mite struggled with the overwhelming odor coming off the lake, his nose ran and his eyes teared. Rayne handed him a scarf to wrap around his nose and mouth.

"Awful, awful. Mite does not like this. He wants to go back to Nemora, yes, yes." He kept mumbling through the scarf.

"I'm sorry about the stench. It's something we've gotten used to because it keeps the curious away."

After passing more than three dozen new buildings, they saw the old storehouses Ponce had described. He pointed out their destination, the fifth building in the second row of older warehouses. Beyond that, the remains of even older buildings could be seen crumbling in on themselves. Rayne shifted his gaze back to the derelict structure Ponce had pointed out. Its blocky two-story frame rose up next to a wide stream of dark water flowing into the lake.

"It may not look it, but this water is fresh," Ponce said as he led them along the stream to a narrow stretch where he and Mite jumped across. "The water turns foul after it enters the lake."

Rayne stopped at the edge of the stream as Mite and Ponce continued walking. He stood without saying a word, waiting for either of them to notice his absence. After a few minutes, they turned to see him still waiting on the far side of the stream.

"If you can't jump it, you're going to have to walk through it," Ponce said. "It's pure here, just plain water. I'm afraid there's no choice."

Rayne looked around, grimaced, and pulled up the hem of his stained and torn robe. Mumbling under his breath, Rayne walked back to a wider but shallower part of the stream and slogged through the water. At least it didn't stink, though it was warm against his feet.

After crossing the stream, they entered the building. It looked as if one small breeze would bring it crashing down around them. Searching the dark, cavernous space to be sure they were alone, Ponce led them through the interior to a door on the far wall. Pulling a chain with a key on it from inside his shirt, he unlocked the door and waved Mite and Rayne in before him. Rayne hesitated, old fears resurfacing. But then, releasing a grunt, he followed Mite into a small room that looked like a closet. Once they were in, Ponce pulled the door shut behind him. The lock clicked, and a door opened to their left, revealing a well-lit stairwell.

They descended heavy wooden stairs, Rayne holding his staff in his left hand and grasping a strong railing with his right as he hobbled downward. A large, rectangular room with lit torches set in sconces spaced evenly on the two longer walls opened before them. When Rayne reached the floor, he lifted his eyes. A network of substantial, dark timber beams threw shadows on the ceiling high above. The uneven flickering of the torches cast the area in wavering light that bounced off the age-darkened walls. The darkness here, though deep in places, felt normal, not oppressive like the shadows now infiltrating Emporium City.

As Ponce led Rayne and Mite toward a group of individuals, Rayne stumbled to a halt. They were the people from his dream. The incredibly care-worn, thin man with the curly red hair and the scarred face; the woman who was missing a hand; the slight man who reminded him of Cai from Veres; and several men and women with the tell-tale marks of having worn slave collars. A few were obviously scarred and looked like they had spent time in the ring. They all looked too thin and were dressed in sad-looking, tattered clothing. Except for one middle-aged lady. Rayne remembered her from his dream, too. She was the one who kept the others fed and helped them find shelter.

"Coralea," Ponce said with a small smile as he approached the well-dressed woman.

Coralea looked up. Her eyes grew large as they caught on Rayne and Mite. "Oh no, Marcus Ponce. What have you done? What were you thinking, bringing strangers here? Careless. You know Pastor Zeb has to meet any new people before they are allowed to come here."

"I know, Coralea." Ponce's small smile faltered. "But this is an exception. I'm sure everyone will understand once I explain."

"Explain what, Marcus?" asked a tall thin man with deep-set, piercing blue eyes and silver hair flowing down around his shoulders, as he came through the doorway of a side room and approached them with a confident bearing.

Several of the men and women who had been talking, trailed him over to where Rayne, Mite, and Ponce were standing with Coralea.

"Explain what?" the tall, silver-haired man asked again, an undercurrent of anger hardening his voice. He strode in front of Rayne and Mite, looking them over with a mixture of curiosity and anger. "Enlighten me as to why you've brought strangers here without first consulting me. That would be a good start."

"I'm sorry, Pastor Zeb," Ponce said. "I've brought these strangers here with good reason. They're believers. I'll vouch for them; they won't betray us."

Grumbling arose among the men and women who walked over behind Pastor Zeb. They stared at Rayne and Mite with open hostility and Pastor Zeb gave his head an irritated shake while frowning at Ponce. These were the very people who were praying for light, the people who needed to hear the message of hope and the One's love.

Without waiting to hear what Ponce or the pastor might say, Rayne turned to face them and declared what the Son had shared with him in the Blessed Hollow. "People of Sorial, do not weep. The One has heard you calling and his heart breaks at your pain. He wants you to know how much he loves you. He sent me with a message for the remnant of his people on Sorial who have been praying for light. You must cling to the truth of his steadfast love, his unfailing, deep, and steadfast love. He is with you, even as the darkness grows, he has sent light to you. He has heard you and sent me to speak his words of light."

Pastor Zeb's look of irritation deepened into one of red-tinged anger. "Who are you to claim that the One has sent you? Why would he speak to us through a stranger? For all we know, you've been sent by the merchants so they can find this place and enslave the last of the believers on Sorial. By what authority do you say these things?"

When Rayne began speaking, others came forward from scattered positions around the room. They joined with those already standing with Pastor Zeb. Coralea, Ponce, Rayne, and Mite became the center of a circle of about fifty people. The wariness on the faces surrounding him touched Rayne's heart. He knew what it felt like to live with that kind of fear and suspicion. Even now, he lived with the need to cap his old fears just to be around Ponce. Rayne bowed his head and prayed for guidance to answer the pastor's questions wisely.

After a few seconds, as the murmuring of the crowd grew in volume, Rayne opened his eyes and met Pastor Zeb's gaze. "The One knows you are persecuted here on Sorial; he knows of your joy even in your trials. He sent me to tell you a time of testing is about to come upon you. But do not despair, for he is with you, and he cares for you deeply. I speak in his name because I'm his chosen Light Bringer. I am the lost and broken. I am the thirtieth generation. I am the true Light Bringer. Let me tell you my story."

Rayne spoke of his childhood, of Warren and how he had taught him about the One. He spoke of his history as a slave and his struggle with darkness and his despair at being forced to kill. He shared how the One had spoken to him and saved him from taking the lives of King Theodor and Queen Rowena, his own parents. He heard the grumbling grow to outright protest.

"This man is old enough to be grandfather to the king and queen, how could he think we would believe he's their son?"

"The crown prince? This pathetic old man?"

"Ridiculous!"

"He was a slave, he understands."

"Can we believe him?"

Speaking over the mumbling, refusing to give in to the increasing pressure to hide, Rayne continued. He told of finding the Words of the One to Corylus, Veres, Amathea, and Glacieria.

Finally, he told about what Sigmund had done to him, taking his body and trapping him in the prison of the old man's body.

"But even though this body is dying," he said to the now quiet crowd, "I won't stop. The One has called me and he's strengthened this frail body so I can keep moving forward. I won't deny my calling. While I was in the Blessed Hollow, retrieving the Words of the One to Nemora, the Son appeared to me. He told me to give you the message of his love. Then the next night I dreamed; I saw you all in my dream. The One told me you were calling for the light and that I must hurry.

"This is the truth of who I am, Rayne Kierkengaard, Crown Prince of all Ochen, and Light Bringer of the One. This is who I am, a young spirit trapped in a body not my own. And I'm here now to reclaim the Words of the One to Sorial.

"My calling is to reclaim all seven Words, bring the light of the One to Ochen, and bind the living darkness. You've seen it yourselves, haven't you? The inexplicable darkness in the air. I know you feel the oppression, the dense, heavy magic weighing on your spirits. Even with both your suns shining, your world is growing dark. You are suffering persecution for your belief in the One. Help me to find the scroll to Sorial so I can stop this evil.

"Time is running out for this body and after I reclaim your scroll, I still must skip to Arisima and reclaim the last scroll before I can return to Corylus and bring all seven together. This is why Ponce brought me here today. He knows me, knows I'm speaking the truth, and is willing to help me in any way he can." Facing Pastor Zeb, Rayne continued. "Please, Pastor Zeb, tell me, what must I do to gain your trust?"

32

꒰

I'm the one you must convince." A woman's strong voice with a bell-like quality rang out from the doorway to the side room. "I am the guardian, the one who has been awaiting the true Light Bringer through the generations. Come, speak with me if you dare. If you speak the truth, I will know; I will see it in you."

She beckoned for Rayne to follow her back into the side room. Mite made to follow, but she held out her hand. "Alone. I will examine him alone." She paused for a moment and tilted her head to the side, staring intently at Mite. "You are an enigma, child. You're more than what you seem." After another moment of silent scrutiny, she straightened her back and said, "I'm sorry, blessed ancient of the One, but I must speak with the man who claims the title of Light Bringer alone. Please accept my apology." She bowed to Mite, then turned to follow Rayne into the room.

"My name is Tindra." She closed the door. "Please be seated."

Rayne sat on one of two straight backed chairs flanking a work table surrounded by a spotless kitchen. Rows of blue cabinets with hand-painted scrollwork and small yellow flowers covered one long wall. The scent of fresh-baked bread filled the air.

Tindra sat on the chair opposite Rayne. "You've laid claim to the title of Light Bringer. You say you've already retrieved five of the seven. Tell me, then, of the guardians you've met."

Rayne looked at Tindra and saw the otherness of her. Although she was even shorter than Naarah, and rounder, with stooped shoulders, she possessed the unique quality of ancient strength he had felt in each of the other guardians. But Tindra also seemed different, more worn and troubled, more human.

"You're different from them," Rayne said.

Tindra gave him a sharp look. "Life on Sorial has been challenging for one such as I. But my query still remains, tell me of my brethren. I would hear you speak, newcomer."

Rayne dipped his head in acknowledgement. "I first met Ari on Veres. She was tall and golden and lovely. She told me of your people and the covenant you had made, giving up everything to serve the One. On Amathea I met Meryn who reminded me of a tall old tree, like he was part of the forest where he lived. He was so full of life and energy. Cleatus was weighed down with sorrow for his brother, Calais, who had been taken by the enemy. He lived with guilt and shame because I was forced to fight and kill Calais. Naarah of Nemora was a young girl filled with joy, who sang and danced and walked with the Son in the Blessed Hollow." Rayne paused, his eyes fixed on Tindra.

"And what of Corylus?"

"It's as I said earlier. Warren had the Words of the One to Corylus. I never met the ancient guardian there. Ari told me he had been her husband. The will of the One was that I receive the scroll to Corylus with a teacher, Warren. That's all I know."

Tindra rose and walked to Rayne. Bending down, she looked into his eyes with keen intensity. Several minutes passed. Rayne's hand began to twitch, and he wished he could turn away from the searching, but then Tindra said, "I see you now. I see the truth in you and hear it in your words. I also see the way you've been broken. Though your spirit is strong, it is weakening. You will not be able to survive much longer severed from your true body."

Tears of compassion pooled in her deep-set, chocolate eyes. "You've suffered much and the end is now near. I will pray to the One for his continued strength for you. As he has said, cling to the truth of his promises. He never fails."

She rose to her full height, straightening her stooped shoulders, and walked to the wall of cabinets. Opening the end cabinet, she reached in and pulled out a familiar looking satchel. Turning she smiled at Rayne's open-mouthed shock.

"You're surprised that this wasn't in a more secure place, aren't you?"

Rayne nodded.

Tindra laughed, a tinkling sound that reminded Rayne of Ari, and he began to understand something of the true strength hidden in her shabby form.

"You're not the only one whose truth is hidden. Many years ago, seeing the persecution of believers on Sorial, I chose to help them. I adopted this form, one that blends in and can walk unnoticed. Through all that time, I and my precious charge have hidden in plain sight with the enemy unaware of the truth. For me, this form has been a shelter from our enemies. Disguised as this woman I've been able to wander Emporium City and move freely among them.

"Within the last year, though, I began feeling the pulse of seals releasing and I knew that the Light Bringer had arisen, but until I examined you myself, I couldn't be sure you weren't another trap.

"It wouldn't be the first time our enemies have tried to lure me out and claim my burden. But now the time has come for me to pass it on to you. Beware though, young Light Bringer. You are being sought here. Our enemies have been watching for you in the form of the old man. When the believers first started meeting here, I set wards of protection over this building. For now, you are safe here, but it won't last."

Bending over Rayne, she cupped his cheek with a warm, work-hardened hand. "Once you touch the Words of the One to Sorial you will be a beacon in the coming night. Our enemies are strong here. They will be drawn to you; they will seek to destroy the light that grows in you."

"I don't think that will happen." Rayne swallowed a lump of sorrow. "When I was myself, on Veres, my body glowed from the Sun Sparrow light. But on Nemora, it was different. Though the light from Ledia entered me, it didn't physically affect me. This body didn't respond to the light. And when I opened the scroll on Nemora there was no release of power."

Tindra shook her head and sighed. "You do not yet understand young one. Every time you've read a scroll, or been exposed to the One's light, your spirit has grown brighter. And the more time you spend with the little light bearer who accompanies you, the brighter your own light becomes. You can't see it with your newcomer eyes, but those born of darkness will. Though your enemy sought to harm you by trapping you in this body, it has acted like a shield to hide the light, like the camouflage of this body I wear. But now that the darkness has grown stronger, and you carry more light within, that body will become insufficient to hide what you are. The deeper the darkness grows, the more your light will stand out.

"You must not remain on Sorial. You are welcome to join us for our worship and evening meal, but then do not linger. Leave this world soon."

Nodding his thanks, Rayne took the bag from Tindra and pulled out the wrapped scroll. He paused for a minute, thinking about the warning Tindra had just given him. But feeling the affirming warmth of the One, he undid the leather, and carefully unrolled the scroll. The warmth intensified, and a faint vibration of energy filtered through his core as he read the first lines.

"The words of the One to the people of Sorial, as recorded by the prophet Neeson. Hear my people and cling to my words, for my words are true. A time is coming when the deceiver will seek to veil my light. Though many will be led astray, do not be dismayed. As your suns still shine behind a cover of clouds, so too, even in the darkness, my light continues to shine behind the veil. Do not turn from my words. Know that I am always with you. My love is never changing and everlasting."

Speak to my remnant on Sorial. Their time of testing is at hand.

Though their trial will be hard, they will not fail. For I am with them. I will be their peace and shelter. Beloved Light Bringer, take the scroll, eat of its truth. The time of judgement is near; Arisima awaits.

"He just spoke to you, didn't he?" Tindra asked.

Rayne nodded. "He says the time of testing is at hand for the believers here. But though they're facing a difficult trial, he's with them and they will not fail. He also warned me that my time is short. I don't think I can stay. I have to skip tonight."

Tindra leaned down to Rayne and hugged him gently. "Please, at least join us for a meal and a short time of worship before you go. Then, leave with the prayers of everyone here. I will not detain you more."

"The One has spoken." Tindra announced as she and Rayne walked back out into the cavernous main room. "Our time of testing is at hand. But take joy, my friends. The Light Bringer has come, and I have passed the burden on to him. The end of darkness approaches, the time of binding is at hand."

"It's true then?" Pastor Zeb asked. "We could see the increasing darkness. Our enemies have grown stronger. I knew the time was close, but now that it is upon us, my heart quails."

He stared into space for a moment, but then, with a shake of his shaggy silver mane, he said, "Quickly now everyone, let us gather for the communal meal. The Light Bringer's presence honors us. Let us show him how the remnant of the One's people on Sorial gather and worship."

While several people hustled to set tables, Coralea helped Tindra carry out steaming pots of potato soup, warm bread, and chunks of softened butter. Soon, everyone was seated and Pastor Zeb said the blessing. Rayne sat between Zeb and Tindra; Ponce joined Coralea at the end of another table, talking with their heads touching. Mite chose to sit at a smaller table of children. Rayne chuckled as they stared with widened eyes while the ancient delighted them with tales of Nemora.

Once again, Rayne found himself enjoying the simple fare of believers who had little but took joy in sharing what they had. Zeb made several attempts to draw Rayne into conversation, but Rayne's thoughts were fixed on the Sorial Scroll and his skip to Arisima. Distracted, he mumbled answers and tried to remain polite. Before he knew it, the table was cleared and Zeb rose to lead his congregation in singing a hymn.

"This has been an eventful evening," Pastor Zeb said after the hymn. "We have met the One's chosen Light Bringer. We have been warned that our time of trial is upon us. And though my heart is joyful that the time of binding approaches, I am full of fear in the face of our trial. I find myself short on words of encouragement. And so, Light Bringer, I ask. Would you speak to us?"

Rayne veiled his frustration. The last thing he wanted to do was to speak encouragement this evening. He hadn't spoken to a group since being trapped in the old body and he felt inadequate. But, as he looked around at the anxious faces raised in expectation, he knew he must speak. Clutching his staff, he rose, took a deep breath, and prayed. Rayne stood, still and silent, gathering his thoughts.

"The One loves you and cares for you, his people, his remnant on Sorial. Even before I met you, he showed you to me in a dream. I know your struggle and your faith." Drawing in another deep breath, he looked around at their faces and compassion welled up within him.

"I know how fear threatens to undo you, how hard it is to cling to faith when the enemy is so strong and everything has been taken from you. But there is one thing the enemy can't take. Your trust in the One. Nothing happens that he has not willed to happen; and all that he has willed to happen, happens with a purpose. He has promised to be your strength and help in the coming trial. Don't let fear keep you from trusting. Be strong. Be courageous. The One is your strong tower. And he never breaks his promises."

Rayne sat down, unable to continue, gasping for air. He was unsure if his message was for the people of Sorial or himself.

"Everyone, please be careful as you head home," Pastor Zeb said after closing the worship.

Ponce turned to Rayne, his mouth set in a determined line. "I'm going with you to Arisima."

"What?" Rayne raised startled eyes to the former rubiate. "I'm going with you. Don't try to stop me. I'm staying with you until the end. No matter what happens."

"You're not a warrior, my dear," Coralea said, touching his arm, worry creasing her brow. "And I don't know what you can do to help. But I'll not gainsay your decision. I do, however, fear that I will not be strong if you leave me."

Ponce put an arm around Coralea's shoulders and squeezed lightly. "I know how strong you really are, how you helped me when I struggled with the guilt of my past. When I fought day after day against the darkness within me, you were there, praying for me, and with me. It was you who brought me here and helped my faith in the One to grow. Your faith is strong, Coralea, I know it is. I promise to return to you as soon as I can. But for now, I need to go with Prince Rayne. If not for him, I would still be trapped in the darkness."

Coralea sniffled and turned to Rayne. "I don't know all that happened, but Ponce told me some of his past. Though you have no reason to trust or care for him, please know, he is a changed man, created anew by the One. You can trust him. His past, what he did to you, still haunts him. Keep him safe for me, please."

"I won't stop Ponce if he wants to come with us, and I can't make any promises for his safety. I can't even do that for myself or Mite. But if you will pray for us, lady, I'm sure the One will hear your prayers."

While they were talking, the last of the worshipers filtered up the stairs and out of the building until only Rayne, Mite, Ponce, Pastor Zeb, Coralea, and Tindra were left.

"We need to get our things from the inn and skip to Corylus tonight," Rayne said as they climbed the stairs and exited the fake closet.

Coralea hugged Ponce, blinking back tears. "I'm going to stay and help Tindra clean up. I don't think I can be alone now."

Tindra wrapped an arm around Coralea's waist. Together they stood in the doorway and waved good-by as Pastor Zeb led Rayne, Mite, and Ponce out into the night. Without warning, a ring of torches whooshed to light. More than two dozen mercenaries wearing Andersen House colors surrounded them.

Beyond the ring, the night was lit with more torches. Rayne ground his teeth. Soldiers were already chaining the worshipers who had left the building and were loading them into the back of a wagon. This was what he had seen in his dream. Then he heard another voice from his past and his heart jumped into his throat. A large, back-lit form moved into the circle to stand in front of them.

"Well, well, well, lookie what spilled out with the trash. If it isn't my old friend Marcus Ponce." Coronus bellowed his pleasure.

Old terror at the sound of the Assassin Master's voice soured the meal that now sat heavy in Rayne's stomach.

Coronus's eyes glittered in the flickering torchlight as he licked his lips. "Do you have any idea how much Sigmund promised to pay to have you delivered to him?" He laughed, a barking sound that dredged up memories of Warren's death and plunged Rayne into an abyss of fear.

No! Not him; not now! Ponce was bad enough, but now to face Ponce and Coronus. What am I going to do? Nothing … he'll never recognize me like this. Unless Ponce is in on this with him. I should never have trusted Ponce!

Coronus's gaze skimmed over Pastor Zeb and dismissed him. Turning his focus on Rayne, Coronus began to turn from him as well when he stopped, took a step closer, and looked at him more intently, his mouth dropping open.

Rayne was certain he saw the man drool. "Woo hoo. Lookie what I've got here. Sigmund is going to make me a rich man for this one. Who would have thought coming to round up a few pathetic One worshipers would lead me to acquire not only the missing traitor, but the old bag of bones Sigmund's been hunting for the last few months."

His eyes lit up and he stroked his thick black beard. In a voice so quiet only Rayne could hear, he said, "Oh, Sigmund wants you real bad old man, or should I say Your Highness? No, wait, even better, *little birdie?*"

Looking back to his men, Coronus shouted, "These two

are the grand prize, men. Someone bring me shackles quick like."

He pointed at Ponce. "Don't go getting any ideas, rubiate. You just stay there and behave."

Focusing on Rayne once again, he said, "I'm right, ain't I?" As Coronus moved forward to stand directly in front of Rayne, Mite forced himself between the two and glared at the man towering over him.

The old assassin master's eyes dropped to study Mite for a moment, then rose back up to Rayne. "I'm sure you remember first-hand how impatient I can be with children. Unless you want some harm to come to your little friend, I suggest you collar him."

"Leave him alone, Coronus," Rayne ground out, standing as tall as he could while he gripped his staff with whitened knuckles. "He's got nothing to do with this."

Releasing the staff with his right hand, he leaned over, grabbed Mite's shoulder and turned the little ancient around so they were face to face. Looking into Mite's eyes and willing him to understand, Rayne flipped the strap of the satchel over his head and onto Mite's shoulder while he whispered, "Run. Take the scroll to Bishop Hedrick in Westvale. Go!"

Mite shook his head no, but Rayne left the little ancient no choice. He pushed Mite from him as hard as he could and stepped up to Coronus.

"I'm here," he said. "I won't fight you. Just let the child go."

Coronus laughed as he grabbed Rayne's arm, his grip like veredium. "Sure, I'll let the brat go, right into the arms of my men. He's a pretty little thing like you used to be, so if you think I'll just let him run off, you don't remember me very well. I'm sure he'll make me a fine profit on the selling block at tomorrow's slave auction, along with the rest of these vermin."

33

Thorvin fumed, his frustration ratcheting up another notch. His Royal Highness had left for Nemora with the new regent in tow five days ago. And now, there were issues arising with no one left to fill the void of leadership—except Thorvin. At least that's what the men sitting across the table from him were saying. He knew he wasn't the only noble of high standing left in Westvale, but not one other person of title was willing to put his life on the line in defiance of the new regent.

"Please, Lord Kraftsmunn, if someone doesn't listen to the citizens' complaints in the name of the king, we're afraid riots will break out. You know better than anyone the strange unrest. Westvale is like a pot set to boil over, especially in the middle and lower quarters." Jeffrey Danton's voice was low but intense.

Before leaving, the regent had ordered the king's chief advisor, Jeffrey Danton, to refrain from holding audiences until he and the prince returned. Unfortunately, the need of the people of Westvale to vent their concerns to a person of authority did not go away just because the prince said so. But none of the nobility who would, under normal circumstances, be striving for more power and authority, was willing to make any decisions that might bring the prince's wrath down on him. In the last month, His Royal Highness' temper had claimed the lives of two nobles accused of usurping his power. They had been hung on the new gallows in the Great Square.

After the first hangings, shopkeepers and homeowners in the craftsmen's quarter began waking to find angry messages critical of Crown Prince Rayne and Regent Woodfield scrawled across walls of houses and shops. Within the last few weeks, the perpetrators had moved into the wealthier neighborhoods, sneaking across manicured lawns and through landscaped areas to leave their angry messages plastered on the houses or stables of the rich.

Captain Marcharn, one of the recruits from Nemora, had been attending a party at a wealthy noble's house when he and several of his friends caught a dozen commoners trying to sneak onto the property with paint and brushes, evidence they were guilty of painting the traitorous messages.

Regent Woodfield immediately announced they were guilty of treason against His Royal Highness and all Ochen, and, as traitors, had no right to a trial. Not even twenty-four hours later, they had been officially condemned and sentenced to hang.

Determined to get to the bottom of the situation, Thorvin talked to aquaintances of the condemned men and learned that they had been drinking at a tavern down by the docks that evening and not one had made it home that night. *Could mean they're guilty. But something doesn't smell right.*

Though Thorvin tried to gain access to the condemned men to determine the truth, he was not permitted. No one except Captain Marcharn and a few select guards were allowed near the prisoners. After questioning several of the men's wives, Thorvin wrestled with his own rising fury. None of the condemned men could write. They were innocent. Though he knew it would do no good, he met with Regent Woodfield to request a formal trial. Despite Thorvin's protest, the prisoners were hung. As their friends spread the truth of their innocence to all who would listen, the city turned even more ugly.

Unnatural rage inundated the city. Soldiers were constantly called out to quell angry groups of citizens who were plundering the shops and homes of their neighbors. Nights were the worst. When the last of the sun's rays gave way to darkness and shadows thickened, a spirit of insanity spread into every corner of the city, robbing people of their common sense and driving them to actions they would never perform under normal circumstances. Westvale had become a dangerous place.

Thorvin, himself had been involved in a few altercations, one right in front of the Kasper's Arms Shop. As Thorvin was asking the angry mob to disperse and go home, someone threw a brick into the head of a soldier. If not for Thorvin's strength of command, the soldiers would have taken their swords to every civilian in the area, involved or not, without mercy. The very air was filled with a tension that fueled the animosity between the populace and soldiers.

Thorvin met with the new captains from Nemora to discuss the situation, but as Captain Fontaine warned months ago, they were useless. Unless the threat was aimed at a wealthy merchant or a noble, no action was taken. Control of the lower sections of the city was left to Thorvin and any troops he assigned to patrol there. He had even unofficially promoted Noah so he could send the young man out with other soldiers under his command.

Now Theodor's advisers were asking Thorvin to take another step closer to getting himself imprisoned or even hung.

"Please," Danton said. "We know Regent Woodfield's orders. But something must be done before riots break out at the docks. We don't know who else to turn to. King Theodor trusted you, the soldiers look up to you, and the townspeople feel the same. You're the only one respected by both sides. And … the regent never forbade you from taking action.

"Just listen to the representatives from the docks. You don't have to take any responsibility, or make any rulings, just be a voice of reason before things get worse. If the fishermen don't stop spreading stories about what's coming across the sea, we're going to face a complete panic. Thorvin, we need your strong presence to calm the situation."

"And will you join with me in conducting this audience?" Thorvin asked, already knowing the answer.

Danton's eyes examined the ground as he chewed his lower lip. "You know I can't, none of us can. We will support you as best we can, but unless we want to hang for treason, we can't openly join you in holding a public audience."

"So, it's okay if I hang, just so long as the rest of you are safe?" Thorvin rose abruptly, angered by the whole insane situation. After looking all five men in the eye, he said, "I'll think about this. But before I make any decision, I want to try talking to King Theodor again."

"Thank you." Danton rose with Thorvin. "We'll await your answer."

Thorvin strode from the small conference room toward the Queen's Chambers where Charlotte greeted him.

"How are they today?" he asked the healer.

"As good as can be expected." When he stared at her, waiting for more, she sighed and said. "While he's gone to Nemora, the Lord Master Mage has the soldiers giving His Majesty that tincture." She pursed her lips. "That just doesn't seem right. Why didn't he give the duty to one of us healers?"

"Yeah," Thorvin rumbled. "I know what you mean. Do you think that medicine is helping the king?"

She shrugged and shook her head. "Honestly, I don't know. The Interplanetary Council trusts him, and he's supposed to be very learned."

Concern zinged through Thorvin, causing his stomach to clench as he walked over to where Theodor was sitting near Rowena, staring at nothing, his eyes glassy mirrors. Thorvin wanted to pull him up and shout 'everything's falling apart around you! Wake up!' He had already actually tried that on a couple occasions. But since the day His Majesty had confronted Brayden and Rayne, nothing seemed to reach past the wall Theodor had erected around himself.

Thorvin ground his teeth. The guards outside the door had refused to let him in until he barked a direct order at them. He didn't recognize any of the four and that rubbed his nerves raw. He suspected the tincture the mage was giving the king was keeping him doped up and unable to function rather than helping him get better. Gazing down at his old friend, Thorvin decided to ask Anne to check out the tincture while the Lord Master Mage, Regent Woodfield, and His Royal Highness were away on Nemora.

Crouching down on his heels and bringing his eyes even with Theodor's, he said, "Hey, Theo, how're you doing today? I don't suppose you'd want to join me meeting with some sailors and fishermen with a story to tell. I hear it's pretty interesting. I sure could use your help with this old friend. I mean, I really need your help. We need ... aw, come on Theo."

For a minute, hope surged within Thorvin as Theodor swiveled his eyes to meet Thorvin's. But then, without any reaction, rotated them back to stare at the empty air over Rowena's head.

Frustration mounted and Thorvin growled. "Come on, Theo, snap out of this and be the king I know you are. You're not helping Rowena like this and the One knows you aren't helping your people either! Darkness is coming, it's right there out on the sea, it's starting to block the sun, and the city is tearing itself apart!"

Thorvin sighed as Theodor continued staring with unseeing eyes. He pushed upright and said, "You know, Theo, sooner or later you're going to have to come out of that place where you're hiding and face things. Face what's been done to Rowena and Rayne. Face what's happening to your realm. You would do us all a big favor if it was sooner. We need you to fight back for your wife and your son—and your kingdom. So, think about it, okay? I have a bad feeling we're running out of time."

He wanted to say more, to shake his friend out of his fog. But he capped his anger and nodding to Charlotte, left the room shaking his head and wondering how he could get a sample of Theodor's medicine for Anne to test.

Returning to the conference room, Thorvin agreed to hold the audience. He hadn't wanted to take the responsibility, but with Theodor and Rowena still incapacitated and the Royal Pain and his sidekick regent gone, someone had to be accountable.

And after thinking about it, Thorvin realized he would rather deal with the situation himself than allow His Royal Highness to do so anyway. Regardless of the consequences.

A hazy, late summer sun filtered into the windows of the main audience chamber as Thorvin sat, sweating, in a heavy straight-back chair set on the floor below Theodor's throne. He listened to the complaints of nearly two dozen sailors and fishermen. His stomach roiled as their words confirmed what he already knew, darkness was approaching. Yesterday he had walked out onto the beach to peer over the waves on the Cameron Sea. The threatening line he had been dreading, boiled on the horizon, tendrils rising as if to blot out the sun before sinking back into the dark, seething mass.

"We been watching it come for a few weeks now," the spokesman for the fishermen said as he crushed his cap in large, calloused hands. "Coming from the direction of the Shattered Continent. Twice we brought this news to Regent Woodfield and His Royal Highness. Each time they told us we were imagining things. 'It's probably nothing more than a storm at sea,' they said. 'Nothing to worry about,' they said. But we've made our living on the sea and we wouldn't mistake the signs of a storm, we wouldn't be very good sailors if we did. This is something different ... something not normal.

"Now, Lord Kraftsmunn, the cloud is closer and blacker, riding right over the top of the water. The fish are vanishing. This ain't our imagination. We're afraid to go out there. We don't know what it is, but now with the fish disappearing, and us full of fear, we can't even make a living."

Another man, with skin like leather, stepped up next to the spokesman. "I been fishin' the Cameron Sea since I was ten, my lord. I'm sixty-two last month. I never seen anythin' like this. Looks like a storm a comin' but it don't act like one. Movin' closer, steady like, day by day. In the last week, we started seein' bodies of dead sea creatures washin' onto the shore, floatin' by the docks. Huge creatures from the depths. You gotta do somethin'."

Thorvin wanted to yell, 'what in the seven do you think I can do about something like this?' But instead, he breathed deeply, questioned his sanity as he thought of the authority he was assuming, then said, "I'll send men out to investigate. Until we know more about what it is, we can't know how to combat the thing. For now, go back to your ships and do the best you can. Stay closer to the coast and don't approach the cloud until we know more."

Thorvin was grateful when the audience finally ended. But just as he was about to rise, he was surprised to see Noah approaching.

"May I speak to you in private Sir?" Noah asked.

"Yeah. I'm done here for now. Come on, we can talk in the small audience room."

Entering the smaller, more comfortable room where Theodor preferred meeting with individuals, Thorvin motioned Noah into a gray leather chair near the dark fireplace as he sat in a matching chair. Once Noah was sitting, he started. "Lord Kraftsmunn, we have a problem."

Thorvin growled, wishing he could spit. "Yeah, tell me something I don't already know. It seems like everyone is having problems. Spit it out boy, what's this about."

Noah's eyes were intense as he asked, "Are you positive you don't know who's been painting these incendiary messages around Westvale?"

Thorvin stared at Noah, a sickening lump working its way up his throat. "Why are you asking me this now? Didn't we just hang twelve men the regent declared guilty of treason for writing those stupid messages?"

"You and I both know those men were innocent." Noah grimaced, made to rise, and then sat back down. "This morning the words death to the impostor were found painted on the wall near the Queen's Garden. This time there was a body ... and the message appeared to have been painted with his blood."

Thorvin cursed under his breath. "All those innocent men

hung for nothing? What a disaster. That idiot, Brayden. This is getting out of hand. We need to find out who's doing this and stop them before more innocent people die."

"Right," Noah said. "Captain Marcharn agrees, even though he has been credited with having already done just that.

"After finding that body, he gave orders to bring in anyone even suspected of knowing anything. And he doesn't care about what condition they're in when they arrive. He's going to use them to show what happens to those who oppose the prince and regent. You know what that means."

Noah sighed and ran his hands through his sandy hair. Then shaking his head, he continued. "The captain is having posters made offering a sizeable reward to anyone who brings information leading to the capture of individuals suspected of being behind the messages."

When Noah stopped speaking, Thorvin sat without a word, his head in his hands. After a bit, he looked up at Noah. "I'll try talking to Captain Marchan and see if I can learn anything. In the meantime, we'll meet tonight so we can discuss what's happening. Of course, it will only be you, me, Anne, Lexi, Kori, Andrew, and Elsie. Mace is still on Nemora and Jonathan's not back from Centerville."

Noah looked at Thorvin and shifted in his chair again. "Still no news from Glacieria?"

Shaking his head, Thorvin huffed out a snort. "Not yet. It's been close to a month now. They should have been back weeks ago. Anne is beside herself with worry for Shaw. But you know her, on the outside she appears calm as ever. Yet with each day that passes now, I see more and more of her composure crumbling."

"I know how she feels," Noah said. "Each day I hope for news of Sashi. The longer they're gone, the more concerned and angrier I get. I can't seem to sit still, everything irritates me. It's like I'm harboring fury I can't explain or release. Every chance I get, I wander over to the portal station. I usually run into Anne or Kori doing the same thing, checking to see if the skipping line to Glacieria has opened yet. Do you think they're alright?"

"Yeah, Noah, I think they're okay, just detained. You know how Shaw can get if something catches his attention. I wouldn't be surprised if he and Tetsuya started talking about prophecies and the like and have no idea how long they've been at it. And though I don't know the reason why Glacieria has closed the portal, I suspect they're still allowing outbound travelers to leave. I'm sure any day now, the three of them will come skipping back to Corylus and wonder why we even worried."

"Thanks." Rising, Noah added, "I'd better get back. I'm supposed to be on duty now. We'll talk more later."

"Just try to stay calm," Thorvin said. "We're all on edge right now."

Thorvin sat in silence for a long while after Noah left, tapping a rhythmic pattern periodically on the wooden table-top. *Okay Lord, you're in charge, right? At least that's what Rayne used to tell me. But if you're in control, why is everything so screwed up? I don't even know who needs prayer more. Rayne? Shaw and the twins? Jonathan? Theodor and Rowena? Or the rest of us waiting here? Anne is missing Shaw. Lexi's still torn between trusting Rayne or accepting Jonathan's theory that the prince is no longer Rayne. Everyone's on edge and people are being murdered. Tell me, what should I do?*

The list goes on. I hope you're getting all this. Jonathan is in Centerville dealing with those scroll worshippers who've now begun burning churches. The fishermen are complaining to anyone who'll listen about that cloud coming across the Cameron Sea. I look around at the people of Westvale and I can see it in their faces; they're angry and afraid. That's a bad combination. We're all feeling the oppression of a coming storm, a violent storm. So, tell me, what do I pray? Help me here, I'm at a loss.

Thorvin felt a slight internal sensation of warmth, as though the midday summer sun beyond the window was warming him from the inside out. He heard the quiet, gentle voice. *Pray for the coming light. Trust.*

Thorvin waited to hear if there was more, wished there would be more, but once he was certain the One wasn't going to speak again, he said, "How in the seven does Rayne deal with your cryptic answers? Well, I guess he's more patient than I am. Okay, I'll pray for the light to come and hope that means the prince is going to be himself again, what with him being the Light Bringer. But if you don't mind, I'd like to pray for everyone else as well. As long as that's alright by you."

34

Ⴈ

Autumn's seasonal brush painted the leaves on the trees of Westvale varied shades of red, orange and burgundy, and the chilly morning breeze sent shivers through Lexi, raising goose-flesh on her arms as she hurried to Anne's cottage. Hugging her chest, she sought warmth for her hands under her arms, clamping them close to her body. The sun was breaching the horizon, sending out golden red rays into the upper leaves. Looking up, Lexi shivered again. This time not from the cold. For even the first rays of the rising sun were not immune to the effects of the ever-present haze that now cast a pall over the city. It was growing denser, tinging the blue above a muted shade of blue-gray.

The cawing of hundreds of crows sounded from the trees, and as Lexi passed, the birds took to the air. The whirring of their wings, ominous in the murky light, caused Lexi to pull her hands from under her arms and cover her head as she rushed past the rising flock.

Seeing huge flocks over Westvale had become a daily affair. Crows were the most common, migrating in vast numbers. But other birds were also moving in unexpected patterns, especially sea birds, fleeing the coming darkness.

Lexi left the main walkway that joined the palace grounds with the church property near the Westvale Cathedral and moved down a smaller path to the guest cottages. Anne would be waiting.

Anxiety over Shaw's and the twin's extended absence had begun to take its toll on Anne and she readily agreed to join Lexi visiting the the church kitchen most mornings, where Elsie offered warm bread and warm company. In the last couple weeks, it had become an enjoyable routine that evolved into baking lessons for the two young ladies.

"Did you hear the news this morning?" Elsie asked Lexi and Anne as they started blending their ingredients together in two large bowls on the heavy work table.

Anne looked up, hope brightening her eyes. "About Shaw? Have you heard something about Shaw? And Stevie and Sashi?"

With a sad shake of her head, Elsie said, "I'm sorry, my dear. I shouldn't have asked like that. I meant the news coming from the docks. They say that storm-like dark mass is coming closer and now the fish are disappearing."

Lexi nodded. "I walked out to the shore yesterday evening after hearing the staff's whispers. It's so much closer now than it was a week ago. Dark and bubbling, filling the horizon. I walked along the beach, my eyes drawn to it. Just watching it made my stomach queezy, like it was pulling all the energy from me, and yet I couldn't look away. I was afraid that if I did, something terrible would happen."

Anne frowned, but then a crooked grin surfaced. "Look at it this way, you already avoided something terrible; the terrible fate of accompanying *His Royal Highness* to Nemora. If I hadn't stepped in, you were actually going to go. Don't tell me you're falling for that innocent and thoughtful persona he's been using around you this past month?"

Lexi turned from Anne and choked back a sob.

"I'm sorry." Anne's smile faded as she regretted her choice of words. "I shouldn't have said that. I know you still struggle with the idea that Rayne is possessed. That you don't know what to think. I didn't want to make you cry. I hoped you'd respond to my words with anger, that I could ignite the spark in you and get your mind off the approaching darkness."

"No, that's not why I'm upset." Lexi took her bottom lip between her teeth. "I mean, yes, I'm upset about this darkness thing, who isn't? But it's more than that this morning."

Lexi got quiet and looked down into her bowl of dough while picking sticky bits off her fingers. Anne glanced at Elsie who walked over and closed the door they had left open to catch the breeze. Once the door was closed, Anne said, "Lexi, what happened?"

"While I stood there watching that *thing*, I couldn't stop thinking about Rayne ... the way he is now. My doubts ... all my fears ... it was like I never had them. There was a voice— no, not a real voice—more like impressions in my mind. I don't even know how to explain it. The thoughts were there like they were my own, and I accepted them as true. 'Rayne hasn't changed. Our so-called friends aren't true friends. They're spreading false rumors because they're jealous.'"

"No!" Elsie's and Anne's response melded into one.

"You've grappled with what to believe for weeks now." Anne shook her head and frowned. "But you can't deny your doubts. Remember the morning after the dinner party? You told us how you had caught His Royal Highness in an outright lie. You admitted to everyone that your heart doesn't sense the truth in him. That it's not the same when he holds you; that something feels wrong. That's why we agreed you shouldn't travel to Nemora with him."

Looking at Lexi, sorrow and compassion twining through her spirit, Anne spoke, her voice quiet but firm. "You need to decide. The One said you would know the truth in Rayne. If you're certain the heart of your heart still resides in him, tell us. We'll believe you and try to understand. But if not, help us find the truth."

Wiping her hands on a towel she picked up from the table, Lexi looked intently at Anne and Elsie. "My heart has whispered within me that His Royal Highness is not Rayne. But I couldn't allow myself to accept it because the alternative is ..." Lexi pulled in a gulp of air and released a sob. "I can't lie to myself any longer." She shook her head, turned away from Anne and Elsie, and squeezed her eyes shut. "Rayne is gone and there's nothing I can do to change that."

Her voice cracked, and she pulled in a shaky breath as she raised trembling hands to her face. "But standing on the shore, watching that darkness seething in the distance, it was all so clear to me. I knew Rayne hadn't changed and that we were wrong. We'd misjudged and misunderstood him. The heart of my heart is right here, I thought, and I need to trust him, no one else, just him. I knew in that moment that everyone else, you Anne, Elsie, all our friends, were the enemy. Those thoughts filled my mind driving out everything else except for an unreasoning fury at any who would seek to harm Rayne. I've never felt that kind of anger before, not even when my father was injured.

"That cloud, or whatever it is, distorted my perspective. Maybe that's what's influencing everyone in Westvale, the real reason why people are attacking each other and getting violent. The cloud over the Cameron Sea, the growing haze blocking out the light, they're both part of that living darkness the prophecies refer to and they're altering everyone's thoughts."

She paused and turned back to her bowl. "The darkness took control of my thoughts. When I went back to my room, I believed that Rayne was perfectly fine. I was ready to accept him and try to work with him as he is now. Do you understand? Without volition, I believed those lies."

"But you don't believe those things now, do you? What changed?" Elsie asked in a hushed voice.

Lexi turned to face Anne and Elsie again. "Last night, I dreamed about an old man. I startled awake and I knew in my heart I had been seduced by a lie born of that coming darkness. It was as if the spirit of that old man reached into my heart and drove the deceit from it.

"Oh, Anne. Elsie. I don't even know who that old man is, but this is the second time I've dreamed of him. He's connected to Rayne in some way, but I don't know how."

"What did you dream?" Anne asked.

"I dreamed that the old man was being enveloped by the

same darkness coming toward Westvale, but he refused to bow to it. A light burned in the heart of him that started glowing brighter and brighter until the darkness drew away from him."

Lexi stopped and flicked her gaze from Anne to Elsie. "Then he looked at me, as if I was standing right in front of him and he saw me. He looked right into my eyes and—oh Anne, Elsie—I felt as if my heart was whole again. Peace and joy, and so much love, filled me. What does it mean?"

Elsie and Anne looked at Lexi shaking their heads.

"I don't know," Anne said, "but I think you're right. There must be some kind of connection between the old man in your dreams and Rayne. Perhaps it means you need to keep trusting that Rayne will come back to you and you will find that peace and love from your dream. It's like Jonathan said, Rayne will have to come back because the prophecy will not fail. I think the dream was telling you that. Keep trusting the One and he will make you strong."

Elsie nodded. "Jonathan knows about these things. I believe what he said is true. I just wish he would get back from Centerville soon. He might know something about interpreting your dream." She paused for a moment, thought lines creasing her forehead. "Doesn't it seem odd that Shaw has been held up on Glacieria where those folks wanted to worship some scroll, while Jonathan is in Centerville, right here on Corylus, dealing with a group of people that sound an awful lot like those worshipers on Glacieria?"

"What if that's why Shaw and the twins aren't back yet?" Fear infected Anne's voice, driving it up an octave. "What if those scroll worshipers weren't so easy to dismiss? What if they captured Shaw? What if ..."

"Now you stop right there, young lady." Elsie's voice took on a firm note. "You just stop thinking things like that. You have no evidence that's what happened and you're getting yourself in a dither for no good reason."

Giving Elsie a sheepish look, Anne said, "I'm sorry. I guess I haven't been too good at keeping my fear under control lately. My apprehension keeps growing and I can't seem to find my old calm with Shaw gone. I wish he would come home already. You're right Elsie, this thing in Centerville sounds too much like what Thorvin said was happening on Glacieria. I want to be strong, but I'm worried something has gone wrong. It's so hard. I feel like I need to hit something and that's not like me."

"It's the coming darkness," Lexi whispered.

Elsie looked at both the young women. "Enough. Ladies, I think your dough is ready. Let's set the bowls on the warm stovetop to rise and sit for a bit. I think we need to spend some time in prayer. Right now."

After putting cloth covers over the bowls of dough and setting them on the stove, Lexi and Anne joined Elsie at the table by the window. They were talking in soft tones when a knock sounded.

Thorvin opened the door a crack. "May I come in?"

"Please, come in," Elsie said as Lexi and Anne nodded.

After closing the door behind him, Thorvin scanned the kitchen. "We need to get everyone together tonight. Can we meet here?"

Elsie nodded. "It's not a problem. With Jonathan and several of his assistants gone and Shaw still away, I'm not cooking nearly as much as usual. Tell everyone to come for supper; it'll feel good to cook for more people again."

"I'll be here," Anne said and Lexi nodded.

"Good," Thorvin said. "We'll talk later. Elsie, could you let Travis and Deven know?"

"I can do that; they usually come by here for lunch anyway," Elsie gave Thorvin a quick nod.

"We'll plan to meet here for a late supper, then. I'm going to walk down to Kori's now to let her and Andrew know."

"Be careful." Elsie said.

Thorvin nodded and, backing out the door, said, "I'm always careful."

The sun, muted and grayed, had already disappeared beyond the dark line on the horizon. The evening breeze drove a raw chill into the air as Rayne's friends gathered at the church house. After everyone had arrived and was settled around the table, Deven stood to say the grace. The slight, dark-eyed Arisimanian delegate to the Reclamation Committee had become a regular at the gatherings. He reminded everyone of Shaw, with his looks, habits, and way of talking. Like Shaw he had studied in a religious community on Arisima before joining the Reclamation Committee, and like Jonathan, he was well trained in both church politics and studies. With both Shaw and Jonathan away, Deven had stepped in as spiritual leader for the group.

After Deven finished praying, Thorvin noticed Anne staring at the man with a sorrowful expression. He suspected Deven's similarity to Shaw was spiking Anne's concern for her husband. Thorvin shook his head. He hoped Shaw and the twins were safe and would return soon. With the Rayne situation still unresolved, and the ominous dark cloud approaching, Thorvin knew they all needed something to pull them out of their deepening despair. Ever since Rayne's birthday, nearly six months ago, things just seemed stuck in a downward spiral. Bad news had dominated their discussions for far too long. Now, as they sat picking at their food, no one seemed willing to break the silence.

"I need to tell you all why I asked you here tonight," Thorvin said, clearing his throat as he rose from his seat. "As you all know, in the last month, political messages began appearing around the city. Each time a message appeared, the rhetoric got more heated and direct. The other day we were all called to the Great Square to witness the execution of twelve men accused of the crime and hung without the benefit of a trial. With the deaths of these men, Regent Woodfield assured the citizens of Westvale, the messages would stop. He was wrong.

"This morning, Noah called me to the wall by the Queen's Garden. 'Death to the impostor' had been scrawled across the wall bordering the Great Square. This time those responsible painted their message in blood and they left a mangled body beneath the message. Whoever is doing this is responsible not only for the deaths of those twelve innocent men, but the death of this unidentified victim as well." Thorvin scanned his friends around the table and pulled in a deep breath.

"I spoke with Captain Marcharn this afternoon. He's ordered wanted posters to be hung throughout Westvale offering a hefty reward for information leading to the arrest of any individuals suspected of being involved with these crimes. He has issued a decree. Any gathering of more than three people, unless they're immediate family, found meeting without his permission, will be arrested.

"From this point forward, we'll have to get creative. I propose we set up a communication chain. Any information that needs to be shared with the group, will be spread one on one, in the proper order, like links in a chain. Does anyone have a better suggestion?"

Thorvin looked around the table but no one would meet his eyes and the silence was complete.

"If no one has any other ideas, we'll give this a try and see if it'll work for us. Are you all in agreement?"

Heads nodded, but it was as if the fire that brought them together when they first returned from Nemora had been doused by a bucket of water. He had never seen these friends so disheartened. He couldn't remember himself ever feeling so hopeless. It was as if something heavy was smothering the life from them. Then Lexi was looking up into Thorvin's eyes, a wild light of understanding blossoming in her eyes.

"This is what happened to me yesterday," she said. "It's the darkness. It's stealing our hope, distorting our thinking, making everyone anxious and angry. Look at us all sitting here as if everything has been lost. Elsie, remember what you said just this morning? How Jonathan was right? We can't give up hope. We all have to be strong for ourselves and for Rayne. He will return and what will he find when he comes? Will he find us holding to our faith? Or will he find us hiding from our own shadows?"

As Lexi's words penetrated the cocoon of despair which had wound around them all, the kitchen door scraped open and the sound of several people entering filtered into the dining room. No one moved or said a word. They held their breath while listening intently and staring at each other with widened eyes. Footsteps echoed up the hallway and a voice said, "Nemora's moons. I'm so hungry I could eat a horse. Something smells good in here. Elsie, Jonathan, where are you guys?"

Sashi strode into the dining room slinging a heavy pack from her shoulders. Stevie was right on her heals. When Shaw walked through the door behind them, Anne let out a little scream and hopped up to embrace him.

The twins looked as if they had just come from a pleasant hike, but Shaw looked haggard, with a month's worth of beard covering the lower half of his face. While Shaw and Anne kissed, Kori rose from where she had been sitting and, smiling her relief, motioned Stevie and Sashi into her arms while tears of joy collected on her eyelashes before splashing down her cheeks.

Thorvin raised his eyes to the ceiling and mouthed a thank you to the One.

35

Somebody grab that brat," Coronus shouted to the men behind him as he wrapped his sausage-like fingers around Rayne's upper arm with a vise-like grip and drew him in close. While a couple of his men scrambled to grab Mite, Coronus hissed a harsh whisper at Rayne, "Now you're going to earn me back all I lost when you turned on Sigmund, boy." Then, taking a moment to look Rayne up and down, he snorted. "You stink old man. What? Have you finally given up on bathing every day?"

Laughing as Rayne glowered at him, he added. "That was a Warren thing, wasn't it? It's a good thing he's dead. If he saw his little prize pupil now he'd probably think what a pathetic creature you've become."

Rayne glared at Coronus. "You're the pathetic one, Coronus. You think you're free when you're nothing more than the Andersen's dog."

Snarling, Coronus raised a hand to strike. The blow never landed. Instead, Coronus flung out his arms, propelling Rayne away as Ponce plowed into the assassin master with a wild yell, propelling the heavier Coronus back several steps.

Gaining his footing, Coronus wiped the front of his jacket as he stepped back to face Ponce. Looking down, a malicious smile tweaking his lips, Coronus said, "Big mistake, little man." His smile growing wider, he buried a ham-like fist in Ponce's unprotected stomach, driving him to his knees, doubled over in pain.

"Just wait your turn *Old Friend*. You stay down there and wait, I'll get to you soon enough." Looking from Ponce to Rayne and back again he shook his head in disbelief. "I never thought I'd see the day when Sigmund's personal rubiate would come to the defense of Sigmund's little slave boy.

"Remember what he was like, Ponce, when you brought him back to me after that year he spent with you and Sigmund? He was so messed up and you kept begging Sigmund for another taste. Not so keen on it now, are you Ponce? Yeah, the blood's not the same rich royal thing it used to be; now it's common, old, and stale.

"Wait a second. Now I get it." Coronus chuckled, low and mean. "You're just hoping to be there when Sigmund gives him back his own body. You think you can apologize to Sigmund, get your old position back, and then beg to taste the boy again." He paused, once again looking between the two, grinning. "Well, I don't know why you're together now, and it doesn't matter to me. I just know I've become a very wealthy man."

Turning back to Rayne, Coronus bent down and scooped up a handful of smelly gray mud. He grabbed Rayne's arm once again and smeared the gritty clay across the front of his robe. "You're nothing but a decrepit, tottering old fool. Why, you can barely stand. And now you smell old too." He laughed at his own humor. "Do I call you boy or old man? Sigmund was brilliant to trap you like this. You're too weak to fight or run. You've finally learned how to be a good slave."

Coronus was still laughing when the sound of wind hissing through feathers ended with a thump and he staggered, losing his hold on Rayne, an arrow jutting from his chest. It seemed to Rayne as if the world stood still for an instant. He watched, his breath catching, as Coronus looked down at the arrow with shocked eyes and reeled in slow motion from the impact. Three more arrows followed in rapid succession, dropping three more soldiers, the one who was approaching Rayne with the chains and the two who were trying to catch Mite.

With Coronus down, his men panicked. Taking advantage of the situation, the prisoners at the wagon who weren't yet chained, turned on their captors, fighting back with their bare hands. Over the sound of grunts and shouts, Rayne heard Tindra's chiming voice rise behind him.

In all the confusion, Tindra and Coralea emerged from the warehouse. Coralea was swinging a short sword in a way that demonstrated she knew what she was doing as she ran to Ponce's side, while Tindra strode quickly past Rayne toward the soldiers at the wagon.

Rayne watched the two for a second with his mouth hanging open, but then yelled, "What are you doing?"

Coralea ignored him, her attention focused on Ponce as she helped him up onto his feet. But with a full smile shining on her face, Tindra glanced back at Rayne and said, "I've waited centuries for this moment. My people weren't called to be guardians without reason. Now, young Light Bringer, go. I will do what I've been called to do, and you must fulfill your own prophecy. Never forget, the One is always with you."

Rayne watched, stunned, as the rather round and sad looking ancient threw off her covering and the truth was revealed in penetrating light. She was even taller and more finely boned than Ari, beautiful and powerful. She marched with full confidence into the chaos that had erupted in the area in front of the warehouse, raising her hands and chiming a sound that disoriented the soldiers while strengthening the believers. She was stunning. Her power magnificent. Rayne watched, frozen, as she moved in dazzling light that pushed the darkness back from the people she loved, forcing the soldiers to retreat.

Without warning, Rayne was seized from behind. In one smooth and swift motion, he was lifted off the ground and flung over a broad shoulder. With his face bouncing against a man's muscular back, Rayne struggled to hold onto his staff as the stranger ducked past Coronus's men and sprinted back toward the bridge. Rayne tried to yell for Mite but bouncing up and down on the moving shoulder kept knocking the breath out of him.

Relief flooded him when he saw Mite on one side and Ponce on the other, running along with the man carrying him. Rayne wasn't sure if the man was friend or foe. For the moment, the stranger was rapidly transporting him away from Coronus and his men, so Rayne just hung on. The man had a bow in one hand and a quiver of arrows slung over his other shoulder. *Must be ... the one ... who shot the arrows. Is Coronus ... dead?*

Once they were back over the bridge and on the island, hidden behind a vendor's stall, Rayne's mysterious liberator stood him on his feet. Rayne looked up into the face of his rescuer and choked. He was the tall blonde man who had been working with the spirit hunter on Nemora. Rayne took a step back and started to speak, "What ..."

But then Mite, face crimson, was there, yelling at the man. "We know who you are, yes, yes, yes. You are the bad man from Nemora. Mite does not forget what you did, no, no, no. Get away from Ray-ray. Now! You leave him alone!"

The man looked to Ponce and said, "Please. I can explain if the little one would give me a chance."

Rayne reached out and placed a calming hand on Mite's shoulder. "Mite, he did just save us."

"You know this man?" Ponce asked.

"Worked with enemy creature on Nemora, filthy disciple of darkness." Mite spat out the words. "Tried to take Ray-ray for Sigmund, he did, he did."

"That was before," the man said. "Please, let me explain. I mean you no harm." The man paused and caught his breath before continuing.

"Yes, I was working with Aquila, that's true. But it was not by choice, I was forced against my will. But then, when that whirlwind thing happened, the demon that possessed me was hurled from me. It was one of the most incredible things I've ever experienced. I was suddenly free of the evil that had kept me a prisoner in my own body for so long. I'm now human again and I have you to thank for that.

C. S. WACHTER

"While I was healing from the wounds I sustained in the whirlwind, I began to understand the full extent of what you'd done for me. I knew I owed you for freeing me, so I decided to see if I could find you again. I searched for your tracks, I'm good at that. When I picked them up coming out of Neth, I followed, hoping I might get a chance to thank you and offer you my services. I'm a man of many talents."

The man dropped to his knees in front of Rayne and, with bowed head, solemnly pronounced, "I pledge from this time forward, to bind myself to you and serve you in any way I can. You freed me; please allow me the honor of serving you." Rising, he continued. "My name's Marius, Sir, and as you've just seen, I can be a big help. Please allow me to stay by your side."

"No, no, no," Mite scrunched his face in distaste. "Can't trust this one. Ray-ray. Leave him. Thank him if you must; but leave him here in the darkness where he belongs. Yes."

Ponce noticed several soldiers observing them. "We can't stay here arguing. We're being watched. Let's head to the inn to get your things. You can decide what to do with him on the way, Sire."

Mite led them down various side streets, peeking around corners and scanning for soldiers as the four worked their way back through the markets toward the inn. As Mite scrambled around buildings and across open areas with the others following, Rayne fell behind.

Dark, potent fear wormed tendrils of doubt through him and he recognized the signs that his body was weakening. The sickness was rising in him like some reanimated corpse. He stumbled to a halt, clutching the staff, his body swaying as he worked to keep the contents of his stomach from creeping up his throat. Foreign thoughts swirled. *Give up. You can't do this, it's too hard. So hard. And you're so weak. Stop running now. Stop and rest. Sweet, sweet rest.*

Mite scurried back with Ponce and Marius behind, and the spell was broken. Rayne blushed. Humiliation and shame flooded him as Marius once again picked him up and slung him over a strong shoulder like a sack of flour. They sprinted up several back alleys with Ponce now in the lead.

Approaching the rear of the inn, Ponce held up a hand, stopping everyone. Marius set Rayne on his feet as Ponce turned to them and whispered, "There are several soldiers loitering at the back door. It may be nothing, but we can't be sure. What do you want to do, Sire?"

Rayne thought for a moment. Looking at Marius, he wavered between conflicting thoughts. *Can I trust him? How much? I don't know ...*

Mite caught Rayne's eyes. "No, no. Can't trust this one, Ray-ray. Please. This one has welcomed darkness. Mite knows, sees it in his spirit."

Rayne ground his teeth. Marius claimed he desired to help Rayne and he was right, he could be a big help if Rayne would let him. On the other hand, Mite knew things, understood things Rayne would probably never understand. His wisdom ran much deeper than Rayne's. But if the soldiers were looking for Rayne, Ponce, and Mite, Marius could be their only option to get the Nemora scroll and their belongings, including what was left of the gems Fallon had given Rayne. Marius could walk right in without raising suspicion and then walk out again with their belongings.

"I'm sorry, Mite," Rayne said, shaking his head. "I have no choice. Marius is the only one who can get past the soldiers without a problem. I have to trust him, at least for now."

Mite turned his back to Rayne, muttering incomprehensible words under his breath.

"Mite, please understand," Rayne pleaded. But Mite refused to turn around.

Facing Marius, Rayne said, "You knelt and pledged yourself to me. You asked me to trust you. I don't know if I can. But it seems, for now, I have no choice."

Rayne gave Marius keys to their rooms and explained where the scroll was hidden. While Marius was retrieving their things, Ponce ran to his boarding house to gather his belongings, and Rayne and Mite made their way to the next market square to wait for Marius and Ponce near the skipping portals.

Though Mite stayed with Rayne, watching for soldiers and possible enemies, he refused to talk and periodically mumbled words in his ancient tongue. Rayne wanted Mite to understand. He wanted Mite to support him, not fight with him.

"Try to understand, Mite," Rayne whispered as they sat together in the shadow of a statue of Lord William. "What should I have done, Mite? Answer me. What else could I have done? Admit it. Marius was the only one of us who could get into the inn. Why are you being so obstinate?"

Mite, shifted, turning his back to Rayne more fully, still not speaking.

Anger seethed to the surface in Rayne. "Go ahead, turn your back on me." His whispered words were harsh and bitter. "Why don't you just leave me like everyone else. No matter what I do, I always end up alone. You don't know what it's been like for me. You've only known me for a little while and you know nothing about my past; what Ponce did to me, what Coronus did, what I lived through."

Rayne clasped his hands together to keep them from shaking, working to calm his breathing and rein in his emotions. "You have no idea how seeing Ponce again shattered me. How hard I've fought to keep the old fears and pain at bay. Seeing Coronus ..." Rayne shuddered. "I can't let him take me. I can't. If he catches me now, it's all over. And Marius saved me, shot Coronus. What do I make of that? It's all too much. I still don't even know if trusting Ponce is the right thing."

He breathed deeply. "Mite, I'm tired. I don't want to fight with you, but I can't keep going like this. If trusting Marius is what I need to do to get off Sorial, I'm going to trust him. At least for now. Nothing else matters, just getting to Arisima, putting one step in front of the other and moving forward. Don't you understand? I'm afraid if I stop moving now, I'll never fulfill the prophecy. So, Mite, I ask you again. What else could I have done?"

At first, Mite didn't respond. Then, releasing a deep sigh, he turned back to Rayne. "Mite's sorry Ray-ray. Ray-ray's right. Mite does not understand. But he will accept Ray-ray's decision. Ray-ray can trust evil dark lover if he must, but Mite will not. Mite will watch the disciple of darkness, yes, yes, yes. He will watch him for Ray-ray. But Ray-ray must also promise to be careful; it is dangerous for light to walk with darkness."

"I promise," Rayne said. "I'll trust him only as much as I need to."

Mite moved next to Rayne and gave him a gentle hug. "Mite knows. Ray-ray is afraid he will not succeed. But Ray-ray will do all the One has set for him to do. The One will give Ray-ray what he needs because his prophecies never fail. Ray-ray will see, yes, yes, yes."

Rayne looked away and mumbled, "thanks, Mite," then stiffened as he saw a figure slipping through the shadows. But when he saw a second figure behind the first, he realized Marius and Ponce were working their way to the market square. At a signal from Marius, Rayne and Mite followed.

Once they gained the deeper shadows of an empty merchant's stall Marius stopped and whispered, "What now, Sir? Shall I purchase passes for Corylus?"

Rayne looked from Ponce to Mite as a flash of lightning from an early spring storm exposed dark, bubbling clouds in the distant sky. Rayne shivered, his spirit flinching from a sensation of hateful eyes watching, as if the clouds themselves were searching for him. "Do we have enough cash left or do we need to trade another gem, Mite?"

"Low, low, funds are low. We must trade here or on Corylus. No choice, no choice."

Thunder rumbled, drowning out part of Mite's answer.

Rayne groaned at the thought of a delay on Sorial, but Ponce spoke up. "I have enough for both skips, Corylus and Arisima. We can trade on Arisima once we're there."

Rayne breathed a sigh of relief. "Thanks." He looked between Ponce and Marius and wondered how he had come to this place where he was trusting his enemies. Gritting his teeth, he said, "Ponce, go with Marius and purchase the passes for the soonest skip we can make. Mite and I will wait behind that book stall near the Corylus portal. And if we can't get passes to skip right away, Mite can trade a gem or two while we're waiting."

Ponce and Marius disappeared into the crowd. Lightning flashed again, this time brighter, closer. Rayne cringed from the flash without even realizing he was reacting. But Mite caught the movement and reached out.

"Soon," he soothed. "Ray-ray will skip away from the darkness soon. Ray-ray more aware now, feels the evil intent in the storm. Ray-ray is growing in the light, even now, even now."

Mite began humming a song Rayne remembered him singing on Nemora. He had called it a song of protection and Rayne found strength in the melody even though the words were unknown to him. He sought out his center of peace as malignant hate seemed to wind around him, like some kind of spiritual serpent trying to penetrate the protection of Mite's magic. It reminded Rayne of the thoughts that had invaded his mind a short while ago, like the tendrils of heavy magic in the cavern on Glacieria.

The air thickened as the storm moved in. By the time Ponce and Marius returned, Rayne no longer possessed the will to fight the compulsion to cower. Red-tinged lightning flashed nonstop and the rolling thunder seemed to go on forever. If not for Mite's protection, Rayne was certain the darkness seeking to take hold of him would have lured him straight into his enemies' waiting arms.

"How long?" He breathed out the question with an effort.

"Now, Sire," Ponce said, taking his elbow. "The portal direction is changing as we speak."

Ponce nodded to Mite who took hold of Rayne's other arm. With Marius leading, they moved through the crowd, their heads bowed against a wind-driven downpour that pounded them and rebounded off the paving around them. Steam rose, reducing visibility even more. Marius shifted his position to behind Rayne as they joined the line moving through the portal to Corylus.

The voices struck again. *Turn back. Turn back. Sweet, sweet rest awaits you. You need it; you want it.* Rayne began struggling. The need to turn away from the portal was so strong, he couldn't think straight. But Ponce and Mite held on, propelling him forward.

11

Once Rayne, Mite, and Ponce disappeared through the portal, Marius stepped out of the line and scanned the wind-swept but already brightening area around the portals. The storm dissolved with uncanny rapidity. Seeing the one he sought striding toward him through the sparkling clear air, Marius waved and nodded. Marius dipped his head to hide a smile as Coronus rubbed his chest and growled. "You didn't have to hit me so hard. My men are going to take weeks to recover."

"You're fine. I didn't hit you that hard," Marius shot back. "I told you that padded vest would be convincing and it worked, didn't it?"

"You just better not be lying about Sigmund's change of orders."

"Trust me," Marius said. "If you'd brought that boy to Sigmund now without the last three scrolls, the only reward you'd get is an agonizing death. As I explained, Coronus, Sigmund decided it's better to let the prince bring the scrolls to Westvale himself. Then Sigmund can destroy him and all seven scrolls at the same time.

"That's why I've made myself necessary to the old man, or should I say boy. This way I can watch the prince's every move without him even suspecting me of working for Sigmund. And this puts me in the right position to make sure that old man stays alive long enough to get back to Westvale. Don't worry, once I tell Sigmund how much help you've been, he'll reward you well. Besides, I'm sure you'll make a decent profit selling those One worshipers at auction."

"Yeah," Coronus rumbled, inadvertently mimicking the thunder now growling in the distance. "I just wish that tall woman didn't get away. She was something special, maybe even an ancient. I could have sold her for a hefty profit. But she up and disappeared just as we were going to take her."

"As much as I would love to stay and discuss your profits, I need to skip before the prince wonders what I'm up to. See you in Westvale once this is over."

"Hey." Coronus stopped Marius. "How'd you like the storm? That was really something. One of Sigmund's colleagues called it up to unhinge the prince. Did it work?"

"Yeah," Marius called back over his shoulder. "He couldn't even think straight, almost ran back to you. It was beautiful."

Marius walked into the portal just as a final distant rumble announced the end of the storm.

36

ॸ

Rayne stumbled out of the Corylus portal into the half-light of the crowded station. His head cleared as soon as he was away from the darkness, the storm, and the voices on Sorial. He caught himself on his staff, gaining his balance and breathing in great gulps. Mite stood in front of him and Ponce behind, but when he looked back to the portal for Marius, he was not among those stepping out.

Mite moved to Rayne's side and looked up at him with concern, "Ray-ray okay now?"

A wavering smile flickered across Rayne's face. "Yeah, Mite. Ray-ray is better now."

"That storm was a product of magic," Ponce muttered, scanning the crowded station.

"No ordinary storm. No, no," Mite said. "Born of darkness, that was, yes, yes, yes. Aimed at Ray-ray. Hurry, hurry, Ponce-man. Must hurry now."

Rayne glanced back toward the Sorial portal, wondering if Marius changed his mind about joining them, then looked back to Ponce, "Mite's right. We can't stay here. I think we're being watched. It's not like what I felt in Emporium City just now, but ... it's evil. I feel it."

"Yes, yes, yes," Mite agreed. "Darkness here, too. And something else." Mite paused, face raised to the sky, eyes closed. "Deep darkness comes. Powerful, powerful. Far off now, far off, but coming. Coming soon."

"Mite?"

"Yes Ray-ray."

"You're going to have to buy the passes for Arisima. Ponce can't do it here in Westvale and neither can I."

Mite looked around and a satisfied smile lit his face. "Only three, three, three. Bad dark lover not come through portal. Yes. Yes. Yes."

Mite's smile soured when Marius emerged from the portal. "Noooo. Ray-ray, please leave the disciple of darkness here. Do not bring him to Arisima. Please."

Marius approached, and Mite turned on him. "What was Marius doing after Mite, Ponce-man, and Ray-ray skipped? Servant of darkness talking to his master. I know, I know. Bad, bad, bad man. Servant of darkness."

Rayne stepped between Mite and Marius. "Thank you for your help back there Marius. You saved us and got us off Sorial. But I trust Mite. If he says to leave you here, then that's what I'm going to do. He's been looking out for me since we met on Nemora and I won't ignore his warning. So, thank you for all you've done. I release you from your pledge." Rayne looked down at Mite who smiled in relief. "Mite, would you please go and buy three passes for Arisima?"

Marius watched, his expression tight, as Ponce helped Rayne to a secluded bench. Mite scurried away through the thin crowd, heading toward the sign announcing Pass Sales. After Mite was out of sight, Marius walked up to Rayne. Squaring his shoulders, he said, "I won't leave you, you know. If I can't travel *with* you, I'll follow." He shook his head and frowned. "Like I said back on Sorial, I owe you a lot and I can't in good conscience let you go skipping to a place like Arisima alone. Excuse me for being blunt, but you three aren't exactly good at defending yourselves. In fact, you have easy targets written all over you. You need me."

"You've been to Arisima?" Ponce asked.

"I've been there a few times," Marius said with a confident swagger. "It's not the easiest place to travel. If the desert doesn't get you, the pirates will. Traveling there with your unique little friend and no protection would be like waving a flag in their faces and saying, 'hey, come attack us. Our little friend will fetch a nice price on the auction block.'"

He paused and looked Rayne and Ponce over then pointed at Ponce. "You they might keep alive. Probably get something for you 'cause you look like you could be a decent clerk." He turned to Rayne. "But you? They'll just kill you outright. You have no material value. Nobody travels on Arisima without protection, nobody. I don't want to see you dead, Sir. So, if you don't take me with you, be prepared. Every time you look behind you, I'll be there."

Marius's demeanor had changed, and Rayne was now convinced that Mite was right about the man. But, was it better to have the enemy traveling with them so he and Mite could keep an eye on him, or to let the man roam freely at their backs? Deciding it was better keeping Marius close, Rayne said, "Go, get yourself a pass. But be quick about it."

With a smirk and a tilt of his head, Marius sprinted in the direction Mite had vanished.

"I don't think it's wise to have that man with us," Ponce said. "I agree with Mite; the man serves Sigmund. I worked for that demon long enough to recognize those who seek dark favor."

"You're right, Ponce. And so is Mite"

"Then why ..."

Rayne held up his hand. "Better the enemy you can see than the one lurking at your back. Thorvin taught me that. As long as Marius thinks he has me fooled, we should be okay. But you and Mite will need to keep a close watch on him."

Minutes later, a scowling Mite returned with Marius on his heels. Mite gave Rayne a hurt look and then stood off by himself, pouting. As they couldn't skip for another hour, Rayne sent Marius to find a vendor near the portal station who would be willing to pay a fair price for two of their gems. While Marius was gone, Rayne explained the situation to Mite who, though not happy about Marius joining them, agreed it was better than having the man at their back.

"Mite, while we're waiting, roam around the station. Keep your ears open and see if you can learn anything about what's happening here in Westvale. Especially any news about the king and queen."

After Mite left, Ponce stood at the side of the bench, blocking Rayne from prying eyes, scanning the crowd. Rayne closed his eyes and rested his head against the back of the bench.

Just being in the Westvale portal station brought back memories of the last time Rayne had been here with Thorvin. He had been so full of hope then, looking forward to reuniting with his parents. Knowing everyone he cared about was so close and yet not being able to see any of them was tearing at him. If he could be certain he wouldn't be recognized, he would take the time now to walk to the Great Square, sit on one of the benches near the palace, and watch to catch sight of his parents or friends.

He missed Shaw, and Sashi and Stevie, all his good friends. He thought about Anne and Shaw and wondered if they had returned to Westvale or had gone back to Cashel. He even missed Thorvin, more than he would admit. Visions of Lexi invaded his thoughts. He could see her beautiful golden eyes and the way her heavy golden hair would fall out from under the hat she had worn on Veres.

With his eyes closed, the images flitted. He heard her voice as she screamed in delight and laughed when swimming with the orphans on Amathea. He wanted so badly to see her, it hurt. He wanted to see his mother and father, feel their love once again. And even though he nurtured a tiny hope Mite would return with good news and things might change, he understood that reality would shatter the fragile hope. He knew with certainty, he was running out of time.

Rayne awoke to the sound of soft voices. Mite had returned and was telling Ponce what he learned about recent happenings in Westvale. Rayne kept his eyes closed, curious to hear what Mite would tell Ponce that he might not tell Rayne.

"Darkness, darkness coming across water," Mite was saying. "Much anger and fear fill people of capital, yes, yes, yes. Darkness sends bad thoughts. Newcomers fight. Bad, bad."

"And what about the prince? What is Sigmund doing about it?" Ponce asked.

"Prince and regent have been on Nemora. Returned this morning. Big, big news. Council all dead. Court all dead. King and queen sick. Now evil prince take all power. No one to stop him. Only Ray-ray. Ray-ray will stop the living darkness. Bad, bad, bad. The darkness grows strong. Maybe too strong." Mite paused and was silent for a moment. Rayne could imagine him shaking his head. "No. Mite will not lose hope. This is of darkness; darkness takes away hope. Mite will trust the One. Yes, yes, yes."

"Are you all ready?" Marius's voice sounded from Rayne's other side, causing his eyes to spring open.

"Where have you been?" Ponce asked, his tone angry. "The skipping line changed direction almost an hour ago."

Marius shrugged. "It took some time to find a fair price for those gems."

Rayne rose stiffly. With both hands clasping the staff, he limped toward the Arisima portal. He didn't speak or look around but moved with a certain focus. Mite ran ahead of him, presenting their passes to the busy portal attendant as Rayne stepped though without pause. His mind was now fixed firmly on Arisima and his purpose. He wouldn't allow himself to lose focus again. With the help of the One, he would put an end to this growing darkness. Then, if he survived, he would think about those he loved.

37

Sigmund strode from the Westvale Portal Station to the large palomino stallion waiting for him in the Station Square, ignoring the waiting crowd. His time on Nemora had been profitable even if the skip had been at the command of the now-defunct Interplanetary Council. He still bristled when he recalled how they accused him of overstepping his bounds when he executed alleged traitors without even bringing them before the Interplanetary Court.

"Your authority extends only to carrying out executions once the accused have been tried and the Interplanetary Court has passed sentence," old man Stewart, representative from Amathea and head of the council, proclaimed in his high nasal voice that had irritated Sigmund for years. Well, it would seem they were the ones to overstep their bounds, and now, Sigmund thought with satisfaction, they were all dead.

Things had gone according to Sigmund's and Heinrich's plans, from the sudden deaths of every council member and judge, to the panic of the remaining officials who, without warning, found themselves without leadership. Fear spread like a wild fire as well-placed rumors of poisoning began to circulate.

Before the situation escalated any further, Heinrich stepped forward as the Interplanetary Council's own Lord Master Mage, and a voice of reason. Heinrich's performance was brilliant, and Sigmund smiled as he recalled how his colleague made a great show of investigating the circumstances before proclaiming the deaths natural.

"It is with extreme sorrow that I report all fifteen council members, all seven judges, as well as several of those serving dinner at the party held in Lord Stewart's house, have succumbed to this virulent illness. Though the whole situation is unimaginable, I have found no evidence of foul play. It was all an unfortunate and wretched coincidence." Heinrich had been most persuasive.

Once people were convinced it was not an attack on the council and court, but an outbreak of an unidentified virus, fear of more deaths from the mysterious illness began to take hold. Anyone who could, rushed to leave Council City. But Sigmund's finest performance was just about to begin. As the panic was escalating, young Prince Rayne had humbly stepped forward and said, "I am not afraid."

Terrified individuals, even Duke and Duchess Woodfield watched as the slight young prince walked into the house of death and dined in the room where the deaths had occurred. He then made a public appearance on the lawn of Senior Councilor Stewart's house to quell the fears. Sigmund's spies reported that everyone who came to hear the prince agreed, he was a brave young man who would make a strong and worthy king. Sigmund had the citizens of Nemora right where he wanted them.

Later, dressed in a uniform of the Interplanetary Council's honor guard, Sigmund once again addressed the assembled crowd, this time from the balcony of the council building where Senior Councilor Stewart had stood just three days before. Brayden Woodfield, Regent of Corylus, stood on his right, and the Lord Master Mage on his left, lending their authority to the address.

With the commanding bearing of a true Kierkengaard descendant, His Royal Highness spoke in a clear, ringing voice.

"Though I am young and unworthy to claim this level of power, I cannot in good conscience leave the people of Ochen without strong leadership. With the serious nature of the situation now upon us, I have no alternative but to declare the right of my heritage. This is not something I chose. It is, rather, a duty I will not shirk because of my love for my people.

"I, by the authority of my position as Royal Heir, do proclaim myself Emperor of All Ochen until such time as that position is no longer necessary. I will do my best to make Ochen strong again. The people of Ochen are my people and their welfare is my highest priority."

Prior to his official speech, Sigmund had taken the step of revealing his true identity to certain influential individuals whom he had spent years grooming to support his bid for power. Whether through promise of reward or promise of punishment, he also called in multiple favors, assuring the prince's offer would be accepted on all seven worlds without question.

Once again reviewing the events of the past week, Sigmund congratulated himself. *Of course, things would have gone differently if Wren had just stayed ignorant of his heritage and obeyed like a good little slave. But as the revised plans have moved forward so smoothly, I am most pleased.*

Upon returning to Westvale this morning, Sigmund drew a hefty dose of magic energy from the advancing darkness. It was finally happening; his plans were all falling into place. After his announcement in Council City the fools whom he had positioned to secure his claim immediately began falling all over themselves to offer him their complete support.

Oh, yes. He nodded, stretching as the dark energy built in him. *There is no one left with the power to stop me now. Soon my master will arrive, and all will be ready.*

His Royal Highness reclined on a deep couch in his suite with his feet resting on a finely crafted wooden table before him. Flames leaped upward from the intense fire blazing in the cool autumn evening. Setting his glass of honeyed sherry on the table to his right, he said, "Once again, your ability to predict the actions of these humans has proven itself, Heinrich. First, on Nemora; now here on Corylus. Thorvin did exactly as you predicted. He took the bait without hesitation and now I just need to be patient a bit longer to get the names of the other traitors in our midst."

Heinrich raised his glass to Sigmund in acknowledgement of the compliment.

"How did you know he would take the chance and hold an audience even though my brother forbade it?" Giles asked.

Heinrich swirled his drink. "It's what he is. The man can't help but do the thing that must be done. He feels compelled by his sense of duty and honor. And, just like it has for so many comparable men in the past, it will prove his undoing."

"What are you going to do with him?" Giles asked.

"For now, nothing," Sigmund said. "I'll let him think he's gotten away with his little strategic maneuver. If those rebels think they're safe, the more likely they are to make a mistake. The longer the rope I give them, the sweeter my final move will be. And with my position now solidified as the sole political head of all Ochen, they have no chance of succeeding in whatever plans they pursue. Besides, when our broken prince returns, as I'm sure he will soon, I suspect the people he will go to for help are those very individuals we've been watching."

"Are you going to have any more of those inflammatory messages scrawled?" Brayden asked in a slurred voice. "From what I've heard since our return, that mutilated body caused quite a stir."

Brayden downed the remains of his drink and snapped his fingers at a diminutive slave girl standing quietly in the corner. He motioned for her to bring him more. When the girl came near with the filled glass, he caught her arm and pulled her down onto his lap.

Smiling, Sigmund watched Brayden run his hands familiarly over the trembling slave. "I think our messages are doing admirably well. Several more well-placed messages accompanied by mutilated bodies should solidify the fear. When I announce we have caught the fiends responsible and hang those loyal to the prince as traitors, the populace will bow at my feet."

Brayden let the girl go but as she tried to rise, he grabbed her wrist and twisting her around, back-handed her across the face, splitting her lip.

"Behave, slave," he snarled as he pulled her back down. While holding her, he gulped from his glass, sloshing wine on himself and the girl. Ignoring the now quiet girl, Brayden looked back up at Sigmund. "Have you decided how we should address you now that you are the prime ruler of Ochen?"

Sigmund pursed his lips in thought for a moment before a broad smile spread across his face. "I believe I would like the title of Imperial Majesty. What do you think? Say it, Brayden. Call me by my new title."

Brayden attempted to focus his bleary eyes on Sigmund. "I believe I will leave your presence now, Your Imperial Majesty, to more properly train this most-tasty little slave girl in my rooms. If that meets with your approval, Your Imperial Majesty."

"Yes, I do like the sound of that." Sigmund saluted Brayden. "And yes, you are dismissed. Enjoy your play my friend. If I didn't have so much on my mind, I'd join you."

Though the girl had stopped struggling, she sobbed quietly as Brayden lifted her over his shoulder and stumbled out the door with Sigmund's and Heinrich's laughter trailing him.

"One of these days I'm going to have to possess that young man," Sigmund said. "He and I could have such fun together. His appetites are so marvelously insatiable. But for the time being, I must remain in this body."

He flexed an arm. "It is indeed a beautiful body, responsive, healthy, and young. And with its help, soon all humans on Ochen will be mine, to use as I please. I look forward to meeting the boy again and showing him all he has helped me achieve."

"Am I one of the humans you plan to enslave?" Giles asked, raising an eyebrow.

A sly grin wormed across Sigmund's lips. "Those who are *perferred* friends of the Emperor, like you my young friend, are quite safe. That is what you wanted to know, isn't it?"

Giles nodded. "Yes, that's what I wanted to know." Looking back to Sigmund he continued. "Brayden is regent here on Corylus, but what about me? Are you planning to give me a position too, or will I just continue following you around like some kind of lap dog?"

Sigmund released a loud and lengthy laugh. "Now I like that. What do you think, Heinrich? Giles is finally growing some teeth."

Sigmund pierced Giles with a discerning look. "I thought you enjoyed being an irresponsible lap dog, but if you want responsibility I can make that happen."

Giles frowned and downed the remains of his drink. "Don't bother. I'm fine just as I am. No responsibility. I'm quite content being a lap dog for the most powerful man in the system. It suits me. I am, after all, a rather worthless individual."

Sigmund and Heinrich laughed.

There was a quiet knock at the door and Sigmund looked to Giles who called out, "What?"

"Sire," a guard's voice sounded through the door. "There's a man here claiming you're expecting him."

Giles sauntered to the door and opened it. "Who is it?"

"He says his name is Marius and he's a friend of His Royal Highness."

Sigmund ground his teeth. "Tomorrow we make the announcement of my new position and title. I am no longer just a Royal Highness and the sooner everyone knows that, the sooner they will honor me as Imperial Majesty." He paused, then said to Giles. "Have Marius shown in. I'm curious as to why he would be here this soon."

After the guard closed the door behind him, Marius bowed to Sigmund. "Thank you for receiving me so quickly, I don't have much time. Oh, and I will need to exchange these for sommes." He held out two gems. "We need funds to skip."

Sigmund motioned for Giles to take the gems. After Giles left the room, Sigmund shifted his focus back on Marius. "*We* need funds? Should I take this to mean you've convinced the prince to allow you to travel with him?"

Marius walked to the sideboard and poured himself a generous glass of wine before walking back to Sigmund and sitting on the arm of the chair Brayden had occupied earlier.

He took a sip and sighed. "Of course, my lord. What better way to keep my prey in sight? He doesn't fully trust me, but with some help from an old friend of yours on Sorial I was able to prove my value as a traveling companion."

Sigmund raised his eyebrows. "Who?"

"Van Coronus. He's been working for Lord William for a while now and when I informed him the broken prince was in Emporium City, he was most eager to see the boy trapped in his current state. At first, he was set on collecting the sizeable bounty you promised for the old man, but I convinced him your plans had changed and now you were best served if the prince remained free for the time being. He asked that I inform you of his willingness to aid you in any way he could.

"We arranged a situation where the prince and his traveling companions would be captured by Coronus, setting the stage for me to rescue them. Coronus was rather put out at losing not only the bounty on the old man but also another little man traveling with the prince. Someone from your past."

"Tell me, who was this man with the prince?" Sigmund's eyes glittered as he considered who from his past would be traveling with the prince now.

"The prince calls him Ponce, a wormy little man. I don't think he trusts this Ponce much more than he trusts me, but they are traveling together, along with a child-like creature from Nemora."

Sigmund pulled in a breath and Heinrich asked, "Is this Ponce a rubiate?"

Marius frowned. "I don't think so. He and the prince talked of believing in the enemy. And when we sprang our trap, the prince and Ponce were meeting with other believers. But, now that I think of it, I believe Coronus did refer to him as Sigmund's personal rubiate."

"Well," Sigmund sat up straight and grinned at Heinrich. "It looks as if our young friend will be returning with more than the scrolls. My dear old friend, Ponce. Imagine that. The boy traveling with the rubiate who tried to turn him. Quite remarkable. I look forward to renewing my relationship with that traitor."

Sigmund closed his eyes. "I only wish I could have seen Ponce's reaction when he realized his grandfather is dead and his body is now the host for that troublesome prince he loved to abuse."

Sigmund purred, deep in his throat, remembering. His eyelids fluttered shut as a vision of sweet revenge flamed to life in his mind. He glanced over at Heinrich, his mind focused on the past. "Ponce was so talented at wringing sweet screams from his playthings, but when he tasted the prince, though, there were no screams." Sigmund chuckled. "But that silence was deafening."

He paused again as he contemplated his plans for Rayne and Ponce. "I've been thinking. As I've made no outright commitment to hand my slave over to our master ... immediately ... I've decided it would be more entertaining to keep him and my rubiate, at least for a bit."

Sigmund licked his lips. "You will appreciate this, Heinrich, as will our young friend Brayden. You've both waited so long to spend some quality time with our enemy's chosen. The boy will return with those last three odious scrolls soon. I will destroy them and defeat the prophecy. Then, Heinrich, you will have the opportunity to study that peculiar fusion of old body and chosen spirit at the border between life and death, just as you've hoped. And, while you're amusing yourself with the prince, Brayden and I can oversee Ponce's retraining. We'll reduce him to the animalistic, blood loving, rubiate I enjoyed so much.

"Once you've finished your experiments and that old-man body is past use, I'll proclaim Brayden Imperial Emperor and possess him, granting him his wish for immortality. That should make the power-hungry fool happy. With the spirit of the failed Light Bringer returned to this body, I'll make him my slave again, and turn Ponce loose on him just like before."

Sigmund smiled and licked his lips. "What joy. At last I'll get to hear that stubborn slave scream. Maybe even be able to touch him without pain. Think of it, Heinrich. Then, when we grow bored, we can present the remains of the failed *Light Bringer* to our master. We will receive renown and praise among our colleagues for delivering that prize. But Ponce, Ponce I will keep for myself. I'll train him to serve me again, but this time as my slave. He'll curse the day he betrayed me."

Sigmund closed his eyes, lost in the pleasure of his day-dreams.

Heinrich's lips flattened, and he stared at Sigmund through slitted eyelids. "Take care, Sigmund. Our master does not appreciate leftovers in the guise of coveted prizes."

Sigmund's eyes popped open and he snarled.

Heinrich raised both hands in a calming gesture. "Think! Do you really want to present our master with a damaged prize? I will not be punished for your obsession with the prince. I will not back you on this."

"Of course. Of course. As usual your *concern* for me is admirable." Sparks flew between Heinrich and Sigmund and heavy magic built in the room. The moment passed, and the pressure eased. Once again in control, Sigmund inclined his head to Heinrigh, then turned to Marius. "What else can you tell me?"

Marius gulped down the last of his wine and began to pace. "I could tell you that if you wanted to take your prey now, the prince and Ponce are in the Corylus portal station at this moment waiting to skip to Arisima."

"He has reclaimed the scrolls to Nemora *and* Sorial? Of course he has. I felt the power release. Excellent." Sigmund stood and paced in front of the fire. "And how is the old body holding up?"

"It appears to be failing. Back on Nemora I think he was close to death at one point. He was quite weak when I first saw him. But the Kindred nursed him for more than a month in Neth. When he left Nemora, he was stronger. That strength was just temporary, though. Between sickness and age, the body is weakening again. The medicine no longer sustains him as it once did."

Sigmund stopped pacing and turned to face Marius, an unfamiliar sensation of concern rising in him. "Will he be able to reclaim the Arisima scroll and return here?"

Marius shrugged. "I don't know. If we don't find it soon,

I would say no. I don't think that worn out old body will last much longer. But if we can locate the scroll quickly, then it is possible he will reclaim it and bring it here. From what I've seen, the prince has an unusually strong will for a human. If it's resilient enough, he may be able to push that body beyond its limitations by sheer will power alone."

Sigmund turned to Heinrich. "What's the situation currently like on Arisima?"

Heinrich swirled the amber liquid in his glass, watching as it caught the light. After a moment, he said, "Since you initiated the accelerated campaign nearly eighteen months ago, almost fifty percent of the population is now worshiping the Scroll of Power on Arisima. However, there are entrenched pockets of enemy worshipers left, especially among the old communities of study. Those citizens not connected to either side resent the violence the scroll worshippers have spawned but they are too afraid to stand up to them.

"The pirates are still a problem. They answer to no one and they have grown bolder lately, even flying their desert ships near the capital. They refuse to negotiate or to accept anything to do with scroll worship although they've never embraced worship of our enemy either. If you remember, as their actions were helpful in increasing feelings of fear in the general populace, we have, for the last nine months, followed a hands-off policy, allowing them to continue preying on whomever they choose.

"The darkness is spreading more slowly than expected. I suspect it has something to do with the strength of belief among the residents of those resistant pockets."

As Giles walked back into the room jiggling a weighty coin purse, Sigmund said to Marius, "For now, I leave things in your hands. But if you do not return with my prizes, not hosting one of my colleagues will be the least of your worries."

Marius bowed. "Understood, my lord. I will not fail." Taking the purse from Giles he slipped out the door.

38

The church house dining room echoed as everyone talked over each other in their excitement, and each person strove to personally greet their long-awaited friends. Anne, seeing how tired Shaw and the twins looked, mentioned it to Elsie, who took control, insisting the travelers sit while she reheated food that had grown cold. Though the three travelers were hungry and exhausted, they took turns explaining all that happened on Glacieria and why they had been gone so long.

Even Sashi's seemingly boundless energy was noticeably absent as she yawned and said in a monotone, "Nemora's moons, Thorvin, not one of us was willing to go back through that tunnel even if it meant spending more than two weeks traveling around the mountain."

Once Elsie had three, heavily laden, plates warmed to her standards, she brought them out to the table. Shaw, looking around, asked, "Where's Jonathan? I need to tell him what we learned."

"Jonathan's in Centerville," Thorvin said. While the hungry travelers ate, the others began telling the travelers the latest news. Noting how tired they looked, Thorvin kept the news to a minimum.

"So, with Regent Woodfield's new restrictions limiting our ability to meet safely as a group, Councilor Danton and I set up a communication chain," Thorvin said. "We figured it this way. Elsie, Anne, and Lexi should continue meeting mornings like nothing's changed. Anne can pass on any news she gets to Shaw. Either Noah or I can stop in to see Elsie daily and one of us can connect with the Kaspers and Andrew. Travis and Deven still take meals with the church staff so they see Elsie daily. That makes Elsie the central contact if anyone needs to spread news quickly."

After explaining the information chain, Thorvin suggested that with all the unrest and increased violence in the city, everyone should head home before it got any later. No one objected.

Noah volunteered to escort the Kaspers home and Thorvin offered to join him.

"Give me a minute," he said, waving for Anne to step away from the others. Clearing his throat and looking a little uncomfortable, Thorvin asked, "How hard would it be to find out what's in that medicine the mage is feeding King Theodor?"

Anne pursed her lips, tapping them with a finger, her brow crinkling. "You must be thinking the same thing I am. It shouldn't be too hard. I just need to get a sample before the Lord Master Mage returns."

"Good. Do it if you can. But don't take any chances."

Her small familiar smile appearing, Anne leaned in and reaching up, planted a sisterly kiss on Thorvin's cheek. "I'll be careful," she said, then added, "Thorvin, I think you should know, I won't be able to meet with Elsie for the next several days. Shaw and I need some time to ourselves. Between that and my duties at the palace and now, trying to get a sample of the Lord Master Mage's tincture ... well, I hope you understand?"

He nodded. "Of course. For now, Lexi will keep you and Shaw informed if anything important comes up."

Anne moved back to take Shaw's arm, and as everyone was leaving, Lexi caught her eyes and inclined her head toward Noah and Sashi. Looking over, Anne noticed the two holding hands. She glanced back at Lexi and grinned, happy to share her joy at the return of the travelers.

A short while later Anne followed a drooping Shaw into their cottage; she realized how truly tired he was when he tripped over the small step. But he insisted on shaving and taking a bath before they went to bed.

Anne snuggled up against his warm back, breathing in the fragrance of the soap he always used. With Shaw back, Anne slept more deeply than she had in weeks, until the sound of a ringing bell shattered her sleep. *Oh no. What now?*

Soon after Shaw and the twins skipped to Glacieria, Regent Woodfield had instituted the early morning bell as a call alerting the citizens of Westvale that he would be speaking in the Great Square at sunrise. The last time the bell rang, they had been summoned to the executions of the twelve men accused of painting the traitorous messages.

Anne groaned. She had hoped Shaw could sleep in this morning and she could surprise him by making him fresh bread. But even more, the bell never signaled good news.

Shaking Shaw's shoulder, Anne whispered, "Shaw, you must get up. I'm sorry but that ridiculous bell of Regent Wood-field's has just rung. We need to eat and get dressed then head to the Great Square."

"What bell?" Shaw mumbled as he wiped sleep from his eyes.

Anne explained about the summons and their need to be in the Great Square in the next hour. After dressing and grabbing a cold breakfast, Shaw and Anne joined the throng filing into the square. In the pre-sunrise twilight, the area was filling rapidly. The tension was palpable as emotions ran high and Anne prayed there would be no violence. Apparently, the regent was thinking violence was unavoidable; scores of mounted soldiers were stationed around the edges of the square. Whatever the regent was going to announce, he was prepared for a violent reaction.

Lexi's right. Anne thought as she and Shaw were jostled from behind. *That dark cloud is influencing everyone in Westvale. Please, Blessed One, keep us all safe. Protect your people from the foul influence of this approaching darkness. Wherever Rayne is now, whether he is trapped in his body or somewhere on the seven, please let him bring your light back to your people. We are stumbling in the darkness.*

As Shaw and Anne moved closer to the platform, Lexi and Thorvin joined them.

"Nice homecoming, eh, Shaw?" Thorvin asked, disgust furrowing the lines of his face.

"How often does this happen?" Shaw asked.

"As often as Regent Woodfield wants." Thorvin's voice rumbled. "Did Anne tell you what happened the last time we were summoned?"

"Yes," Shaw shuddered. "Those poor people. She also told me about the new development of the messages painted in blood and bodies left at the scene. Do you have any idea who's doing this?"

"At this point, not a clue," Thorvin answered as they watched Regent Woodfield strut across the platform.

"My fellow citizens." Brayden's voice echoed off the buildings surrounding the square. "It is with both profound sadness and immense pleasure I call you here this day."

He paused and scanned the square. A strange expression tweaked his lips then disappeared. "This morning we join with all the people of Ochen in mourning the deaths of the members of both the Interplanetary Council and the Interplanetary Court. A few days ago they were taken by a sudden, inexplicable illness that struck while they were dining together at Senior Councilor Stewart's home outside Council City."

A wave of shock and murmuring crashed through the crowded square. Brayden held up his hands in a supplication for quiet. When the level of noise dropped, he continued. "All across Ochen, people like you are hearing the news and wondering what will become of us now. Who will step forward to snatch us from chaos? Who will come to our aid and lead us in this time of loss? Who will save us?

"Last week, the Interplanetary Council requested that His Royal Highness, Prince Rayne, and I join them for a special meeting. It was with great humility that we met with them to discuss future plans for Ochen. Then, just two days later, while we were still visiting family in Inverness, we received news of the calamity. We groaned as the weight of this tragedy that has left all the inhabitants of Ochen orphans, descended upon us."

He paused, as the murmuring once again rose in volume. This time he gave the crowd a few minutes to settle before continuing.

"This is bad." Anne heard Thorvin mumble. "This is really bad."

Anne, Lexi, Shaw, and Thorvin exchanged glances. Then Brayden was speaking again.

"But fear not, stricken orphans of Ochen. For we are not without hope. Our very own prince, His Royal Highness, Prince Rayne of all Ochen, has stepped into the gap for his people. Though it is against his very nature to grab power for himself, he has agreed to take on the title of Emperor, so you, his people would not be cast to the wind like foundlings with no leadership or protection. He is our savior!"

There was a stirring in the crowd as a figure appeared on the platform as if out of thin air.

"His Imperial Majesty, Emperor Rayne Kierkengaard!" Regent Woodfield shouted as Rayne, clothed in armor of gold and a flowing cape of gold with an iridescent purple lining strode with majestic grace across the platform. He looked bigger than life, his eyes reflecting the color of the cape lining, his hair a loose mane of midnight black around his shoulders.

"All bow!" Regent Woodfield shouted.

Horror, like a leaden lump, soured Anne's stomach as people by the hundreds began kneeling and bowing to the golden emperor. Then, from the edge of the crowd, a woman shouted, "Where is the Light Bringer? We want the Light Bringer! We need words of truth and we need protection from the coming darkness, not a phony emperor! People of West-vale, don't you see ..."

But her words were cut off as two of the soldiers closest to the woman rode to her. One drew his sword and slammed the hilt down on her head. The second grabbed the uncon-scious woman and flung her over his saddle. The air grew heavy and time itself seemed frozen as the guards disappeared around the side of the palace with the woman.

For a brief moment, silence reigned, then angry voices rose, echoing in imitation of the regent's announcement minutes earlier. His Imperial Majesty raised his hands for quiet; his golden presence demanding confidence. The voices silenced.

"My beloved people." His smooth-as-silk voice stretched over the square like a comforting blanket. "Do not let the mistaken notions of one poor deceived woman lead you astray. I am your protector, your kind and loving father. Trust me and I will serve you like no other. Be at peace. Disperse now to your homes and businesses. Do not be anxious. I will speak to you again soon. Remember I am your savior. Trust me."

Then he and Regent Woodfield left the platform, mounted horses, and made their way to the main entrance of the palace surrounded by a contingent of palace guards.

Hopeful voices sounded as the sun's first beams broke over the black horizon.

"He's so kind."

"Our emperor will protect us."

"Our savior has come."

"The golden emperor, our father."

Anne trembled, despair seeping into her bones.

"We need to talk," Thorvin snarled before marching away, growling to himself.

As Anne watched, he disappeared into the crowd. *Yes. We need to talk. Blessed One, please save us!*

Looking up, she was surprised to see Bishop Hedrick; he must have just returned from Centerville. He looked old and stricken as he stared off toward where the emperor had just disappeared into the palace, his eyes glazed. He caught Anne's eyes and shook his head before turning. His shoulders stooped and his back bent, Anne watched Jonathan walk slowly toward the church grounds.

39

Ponce, Mite, and Marius followed Rayne out of the skipping portal on Arisima, blending in with the throng of people streaming in from the surrounding portals. Rayne stopped short. Nothing had prepared him for the size and splendor of the portal station in Zoraya, the capital of Arisima.

The cool beauty of the station filled him with its calm wonder. The walls were smooth stucco, stained in a random pattern; muted shades of gold, bronze, and burnt umber drew his eyes. Brightly colored artwork decorated the walls between large copper sconces holding massive, spicy-scented candles. Craning his neck, he studied the ceiling. Wide planks of well-polished burgundy-colored wood were held in place by dark, heavy timber beams. The floor was tiled in a geometric pattern in hues mimicking the colors on the walls, but with the addition of bright blue tiles interspersed. Well-dressed people were scattered through the station, talking in small groups or sitting, sipping drinks on oversized, leather chairs. This was not what he expected.

"This isn't anything like what Shaw described," Rayne whispered. Mite looked as stunned as he felt.

Marius chuckled. "I guess no one told you. Arisima has become the world of choice for those who can afford to vacation here."

Rayne's eyes grew larger. "No. From what Shaw told me, I expected dry empty desert and small religious communities of studious monks."

"You'll find that too," Marius said. "Arisima is mostly what you've described, dry, sandy, desert. But it also has areas of intense fertility over pockets of underground water called oases. The city of Zoraya is set over the largest of these underground lakes. Walk a short distance away from an oasis and you'll find hot, dry days and freezing, inhospitable nights. But where the water and vegetation moderate the changes, the temperatures remain most comfortable both day and night.

"The first people to understand the value of this situation were several powerful Sorial merchants. Initially, they just used Arisima as a personal vacation resort. But then, they realized the profits they could make by building complexes and spreading the word of the beauty and comfort to be had here. Now, they own most of the larger vacation complexes not only in Zoraya, but in the other oases close to the capital."

Rayne noticed Ponce giving him a curious look. "What?"

"You don't remember, do you?"

"Remember what?"

Ponce released a ragged sigh. "Nothing."

Rayne's chest grew tight as the truth sank in. "I've been here before, haven't I?"

Without turning to face Rayne, Ponce nodded. "Sigmund and I brought you once and Coronus had you here a couple times. When the wealthy and powerful came to Arisima to relax or party, they tended to have looser security. This was a good place for assassinations, until people caught on and increased security." He paused, guilt deepening the lines around his eyes. "The games here rival those on Veres. Keep those memories buried. It's better if you don't revisit your times here."

Rayne stared at Ponce for a minute, his mind chipping at old walls of protection. "Better for me or better for you?" Stifling his loathing, Rayne turned from Ponce and asked Marius,

"Where would you suggest we stay while I decide my next move?"

Marius smiled broadly. "With your funds, we can afford the luxury of the best place here. Besides, you could really do with some pampering, you look like crap, Sir. My recommendation is the Sterling Pony Resort."

"No." Ponce practically shouted. "No, not there."

Rayne, Marius, and Mite all looked at him and Ponce said, "Sigmund and Lord William own that place."

"You're right, it's best to avoid any place where we might be recognized." Focusing on Marius, Rayne said, "Someplace reasonable. I wasn't given these gems to stay in luxury, but to use wisely as needed."

Marius scowled his dissatisfaction and looked as if he was going to protest. Gripping his staff as frustration built within him, Rayne turned to back Ponce. "What do you suggest?"

Ponce looked down at the floor. "I know an inn not far from here. If it hasn't changed, it should be reasonable and clean, with good food."

Rayne took his time, moving through the city, taking in the sights of Zoraya. *How could Shaw have failed to tell me how beautiful this place is?* He caught sight of a waterfall to his right. A red rock formation that rose to a height of more than thirty feet stood in the center of a large open square at the end of the street. The water splashed, clean and sparkling, out of a small cave-like opening near the top, down into a green-tinged pool surrounded by sand, orange rocks, and stately trees. The tall trees were unlike any other trees Rayne remembered. Single trunks grew upward almost to the height of the rock formation before spreading out large compound leaves in all directions, like a mop of unruly hair. People sat at tables set around the pool, colorful umbrellas sheltering them from the sun as they ate. The buzz of conversations filled the air, mingling with the chatter of falling water.

Curious, Rayne swerved away from Ponce and walked past the tables toward the water. A large man in an understated, well-tailored, blue uniform stepped in front of him. Looking Rayne up and down and wrinkling his nose, he said, "What do you think you're doing? You don't intimidate me, and I'll not allow you to disturb the guests with your crazy talk. Leave now Vagrant before I call the patrol and have you arrested."

Mite's face turned deep red. He stammered as if ready to spew something caustic, until Rayne rested a hand on his shoulder, and said, "Yes, sir. Sorry to have caused a problem. I've not been on Arisima before and was drawn by the water. My apologies."

Ponce scurried over with Marius strutting behind. Mite stared up at the guard, his mouth twisted in disgust, hands on his hips. "Green water not so nice as blue water of Nemora. Mite not want to see stinky green water anyway, no, no, no."

"Please excuse my young friend." Rayne kept his voice soft, controlled, as he turned from the man and the waterfall. "His manners tend to disappear when he's angry."

"Don't come back here again, you filthy Vagrant," the man shouted as Ponce turned to follow. Marius stood for a moment and waved a large stack of sommes under the man's nose, then flashed a smile before swaggering away.

They passed several more eating establishments set around the green, tree-shaded pools beneath sparkling waterfalls. Wanting to avoid any undue attention another incident would bring, Rayne stifled the urge to take a closer look. He and Mite stayed close behind Ponce until they reached the inn.

Though small and plain, the Green Palms Inn was, as Ponce had promised, clean and neat. Savory aromas drifted across a narrow common room from what must have been the kitchen. The proprietor stood behind a tall desk near the door and looked up over small glasses balanced precariously on the edge of his long, narrow nose. He pinched his lips as he watched Rayne and his companions enter, suspicion evident in his deep, black eyes.

Rayne and Mite stayed by the door, allowing Ponce and Marius to approach the man.

Ponce took the lead. "Sir, we're looking for two adjoining rooms for the next couple nights."

The man looked Ponce and Marius over, but glancing back to Rayne, he said, "Please, I want no trouble, but I don't rent rooms to Vagrants. There's free housing offered farther down the street at the edge of town."

With a confused look, Ponce said, "Sir, we're quite willing and able to pay. What seems to be the problem?"

The man cleared his throat. "I don't understand why two upstanding men and a child would be traveling with someone like him."

"What do you mean, like him?" Marius asked.

"You know," the man said. "A Vagrant."

Rayne took several steps toward the innkeeper. "I don't know what you're talking about. We just arrived here from Corylus and know nothing about any Vagrants. Who are they?"

The man's eyes opened wide over his glasses. "I'm sorry, sir, to have mistaken you for a Vagrant, but you are dressed like one. They dress in dark, filthy robes like the one you're wearing; and, sir, I hate to say it, but I can smell you from here.

"They call themselves Vagrants of the Scroll and travel across the desert from oasis to oasis. They don't believe in bathing or carrying money. They preach about the power of the Scroll of Arisima to any who will listen. Many now follow their ways, though no one really understands much about this scroll they worship. In return for their teaching, they expect others to feed and house them for nothing. One or two are not usually a bother, but lately, they've taken to traveling in larger groups. And, when refused food or lodging, they've attacked and even killed those who deny them.

"At first, I allowed them to stay and fed them out of a sense of duty. Their words seemed to hold many answers and sounded wise. But I do so no longer. Most everyone now chases away one or two Vagrants, but if they come in greater numbers, the city guard is called. Those Vagrants are almost as bad as the thieving pirates."

"I understand now," Rayne said, groaning inside at the thought of scroll worshipers on Arisima. "You're talking about scroll worshipers. When did they come to Arisima?"

"Initially we saw only a few of them in the city. That was … oh, almost eight or nine years ago. At first, we didn't think much of it and welcomed them as peaceful religious travelers, like our native monks. But then, about five years ago, they started arriving by the hundreds and spreading through the desert to other oases. Within the last year, things began to change. The violence started. Many of the traditional religious communities that studied the writings of the One have been destroyed by roving bands of Vagrants. Though the pirates have always been a lawless lot, they at least honored the sanctity of the holy communities. But the Vagrants have no such scruples.

"I guess I do look like a Vagrant. And you're right, I smell; I'm long overdue for a bath. My robes ... well ... they looked much better a few weeks ago. I would really like a bath. We could all use one. And to avoid any more confusion, I need new clothes. Is there a clothier near who could help me? Those who worship the scrolls are no friends of mine and I would rather not be mistaken for one."

"Yes, sir," the innkeeper said. "I know just the man. He's quiet and discrete and will come here with some samples if I ask him." An apologetic expression crossed the man's face. "But I have to ask, do you have the means to pay him?"

Marius smiled as he pulled out the bundle of sommes. "How much will it cost for two adjoining rooms for two nights, and food, while we're here? And, let's say, a new set of clothes for each of us?"

The innkeeper sent one of his daughters to fetch the clothier while Rayne, Mite, Ponce, and Marius settled in their rooms. It didn't take long for the girl to return with a frail little man who looked almost as old as Rayne, and two of his assistants. He spread samples of his clothing out on the beds while he made suggestions for what would be best after Rayne explained they needed sensible clothing suited for desert travel.

"I have supplied these robes to several of the holy communities surrounding Zoraya for a long time now," the clothier said. "This is the material and style they prefer. It is the most comfortable of clothing for desert living. You will see, you will be comfortable."

In the end, Rayne was the only one to select an ankle-length, long-sleeved tunic of light material with a matching sleeveless cloak. If he was in his own body, he would have chosen something more to his taste, but for now, it was the most sensible choice for him. Mite and Ponce chose loose fitting trousers with matching long-sleeved, thigh-length tunics in the same material as Rayne's. Marius insisted on leather leggings and a sleeveless tunic.

The clothier shook his head saying, "the leather will be hot when you go into the desert. You will not be happy with your choice. At least wear a long-sleeved cloak to protect your arms from the sun."

After everyone had made their choices, the clothier informed Rayne the tailored garments would be ready by the next afternoon. As Rayne's choices were items normally kept in stock, the man gave him the samples he had brought with him. While the clothier's assistants gathered their things, Rayne asked him, "What can you tell me about the local religious communities?"

The little man glanced at Rayne, blinking. "What would you like to know?"

"I need to find a certain community where a friend of mine lived before he moved to Corylus. I don't remember the name of the community, but my friend studied under a man named Behnam. In your dealings with the communities, have you met anyone of that name?"

The clothier's face lit up. "As a matter of fact, I know Behnam quite well. I have supplied robes to Aleppo Monastery for many years. What would your friend's name be?"

"Shaw. His name is Shaw Radinajan."

The man's smile broadened. "Shaw, yes. I have known Shaw since he was a little boy, though I have not seen him for a few years. What a bright young man. How do you know Shaw?"

"I met him in Westvale. We studied the Words of the One together. He's a good friend."

"I'm glad to hear that. But I hope he's found some friends closer to his own age. Shaw's always been drawn to relationships with older people like you and me. Even as a child, he was so serious. Tell me, has he found any friends his own age, or does he still spend his time among old graybeards?"

Rayne could have laughed at the description of Shaw if the

reality of his situation wasn't so painful. Because of what had been done to him, the man couldn't know Rayne was Shaw's younger friend. To the clothier, he was just another grandfather. "No," he replied. "He's got younger friends. In fact, the last time I saw him was the day he married a very special friend of mine who is like a sister to me."

Seeing the incredulous look on the man's face, Rayne said, "I mean daughter ... uh, no, granddaughter. She's like a granddaughter to me."

The man's confused expression morphed into a smile. "I see, I see. I'm so glad that young Shaw has gotten married. You should try to meet with Benham while you're on Arisima. You can tell him about Shaw getting married. I know he wonders how his student is doing and would appreciate any news."

"Actually, one of the reasons I came to Arisima was to meet Shaw's mentor. Can you tell me how to find him?"

The man paused in thought. He puffed out a stream of air, then, thinking out loud, said, "The community where Benham lives is quite remote. And the pirates in the area make the trip even more dangerous, not to mention the roving Vagrants. Lately, they've been seeking out the smaller communities and monasteries and destroying them. Many of the monks have fled to Aleppo. Those Vagrants haven't attempted to attack there yet. It's too large, remote, and well protected."

He paused again and his eyes lit up. "But wait, I know of a caravan heading past the Aleppo Monastery. One of the merchants will be stopping briefly at the monastery to drop off some supplies. I'm sure he'd be willing to take you with him. The more people in a caravan, the safer the caravan. But they will be leaving in the morning. I don't suppose you and your friends can be ready by then?"

"Can you get my friends' clothes done in time?"

"I suppose I can set aside our other orders for a few hours," the tailor said, brow scrunched in thought. "Yes, it can be done. I'll have my assistants make the alterations as soon as I get back to my shop. Your clothes will be delivered this evening."

"I'll pay extra for the quick work," Rayne said. "That settled, we'll be ready to leave tomorrow morning. Talk to your friend. Make sure he's willing to take us."

The man's face dropped. "There is another problem, though. The caravan moves swiftly; you will need horses. I doubt you'll be able to acquire any at such short notice."

"One way or another," Rayne said. "We'll have horses, come morning. Talk to your friend."

The man nodded and bowed out.

A short while later Rayne groaned with pleasure as he scrubbed the last of the dirt and sweat from Sorial off his body and soaked in the comfort of a bath. He relaxed in the quiet and stillness of an uninterrupted time for thought, while the heated water eased the aches in his hip and back. Knowing Ponce and Marius would be gone for a while, he planned to fully enjoy his time alone. The two had left the inn arguing about which horse trader in Zoraya would give them the best deal.

Arisima was different from what he had expected. *I didn't even know what I expected. Once again, I've skipped to a world with no idea of how to find its scroll. I hope Benham has some answers for me. What if we run into pirates on our way to Aleppo? Would they kill us outright? Take us as slaves? And then there are the scroll worshipers. Their presence here is definitely another complication I could do without.* Rayne leaned his head against the side of the tub as his thoughts drifted back to his time at Coronus's compound and memories of Warren swam to the surface.

What do I do, Warren? The tincture from Ean and Elspeth is almost gone and I'm getting weaker by the day. I don't know how long I can keep going. I wish you were here, or Shaw. I don't know if this Benham will even talk to me. Mite's a big help, but he knows no more about Arisima than I do. And then there's Ponce—and Marius—I'm stuck between a rock and a hard place, Warren, and I don't know what to do. Trusting them is probably a big mistake, but at this point, I have no choice.

Rayne allowed his eyes to drift shut. An image of Warren filled his mind; standing in the library, his arm raised in a stance he had taken so often when he was trying to help Rayne understand something important. Suddenly the word was there, just as if Warren had whispered it into Rayne's ear. *Pray.*

Rayne's eyes popped open. Since skipping from Sorial, he

had allowed his confusion and frustration to drive prayer from his mind. Knowing he needed guidance, he decided to get dressed and spend time in prayer. Moving to get out of the tub, he released a frustrated puff of air. He didn't have the strength to pull himself up.

No, Rayne rebelled in his mind, grinding his teeth. *I will get out of this tub without help. I refuse to be so helpless.*

But five minutes later he succumbed to the reality that he was unable to even climb out of a tub himself. He would have to call for help, and his cheeks burned with the humiliation.

As if he was aware of Rayne's need, Mite poked his head in the door and said, "Ray-ray ready to get dressed now? Yes, yes, yes."

Rayne let Mite help him out of the tub and bring him a warm towel. After he was dry, it felt good to put on clean clothing. In place of the torn and stained robe Rayne had been given by the Kindred, Mite helped him into an Arisimanian robe similar to the one Shaw wore. The long-sleeved inner tunic was lightly woven beige material that tied at the waist with a leather belt. Over the tunic, Mite helped Rayne into the sleeveless, hooded cloak of deep brown.

"Sit, sit, Ray-ray," Mite said. When Rayne was sitting, Mite fastened sandals with long leather ties to his feet. When he was done, Mite said, "Now Ray-ray look like native, not Vagrant. Nice, nice, very nice."

Mite called for fresh water and ushered Rayne out of the bathing chamber. As Rayne made his way to the common room, he ran his hand over the soft material on his arm. The clothier had patiently explained that long sleeves were important if Rayne planned to travel in the desert. The sun there would burn his skin if it wasn't protected. And this material would also absorb his sweat in the heat.

Rayne stopped at the innkeeper's desk and asked that coffee be sent up to his room. As he was talking to the man, the quiet voice of the One spoke into his spirit. *Trust the scrolls to this man. He will keep them safe until you return.*

After studying the innkeeper for a moment, Rayne asked, "What's your name?"

"Kaydin, sir."

"Do you believe in the One?"

Kaydin scanned the room before saying, "Yes. I have believed in the One since I was a child and I've raised my own children in that faith. Even with the Vagrants threatening, I wouldn't deny my Lord. Why do you ask?"

Rayne smiled. "Because he's asked me to trust you with something precious beyond measure, Kaydin. I have with me two scrolls, the Words of the One to Nemora and Sorial."

Kaydin's jaw dropped open. "How can this be? I have always thought the scrolls were nothing more than legend."

"But legends are founded on reality. If I ask, will you hold the scrolls for me, keep them safe, until I return?"

At first Kaydin screwed up his eyes and looked at Rayne with mistrust, as if he thought Rayne was trying to trick him. But then his expression changed to one of amazement. "Yes. Yes, I will keep this treasure safe until you return."

"Have someone you trust bring the coffee to my room. I will give that person the scrolls. Don't tell anyone else about this, not even my companions. Understand?"

"Who are you?" Kaydin asked.

"You wouldn't believe me if I told you. But what you're doing—keeping the scrolls safe—you're doing for the One."

Peace permeated Rayne as he made his way up the stairs to the second floor. Once alone, he pulled the satchels from where he had hidden them and set them on a small table. As an afterthought, he pulled a gem from his bag and placed it on top of the sacks.

Lowering himself onto a cushioned chair, Rayne closed his eyes to pray. Before he began, there was a knock at the door. "Please come in," he called.

The innkeeper's daughter entered with a tray that held a stoneware carafe of the strong local coffee and a tiny stoneware cup. She smiled and filled the cup with the steaming brew. As the aroma of strong coffee wafted through the room, Rayne nodded his thanks and pointed to the satchels. Her eyes widened when she saw the gem. She met Rayne's eyes, hers still wide and questioning.

"For when we return," he said. "Tell your father that's for when we return."

She gave him a sweet smile as she took the bags, draped them over a shoulder and then bowed out, leaving Rayne alone once again.

He had been meditating on a portion of The Words of the One to Sorial for almost an hour when warmth enveloped him. The voice spoke into his spirit. *My beloved servant. When all seems lost and hope is shattered, trust me. I am with you. When you return to Westvale and stand alone before the darkness, be strong. I am with you. The end approaches. What I have purposed, that will I accomplish. In dying is death destroyed and the cup of wrath filled to the brim. Be strong and of good courage. You are never alone my beloved Light Bringer.*

Rayne sat in silence, unmoving, for a long while, sifting through the words the One had just spoken. Eventually, he realized Mite had come in and was sitting across from him, watching, his eyes pools of sorrow.

Mite sat still and quiet for another minute before saying, "The One spoke to Ray-ray again, yes? Mite will not leave Ray-ray. He will walk with his friend always. Ray-ray not face darkness alone.

"Until that time comes when I must walk alone, right?" Rayne whispered.

Compressing his lips, Mite just nodded and then covered his face with his hands.

40

The morning sun was a faint promise on the horizon as Rayne, Mite, Ponce, and Marius mounted and fell into position in the long line of the caravan. At first the merchant was uncertain, complaining. "I will not be responsible for some old man dying out in the desert heat."

However, when Marius volunteered to act as an additional guard, and Rayne handed over one of his remaining gems, the merchant agreed to let them come. "But," he snarled. "I will not be responsible if you die."

The raw-boned man climbed onto the saddle of his lead animal, still mumbling about crazy off-worlders. Rayne stared at the man's line of large pack animals, curious about the unusual creatures. The merchant held the lead rope to a line of five of the animals he called Nars. Another associate held the lead to five more Nars, each carrying a hefty amount of merchandise. The beasts were large and hairy, strange looking, with long faces and a hump in the middle of their backs. One of the guards told Rayne the humps held enough water for the animals to travel long distances across the desert before needing to drink again. But before Rayne could ask him any more, the informative guard rode off when the merchant yelled, "If you don't want to lose your job, stop answering stupid questions for off-worlders and get to work. And you, off-worlders. you'd better start moving or I'll go without you."

Leaving the oasis of Zoraya behind, Rayne began to understand Shaw's descriptions of Arisima. Beyond the greenery of the oasis, lay a world of scrubby brown, broken by plants that defied description. Some were greenish-brown and thin, with fine, spindly arms, standing taller than the men riding the Nars. Others were orange and yellow, short and squat. But no matter what size or color, they all seemed to be covered with sharp spines. Rayne quickly decided he would keep his distance from the painful-looking thorns. The brown scrubby flat land ran right up to severe, red-hued mountains in the near distance.

The clothier had given Rayne and his companions each a scarf to wrap around their faces or heads as needed and after watching the merchant, Rayne, Mite, and Ponce, copied his behavior, soaking theirs in some water and wearing them on the back of their necks to keep cool. Realizing the importance of his hood, Rayne kept the sun off his rather hairless scalp by pulling it up, over the moistened scarf.

Two days later they reached the foothills. After scrambling up a narrow trail and cresting a gap between two dusty red tors, Rayne caught his breath at what lay before them—the desert proper. Here was the sand Shaw had described, mounded into ridges and humps like small mountains marching off into the distance, reflecting the sunlight in shades of white so bright, Rayne's eyes hurt looking at it.

Marius, who had been flanking the caravan as a guard, rode up to Rayne. "Have you ever seen anything like it?" he asked. Marius seemed to thrive in the desert heat, as if he had been born there. He smiled. "If we're lucky, we'll see a storm. There's nothing as beautiful as a storm in the desert."

"Were you originally from Arisima?" Rayne asked.

"No." Marius studied Rayne, his brow furrowed. "But I did spend time a few years ago working as a caravan guard. I love the desert. It's harsh and tough, but to those strong enough to survive, it shows its beauty, especially after a storm."

Mite, riding a large pony next to Rayne's horse said through his scarf, "Mite does not like sand, gets in mouth, gets in nose. Too hot, too red, too, too sharp. Everything sharp here. Mite misses soft blue Nemora, yes, yes, yes."

Ponce sat his horse in silence, staring out across the rolling dunes of sand.

The next day, they arrived at the first of several oases where the merchants planned to trade, buying and selling their goods. Rayne hadn't realized how sore his eyes were until the soft green beyond the rock cut they rode through eased the ache. As they waited in line for their turn to fill water jugs and canteens, Rayne watched, his jaw hanging loose, as the Nar drank. The humps that had diminished as they traveled, quickly swelled again as the animals drank gallons of water from an outer pool where caravans were allowed to water their animals.

While the merchants continued on into the oasis to conduct business, the caravan workers and guards set up a camp near the pool to rest for the remainder of the day. From now on, they would rest during the day and travel at night, avoiding the burning heat of midday and taking advantage of the cooler air after sunset.

Rayne and his companions watered their horses and filled their water bags, they rode into the oasis to find an inn where they could bathe, eat, then rest for the next several hours.

Marius led them to a small place he had stayed at before. He arranged for a room with four beds where they could sleep once they had bathed and eaten. After leaving their horses in the care of a young stable boy for some well-deserved food, more water, and a chance to rest in a shady stable, the four sat down to a meal in the cool interior of the inn.

The common room was bright and airy with a wall of glass doors set open to catch the breeze which carried the sweet, earthy scent of things in bloom. Beyond the doors was a large green pond surrounded by a verdant garden, the source of the myriad fragrances. The lower plants, most of which were blooming in shades of red and orange, were shaded by the tall trees Rayne recognized from Zoraya.

Their meal, like most Rayne had eaten since arriving on

Arisima, included fruit from the tall trees surrounding the pond, as well as a different kind of fruit he had not tasted before. The server explained the other fruit came from the smaller trees scattered through the garden. Both were sweet and complemented the highly-spiced desert grain and shredded meat they were mixed with before being stuffed into large edible leaves. Tall glasses of cool water were served with the meal, which ended with fresh fruit and tiny cups of the strong local coffee.

After traveling in the daytime heat for the last few days, then eating well, Rayne and Ponce were ready to nap. Marius and Mite went out to investigate the oasis. Marius walked alongside Mite and tried to strike up a conversation, but Mite just ignored the tall blonde.

"How long have you known this old man we're following? I mean, I can see you're committed to him. So am I. For now. But, honestly, he looks like he's on death's door. How much longer do you think he's going to last? What will you do when he croaks?"

Mite pulled up short, anger warming his blood. "Dark worshiper, servant of evil, not worthy to even speak of Ray-ray. Dark lover knows nothing. Mite will not allow him to speak of friend with disrespect."

"So, tell me, O fearsome little one," Marius said. "What makes this *Ray-ray* so important. Powerful enemies hunt him. I know. I worked for one until I was freed. Tell me, what makes him so special? I know you're an ancient. Why do you even follow him?"

Mite scrunched up his eyes and stared at Marius wondering if the tall dark worshiper was asking an honest question, and, if so, how much he should tell the man. Deciding it was okay to tell Marius something, Mite said, "Mite follow Ray-ray because Ray-ray is Light Bringer, chosen by Creator-Father to bind the darkness and bring light back to all Ochen."

"Have you ever stopped to think," Marius asked, "if

Ochen even wants to be saved from the darkness? What if people want the dark to come?"

Mite shook his head, his blue braids bouncing. "Marius not understand. Too sad, too sad. All lies lead to darkness; and darkness births lies. Where there is darkness, newcomers hide behind lies; lies to self and lies to others. Light and truth bring life. Darkness brings slavery and death."

Mite rested his fingers on Marius's chest. "Marius knows truth, in here. But too sad, too sad, Marius still slave to the dark."

Marius harrumphed. "I'm a slave to no man. So, you just keep your foolish lectures to yourself. Or, if you need to share them, share them with that ex-rubiate Ponce. He's full of self-loathing and looking to find forgiveness. That's why he hangs around your Ray-ray. Or should I say Rayne."

Mite startled, his eyes rounding like Nemorian moons.

"Yes, I know who he really is inside that body, and I know why Sigmund wants him. I've known since Nemora. But I'm still here helping him. So, don't spit your anger at me. I'm here by my own free will. I promised I'd help him, and I'll help him find what he came for, then get him safely to Westvale."

Mite shook his head. "Marius wrong, still slave, always slave. No hope, no hope."

"Oh shut up." Marius growled and then stalked away.

It was almost sundown when the companions walked their horses back to the outer pool. The caravan looked like a disturbed bee hive. The need to repack their wares and be on their way by sunset prompted a flurry of activity that had merchants and their crews scrambling.

As the last of the Nar were loaded and the beasts were grunting and groaning to each other, a strange sound drifted in from beyond the opening to the oasis. Rayne was about to ask Marius what it was, when shouting and panic erupted.

"Pirates!"

"Pirates!"

"No! It can't be!"

"They wouldn't attack this close to the oasis!"

Without warning, Rayne, once again, found himself lifted off his feet by Marius. This time Marius pushed him up onto his horse. "Hurry," the man yelled. "Move now, or we die." Bent low, he ran to his own mount, dragging Rayne's behind. Mounting, he spurred his horse into a full run, leading Rayne through the cut in the rocks, out into the desert. Ponce and Mite followed, pushing their horses, clinging low over their necks. They raced across the now dark sand for several minutes. Rayne was breathing out a sigh of relief, thinking they had escaped, when something slammed into his chest driving him back over his horse's rump and down onto his back. He lay stunned, struggling to draw in the breath that had been knocked from him. Then something dark swooped between him and the stars sparkling above.

Rayne woke still on his back. He squinted into the bright light of midday and tried to lick his lips. His parched mouth was dry as the the desert floor. Releasing a grunt, he pushed himself into a sitting position. His head spun and his stomach threatened revolt at the motion. Looking down he concluded he must have been lying unconscious out in the sun, his arms were an alarming shade of cherry red. Above him was light blue sky and beneath him, not the sand he expected, but a hard, wooden floor that hummed and vibrated. Around him sat several people he recognized from the caravan, hands bound. He scanned the sorry-looking group, searching for Mite, Ponce, and Marius. He caught sight of them a short distance away with another group of prisoners.

Two pirates grabbed the arms of a protesting merchant sitting near Rayne and dragged the man in front of a large pirate reclining on a tan leather chair. The chair's arms resembled animal paws and the cushions were worn so thin in places, stuffing stuck out at various angles. The pirate, who Rayne suspected was the captain, reminded him of Coronus, large and overweight, with a full, black beard and thick black hair worn in a braid that draped over the man's broad shoulder.

The pirate captain looked the now pleading merchant

over, as if he was assessing the man's value. Rayne realized with a start that was exactly what the pirate was doing. He wrote something in a black ledger and then waved the man over to the other group where he was allowed a sip of water before being pushed down to the floor. When the two pirates returned to Rayne's group and grabbed another man, he concluded he was in the group yet to be assessed. He caught Mite's eye. The little ancient mouthed, "So sorry, so sorry."

Rayne understood. Like on Sorial, Mite could not help him here. Away from Nemora, away from the Source, Mite's abilities were diminished and the pirates too focused to mislead with illusion.

Rayne understood something else as well, in the pirates' eyes he had no worth. As he was, no one would purchase him for a slave. Scanning the few remaining people in his group, Rayne knew, he was going to be judged very soon and he was the only one unbound. They knew; he wasn't even worth the effort of binding.

When there was no one else left, the two pirates came for Rayne. He desperately wanted to rise on his own power, but he couldn't even manage that and was forced to wait until the two hauled him to his feet and dragged him before their captain. Without his staff, which was now resting in the crook of the captain's elbow, he couldn't even stand for more than a few minutes on his own. But with an effort, he determined to remain upright—at least until he collapsed. Standing tall on unsteady legs, Rayne faced the pirate captain with a show of confidence.

A cruel smile splitting his beard, the captain leisurely scanned Rayne from head to foot. "And what have we dragged up in our net this time? Something dead and awaiting burial?"

Speaking past his swollen tongue, Rayne rasped out, "Sir, may I please have some water?"

The man gave him an incredulous look. "Look around you, old man. You're in the desert where water is costly. I don't waste anything of value."

Trying to pull every shred of moisture to his dry mouth, Rayne whispered, "I know you're assessing the value of your prisoners and I'm sure you can see, as a slave, I am without worth. But I'm not without means. If you're willing, I can pay you well for the freedom of myself and my companions."

"Ho, ho. Just listen to this one speak. He sounds like some high and mighty noble. That must have been your horse where I found this." He held up Rayne's staff. "I suppose you would like it back, huh? And this, too?" The captain held up the pouch containing the remaining gems and money.

"Yes, sir," Rayne gritted out as his head pounded to the beat of his heart. "That was my horse and those are mine."

"Carrying this kind of wealth, I must assume you are of importance to someone. I'd be willing to keep you alive as a prisoner if we could arrange for a hefty ransom. Who values you?"

Thoughts scurried through Rayne's mind. *Who values me? No one even knows who I am except Sigmund and his associates. Sigmund? No, I'd die first. Broken as I am, there is no one who will even know me. I will not hand myself over to that demon. Not ... going ... to ... happen!*

"No." Rayne murmured. "There is no one."

The pirate's smile broadened. "Then the only value you have is to provide some entertainment for my men and me."

He nodded to the two pirates who grabbed Rayne's arms again, dragging him to the rail at the back of the ship. Looking over the side for the first time, Rayne gasped. They were sailing through the air far above the red-tinged sand of the desert.

The captain laughed as he rose and walked up next to Rayne. "Never been on an airship before, have you, off worlder?" The man ran his hand lovingly over the rail. "It's something to behold, yes? Only a few of the oldest desert families have retained the knowledge of how to make our ships fly. It does give us the advantage. No one can catch us. Those with the strength of Arisima can summon the magic energy to raise a ship into the air where the sails pick up the desert winds and propel us forward. Old, old magic. Of much value, unlike you."

The airship had changed course and picked up speed. They were now plunging forward, the wind filling the sails, so they billowed out like pillows. For the next hour, the ship raced over red sand dunes. At one point, they passed what looked like an oasis off in the distance.

If not for the railing, Rayne would never have been able to remain upright. Even with its support, his legs were quivering with the effort. He didn't know how much longer he could last. Rayne flicked his gaze to the pirate captain. *No help there. Still …* "What's your name?"

The man chuckled. "What does it matter if you know my name? You won't know it for long."

"Long enough to ask a favor."

"Nail," the captain said. "My name's Nail. Captain of the Flying Arrow."

Rayne nodded. "My name's Rayne."

"And the favor you would ask?"

"Well. I've been standing for a long time. And not only am I thirsty beyond belief, I think my knees are giving out. I wonder if you would mind lending me my staff? At least until you kill me?"

Nail ran his fingers through his beard and stared at Rayne for a moment before saying, "Naw. I've decided I like your staff. It's sturdy. I think I'll keep it. You won't need it any more. I wonder if you realize that it's of more worth than you, old man." He gave a short barking laugh. "Pathetic, no? You've outlived your usefulness as a human. Good for nothing but to provide some meager entertainment for this motley crew while you die."

Suddenly Mite's voice rose above the sound of wind in the sails. "Stop, stop, stop. Leave him alone."

"That one of your companions?" Nail asked Rayne.

"Yes."

"Then you'd better shut him up, or I will." Nail frowned, then asked, "What kind of creature is he? He's not human, that much is obvious."

Rayne just stared at the man, refusing to answer.

Nail laughed and then waved at one of the men watching over the prisoners. "Bring the little one here. And those two who were with him when we picked them up."

Three more men came forward, pulled Ponce, Marius, and

Mite to their feet, and propelled them to the rail where Nail and Rayne were standing.

Nail took time to look each one over. "You're truly an unusual assortment of individuals. One wasted old man. One child-like creature … ancient maybe? Definitely magical. One warrior ... hunter perhaps. And one ... clerk? I must say you've made me curious. What brought such a peculiar group together?"

Rayne and his companions remained silent as they watched the desert swiftly slipping away beneath them.

With a snarl, Nail grabbed the back of Rayne's neck, slammed his head into the rail, and said, "You will not ignore me. I have your life in my hands, fool. You will respect me."

Mite jumped at Nail and yelled, "No, no, no. Bad man must not hurt Light Bringer. Darkness, darkness will destroy all if Light Bringer doesn't bind. Please, please, please let him go. Mite will stay and do anything bad man says. Just let Light Bringer go. He must, or all will be lost, lost, lost."

Mite dropped to his knees, his head in his hands.

Nail stared down at Mite for a second, then raised his eyes to meet Rayne's, now blinking as blood seeped down from his split forehead. Mustering his flagging courage, Rayne met the pirate's eyes with a hard look of his own.

"Superstition?" Nail spat out. "Your friend would sacrifice himself for worthless superstition? Begging is weakness. He's a weak creature. Be glad he'll bring a good price on the auction block, otherwise he would be joining you in death."

With his hand still gripping Rayne's neck, Nail pointed to a spot the ship was racing toward, where the sand reflected the light of the sun like a mirror. There it is. See it? That's the place where the desert drinks itself. That's where we dump our garbage."

When they were close, Nail waved, bringing the ship to a hovering stop over the spot. Looking at Rayne, he smiled. "This should be good."

Still smiling, Nail shifted and flipped Rayne over the railing with a swift motion, dropping him to the mirror-like sand. It happened so fast, the companions never had a chance to respond before Rayne was over the side and falling.

Mite's scream, like that of a pained animal followed Rayne as he fell. "Nooooo!"

41

Rayne heard Mite's cry as he plummeted toward the ground. He landed on his back, hitting the sand with force. Air exploded from his lungs, snatching away the scream that rose within him. He heard the sickening sound of bones breaking and intense pain seared through his torso. At least one rib was broken. But that was the least of his problems as the sand beneath him began to shift, drawing him down. He tried to clutch at the sides of the funnel his descent was creating, but the sand kept slipping away. Laughter drifted down from above, Nail and his crew were enjoying Rayne's struggle to overcome, to survive. It was hopeless.

Please, Lord. I don't want to die! Please. Save me! Help me! Don't let me die here. Not like this!

But he was sinking. Soon the sand would cover him, and he would die. Lexi, his parents, and his friends back on Corylus would never know the truth of what Sigmund had done or that Rayne had died an old man. As the sand began covering him completely, crusting his eyes and liming his nose and lips, something bizarre happened. He slipped beneath a partition that blocked out the shifting sand. Fresh air blew across his face, disbursing the remaining sand. He choked and spit out gritty clods, while a gentle presence upheld him. It felt as if woven branches were holding and sheltering him. To his amazement, they were. Here beneath the scorching desert of Sorial, he was being lowered through the center of a vast tree covered in tiny, deep red leaves, by the tree itself.

Rayne felt the movement as each strong limb rose up to accept him and then lowered, shifting his body to the one beneath until, finally, he was placed on the ground with a gentle motion. Blinking in disbelief, Rayne looked up through the tree that had saved him, at what appeared to be a ceiling of crystal. The sand that had looked like a mirror from above, here below, looked like a faceted jewel through which the sun shone in dappled rays of soft, pink light.

What just happened? It was so unreal, Rayne wondered if he was imagining the whole thing while in truth, he was buried in the sand. *Maybe I'm really dead now. But if I'm dead, how could I be wondering if I'm dead?*

He wanted to thank the tree, but he couldn't get his gritty, swollen tongue to work. His head thrummed like the inside of a beaten drum and he wished it would stop spinning.

His befuddled mind struggled to comprehend what just happened. *I need to thank the tree … thing. I think. Thank a tree? I'm losing my mind.* The pain in his ribs and his lack of air, the pounding and spinning of his head, and his inability to work any moisture into his swollen tongue, combined with an overwhelming exhaustion, and Rayne gave up the battle for consciousness. With one last look up at the crystal ceiling, he closed his gritty, tired eyes and allowed the oblivion of unconsciousness to take him.

Rayne woke. He didn't know how long he had been unconscious; it could have been a minute or days. He had no way of knowing. But he was alive. Something wet dripped onto his parched lips, and though his cracked lips split with the effort, Rayne opened his mouth and let the moisture trickle onto his tongue. It wasn't more than a tiny drip at a time, but it felt wonderful. At the sound of movement above, he cracked his eyes open a sliver and watched as the tiny red leaves rustled and dipped, dropping the little gems of fresh water on him.

After a time of just lying and soaking in the moisture, Rayne felt ready to talk. Looking up into the still-quivering branches, he croaked, "I guess I have you to thank."

The effort of speaking drew a groan from him and he carefully wrapped an arm around his painful ribs. The tree rustled harder and waved its branches as if it understood Rayne's words. He looked up in wonder and asked, "You ... understand?"

The massive trunk swayed, and the leaves fluttered, dropping cascades of water. The cool liquid caressed Rayne's skin as it ran down in tiny rivulets off his hands and face.

"I don't understand what's happening," Rayne mumbled faintly. He closed his eyes and slept.

𝕽

While Rayne lay sleeping and the tree continued to drop moisture to him, footsteps sounded from a tunnel-like opening in the crystal-ceilinged cavern. Soon, a deep, bell-like singing blended with the footsteps and heralded the entrance of a tall, broad-shouldered figure into the cavern. The ancient spoke briefly with the red tree, then strode to where Rayne was lying. Looking down, his expression changed to one of frustration.

"Yes. Yes. I see. Those dirty pirates have dropped another body on us. I wish they would find a better way to dispose of the dying than to watch them struggle against the sand and end up here," he said in the common tongue, his voice sharp and angry. "I guess I'll have to bury this one too."

The tree swayed and rustled more intensely. A whistle started from somewhere deep within the old trunk and worked its way out to become a shrill note of warning.

𝕽

Badr looked up at the branches as they quivered and after a minute shook his head. "No." He sighed. "I know you feel

361

sorry for all of them but trying to convince me this one is the Light Bringer I've been waiting for isn't going to work. He doesn't fit the prophecies. Remember, in his sixteenth year? This walking corpse is way too old.

"As with the others who've made it this far still clinging to life, I'll ease his passing and then bury him in the tunnel of holes just like the rest."

Terev's color shifted from a deep burgundy to a bright cherry-apple red, starting at the inner veins of the leaves and working outward.

"Don't you get snippety with me," Badr grumbled. "There's no cause to take that tone."

He listened a bit longer. *Terev does have a good point. Perhaps* … A thoughtful expression furrowed his strong, chiseled features. He sniffed in a deep breath and huffed it out. "Yes, yes, I see. The prophecies mention him being broken. Are you sure you saw the light within him?"

Terev settled until perfectly still, its color restored. With what seemed like a deep inhalation, the tree pulled magic energy from within the cavern into itself, then burst into a brilliant red glow as if on fire, but not one leaf was burning. Each leaf and bud blazed from within, casting red-hued light through the cavern.

As the light reached the unconscious old man, Badr's eyes widened. Coruscating light in shades of gold and blue began rising in streams from the body, blending and dancing with the tree's red light.

Badr fell to his knees watching the lights blend into rainbows of splashing brilliance. The lights danced for several minutes in their combined glory. Colors flashed and faded only to flash again in new combinations. Beauty beyond beauty. Then the light began descending, merging into streams that poured into the old body lying asleep and unaware before Badr. Just as the last of the combined light entered the body, a blinding flash shot down from the sun, through the crystal above, turning the body into a transparent, shimmering form. And for a brief instant, Badr saw the heart-wrenching beauty of the spirit trapped within.

The voice of the One echoed through the chamber. *Know that you have glimpsed the true form of my beloved Light Bringer. Even broken and lost he has clung to me and trusted. Honor him as he has honored me.*

The last echoes of the One's voice were fading as Rayne blinked his eyes open to see a tall, imposing ancient, kneeling next to him. He watched the ancient with interest as he knelt with closed eyes as if in prayer. The tree rustled overhead, and Rayne could almost make out words that sounded like *told you so.*

The ancient opened his eyes and Rayne found himself looking into twin rubies. He had never seen red eyes before and it was startlingly beautiful and alien at the same time. The two stared at each other for a long moment and Rayne wondered if he was hallucinating or dreaming.

Rayne spoke first, his voice a dry whisper. "Are you real or am I dreaming?"

Badr shook as if coming out of water, suddenly impaled by the reality of the person before him. He looked closely to see if he could discern what he had seen just moments before, but now, all he saw was a very old and very frail newcomer who needed his help.

"Welcome, Light Bringer, blessed of the One," Badr said, his voice resonating like a very large, deep-throated bell.

"You know who I am?"

Badr inclined his head. "Please accept my apologies for not recognizing you immediately. There's no excuse for my ignorance."

The newcomer chuckled lightly then grunted. "I understand. I'm not a very imposing figure now, am I?"

"Formality aside," Badr said. "We must treat your injuries without delay. Excuse me, don't move while I get my supplies."

"I don't think I could move even if I wanted to."

11

The ancient bowed deeply and slipped from the cavern while Rayne closed his eyes. He focused on his breathing for a few minutes, then said, "Am I losing my mind, or did I really hear you talk, Mr. Tree?"

The tree's limbs rustled lightly, and words seemed to float through the air, *most honored ... meet ... Light Bringer.*

Rayne whispered, "The honor is mine. If not for you, I'd be dead. It's strange though, talking to a tree. Do many of your kind talk or are you unique?"

Rayne barely caught the words as they drifted past him this time. *Unique ... result growing in magic energy ... here. Gift of Creator-Father ... for Badr.*

"Badr?"

Friend who just left. Will heal you. Badr ... master healer.

Badr hustled back into the crystal-ceilinged cavern with a large bag hanging from a strap pulled over his shoulder. Kneeling next to Rayne once again, he set the bag on the floor and reaching in, began rummaging through it mumbling to himself in his deep bass voice.

After giving Rayne more water, Badr cleaned the wound on his head and then rubbed a healing salve on the wound and the burns to his face and arms. He helped Rayne to a sitting position to check his ribs. Sucking in his breath at the pain, Rayne wheezed out, "There are at least two broken."

"I'll be the judge of that," Badr said. "Unless you are a healer."

"No, not a healer." Rayne grimaced. "But I heard the break and I've had broken ribs before. I know what they feel like. You'll need to wrap them well so they don't puncture a lung."

Badr harrumphed, mumbled something about who was the healer and who was the patient, then helped Rayne unwrap his belt and ease the robe off his upper body, letting it rest around his hips. Badr examined Rayne's torso, probing with skilled hands. After a few painful moments, Badr admitted Rayne was right. He felt two broken ribs and it looked as if another was bruised. Once the ribs were wrapped tightly, Badr returned his things to his bag, helped Rayne back into his robe, and held the water skin while Rayne took another long drink.

Badr sat back, cross-legged, after taking the water skin from Rayne and setting it next to his bag. He gave Rayne a curious look and asked, "Are you up to sharing your story? Judging by what I've seen, it must be quite something."

Rayne started to explain how the caravan had been attacked by pirates, but Badr stopped him right away.

"No," he said. That's the end of the story. I want the whole thing, from the beginning. I know you're not some old man; I know what you are. Now I would like to hear about who you are and how you came to be here, like this."

Rayne eyed Badr. "How far back do you want me to go?"

Badr closed his eyes and thought for a moment chiming quietly to himself, then said, "Well, seeing as I've waited hundreds of years for you to come, and as I have been lonely for most of that time."

The tree above them began to rustle furiously.

Looking up into the branches Badr said, "You shut up. I know you've kept me company for a long time now. But I also know you want to hear this story as much as I do. So don't get your leaves in a snit."

Turning back to Rayne, Badr smiled. "And being as I love long stories. Why don't you start from the beginning? Start with where and when you were born, your parents, growing up years, things like that. From the looks of those ribs, you're not going anywhere soon and Terev and I love a good story."

"Who?"

"Our tree friend, Terev. And just to let you know, he doesn't like newcomers. But for some reason, he has affection for you. Right from the start he wouldn't let me just bury you."

"Bury me! You would bury me because of a couple broken ribs?"

Badr gave Rayne a disgusted look. "Be honest, when you fell through the sand, you were almost dead. Weren't you? If not for Terev and me, you would be dead now. Right?"

Unable to argue the point, Rayne nodded.

"Good." Badr leaned back into a smooth rock formation. "Now, don't leave anything out."

Over the next week, Rayne's story unfolded in short segments. Unable to leave the cavern, he rested on a bed of leaves Badr made for him, sleeping most of the time. When he was awake, he ate what Badr brought for meals. Every day, the ancient would check Rayne's ribs and pronounce them mending. And every day, Rayne would share more of his story. He told Badr things he had never told anyone else. When he talked of his time with Sigmund and Ponce, Terev shook with anger. And when he told of waking up in the old body, Terev hung his branches in sorrow. Finally, he shared what happened on the pirate's ship and how he was thrown overboard to die.

"I pray for my friends' safety." Rayne said, sorrow turning the corners of his lips down. "They are in trouble because of me, especially Mite. The thought of him as someone's slave makes me wish he had never helped me—that I never accepted help from any of them."

"And yet, it was their decision to make, and each one chose to help you. Do not diminish their choice by taking blame that is not yours. You trust the One for yourself. Now you must trust him for your friends, those waiting on Corylus and those who came with you to Arisima."

With his story laid out fully for the first time, Rayne felt a sense of contentment. At least someone knew the whole story, even if Badr would be leaving to be with the One soon.

Badr rose to check Rayne's ribs. "They are healing nicely, but …"

Rayne noticed the look of concern on the ancient's face. "But, I'm dying."

Badr nodded and Rayne continued. "I haven't had the tea or tincture from Ean and Elspeth for over a week now. It doesn't matter, I was running out of time anyway."

Rayne looked up at Badr. "I think our time together has

come to an end. As long as I have the energy to skip to West-vale with the scrolls, I'm going to trust the rest to the One. But now I must ask for the scroll to Arisima. I know you're its guardian and you know who I am. It's time."

Sadness permeated the air around Rayne as Terev began dropping leaves. Looking up at the tree, Rayne said, "Hey, none of that now. Please, don't diminish my sacrifice by refusing to go on living just because I have to die. Knowing you're here and strong, just like knowing all my friends are okay, gives me the strength to do what must be done. And though I can't be sure what's happened to all my friends, I pray for them. Like Badr said, I have to trust them to the One."

Badr gave Rayne a hand up. He swayed for a bit before finding his balance. As the two stood there for a moment, Terev began to shake and suddenly there was a great crack. Rayne and Badr both looked up at the tree with concern. Waves of contentment surrounded them as a perfectly straight branch dropped to the cavern floor.

Badr bent down and picked up the branch and Rayne looked at it in awe. It was arrow straight for its entire length, with no discernible knots or defects, and stood as tall as Rayne. On closer examination a design could be seen worked into the wood. As Rayne studied the design, he realized it was made up of pictures etched into the wood. Each picture depicted a part of his own story, from his childhood to his time with Terev and Badr.

Rayne looked up at Terev. "This is beautiful. I don't even know how to thank you for this, my friend. You've humbled me with such a gift."

Terev shook again and Rayne felt words echoing through his whole body. *Live! Remember the promises in the prophecies and live!*

Using Terev's staff, Rayne walked up to the huge trunk and placed his hand against the rough, warm bark. He stood like that for several minutes before saying, "Thank you for everything."

He turned to Badr and nodded. Badr led him from the cavern through the tunnel to another, smaller cave, Badr's home. It had the same crystal ceiling as the larger cavern, allowing light to shine into the area. There was a kitchen with a heavy wooden work table and a spring that fed into a trough which ran out into the tunnel. A tall stone table with matching chairs was set just beyond the kitchen and to the other side of it was a recessed alcove with a fireplace and two large padded chairs. With the pink-tinged sunlight shining down, everything looked warm and inviting, like a home, not a cold rock cave.

"Have you stayed in here the entire time?"

Badr chuckled. "Of course not. Over the years, I've visited the oases and communities often. I have many friends among the newcomers here on Arisima. Your friend Shaw studied with one of them. I believe you mentioned looking for Benham. His community is not far from where we stand right now. If you had succeeded in reaching Benham, he would have tested you, and if you convinced him of the truth of your identity, he would have brought you to me. So, you see, Rayne, you were on the right path."

Badr sighed, looking around his home. "It is time. Come."

Badr led Rayne through his kitchen into another tunnel. Following close behind the ancient, Rayne realized for the first time how truly large he was, taller and much broader than any of the other guardians Rayne had met while reclaiming the scrolls. As they walked, he asked the question that had bothered him since meeting Badr. "Are you the same as the other guardians? You seem different, you're much larger and you have red eyes."

Badr turned back to Rayne and gave him a hard look. "What? Don't you like my red eyes?"

"No," Rayne said. "That's not it. I've grown used to your eyes. It's just that you seem ... I don't know ... different. Somehow."

"And so I am. But my story, like yours, would take many days to tell, days we do not have. For now, what you need to know is, whatever I was or did in the past was forgiven by the One. Now I serve him and him alone."

Allowing a bittersweet half-smile to surface, Rayne said, "I think I understand. Whatever I was or whatever I did in the past was also forgiven by the One. We're not so different, are we?"

"True, my young friend. We're not so different. I'm saddened that our time together has been so short. When the hour comes for you to leave this life and join those of us already in the presence of the One, I look forward to some long talks with you, chosen Light Bringer who has come through so much."

Rayne grimaced. "It doesn't look like you'll have to wait long."

Badr's smile faded. "You must remember to trust the One. His prophecies are always true."

As they moved farther away from the crystal ceiling, Badr grabbed a torch from one of the sconces positioned at intervals through the tunnel and lit it. After walking a while longer, just as Rayne was wondering how much farther they would have to go, they rounded a bend and Rayne saw light ahead. Badr moved to the side and motioned for Rayne to continue alone.

Approaching the opening where the light poured into the tunnel, Rayne saw another room, this one cut out of the same red rock that formed the mountains surrounding the sand desert. The ceiling above shown like the crystal from the other rooms, but here it was tinged a deeper pink, casting the whole room in a pinkish light which made the smooth, red sides of the cave look a deep maroon. Seeing the scroll setting on a flat-topped rock of the same red hue, Rayne stumbled.

This was it, the final scroll. Every action took on a dreamlike quality as he walked to the rock using Terev's staff. He felt unreal. All that he had struggled for, all that he had suffered to achieve, was finally within his reach. With this, the last Words of the One, he could now return to Westvale. But questions slithered through his mind like poisonous snakes. *Will I be strong enough to face Sigmund? Will I be able to bind the darkness? What does that mean anyway? How do I bind Sigmund?*

Reaching out, he pulled the leather bag to him. Taking the scroll from the bag, he unwrapped the cover, and ran his fingers over the scroll. Warmth blossomed around him. Energy pulsed outward with force, raw and powerful.

My beloved Light Bringer. With you I am well pleased. Do not doubt. In your weakness, I will be your strength. Read my words and be strong.

"Yes, my Lord."

Your friends await you at the inn. You will know the traitor by his words; he is the one you must take with you to face the living darkness so all will be fulfilled as foretold. When the cup of wrath overflows, the judgment will descend. You now know this to be true. Be strong and courageous. Trust that I am with you even at the end.

42

Mite had been curled up, trying to rest as visions of Rayne disappearing over the railing of the airship drove all possibility of sleep from him.

Why? He asked the One. *Why send Mite to protect if Mite can't protect? Ray-ray gone, gone, gone. What will Mite do now?*

Six days had passed since Nail had dropped Rayne and locked the rest of his prisoners in the hold of his ship. Twice more, the pirates attacked caravans and added more prisoners to those already in the hold. Though Mite, Ponce, and Marius were chained next to each other, they barely talked. Mite was inconsolable, Ponce retreated into himself, and Marius ate as much food as he could and slept most of the time. He claimed he was building his strength for the moment when they could escape.

With a creaking sound, the hatch above the prisoners opened and a shaft of too-bright light pierced the darkness in the hold. Mite didn't react. The pirates were probably bringing the mash they called food down to their captives. Mite hadn't eaten since Rayne's death, and still had no desire to do so. In all his long life, he never experienced the depth of sorrow he now felt. Anger and guilt at his failure to protect the Light Bringer, self-hatred at being the reason darkness would now cover Ochen, blended with the pain of losing his friend and soured his stomach. Even if he ate, Mite was sure the food wouldn't stay down.

But rather than two pirates bringing down a pot of food, six pirates descended into the underbelly of the ship. While four stood with weapons ready, two began moving through the prisoners releasing their shackles from the long chain bolted to the floor.

"Move, scum. Up on deck," one of the men with a drawn weapon growled. "It's auction day. Time to pay us back for not killing the lot of you."

The pirates prodded everyone up the steep, narrow stairs into the glaring sunlight on the deck. They were lined up and forced to stand under the burning sun, waiting. After more than an hour, Nail emerged from his cabin and walked down the line of prisoners, stopping in front of each one as if to reassess their value.

When he stepped in front of Mite he paused. "You don't look so good, little ancient. I'll not allow you to reduce my profit by refusing to eat."

Nail grabbed Mite's jaw as one of the guards brought over a bowl of gruel. "I hear you don't appreciate the food I feed my merchandise." Reaching behind him, Nail grabbed a handful of gruel from the bowl and squeezing Mite's jaw until he opened his mouth, Nail forced the mash into Mite's mouth, smearing the mess over his face.

"Can't you just leave him alone," Ponce moaned from his position next to Mite. "Haven't you hurt him enough already?"

Nail's eyes swiveled from Mite to Ponce. "Nobody asked your opinion, slave. I see you too need to learn your place. If you weren't going on the block in the next couple hours, I would teach you some respect. But I'll just have to leave that lesson to your new owner."

The moment Nail returned his attention to Mite, he spit the gruel he had been holding in his mouth at the captain's face. Venom laced his words. "Stupid, stupid newcomer.

C. S. WACHTER

Stupid newcomer worries about profit when he has condemned all Ochen to darkness. The One will avenge his Light
Bringer. Tremble, tremble, stupid newcomer. Your fate is
sealed."

Nail stood frozen, staring at Mite as the gooey mess
slipped from his face and plopped onto the deck. Mite met his
gaze, unflinching, anger bubbling through him. The crew and
every prisoner watched as if waiting to see Nail kill Mite on the
spot. But with a grunt of disgust, Nail turned away and
marched into his cabin.

Ponce leaned into Mite. "What was that? What did you
do?"

"Mite just gave filthy light killer something to think about.
He did, he did."

Another hour passed as they stood under the pale blue
sky, baking in the heat. Then the airship vibrated as it came to
a halt. Nail strode out onto the deck as if nothing had happened between him and Mite and began barking orders to his
men. The ship started to descend and as it dropped, Mite got
his first glimpse of the oasis. Shock seized him, dropping his
jaw. They had been brought back to the capital. They were
going to be sold in Zoraya.

The main entrance to Zoraya shrank behind them as the
ship skirted the perimeter of the oasis. A few minutes later,
they dropped lower and landed by a smaller, all but invisible,
passage into the city. The prisoners were ushered off the
airship while Nail barked a few last orders before walking
down the plank to the ground as well. The skeleton crew took
the ship back up while Nail and the bulk of his men herded
their merchandise through a shadow-filled tunnel.

As the first pirates stepped out of the tunnel into the city,
Nail positioned himself next to Mite. "Don't think I've forgotten what you did. I haven't. While your friends are being sold,
I'm taking you to someone who can block your magic, boy.
When he's done with you, you'll learn to be a good slave. He's
an old acquaintance of mine, a manipulator. Maybe even the
last manipulator left on the seven."

Nail looked down at Mite as if expecting a reaction, but

373

Mite just stared straight ahead refusing to give Nail the satisfaction of a response.

"In fact," Nail continued. "I think, once you're fixed, I'll keep you for myself. With the proper training, I'm sure you'll make a good little cabin boy …"

Nail's words died on his lips as several of his men cried out a warning before dropping under a rain of lethal arrows. He ground out a curse, pulled a large sword, and charged toward an advancing wave of soldiers. Within seconds, Marius was pulling Ponce and Mite back and away. He had managed to undo his shackles and was now furiously working to free Ponce.

"We have to hide," he said as Ponce's chains dropped with a clatter and he turned to release Mite.

"No," Ponce ground out, a determined look on his face. "We have to help those soldiers."

Marius dropped Mite's chains and turning to Ponce asked in a harsh whisper, "And just how do you plan to do that? Do you know how to use a sword, a knife, any weapon? No? Those are trained men. If we try to help now, we'll just get in their way. Look, even now, they've taken down most of the pirates."

Mite watched as the soldiers dominated the pirates, except for Nail. He was skilled and fierce. Several bodies littered the ground around him as he swung his massive sword into the side of another man, dropping him.

With a hard look, Ponce turned back to Marius. "You're a warrior. You fight him."

Marius shook his head. "No way. I don't take chances like that. Nail is too good, we'd be too evenly matched. I'll let the soldiers do their job."

Giving Marius a disgusted look, Ponce shook his head and turned his attention back to the action between the pirates and soldiers. But now, there was only one pirate left standing, Nail.

Mite chafed at his inability to help as he watched another soldier succumb to Nail's blade. A powerful voice cut through the noise, shouting something Mite couldn't understand and instantly a dozen archers moved in around Nail with nocked arrows pointing at the pirate captain.

"Give up or die," the powerful voice shouted.

A grimace darkened Nail's face as he growled. He swung his massive sword and yelled, "Then I die."

He started toward the man who was shouting the orders, but before he could take three steps, he was peppered with arrows like a human pincushion, and dropped to his knees. The archers nocked again and Nail, shouting curses at the One, collapsed under the barrage of arrows.

With the pirates all dead or taken prisoner, the captives began to come forward, fearful and hesitant, asking the soldiers to release them. Marius led Ponce and Mite right up to the man who was in charge and with an air of authority said, "Thank you my good man. You've saved us from a terrible fate. May I ask who it is that has freed us?"

Giving Marius a curious look, the man said, "How is it you're not chained like the others?"

Ponce spoke up. "Please, my companion just undid our shackles back there by that wagon. You can see them on the ground. Once we were free, I wanted to help your men as they were fighting, but I fear I am no warrior. My name is Marcus Ponce and my companions are Marius and Mite. We were taken prisoner several days ago when our caravan was attacked ..."

Mite jumped in front of the man. "Please, please. You must find our friend. Alive, alive, alive. Yes, yes. We must find him. Please, please. Or the darkness will come, take all Ochen. We must go look now."

The man held up his hands to stop the rapid flow of words pouring from Mite. "Hold on there, kid. Just a minute. Just give me a minute. You're not making any sense and I need to talk with my men. Wait here and I'll be right back."

When the man walked away, Marius said, "Let's get out of here before he asks any more questions."

Mite turned on Marius, his need to find Rayne, battling with his mistrust of the darkness in Marius. "Why? Why? Mite has nothing to hide. Mite asks for help. Soldiers can help find Ray-ray."

Marius's brows lowered like thunder clouds. "You may not want to hear this, but your friend is dead. Even if the fall didn't kill him, being stuck out in the desert with no water and no supplies for days would kill even a young healthy man, let alone someone like him. Resign yourself to the fact, he's dead. I have. Because of him, I'll have to disappear." Marius cursed, a sick look on his face. "What am I going to do with that old man dead?"

Ponce released a huff. "Stop upsetting Mite. Maybe he's right. If anyone could survive, it would be the prince. We can't know for sure unless we go back and look. Make sure."

"Are you nuts?" Marius hissed. "Do you even hear yourself? Survive the sand desert of Arisima for days with no water? I know the prince is something special, but he was trapped in that old body and already on the edge."

Marius looked from Ponce to Mite as both stared at him. "I need my head examined. I've caught insanity from you two. Yeah, sure, we'll ask the soldiers for help."

"Help for what?" the man in charge asked as he walked over.

Just as Mite was set to start talking again, the man held out his hands, stopping him, and looked at Ponce. "Why don't you tell me."

After Ponce explained, the man shook his head. "No. It's not possible for anyone to survive that. The glass sand has no bottom. Anything dropped on it, just keeps sinking and is never seen again. Even if we went back to look for your friend's remains we would find nothing, and I can't spare any men to go off on a wild goose chase. As it is we're shorthanded and with the political upheaval in Westvale, I doubt that's going to get any better.

"Our division was commissioned by King Theodor himself almost three years ago to combat the pirates. For the last year and a half, we've had no reinforcements or updates. And now, with King Theodor ill, a new regent, and Prince Rayne taking control of the seven, we don't know what's going to happen."

"What?" Ponce and Mite exclaimed in unison.

"You don't know, do you? A few few weeks ago, the members of the Interplanetary Council and the Interplanetary court all died from some mysterious illness. They were together at a feast when it struck quickly. Within hours, they were all dead. I don't know much about the details, but the Prince of Corylus received the backing of those with any power left and proclaimed himself Imperial Majesty, Emperor Rayne Kierkengaard.

"Look, I'm sorry I can't help you but between thieving pirates and marauding scroll worshipers, I have enough problems of my own." He paused, chewing the ends of a long mustache that grew over his upper lip. "Look, I know it's a long shot, but I can tell you're not going to listen to common sense. Check out the independent guides here in the city. Perhaps one of them will help you. But, be forewarned, they don't come cheap."

After the soldiers left, Ponce, Mite, and Marius stood in silence, pondering the soldier's words. After a bit, Mite looked up at Ponce and said, "Darkness, darkness has done this. Sigmund took body of power and now has power, power, and even more power. No time, no time left, quick, quick now. Ray-ray must live, must stop darkness from spreading."

Marius squinted, scanning the area. "Well, standing here talking isn't getting anything done. We should go back to the inn. Rayne paid that innkeeper well, more than he asked. Maybe he'll front us a room to stay in until we get some funds."

"Good idea," Ponce said, nodding. "And if he won't, I still have a little something sewn inside the seam of my pants."

"You have what?" Marius asked.

Ponce smiled, and Marius grinned back. "You're a smart little sneak, aren't you? We might just pull this off yet. Come on."

Marius had a pretty good idea of the way back to the inn so with only a few detours, the three entered the common room to find Kaydin behind his tall desk just as they had first seen him.

"Welcome back, good sirs," he said with a large smile. "I will have rooms ready for you shortly. Is there anything else I can do for you?"

The three exchanged looks and Ponce said, "You knew we would be coming back?"

"Of course," Kaydin said.

"We don't have any money," Marius said.

"That's not a problem. Your friend made provision for your return the last time you were here." Kaydin looked past the three. His smile faltered. "Isn't he with you?"

While Ponce shook his head sadly, Mite spoke up. "Mite find friend. Yes, yes, yes. Ray-ray come back with us soon, soon."

"Yeah," Marius said. "We need to hire a guide. It seems our friend has gone missing."

Kaydin's face blanched. "In the desert?"

"Look," Marius growled. "We're going to find him. We just need to stay long enough to hire a guide. Okay?"

Kaydin bowed. "Of course, of course. Stay as long as you need. As I said, your friend already paid for your rooms. Do you want me to ask about for a guide?"

"Yes, yes," said Mite. "No time left, no time. Must hunt now."

Kaydin nodded, handing them a key. As Ponce walked past the desk, he said, "Reserve the bathing room for us as well."

𝕸

Later that evening, the three companions sat by the open glass doors eating a late dinner. Mite picked at his food.

"Eat something," Ponce said. "You can't help Rayne if you're weak from hunger."

With a sigh Mite stopped picking and popped a bit of fruit in his mouth. "Ponce-man right." He spoke around the food. "Ray-ray will need Mite to be strong."

"I don't think turning around requires that much strength," a reed-thin voice spoke from behind them.

Mite's fork clattered to the floor as all three turned in shock to focus on a slight old man clutching a tall staff.

"Ray-ray," Mite screamed as he jumped from his seat and scrambled to Rayne.

A pained expression crossed Rayne's face and he held up a hand, stopping Mite. "No, Mite. Don't touch me. Don't."

Mite backed off quickly, his eyes rounding.

"I'm sorry, my friend." Rayne's whispy voice drifted on the evening air. "Broken ribs."

Ponce rose, knocking back his chair. With Mite on one side and Ponce on the other, they guided Rayne to a chair Marius brought over to their table.

He eased down, releasing a groan as a shaft of pain took him. Then, looking around at the faces of his friends, Rayne smiled weakly.

"I didn't think I would ever see you again when I was thrown from that airship," Rayne said, his voice reedy and thin. "But it seems the One isn't done with me yet."

Ponce ran to order more food. When he returned, he asked, "What happened to you? We thought you were dead. But Mite wouldn't let us give up. He kept insisting you were alive. We were going to hire a guide and look for youe. How, Sire, how did you do it?"

Rayne breathed out a soft, tired sigh. "It's too long a story and I don't have the energy to tell it. Later, Ponce, okay?"

"Of course, Your Highness. Whenever you're ready. I just can't believe you're really still with us."

Kaydin arrived at that moment, bringing a steaming plate of food. Setting the serving in front of Rayne, he bowed. "I am truly happy to see you again, sir. As per our arrangement, I have kept my word."

Rayne whispered as Kaydin rose. "Just as I knew you would. I will retrieve my things later."

After Kaydin left, Rayne turned to Mite. "So, tell me, Mite, how did you escape the pirates?"

Mite and Ponce took turns telling Rayne all that had happened to them while Marius sat like a statue, staring at Rayne. When the story ended, Marius leaned forward, an eager look in his eyes. "Did you find the scroll?"

Mite and Ponce glared at Marius, and Mite said, "Dark lover still dark lover. Thinks only of scroll not of Ray-ray."

Marius returned the glares, and said, "That's what he went into the desert for, isn't it? I just asked. Sure, I'm glad he's still alive but I don't see why you're attacking me for asking a simple question."

"It's okay." Rayne raised his hand in a soothing gesture, his eyes fixed on Marius. "I have the Words of the One to Arisima."

Looking down at his plate, Marius fisted his hands. "And the other scrolls, the ones from Nemora and Sorial, did the pirates take them?"

Rayne didn't answer, just stared at Marius. Something sparked between them. After a couple minutes, Rayne let out a puff of air and said, "What do you think?"

Still keeping eye contact, Marius answered, "I think the Light Bringer of the One would not risk returning to Westvale unless he possessed the final three. You left the scrolls here, at the inn, didn't you? That's why you paid for rooms in advance. You planned to return."

Rayne dipped his head to Marius, acknowledging the truth.

After picking at his food, eating very little, and drinking only one glass of water, Rayne excused himself saying he needed to rest. He stood and reached for his staff, but Mite beat him to it. Lifting the carved wood, Mite exclaimed, "Old, old, old, wood. Living wood from before time of newcomers, yes, yes."

He paused, examining the staff with sharp eyes, running his hands over the etchings. Looking up at Rayne, his eyes filled with wonder, he said, "All Ray-ray, yes?"

"Yes," Rayne took the staff and ran his hand tenderly over the pictures. "All Ray-ray."

Several hours later, while Ponce and Mite were sleeping, Marius slipped out the front door of the inn to find Rayne already waiting for him.

"How long have you known?" he asked.

Rayne looked up to the stars sparkling through the leaves of one of the tall, local trees. "I wasn't certain until tonight." He sighed. "But I know now. Let's go."

Marius climbed down the two steps of the inn entrance and started walking but then turned back to Rayne. "Why?"

"Why what?"

"You know what," Marius hissed. "Why leave them and take me when you know what I'm going to do? With the remaining money, you could even hire someone to kill me in the street and no one would ever know. Why?"

"Because it was foretold."

"And you're okay with this?" Marius asked, confusion and anger lacing his words.

Rayne kept walking, clutching the wooden staff in a vise-like grip.

Marius reached out and spun Rayne around to face him. "Why are you doing this? Why don't you let someone else face Sigmund? I know who you really are in there. You're just a good kid who's had a lot of crap dumped on him. You're not like me. Why does it have to be you?"

Compassion for the lost man rose in Rayne, smoothing his wrinkled face. "Perhaps you should ask yourself the same question. Maybe you will before it's too late. As for me, I made a commitment to a friend a long time ago to trust the One. Since then, I've made that same commitment to the One himself. I will not turn from my destiny. I will do what must be done."

He turned, and with a veredium like determination propelling him forward, strode toward the portal station and Corylus.

"Stupid prophecies," Marius spit. He shook his head and ground his teeth. "I'll get the passes and meet you at the portal." He sprinted ahead of Rayne, down the street.

43

Rayne and Marius stood silently facing each other after exiting the Arisima portal in Westvale.

"You're a stubborn fool, Rayne," Marius said softly.

"So are you Marius."

"You know the next time we see each other, we'll be enemies."

"I know. You do what you have to do; I'll do what must be done. But do me a favor, if you will. Give me a few hours. Tell Sigmund he can find me in the cathedral after midday."

With a nod, Marius jogged off through the half-empty portal station, out into the square. Rayne hobbled at his own slow pace through the hushed station. He crossed Portal Square, heading toward the cathedral, his ribs aching with every breath and every movement. But he wouldn't stop, would not allow himself to give up now.

He was surprised at the lack of people. At this hour of the morning, Portal Station Square and the main thoroughfare to the Great Square should be bustling with activity, but now he saw few people. And those he saw scanned their surroundings, their movements erratic, their faces masks of suspicion and fear. Rayne felt it too, a sense of foreboding. *The light. It's wrong.* Glancing up at the sky, his breath caught. A large dark mass boiled high overhead, casting a sickly yellow-gray hue over the city. It looked like an approaching squall. But this was no natural storm.

He struggled against the weight of the scrolls, as if they were growing heavier with each step. The effort of taking in enough air without being able to draw deep breaths taxed his remaining strength. The air, which should have been crisp and clear, was heavy, and the strange color he'd noticed muted the beauty of the autumn morning.

I'm too late. Fear, like a burning clump of half-eaten food, lodged in his throat. At least he was stronger this morning. Though he had spent the night awake, studying the Words of the One to Arisima, he felt rested, as if he had slept a full night.

He also sensed a new source of strength within him. Something happened to him in the crystal cavern and Rayne suspected he now carried another light. The sensation of reserved energy within his spirit reminded him of the Sun Sparrows on Veres and Ledia's light on Nemora. Whatever it was, it was fueling his internal spark. The smoldering wick of rebellion that Sigmund had despised and tried to extinguish over the years was growing stronger. Rayne remembered how it blossomed into flame when the One strengthened him as he battled Sigmund's will.

Why? Why do you give me more light, fuel the spark you set in me so long ago, when I can't even use it in this body?

Like so often before, the only answer he received was the single word spoken quietly in his spirit, *trust*.

He nodded. "I'm trusting."

As he moved toward the cathedral, Rayne sensed the darkness battering at him, seeking to extinguish the light within. But the shell of the old man was as resistant to the outside forces of spiritual energy as it was to allowing energy to flow from it.

While he had been healing in the crystal cavern, talking with Badr and Terev, Rayne thought about why the One allowed his spirit to be torn from his own body and trapped in this one. He began to understand. The old man body acted like a kind of magic-resistant protection for his spirit. He wondered if his spirit could have survived as unscathed if he had remained himself, sensitive to and receptive of magic energies.

It had been hard living in a dying, pain-infested body, but his spirit had matured and grown strong through the struggle. His faltering trust in the One was now solid, firmly planted on the promises embedded in the prophecies. Rayne no longer doubted that the One was in control. And if the One was truly in control, all that had happened to him, all he had yet to face, was part of the One's weave of events. And if Rayne must die, that too was part of the prophecy even if Rayne couldn't understand it.

He crossed the Great Square, his mind racing. Rayne had thought much about what would be needed to bind the living darkness, and he had come to one conclusion: he couldn't be the final piece; he was physically too weak. He had done his part, finding and collecting the scrolls. He would deliver the final three to Jonathan, then someone else would have to finish the job.

But Rayne still had another task. A role in the One's plan to bring judgement down on Sigmund and his kind. Rayne wasn't certain how it would all work out, but he was certain he needed to meet with Sigmund and somehow keep the demon's attention away from the scrolls.

To make that happen, Rayne planned to have Jonathan keep the originals while Rayne carried fake scrolls with him to the cathedral. *That should hold that demon's attention.* Jonathan would hide the seven originals until they were needed.

His weakened state forced Rayne to stop and catch his breath several times before he stood in front of the grand Westvale Cathedral. He considered going around the back to the church house, slipping into Elsie's kitchen, and asking her to bring Jonathan to him, but he discarded the idea. Jonathan would be in his office by this time and it would be best to meet with him there. He climbed the couple steps to the walkway and following it around the large building, entered through a small side door that opened onto a hallway leading to the church offices.

As he approached the large suite of rooms that housed the high office, Rayne saw Bishop Hedrick's secretary Simon sitting at his small desk, shuffling papers. Turning to lean against the wall, Rayne closed his eyes and huffed in frustration. Simon was a fastidious and fussy man and Rayne knew he would have difficulties getting past him to see Jonathan without an appointment. The balding, middle-aged secretary guarded the bishop's time as if it was the most valuable commodity on Corylus.

Though Rayne was loathed to give one of the scrolls to the man, he knew it might be the only way to gain Jonathan's attention. Lifting a prayer to the One, Rayne eased off the wall and walked up to Simon. He stood, silent, waiting, until Simon looked up. "Well, what do you want?"

"I seek an audience with His Eminence, Bishop Hedrick."

Simon scrutinized Rayne, a sour frown set on his pinced features. "I don't suppose you have an appointment?"

He fixed Rayne with a questioning gaze, then began to shuffle his papers again. "His Eminence is a very important and busy man. He does not have time to meet with every itinerant monk who happens to come to Westvale. Next time, think ahead and schedule an appointment. I currently have a few available two months from now."

Taking as deep a breath as he dared, Rayne leaned his staff against Simon's desk, eliciting a dirty look from the man. Grunting from the effort, he lifted the strap of the Nemora satchel over his head, then placed the bag on Simon's desk.

Simon looked at the satchel as if it was about to bite him. "His Eminence doesn't accept gifts. Please remove your *thing*."

"You don't recognize this satchel, do you?" Rayne asked, his voice breathy and weak.

"I've never seen it before in my life." Simon huffed.

"Or any like it?"

"Perhaps," Simon said, looking away.

"Well, Bishop Hedrick will recognize it. He will know what it contains. And he will want to see me. Tell him I have two more just like it."

"I do not interrupt His Eminence when he is busy." Simon waved for Rayne to take the sack from his desk.

"Look, Simon. I don't have much time here. Actually, I don't have *any* time to argue with you. Take the satchel to Jonathan *now*! Give him my message. And tell him it's urgent!"

Relief eased some of Rayne's tension when Simon responded to his emphatic order by scurrying into the bishop's office with the scroll. After Simon vanished, Rayne sat down on one of the few straight-back, black chairs set in the hall for those waiting to meet with the bishop. He didn't wait long. Jonathan himself barreled out the door moments later, with the bag in hand and Simon trailing on his heels. When he saw Rayne, a look of confusion passed over his face. Dismissing him, the bishop began scanning the hall.

"That's him," Simon said, pointing to Rayne.

"*You* brought this?" Jonathan asked, glancing at Rayne before checking up and down the hall once again.

"Yes." Rayne pushed upright and wobbled a moment before finding his balance.

Jonathan stopped, stared intently at Rayne, then waved him into his office saying, "We must talk."

Gesturing at a blue brocade, wing-back chair as he took a seat behind his massive, oak desk, Jonathan said, "Please, sit."

After propping his staff against the desk, Rayne sat. He didn't want to show weakness at this point, but he couldn't avoid the grimace of pain or the groan as he lowered onto the soft cushion.

"Are you alright?" Jonathan asked, his brow furrowed.

Rayne closed his eyes for a moment, struggling with an unexpected surge of emotion. Being in Westvale, sitting across from his friend, was fueling feelings Rayne refused to acknowledge. He couldn't let his feelings shake his resolve. Not now.

Opening his eyes to see Jonathan's blue ones gazing over the top of his glasses, brought back memories of Warren that almost undid Rayne right then. With an internal effort, he clamped down the roiling emotions. "Just some broken ribs, but that is not the issue. The important thing is the seven scrolls."

Jonathan stood up and paced behind his desk for a minute, then turned to Rayne and pointed at the scrolls still draped over his shoulders. "Who are you? And how did you come to possess these scrolls?"

Giving Jonathan an even look and fully aware of the answer, Rayne asked, "You don't recognize me, do you?"

"Should I?" Irritation oozed through the the bishop's words.

"Remember the day you caught up with me on the steps of the library?" Rayne's thoughts returned to the day Jonathan had confronted him about the Corylus scroll. "You asked to see the Words of the One to Corylus? That was before you joined Shaw, Anne, and me in studying the scroll."

Jonathan's lips flattened, and his eyes turned into pools of blue suspicion. "What kind of game are you playing? There is only one person who would know about that. And, you're not him. I don't know you."

"Are you certain?" Rayne caught Jonathan's eyes, willing him to see the truth. "I remember that morning. You're words. That I claimed to be the Light Bringer, an unverified person from an unverified prophecy, that I was a trained assassin with blood on my hands. You were right. You said, 'If this scroll is indeed what you claim it to be, it should have been brought to me as the head of the church on Corylus and studied by officials of the church, not studied by an off-world monk, a woman, and a former assassin.'"

Jonathan dropped into his seat. He stammered, but no words came. He reminded Rayne of a fish as his mouth opened and closed, until finally, he said, "How could you know that?" Blinking rapidly, Jonathan cleared his throat. "Rayne?"

"Yes, yes." Rayne moaned, dropping his face into his hands. *Thank you, my Lord.*

"It's really you, isn't it?" Disbelief reduced Jonathan's voice to a whisper. "How?"

Rayne shook his head. "It's too long a story. Just tell me this, Jonathan, do you believe me?" Rayne paused, blinking back threatening tears. "Do you believe I'm who I say I am?"

"I believe that only the true Light Bringer could have reclaimed the last three scrolls." He stopped and stared intently at Rayne, compassion and understanding infusing his features.

"Oh, my poor boy! You being here now, like this." He waved his hands at Rayne. "This explains so much we didn't understand. It's what we suspected, an alternate body. You truly are the broken. The lost and the broken from the prophecies. Tetsuya's prophecy said as much. 'I will guide his steps by the least of lights until the three are found and the cup of wrath is full. Then the true heart will be known by the bond I have made and *the broken made whole* once again.'"

Rayne's thoughts raced. "Yes. Yes. Mite guided me. He must be the least of lights. And the three must be the final scrolls. They're here now. It's time. The cup of wrath is almost full." He paused and sucked in a painful breath. "Jonathan, please, I need your help. Are the other scrolls here? Please say they're here."

"They are all close. But because we mistrusted you, I mean His Imperial Majesty, we've kept them hidden."

"How long? How long will it take to get them together?"

"About an hour if I can get hold of everyone."

"Good, good ..." Rayne mumbled, closing his eyes. "And the sword. I need the King's sword. Can you get it?" Rayne cracked his eyes open when Jonathan didn't respond.

Dropping his gaze to his desk, Jonathan said, "The King's sword went missing days ago. The emperor—I mean His Imperial Majesty—I mean ... you." Jonathan shook his head. "His Imperial Majesty has been tearing the palace apart looking for it."

Jonathan stopped and scrutinized Rayne. "It's Sigmund? It's him in your body, isn't it? Ever since the incident on Nemora, Thorvin and Anne insisted you weren't you."

Rayne nodded. He closed his eyes for a few seconds digesting Jonathan's words. Trying to release some of the tension building in his neck, he shook his head. "I wish I knew what I'm supposed to do here. I'm so confused. I was certain I needed the sword, but ..." He huffed out a breath of air. "We'll have to make do without the sword and trust the One for the rest. Soon Sigmund will know I'm here. He must believe I have the scrolls when he comes for me, so I'll need seven blank scrolls."

Jonathan stood silent as lines of concentration gathered on his face, then he nodded. "I can get those."

"Good." Rayne studied Jonathan for a minute, considering the danger inherent in what he was asking of the man. "Someone will need to keep the original scrolls safe. It will be dangerous. Are you willing?"

"What are you planning?" Jonathan asked, a determined light blooming in his eyes.

Rayne groaned. *Am I doing the right thing here? I don't know. Please stop me if I'm wrong.*

"I'm going to wait for Sigmund in the cathedral, draw his attention. I think the scrolls need to be close so somewhere near the sanctuary should be good. That way, when the One reveals what needs to be done to bind the darkness, you'll be ready. But, for this to work, Sigmund can't suspect that I don't have the original scrolls."

Rayne's voice dropped a notch. "Listen to me now, Jonathan. This is important. You must do what I ask no matter what happens. Do you understand? No matter what you see, no matter what happens, you must keep the scrolls safe. Promise me. In the end, you will have to trust the One to guide you. Can you do that?"

"I promise." Concern etched deep lines on Jonathan face.

Shifting painfully, Rayne pulled the two remaining satchels over his head and placed them on Jonathan's desk. "Here." He sighed and looked out the window as he ran a hand down his face. He returned his gaze to Jonathan. "When Sigmund comes for me, I must let him take me."

"What?" Jonathan cried.

"Remember. You must not interfere no matter what happens. You'll know what to do when the time comes. Just accept this is the way it must be. Help me do what must be done while I'm still able. And please, don't try to stop me."

"Are you absolutely certain, Rayne?" Jonathan's voice cracked.

"Yes. It's the only way to drive back the darkness that's overtaking Ochen. I must not falter. The One has promised to be with me. I trust him."

"Rayne. There's something you need to know. We, all your friends, have worried about you and prayed for you these last months. We were never sure if you were still in your body, or even ... still alive. Everyone is going to want to see you. I can contact them and have them meet with you in the sanctuary. You have time for that, surely. I'll send word to Thorvin and he can gather the others. Elsie, Shaw, and Anne are all here on the church grounds. And Lexi ..." Jonathan paused, thought crinkling his already wrinkled brow.

"Oh, Rayne ... it is imperative you meet with Lexi. That's got to be what the prophecy means when it says, the true heart will be known by the bond I have made and the broken made whole once again. You must talk to Lexi. Don't you see? She's part of what needs to happen."

Rayne closed himself off from Jonathan's words, going still and quiet.

"Sire?" Jonathan asked.

"Lexi," Rayne mumbled. "Only Lexi." He shook his head, frowning. "I will not put them in danger. But I ... need to see ... No, it's too selfish. I can't put her in danger."

"She won't care. Just Lexi, Rayne. Okay? Just Lexi."

Rayne nodded. His eyes closed, and his head fell forward as exhaustion overcame his will to keep moving.

𝕟

Jonathan watched as the old man's breathing evened in sleep, sorrow compressing his heart.

O merciful One, I can't believe what's happened even though this was what we suspected. But he's here; your Light Bringer has come home, as prophesied. I can't even begin to imagine what that young man has been through and yet here he sits. Please tell me what to do. How can I help him?

Grabbing a pen and paper, Jonathan scribbled three notes. After looking them over, he nodded to himself, ran to his door, and cracking it just a bit, called, "Simon, get this to Thorvin, immediately." He handed his secretary one note. "Then, find Lady Alexianndra and give her this." He handed Simon the second note.

"Once you've delivered these, run to the copy room and give Brother Felix this note. Quick man, quick. We have no time to waste." As Simon started to sprint down the hall, Jonathan shouted after him. "Simon, stop in the kitchen first. Have Elsie send me some tea and bread, straightaway … and … honey. Yes, of course, honey too."

Simon stopped in the middle of the hall and turned back, nodding.

"Go, go, go!" Jonathan shouted, then ducked back into his office, closing the door with a soft snick behind him.

Twenty minutes later, Rayne woke with a start followed by a groan as he wrapped his arms over his torso. Jonathan, who had been pacing behind his desk, looked up. "Are you alright?"

Blinking the sleep from his eyes, Rayne said, "Better. Not so tired."

"This might help," Jonathan indicated a tray of sliced bread, honey, tea, and a large glass of water on the table by Rayne's side.

Rayne sniffed and then a smile raised the corners of his mouth. "Is this what I think it is?"

"Elsie's bread, yes. You know she's going to refuse to make it for me anymore once she finds out you were here and I didn't tell her."

"The fewer people who know, the better. I don't like putting anyone at risk. Yet now I've put you in danger by asking for your help. And my need to see Lexi has driven me to put her at risk as well. I should have said no when you asked. Is it too late to stop her?"

"I'm afraid so. She's already agreed to come to the sanctuary. She thinks she's meeting an old friend of mine from Veres. She should be there at the midday hour, so you have time to eat something more filling before you go. I can ask Elsie to send up a full meal, if you want. It will strengthen you. From the looks of you, I would say you haven't been eating well for some time now."

"Nothing more, Jonathan. The bread and honey are enough. I haven't had much of an appetite since I moved into this body. It's pretty weak and can't hold down more than a little at a time."

Jonathan poured Rayne some tea and watched while he nibbled around the edge of a plain piece of bread.

"I almost asked Elsie to send some bacon as well, but then thought better of that. She would have stormed over here and yelled at me for making her think of you and how you always loved those bacon sandwiches. But I can see now, even if I had taken the chance, it would have been for naught. You really can't eat more?"

Rayne had returned most of the slice of bread to the plate and just sipped the warm tea. He shook his head. "No. But thanks for this. It's helped a lot to eat Elsie's bread. I feel much better now. Stronger."

While Rayne was finishing up his tea, there was a knock at the door. Jonathan rose and after a brief dialog with Simon, walked back to his desk holding three carry bags, one containing the seven blank scrolls, and two with originals.

"Will you be able to carry all seven?" Jonathan asked, looking at Rayne, doubt clouding his thoughts.

"I have no choice. Do you have the seven originals now?"

"I have your three, plus these two. The last two are coming as we speak. I should have them shortly."

"And will *you* be able to carry all seven?"

"If you can manage, Sire, so can I," Jonathan returned, a half-smile worming its way onto his face. But then the smile faltered, and sorrow creased his brow.

Rayne grabbed his staff with both hands and levered his body upright. When he was stable, he walked to Jonathan and held out his hand. "Thank you for everything."

"I truly wish I could do more, Your Highness."

The two stood blinking back tears, then Jonathan stepped up to Rayne and gently hugged the old man. With care, he lowered the straps of the heavy bag over Rayne's head, settling the scrolls evenly on Rayne's back. Once they were balanced, Rayne took a couple steps and nodded. "This will work. Be careful carrying the scrolls, the dark can sense the power in them. Hopefully, Sigmund will be so focused on me, he'll ignore everything else."

"You be careful, too, my friend."

"Always," Rayne whispered. He turned without another word while Jonathan stood, staring at nothing until the door closed behind Rayne.

44

Andrew slipped through the narrow, web-infested passage that Rayne had found so disturbing when he had first returned to Westvale. Andrew shuffled sideways in places, clutching a heavy, awkward package that was nearly as tall as he. It was his eighth time through in the last four days, and still he was pulling cobwebs off as he emerged in the Queens Chambers. Charlotte was asleep as she usually was by this time of the morning, snoring through her open mouth, head tilted back into the soft padding of the overstuffed arm chair.

Queen Rowena lay unchanged on her bed, while King Theodor sat with eyes closed, resting his head against the tall back of the wooden-armed chair he favored.

Andrew tiptoed across the room to stand in front of the king before clearing his throat and whispering, "I'm back, Your Majesty."

Without opening his eyes, Theodor rumbled in a rough voice, "Do you have it?"

"Yes, Your Majesty." Andrew heaved the package out toward the king. Theodor opened blood-shot eyes and pulling up, straightened his spine, and reached for the package.

"And were you able to find out what that Imperial Impostor is up to now?"

"Yes … um … Your Majesty." Andrew bit his lip. "Are you certain this is the right thing to do, Your Majesty. I know it's not my place to question you, Sire, but ... I don't know if I can do this. I don't think I can. Your Majesty, he is still your son … and my friend."

Andrew backed up a step as the red-eyed, scruffy-bearded sovereign snarled at him. "That may be Rayne's body but the thing inside it is pure evil. My son is dead! He's dead! It's time his body joined him at rest.

"Did you think it was coincidence that you happened to come into the secret passages to spy on that impostor at the same moment I was making my way to the wall behind his sitting room? No, it was no accident I found you. I've been using the hidden passages for over a week to spy on that demon and his associates. Ever since my mind began to clear. At first it was disorienting but the more I walked, the sharper my wits grew. That too was no coincidence.

"Though I grew stronger, I continued acting as if I was still frozen in a drugged stupor whenever that thing came to mock Rowena and me. But I had to do it; I had to be sly to trick the demon. But I've done it. I fooled Sigmund. He has no idea I've been using the passages to gain information about what's been happening not only on Corylus, but throughout Ochen.

"Today, I put an end to this mockery. I've allowed the deaths of good men and women. I've waited too long, been too hesitant. No more! I've been a fool. It's time I faced the truth that the only way to save my people is to kill that monster parading as my son."

Theodor unwrapped the package resting across his knees, laying bare the King's Sword. Allowing the sheath to fall at his feet, Theodor lifted the sword and Andrew watched as light and determination grew in the monarch's eyes.

"Thank you for this, Andrew," Theodor said, watching the blade catch beams of sunlight as he turned the ancient weapon in his hand.

At Theodor's command, Andrew had taken the sword from the vault days ago. But struggling with what Theodor planned to do with it, Andrew had kept it hidden. Then yesterday, when Theodor said he was going to act today, whether he had the sword or not, Andrew knew he needed to bring it to the king. He had no choice.

Theodor seemed to grow in stature as he stood and began swinging the blade in figure eights in front of him.

"Oh my!" Charlotte suddenly gasped with a breathy scream as she came awake. "What's going on here?"

"What's going on here, madam, is your king has finally decided to act like a king once again." Theodor walked to the healer. Standing over her, his face a stern mask, he asked, "Do you still honor your king, or do you bow down to the darkness that masquerades as my son?"

Charlotte raised widened eyes. "Y-y-you, Y-y-your Majesty and the Q-q-queen, I'm loyal to you."

"Then keep quiet and don't alert the guards." Turning back to Andrew, Theodor said, "Now, Andrew, tell me what the emperor is doing."

"Well." Andrew chewed his lip again, still unsure if Theodor's mind was stable enough to make this decision. At times, the look in the king's eyes scared him. He could be helping the king make the most horrendous mistake of his life.

But then Andrew remembered how Rayne had acted when he returned from Nemora after his birthday, and the horror he had felt when Rayne kicked Boone while the dog barked and snapped. *Boone knew. She knew from the start.* Faces of the people executed in the last few months rose in his mind, twisting his stomach. All that happened since Rayne's return, even the sudden and questionable deaths of the councilors and judges, pointed to the fact that something evil had taken hold of Andrew's friend. But most of all, Andrew thought about the things that were said in the church dining room.

If Rayne was really still trapped in his own body, then he would be fighting against the evil, I know he would. But he hasn't. And if Rayne was still there, Boone would know. I hope I'm doing the right thing.

Lifting a heartfelt prayer for guidance, Andrew looked up

into King Theodor's eyes. "I'll tell you, Your Majesty. But you have to promise me you'll wait to see how Boone reacts first. If she still hates the prince—I mean, His Imperial Majesty— then we'll know for sure Rayne isn't there anymore. But please promise me you'll give Rayne that chance and wait to see what Boone does. Please? Just in case."

Theodor grimaced, but then his eyes softened. "Son, I wish you were right. But I've talked to that thing inside Rayne's body. It has come by often in these last weeks to mock my helplessness. And Rowena's. He has her trapped by some magical thing he calls a spike, but she can hear everything we say. It's an abomination!

"Andrew, try to understand. Heinrich helped Sigmund take Rayne's body for himself and now he's using it to overthrow Ochen and deliver everyone to the darkness. He's quite proud of what he and his evil colleague have done. They laugh in my face, Andrew. You must accept that they are pure evil incarnate. And Brayden, our own nephew; we trusted him and loved him like a son. We were fools. All this time, he's been working for Sigmund.

"I don't even know if Rayne is alive or dead. Sigmund taunts me with unbelievable stories of how he has imprisoned my son's spirit in someone else's body. He believes I'm too broken to try and defy him. He's wrong."

Theodor sighed. "Andrew, I know how much you care for my son, but we must be strong. If Rayne *is* still in his body, dominated by Sigmund, don't you think he'd want to be released from that?"

Tears began to leak from Theodor's eyes as he tried without success to blink them back. "He's my son. My only child. Don't you think this hurts me too? But Andrew, I can't allow my personal feelings to cloud my judgement; a king doesn't have that luxury. I owe it to the people of Ochen to stop this monster even at the cost of my own son ... and wife." His voice cracked. "You know what Sigmund promised to do to Rowena if I hindered him. I've told you. At first, I couldn't face that. But now that I'm free of the tincture-induced fog, I can't stand aside and watch this evil overtake my people. No! This must end now. Today."

Theodor pulled in a quivering breath and walked over to the large bed where Rowena rested. Andrew came up next to him and taking his hand said, "Sire, Boone and I will help you any way we can.

"The emperor's planning to meet someone important in the sanctuary during the midday meal. It must be something special because Martin, his page, told me the emperor, the Lord Master Mage, Regent Woodfield, and his brother Giles have all been talking about it in the royal suite with a man who arrived from Arisima this morning. Even the captains from the royal guard have been coming and going. And Jason Andersen was summoned from Sorial. But, from what Martin overheard, only His Imperial Majesty, the mage, Brayden, and Giles will be in the sanctuary during the meeting. The guards are supposed to all remain in the Great Square in front of the cathedral until they're called."

Rowena's chest rose and fell in a steady rhythm as the king listened to Andrew, then asked, "Who is this important person they're meeting?"

"No idea, Sire. Only the emperor's inner circle knows for sure. Martin tried to listen in so he could get me more information, but they were being really secretive. One thing Martin did learn though, they plan to have a big celebration after the meeting."

"It's almost time for the midday meal," Theodor murmured. "In the Westvale Cathedral sanctuary, you say? That's an odd place to meet with a dignitary. That's an odd place for Sigmund to even venture into." He paused, eyes crinkled. "But it's a perfect place to confront the demon, right there in the sanctuary of the One when he's surrounded by so few allies."

The door knob rattled. Theodor bent to slide the sword under Rowena's bed before scrambling into his chair and assuming the look of unknowing the tincture always produced. Andrew slunk back through the hidden door, into the secret passage.

"What's going on here?" Anne asked, confused by the feeling of activity and Charlotte's guilty expression.

"Nothing," Charlotte said, putting her hands to her mouth and shaking her head. "Absolutely nothing at all."

Anne looked at Charlotte, suspicion creasing her brow. She scanned the room, certain that something was indeed going on in the Queen's Chambers. But she had no idea what, and no time to try to pin down whatever it was that had Charlotte acting so strange. The woman was always a bit flighty anyway. Anne had gotten a cryptic message from Thorvin nearly an hour ago about meeting in the church house for lunch. She hoped Charlotte wouldn't mind staying with the royals a bit longer.

Ignoring the impression that Charlotte was hiding something, Anne walked over to look at Theodor. She was pleased to see that he seemed more alert. "Soon, Your Majesty. The effects of the tincture are wearing off and soon you should be yourself. I just hope no one notices the changes I made to the Lord Master Mage's ingredients until it's too late."

Turning back to Charlotte, she said, "Charlotte, something's come up. Would you mind watching over the king and queen for another hour or so. I'll return as soon as I can."

Charlotte jumped up from her chair and ushered Anne from the room saying, "You just go ahead and take all the time you need dearie. I'll be here when you get back. We'll all be here when you get back. Just like always." Charlotte giggled as she pushed Anne out the door.

After closing the door behind Anne, Charlotte plopped her frame down into her chair, fanning herself with her hands. "This is too much excitement for someone my age."

Andrew peeked from the hidden door and after scanning the room, came out.

Theodor rose. As he went to Rowena's bed to retrieve the sword, he shook his head. "So, Anne was behind that change in the tincture. I should have known." He released a slight chuckle.

"Here, Andrew. Take the sword, set it in the passage, and be ready to hide. The midday meal will be coming soon. We'll wait until after it's been delivered to leave.

"Charlotte, if we're not back before they return, set the empty dishes outside the door so no one enters."

"Your Highness, what am I supposed to do with your food?"

Theodor gave Charlotte a level look. "Madam, I don't care. Eat it, throw it out the window, whatever. Just make certain no one comes in this suite after I've left. Do you understand?"

"Yes, Your Majesty, of course."

"Andrew, you and I will head out through the passage and cut across the lawn to the cathedral. It would be better if we could do this in the dark, but I refuse to wait any longer. If I hesitate, I may lose the will to do what must be done."

After the meal was delivered, Theodor said, "Andrew, it's time. Is Boone ready?"

"Yes, Your Majesty. I told her to stay down near the passage entrance. She'll be happy to get outside again. And, Sire," Andrew added. "Thanks again for giving it one more chance before you do what you feel ... what you need to do with that sword."

A sad smile ghosted across Theodor's face. "You're a good man, Andrew. I can see why Rayne liked you so much. I'm glad I don't have to face this alone."

Despair erased Theodor's faltering smile, and he whispered, "I hope I have the strength to do what I must. The need to take the life of my only child is ripping my heart to shreds. I know now Sigmund was counting on that. But he failed to realize I would, in time, overcome that restraint and fulfill my duty as King of Ochen."

Theodor walked over to where Rowena was now propped up, so Charlotte could feed her. "Andrew. Charlotte. Please give us a few minutes."

Andrew moved to the secret door while Charlotte busied herself with some needlework.

Theodor sat on the side of the bed and took Rowena's hand. "I'm so sorry, my love. But I need to believe you understand. You know I must do this. I have no choice. I kept praying something would change, but things have only gotten worse."

He kissed her cold hand and rubbed his fingers over her knuckles and across her signet ring. "I know that if something goes wrong, Sigmund will carry out his threat against you. I pray that doesn't happen. But if it does, my love, please believe that if I could, I would take every bit of pain for you.

"Oh, my dear, dear beloved, how could it have all gone so wrong?" Theodor cried out his mental anguish. "I love you, I will always love you, but I have to do this for Ochen. You know this is true.

"We must accept that our son is dead and my duty compels me to kill the demon using his body. It's only through my faith in the One that I find any relief to this overwhelming pain. I cling to the hope of our reuniting as a family once again when we go to be with the One. Maybe then, if Rayne could forgive us, we'll finally find some peace. Please, my love, pray for me, that I will have the strength to defeat Sigmund."

As he bent to kiss Rowena, Theodor noticed two tears tracking from the corners of her beautiful but empty amethyst eyes. With a groan, he pulled himself away and followed Andrew into the passage in the wall.

45

⊓

Odd, very odd, Anne thought as she hurried down the stairs to meet Thorvin at the church house. As she cut across the dining hall, she spotted Lexi eating by herself and walked over to join her.

Looking up as Anne approached, Lexi said, "Anne, I'm glad you're here. I was hoping to see you before you started your shift with the king and queen." Then with a quizzical look she said, "Wait, you should be up there now, shouldn't you?"

"Normally, yes. But I got a strange note from Thorvin asking me to meet him at the church house for the midday meal. He said it was important, so I asked Charlotte if she could cover for a bit. I'm not sure I should have done that, though. She was acting very peculiar, not like herself, when I left." Anne shook her head, but then looked up at Lexi. "Did you get a note from Thorvin?"

"Thorvin asked you to meet him at the church house? Now? No. I didn't get that message. But I did get an unusual request from Jonathan. He sent me a note saying it was *imperative* I meet a friend in the sanctuary *during* the noon hour today." Lexi's brow scrunched. "Doesn't it seem rather peculiar that both meetings are scheduled for the same time and both are *important*?

"I don't know, but now that you mention it …" Anne shook her head. "Why?"

"Just a feeling. It seems too coincidental. I must admit I'm curious to meet this friend Jonathan insisted I see. He said the man is from Veres and he knew things about me that a stranger couldn't possibly know, so I think he must know my father. But the real question is, if he's from Veres how did he get off world? If the situation there has changed, that would mean I can go home. Anyway, with the way things have been going, I don't think it's farfetched to believe the two meetings are connected in some way. In fact, I ate early and was just about to head to the cathedral. We could walk over together."

"I'd like that," Anne said. "After you've met Jonathan's friend, why don't you stop by the church house. I'm sure Thorvin wouldn't mind. In fact, he probably would have asked you to come, but he must have talked to Jonathan and learned you were already meeting his friend."

"That, or he only wants to talk to one or two people then have you spread the news, like we planned." Lexi finished munching on a roll.

"Yes," Anne said. "That makes sense. Stop by the Queen's Chambers later, and I'll fill you in on whatever is so important Thorvin said it couldn't wait, and you can tell me all about your meeting with this mysterious stranger."

The two walked out together into the shrouded afternoon air.

"This is getting worse," Anne said, waving at the sickly fog that blanketed the area and dimmed the autumn sun.

Looking upward, they stood for a few minutes and watched the bank of dark storm clouds now boiling over the city. Lexi shivered. "It's darker here now than it was on Veres before Rayne brought the light back. And that cloud! It feels evil. It looks like it's boiling right over us. Anne, I'm afraid."

"Me too," Anne admitted. "But we have to keep trusting the One is in control. That's what Rayne would say if he was here." Tired of the ever-present topic of the growing darkness,

Anne change the subject and asked, "Has His Imperial Majesty invited you to Sorial again?"

Lexi rolled her eyes and flipped a strand of golden hair from her face. "Yes. Just this morning. He seemed to be in an extraordinarily good mood and insisted I would want to join him in some kind of celebration there. He even hinted at inviting a special guest from my past.

"Oh, Anne, he doesn't give up. This is the third time he's asked me in three days. I wish he would just get the hint and stop asking. I have no desire to be near him, let alone go watch some poor slaves fight to the death while he and his friends get drunk and gorge themselves on rich food. After which, I'll have to fight off His Imperial Majesty's very persistent advances.

"I'm so tired of it. I don't even see Rayne anymore when I look at him. His eyes used to stir me with their beauty and kindness, now they just terrorize me. They're so cold and empty. He's a total stranger. And yet, I don't know how much longer I'll have the strength to oppose him. He's growing stronger while my will seems to be shattering into weak slivers of hopelessness."

Anne nodded. She didn't know what to say to comfort her friend. The growing darkness was sapping everyone's energy and will. Anne didn't know how much longer Lexi would be able to hold off the most powerful man in Ochen.

"Anne?" Lexi said. "Could I ask you something?"

"Of course."

"I know we've talked about this so much, and you're probably sick of my inability to let it go, but do you think Rayne's still ... oh, here I go again. No. I will not continue to hold onto an empty hope. He's dead. I've known it for a while, ever since my heart began to feel so empty. I need to accept it."

Lexi met Anne's gaze, confusion flickering in her eyes. "It's just that when I have those dreams about that curious old man, I feel like I'm connected to Rayne in some way. It's as if he's still alive, somewhere, somehow, and my heart longs to reunite with his. Do you think that might be so, or am I just too stubborn to let go of a senseless hope and accept the truth?"

Anne hugged Lexi. "No. You keep holding on to that hope. Until we know for certain it's senseless, don't let go of your hope. Maybe the One is telling you to keep hoping by sending you these dreams."

"Thanks, Anne. You're a good friend."

Anne smiled. "Stop by the Queen's Chamber later and we'll talk some more."

"You don't mind that I can't stop talking about Rayne, even now?"

"Lexi, he's my little brother. You can talk about him all you want."

"Thanks for being a big sister to me too." Lexi said as she veered toward the sanctuary while Anne kept straight on toward the church house. "See you later."

46

Rayne sat in the deep shadows behind one of the tall columns in the dim, comforting half-light of the nave of the Westvale Cathedral. It was peaceful here, surrounded by the familiar echoing sounds he had grown to love when he would come here alone for time to think, before everything changed, and he was forced to leave. He could close his eyes and pretend nothing had changed and all was as it should be.

The outside darkness brought on by Sigmund couldn't penetrate the sanctuary and Rayne was alone with his thoughts. He ran his hand over the worn wood of the bench where he sat, feeling the faint groves of the original wood still evident despite centuries of use. Nearly a year had passed since he had been here last, and he could never have imagined he would be here now, at seventeen, facing the end of his life in someone else's body. But where better to confront Sigmund than here in this sanctuary dedicated to worship of the One.

He should never have let Jonathan convince him to meet with Lexi though, to let her come here when Sigmund could arrive at any moment.

Foolish, idiot. But his heart had cried out to see her one last time, to feel her heart beating with his own, joined in some mysterious way by the One himself. His mind drifted to another time of quiet prayer, back when he nearly died on Nemora and the Kindred had taken him and Mite into the Heart of Neth. He remembered the One's words.

Will you trust me Light Bringer? If my will is for your life to come to an end, at this time and in this body, will you still trust me?

The words echoed in his mind like a knell of doom. And still he struggled with all that question implied. *Do you trust me?*

Yes, my Lord, he had replied then, though his spirit was in turmoil. But could he still hold to that answer now, when death was imminent, not some future possibility?

And he felt the pressing upon him of all that had brought him to this point. His mind staggered as the weight of the memories overwhelmed him. His fear and pain at being Sigmund's slave when he was six rose up, snatching his breath. But then Warren was there, comforting, teaching, easing his spiritual pain. Warren, leading him to a renewed trust in the One after the year when Sigmund had torn his spirit to shreds. He rested in the strength of the memory of his reunion with his parents. He recalled the bathing warmth of the One when he first unlocked the Words to Corylus. Each world and the people he had met there; each ancient guardian, came to the forefront of his mind in stark relief. His knowledge of the love of the One and his trust had grown through all that he had faced in reclaiming each world's scroll. And Rayne knew he had never been alone. Through it all, every step of the way, the One had been an ever-present source of strength when he was weak, and peace when his spirit was in turmoil.

"I'm afraid." He breathed out into the soft silence of the sanctuary. "I know all that has happened and all that is before me now, is according to your will, and your will is perfect, Father One. But I'm afraid. There's so much I don't understand.

"The broken will be made whole? The lost will be found? Yet, you have called me to give up my life so the last full measure will be added to the cup of wrath you will pour out upon Sigmund, his master, and all his kind. I understand this.

But Father One, I don't understand how that can be. How can I die and yet be made whole again? I don't think I can do this. If I die here today, doesn't that void the prophecy? How can I be made whole if I'm dead? Or is the wholeness you speak of not a physical thing? I don't know how to make sense of this."

Rayne sat still and quiet for long minutes trying to comprehend how two ideas that seemed to contradict each other could both be true. But, in the end, it all boiled down to one question for him. And one answer. *Do you trust me?* But was Rayne strong enough to still answer yes, now at the end?

Ever since Nemora, he had struggled with the knowledge that he would have to face this question when the One asked it this last time, when his yes would mean his death. He lived with the dread ever since he had begun to understand what the One was calling him to do. And now that time was here.

"I am afraid." He whispered into the silence once again. "But my fear is in your hands, my Lord. And even though my sorrow, like a swollen, rushing river after a storm, seeks to drown me in rising grief and pain, this too is in your hands. You, you alone are my source and my strength. Where can I turn but to you? You are my hope and my life. Where can I find peace, except in you?"

Rayne leaned his head back against the bench and rested while his spirit sought the very core of his faith. Taking as deep a breath as he could and slowly releasing it into the stillness surrounding him, he said, "My life is in your hands, my Lord. Use me as you will. I trust you."

With the final decision made, Rayne felt intense, comforting peace suffuse his spirit. He felt light. However it all worked out, he was now resting firmly in the center of the One's will. And there was no place he would rather be, even if it meant losing everything he had ever desired; Lexi, his parents, his friends, life as a normal teenager, life itself. Because it meant he had gained a treasure of immeasurable worth, the honor of serving the Creator-Father. In the end, he chose to trust the One in spite of all he was losing. Resting in the peace of his resolution, he turned his focus to his friends, praying for them.

Rayne lifted his eyes. An echo curled through the empty

sanctuary as one of the small side doors opened and closed, pulling his gaze toward the source of the sound.

Lexi, so petite and so beautiful, stepped lightly into the vast room. Rayne's eyes stung, and his chest ached with the love of her. He could see her looking around, searching. She noticed him in the dim light and moved forward. As she approached his bench he spoke, his voice the breathy and hollow thing it had become since his time in the desert of Arisima. "Come no closer. I would not have you look on me. Please sit. We need to talk."

She paused for a moment before taking a seat on the bench behind his. He could hear her settling in and he knew she was taking time to think through what to say to the stranger Jonathan had insisted she meet.

"Who are you?" she asked, her voice soft in the hollow sanctuary. "Jonathan mentioned you know my family. He also told me you know things you could not possibly know. I've told only a few close friends of my doubts, my feelings. How can you know these things?"

He swiped his eyes as unwelcome tears came at just hearing her voice. Speaking around the lump lodged in his throat, he said, "I know because I know you, heart of my heart."

He heard Lexi's intake of breath, then anger filled her voice and raised its volume. "How dare you speak to me in that manner? Who are you? I don't know you."

"I know you don't trust His Imperial Highness. You believe he's an impostor because the prince has changed since he was poisoned on Nemora. This is true, isn't it?"

"Yes," she hissed. "Who are you? Please tell me." Lexi paused, then with her voice breaking, asked again, "Who are you?"

"Don't listen to the voice. You know who I am. Let your heart feel the heart of the one speaking and your heart will know the truth of me." He paused for a moment, allowing Lexi to take in the words he had spoken. "I'm sorry. I shouldn't have let Jonathan call you here. But ... I ... needed to see you one last time, hear your voice, feel you near, and tell you I love you, before I face Sigmund."

"Rayne?" Lexi breathed out the name in an almost inaudible whisper. "No. No, it can't be. What kind of trick is this? Rayne is in the palace. You can't be him."

Silence filled the sanctuary. Lexi spoke again, thoughts finding outlet in her spoken words. "But you are right. I have doubts. They haunt me. That isn't Rayne in the palace, is it? It looks like him, but he's not the man I fell in love with. That man's heart is cold. The man I fell in love with earned my forgiveness and love because he was forgiving and so full of love himself. The man back in the palace is nothing like the man I love."

Lexi sucked in a quick breath. "This can't be real. But it is. I feel it just sitting near you. Like the One said that day on Veres, I feel the truth of you. You *are* Rayne. But how can this be?"

She bolted upright, moving out of her pew to come to him, but Rayne stopped her.

"No." The word burst forth harsher than he wanted, but he knew it was for the best. "I don't want you to see me like this. Listen carefully, Lexi. There are things you need to know. The person you know as Rayne is Sigmund. When I was poisoned on Nemora, he took my body and drove my spirit into this form."

"It *is* you!" Lexi interrupted. "I knew it. Please, Rayne, let me come to you."

"No," Rayne said again though it tore him up inside. "We must be strong now, you and I. You've seen the darkness. Even now, even in this place, I feel it battering against me, searching me. You feel it too, don't you? Wearing you down until you have no strength left to fight, stirring up hate and violence. I must stop Sigmund before it's too late. Jonathan has the scrolls. He's agreed to keep them hidden until the One tells him what to do.

"Lexi. Sigmund knows I'm here. He'll be coming soon. I have to face him. I must keep him from getting the scrolls. If he gets even one of them before they're united, he will try to shatter the prophecy. That must not happen."

"But why does it have to be *you*?" Lexi asked, and he could tell she was crying. "Why can't you run away. Take me with you and run away. I don't care what you look like. I can feel your beating heart from here. The heart that calls my own heart to beat with it."

"You know I can't do that. This chance to speak with you again has meant everything to me, but now you must go."

Rayne paused as the pain of saying good-bye threatened to undo his resolve. "Always remember how much I loved you. When this is over, tell everyone good-bye for me, especially my parents. We parted in anger and I need them to know ... I'm not angry and ... I'm sorry. Now, go."

The side door where Lexi had entered creaked open, letting in a shaft of yellow light. A group of worshippers shuffled in, talking in hushed voices. Rayne wanted to scream, 'No! Not now. Leave!' But movement at the front of the sanctuary caught his eye, drawing his attention from the worshipers. Jonathan. The bishop approached Rayne from the door leading to the church offices beyond the altar.

"What are you doing?" he hissed at Jonathan when the bishop got close enough to hear. "You're not supposed to be here."

Clutching his staff Rayne rose and turned to step into the main aisle. He came face to face with Lexi at the end of his bench. It took all his willpower to refrain from flinging his arms around her as she stood before him, chewing her lip and looking so vulnerable. Refusing to meet her eyes, he lowered his to the floor and cringed, painfully aware of what she was seeing; not the youth she had fallen in love with, but a sickly old man she couldn't even recognize.

But his shock knew no bounds as she reached out, cupped his cheek, raised his face to hers, and looked into his rheumy old-man eyes with love-filled golden eyes. Then, with a sad smile and tears falling unnoticed to her cheeks, she threw her arms around him. "I love you Rayne. No matter how you look on the outside, I will always love the heart of you."

He hesitated but then reached around and embraced her, feeling her warmth. Closing his eyes, he reveled in the embrace. *Thank you! With all that I am I thank you for this!*

For that one moment Rayne clung to the dream of what he had hoped his life would be. He imagined he was whole, and the darkness was not consuming Ochen. He allowed the dream of loving Lexi, taking her as his wife and having a family, to unfold in his mind. But then he let it go. It was no longer the reality of his life. He unfolded his arms from around the crying girl, and, gently placing his hands on Lexi's shoulders, pushed her away. "Now leave me." He forced the words out hard and bitter.

"Lexi, is it true? Is that Rayne?"

The worshipers had gathered in the large, central aisle behind Lexi. They weren't strangers who happened to come to the sanctuary at this time, but his closest friends. And it was Anne's voice he heard. She walked up to stand just behind Lexi with a sad but determined look on her face. "Oh, Rayne, I'm so sorry. But, honestly, you didn't think we would turn our backs on you just because you look different now, did you?"

Then Rayne was knocked back down onto the pew. Boone had scooted between Shaw's and Anne's legs and jumped up onto Rayne with her paws planted on his chest. She licked his face while whining in pure doggie joy, her tail thumping the back of the pew. Smiling, Rayne reveled in her enthusiastic greeting, just enjoying the normalcy of it. Then Boone laid down next to him and lowered her head onto his lap with a contented sigh.

"Where did you come from?" Rayne asked. "You know me, don't you, girl?" She looked up at him with wide, trusting eyes, wagging her tail even harder.

They were all here; Lexi, Anne and Shaw, Sashi and Noah, Stevie, Kori and Mace, and Thorvin, Travis and a man Rayne recognized from the Reclamation Committee, even Danton, Theodor's advisor. Jonathan stood behind the group, looking over the tops of his glasses with guilty eyes. "I'm sorry if I overstepped my bounds, Sire. I had to tell them the truth. I couldn't deny them the chance to see you."

Rayne knew Jonathan was right, but he wanted to hide. There was a part of him that recoiled at his friends seeing him like this, especially Lexi.

"We knew it," Anne said. "We all knew Sigmund had done something to you. We were so worried not knowing what he'd done, or if you were even still alive."

"Nemora's moons!" Sashi murmured. Rayne could have cried at the familiar sound of Sashi speaking those words.

"Nemora's moons," Sashi said again. "Is that really you, Rayne?"

Lexi sat down next to Rayne. Jonathan walked over to stand where she had been, and said, "It's an evil thing Sigmund has done. I still don't understand how he was able to do this."

Rayne cringed as Lexi grabbed his gnarled right hand and held it tightly. He looked at her with a pained expression and then up at the faces of all his friends. "You deserve to hear the whole story. But we don't have time. Sigmund will be coming. By now, he knows I'm here. I need to face him. Alone. Please, you all need to go, now."

Thorvin growled, his face a cold mask. "There are palace guards forming ranks out in the square. Tell me, what's going on here?"

Panic seized Rayne. "Sigmund's here already! I'm out of time. Go!"

He gestured to Jonathan. "Please, help me. Get them out of here."

But then, drowning out Rayne's words, the grating of heavy movement filled the sanctuary as the rarely used massive doors of the narthex shifted and opened. Rayne's heart beat a tattoo in his chest as he turned. Sigmund strode in, shadowed by Brayden, Heinrich, Marius, and Giles. Behind them, to Rayne's horror, Theodor, Andrew, Mite, and Ponce were herded through the doors, surrounded by a contingent of palace guards.

47

His Imperial Majesty smiled and clapped his hands while calling orders to the soldiers. "Move, you idiots. These are the traitors who've been painting those treasonous messages and leaving bloody bodies all over Westvale. Don't let any of them get away."

Leaving several soldiers to guard the prisoners, the rest moved forward and surrounded Rayne and his friends.

Andrew's eyes were wide and his face pale, but he stood tall next to Theodor whose eyes burned with a fire of indignation.

Catching Mite's eyes, Rayne saw the anger burning deep within the ancient. Shaking his head, he mouthed, *no*. Mite looked as if he wanted to argue, but Rayne shook his head and Mite reluctantly nodded acquiescence.

Then, for the first time since the shack on Nemora, Rayne faced Sigmund. Seeing his body inhabited by the demon, clothed in elaborate finery, a superior smile pasted across his face, repelled Rayne. It was all so wrong. He shivered

From his cream-colored, suede shoes with gold buckles and matching hose with gold-trimmed garters, to a heavy velvet skirt set beneath an equally heavy sleeveless jerkin of the same amber shade, Sigmund looked like a golden idol. Under the jerkin he worn a pure white, linen shirt lavishly embroidered with gold threads, wide puffed sleeves drooping over ring bedecked hands. His long black hair fell loose over his shoulders and a heavy golden crown set with jewels held the curled, and coiffed hair off his face. Rayne also noticed flecks of gold leaf scattered through the curls. Rayne would have laughed at the ridiculously overdone outfit if the whole situation wasn't so horrifying. *Why not? Why not insult Sigmund? I can't get out of this now, why not at least get some satisfaction before he ends me. He looks ridiculous and it might help keep his focus off the others. Holy One, it's all in your hands now. Please guide Jonathan.*

Rayne turned back to Lexi and his heart swelled. He would protect her and everyone else. Meeting her eyes, he smiled. Then he turned to Sigmund. "What are you supposed to be?" Rayne's voice was a hollow, wispy thing as he faced Sigmund with a bravado he really didn't feel. "You look like a cheap party favor. Ridiculous and tacky. I'd be laughing now, except you're such a dimwitted fool you wouldn't realize I'm laughing at you."

The smug smile Sigmund was wearing, fell into a sneer. Without taking his eyes off Rayne, he yelled back to a guard holding heavy iron shackles. "Drag him out of there and secure him. We'll see who the fool really is."

As the soldier approached Rayne, Boone rose on the bench, her hackles up, growling. The guard took a step back.

"Just kill the animal and get on with it," Sigmund hissed.

"No," Rayne and Andrew yelled together. Grabbing Boone's collar, Rayne commanded her attention. He whispered something to her. At first, she just stared at him. But then, with a whine, she jumped from the pew and bolted toward the interior of the cathedral. The guard looked as if he would chase her, but instead, he grabbed Lexi and pulled her out of his way. Then seizing the front of Rayne's robe, dragged him out into the central aisle.

Rayne struggled for balance as the man chained his hands then pushed him down the aisle toward Sigmund. Unable to stay upright without his staff, he crashed to the floor amid loud, angry protests from his friends.

Glaring down at him, Sigmund said, "Give the old fool his staff. We wouldn't want him tripping and dying before his time."

While the first guard hefted Rayne back to his feet, another shuffled up the row and grabbed the staff and brought it to Rayne. As the guards herded him toward his friends who had been moved into the narthex, Sigmund said, "No. Not with the others. Brayden, you watch him."

With his signature wolf grin in place, Brayden nodded and took Rayne's arm, pulling him to the side.

Sigmund waved to Heinrich. "Check. Are the scrolls there?"

Heinrich went to the bench and after scooting in, turned to Sigmund with a smile and lifted the sack containing the seven blank scrolls. "I have them."

Heinrich brought the sack to Sigmund, but after a quick glance at the contents, anger flared across both demon's faces. Sigmund glared at Rayne and raised his hand to summon energy from the darkened air around him. "Where are they, boy? I'm past patience with you. Where are the scrolls?"

Before Rayne could say anything, Heinrich said, "They're here Sire. I can feel them."

Nausea seized Rayne as the two demons paused, sensing the air for the energy they sought. After a moment, they moved to the doorway that led to the back offices.

"No," Jonathan cried, slipping past the guards and darting toward the two. While Sigmund continued forward into the hallway, Heinrich turned back, grinning. With a lazy wave of his hand, and a few words muttered under his breath, Heinrich leveled dark fire at Jonathan.

The bishop staggered to a stop, his eyes and mouth growing wide. Then with a scream of anguish he dropped to the floor, his body jerking and shuddering as oily black smoke rose from his back.

Anger, deep and complete, coursed through Rayne as Jonathan's body stilled in death. Swallowing bile and blinking back stinging tears, Rayne watched in horror as Sigmund reappeared in the doorway holding a satchel. He smiled at Heinrich as he handed him the bag. Then, focusing his attention on Rayne, strode up to him with Heinrich following.

"Who's the fool now? You've lost, my little bird. This game of Kings and Swords is mine. You belong to me, you pathetic creature, you always have. And nothing you can do will change that."

With a wink at Rayne, Sigmund shifted his attention to Theodor. "And you, my loving Daddy. I'm disappointed in you. All this time you led me to believe you cared about me, your faithful son. Only now do I find that's a lie. You knew I was searching for the King's Sword and yet you hid it from me. What did you think you were going to do with it anyway?" Sigmund smiled, "Oh, I see, you were trying to attack your son and sovereign with his own sword. Tsk, tsk, tsk."

With his gaze steady and back straight, Theodor said, "You're not my son. You're a demon."

Sigmund laughed as he walked up to the king. Leaning in, he flung an arm around the monarch's shoulders and whispered in his ear. Suddenly Theodor's eyes went wide and he turned his head, searching Sigmund's face with a look of disbelief. Theodor shifted his gaze to Rayne. Understanding blossomed in his eyes and he wrenched away from Sigmund. "You monster," he hissed.

As two guards stepped in to grab Theodor's arms, Sigmund walked away and looked to Heinrich. "The scrolls?"

Heinrich nodded. "These are the originals. All seven. Nothing. Nothing's happening. There's power here, but it's latent, not active."

Sigmund strode back over to Rayne. "You see. You never had a chance. Before you were even born, you were destined to fall under the shadow of my master. He will be delighted with my gifts, especially you. You chose to serve the wrong master and now you will pay for that mistake."

Sigmund turned to the men guarding the prisoners in the narthex. "Gaines, you and your men remain here with me. The rest of you are no longer needed. Leave the little ancient and the man you found with him, Lady Alexianndra, and Lord Kraftsmunn here with Gaines, and escort the rest of these traitors to the dungeon. Then go help our colleagues secure the city. They should have arrived by now. Tell the human livestock that martial law has been declared and they are to remain in their homes until further notice. Kill anyone who questions your authority. And be certain to destroy any soldiers who remain loyal to the old order. Our master approaches. We must be ready."

Theodor protested and struggled as he was dragged from the sanctuary along with Rayne's friends. After the large doors groaned and slammed shut, silence claimed the sanctuary for a few moments, until Sigmund said, "Heinrich, give me a hand."

With a show of power, the two demons blasted the rows of pews across the floor into piles of debris against the walls. Sigmund grinned at Rayne and with the exaggerated movements of a performer, he raised his arms above his head, shook the billowy sleeves down to his elbows, and ignited the torches that ran around the outer walls of the sanctuary. They burned with an oily light, casting red shadows on the once white pillars that were now murky gray.

Then, stepping next to Rayne, he whispered in a conspiratorial tone, "The livestock who are even now returning to their pens trust me, thanks to you; I have become a golden god to them. Tomorrow I'll oversee the executions of the traitors who have been disturbing the peace of Westvale. Like the mindless animals they are, the people will cheer me for my swift and just action." He chuckled, "Newcomers have always been so easy to manipulate. Possessing your body has proven to be most profitable. With your pedigree, I have achieved in a few months what would have taken me years otherwise."

Sigmund turned and motioned to one of the remaining soldiers. The man came forward carrying a long slender package wrapped in heavy cloth. Sigmund slipped the wrapping off one end, revealing the grip of a sword, while the soldier pulled the remaining cloth away. Then, swinging it before him, Sigmund turned back to Rayne. "You recognize this, don't you? It belongs to me now."

Seeing the King's Sword in Sigmund's hands drove Rayne's anger a notch higher. Taking note of the sword's lack of response to the demon's touch, Rayne allowed his anger to fuel his words. "At least it recognized me. You can swing it all you like, but the King's Sword isn't even flickering at your touch. That alone is proof you're not who you claim to be. It doesn't recognize garbage like you as its master. Remember the day I first held it? How it flamed for me? You were afraid then. I saw it in your eyes. Give it to me now; even in this body, I'll show you how it responds to true royalty."

Sigmund's eyes sparked; he swung the sword up so its tip rested at Rayne's throat.

"Don't let him provoke you," Heinrich muttered. "He's good at that."

"You think I won't kill you?" Sigmund growled.

"I don't think you can." Rayne shrugged. "I think you're afraid to kill me. But feel free to prove me wrong—if you can."

Snarling, Sigmund swung the King's Sword in an arc, stopping at Rayne's right shoulder. His eyes grew bright and a grin emerged as he lowered the tip of the blade. He paused, made a show of checking its position, then, slowly and with great care, drove the tip of the blade into Rayne's shoulder until it slid through muscle and buried itself in the soft tissue at the joint.

Rayne huffed in pain, fighting the agony blossoming through his arm and the encroaching dizziness that heralded unconsciousness. Sigmund pulled the sword out. Rayne lost his grip on the staff and groaning, dropped to his knees as the staff clattered on the marble floor and blood ran down the sleeve of his robe.

Brayden laughed. "Do it again, Sigmund. Come on, take out his other shoulder. Make him grovel."

"Stop this," Lexi begged. "Please stop!"

Rayne swiveled his eyes toward the narthex. Even with his sight blurred by pain, Rayne saw Thorvin's and Mite's massive anger and Ponce's unremitting fear. He regretted their captivity and wished he could spare them what was to come. But it was out of his hands. Biting back another groan, Rayne grasped his staff with his good hand while his injured arm hung lifeless. Sheer determination drove him to lever himself upright and glare at Sigmund.

"Oh, this is promising." Sigmund grinned. "I see you still have fight left in you. I admit I was afraid you might have lost your spark of defiance after being imprisoned in that pathetic excuse of a body for so long."

48

$\mathcal{W}$

Sigmund stared into Rayne's smoldering eyes as if looking for something. With a sigh, he shook his head and continued. "But despite Brayden's desire to cause you more pain, I know you too well. Subjecting you to pain isn't nearly as effective as threatening harm to those you care about. No, you're too familiar with suffering and you're still far too stubborn to beg for yourself. But you would do anything to protect your friends, wouldn't you? The need to protect others has always been your weakness.

"Tell me my little Wren, whom shall I play with first? Thorvin? Your little ancient friend? Or, how about the lovely Lexi?"

He tilted his head and pursed his lips as if considering his options. "No, not Lexi. Not yet, at least. She'll be a more pleasurable bedmate unscarred. When we're finished here, I'll have her escorted to my chambers to begin her training."

Sigmund licked his lips. "I'm getting excited just thinking about it. And for added pleasure, I'll even chain you to the foot of my bed to watch. Helpless, incapable of stopping me. You've been there before, remember. I'm sure you haven't forgotten how adept I am at forcing compliance. Your pain at watching me begin her training will be delicious."

Sigmund walked to Lexi and grabbed a handful of her hair. Lifting it to his face, he sniffed. "So sweet."

Lexi glowered at him. "Don't you touch me, you loathsome demon. I'll never submit to you."

Sigmund chuckled. "Oh, how precious. You actually think you have a say in the matter. You're quite mistaken, my dear. In time, you *will* learn to be a proper slave. And when I tire of you, I'll give you to Jason to sell in Emporium City. Of course, by that time you won't be worth much, but I will enjoy your horror at being displayed on the selling block."

Lexi leaned away from Sigmund. "I'll die before I let you take me."

Sigmund threw back his head and laughed. He turned to Brayden. "This should be fun. I'll share her with you. I think, together, we can tame the shrew."

Rayne struggled against his weak body. His need to grab the King's Sword and ram it down Sigmund's throat, even if it meant he was killing his own body, rose like a tidal wave within him. But he was physically incapable of any action. His only recourse was words. Praying for the One's guidance, Rayne channeled his fury toward Sigmund into words designed to push the demon into uncontrollable rage and reckless action. With Rayne's death, the cup of wrath would be filled, and the One's justice would be unleashed.

Remembering Sigmund's past fury whenever the name of the One was spoken, Rayne closed his eyes and prayed aloud. "Blessed Creator One. Lord of all Ochen and all that exists beyond Ochen, I praise your name … Holy One … merciful Creator-Father …"

Rayne felt the shift of air as the sword swung in from the side toward his chest. He waited for the pain to follow, but then Heinrich was there blocking the swing with his mage's staff.

"No," Heinrich hissed at Sigmund. "Our master wants him alive. Do what you will to the others, but you must not kill the Light Bringer."

Frustration colored Sigmund's face a deep red, but he lowered his weapon, disengaging with the staff. Then, rotating the blade in an arc he swung back at Heinrich, but pulled up short. His face a cold mask, he bowed. "Apologies, my colleague. You are right."

Turning back to Rayne, Sigmund spat. Rayne grimaced, as spittle ran down his face. Sigmund looked sideways at Heinrich. "I think it's time we tested how well those ineffectual old scrolls hold up to dark fire, *my friend.*"

Rayne's heart raced as Heinrich dumped the scrolls on the floor. Heinrich and Sigmund studied them, alert, cautious, as the scrolls rolled in different directions across the polished floor. Sigmund laughed out loud and Heinrich smiled. The scrolls stopped rolling and lay there, impotent, nothing more than old scrolls.

"How does it make you feel, boy?" Sigmund crowed, striding back to Rayne, shaking his head as he gazed at him with his mouth turned down in scorn. "You must feel so used. All your work, all your pain, all for nothing. Soon you will see real power. My master is close now."

With a quick turn, Sigmund rounded on the scrolls and, as Heinrich laughed, bent, seized one and held it into the oily blood-red flames of the closest torch.

Rayne shuddered and cried out in protest as tears ran down his face. The scroll ignited, and Sigmund carried it back to the others, lighting each in turn.

"No," Rayne moaned, anguish filling him. He clutched his staff as his weakened body swayed in defeat. But Sigmund wasn't satisfied. Striding back to Rayne, he tore the staff from him, grabbed him by the back of the neck and dragged him to the burning pile.

"Serve me, slave." Cupping Rayne's manacled hands in his own, Sigmund sent a blast of dark fire through Rayne's hands into the burning pile, sending the flames higher and engulfing the burning scrolls with the oily flames, until nothing but cinders remained.

Rayne screamed as the physical pain exploded in his hands and the spiritual pain shredded his spirit. Sigmund released him, and he fell to his knees, sobbing, covering his face in his ruined hands, shattered and inconsolable.

Thorvin was swearing and struggling as four guards wrestled him to his knees, shackled, and gagged him. Mite battered against the man holding him, while Lexi stood straight and proud, held by two guards, glaring, but silent."

Sigmund's gaze focused on Ponce, cowering behind the others. "Don't think I've forgotten about you, old friend. Your turn will come. Resurrecting your identity as a rubiate will give me great pleasure."

Rayne held conscious awareness with tenuous threads as the darkness saturating the sanctuary deepened. Oily, red-hued darkness, like the flames Sigmund had forced through Rayne's hands to destroy the scrolls, called out to the quiescent darkness within Rayne. It pounded against the bonds he had set around it. Sorrow swept through him and he shuddered, knowing the walls he'd built to hold the coiling darkness were crumbling. It was at that moment of despair that the first hint of warmth trickled through him. The pain in his hands receded and he heard the words, *look up.*

Licking parched lips, Rayne raised his eyes from his blistered palms to see Elsie standing in the shadows of the doorway that led to the church offices. She was holding Boone's collar with a white-knuckled grip as she watched, her eyes round with horror. Fear for her blossomed in Rayne. He wanted to tell her to run, take Boone and run. But all he could do was stare at the two while in his mind he wailed, *Run!*

Finally the word erupted, harsh and hollow under the high, vaulted ceiling.

"Run!"

More warmth filtered through him, easing his pain. *Be strong, the time is at hand.*

Hope grew and warmth flooded Rayne's spirit. He watched with relief as Elsie pulled Boone back into the recesses of the hallway and disappeared. But his utterance had drawn Brayden's attention. Striding over to stand above Rayne, Brayden said to Sigmund, "It's my turn. Let me hurt him."

Thorvin continued to struggle against his guards. "You

slimy piece of crap," he yelled at Brayden. "Fight me instead of picking on a defenseless old man, you coward."

ᛉ

Sigmund chuckled. "Keep that up, Thorvin and I'll sell you to the Andersen's for their games, even if it would be a waste of your talents." His face turned thoughtful. "Think about it, man. I can offer you a position training my people."

Thorvin snarled and almost broke away. Sigmund shook his head and turned his focus back to Brayden. "As always, your appetite for inflicting pain pleases me, my young friend. You may cut him." Threat filtered into Sigmund's voice as he handed Brayden the King's Sword, "But ... do not damage him seriously. He belongs to our master now."

Brayden's eyes glinted as Sigmund turned to Rayne and said, "Your blood-thirsty cousin wants another piece of you before he loses his chance." He shook his head, and laughed. "It must have frustrated you even as a child. Every time you tried to get your parents to believe the truth about Brayden, they would just dismiss your words. Do you remember the time Brayden brought you to me at the sacrificial rock outside Inverness, begging me to let him strike the killing blow in the sacrifice? Even then he was my obedient apprentice."

Curiosity crinkling his eyes, Sigmund moved over and knelt in front of Rayne. "Do you even remember? Do you remember how your stupid aunt stopped us from sacrificing you but never breathed a word of it to anyone, she was so afraid of her own son? You don't even remember that, do you? Your mind is so damaged by what we did to you as a child." Watching Rayne's eyes with anticipation, he said to Brayden, "Do it. Let me see the pain."

Sigmund scrutinized Rayne's eyes to see the pain reflected there when Brayden struck. Turning in a complete circle Brayden grinned and swung the sword downward, slowly, almost gently, slicing Rayne's left cheek.

"Was that careful enough? Can I do it again?"

"It was beautiful. The moment you cut him, I could see the agony in his eyes. Marvelous." Sigmund licked his lips.

"What are you doing?" Heinrich said. "Stop playing with Brayden and end this now."

Sigmund purred as he watched the blood dripping from Rayne's chin. "What's the problem, Heinrich. You used to enjoy these games. We have time. Don't you realize what we've just accomplished here; the scrolls are gone; the prophecy thwarted; the Light Bringer reduced to this quivering excuse of a newcomer. What's the harm in a little diversion while we wait?"

Taking the King's Sword back from Brayden, Sigmund began pacing in front of Rayne. With a smooth, controlled voice, he said, "Do you know why I have this sword? Your daddy snuck it out of the treasury and sought to kill me with it. He tried to kill me! Can you believe that? His own son? But now I'll use it on you."

"Sigmund!" Heinrich growled deep in his throat. "You've had your fun. Stop playing around."

"You fools," Rayne ground out, his voice reduced to a dried husky whisper that penetrated every inch of the sanctuary. "Don't you know you've already lost?" He gathered strength and his voice rose in volume. "Your master is nothing before the power of the One. And his justice will descend on you for what you have done."

"No!" Sigmund shouted, continuing to pace back and forth in front of Rayne. "*You're* the one who doesn't see. You're the fool. It is your master who is weak, just like you. Why, you've never been anything more to him than a weak pathetic pawn. The power is mine, mine!"

Sigmund's fury almost drove him to strike, but he drew back again, gaining control over his rage. After a few minutes, Sigmund retrieved Rayne's staff, pulled him upright and handed it to him. As he turned to face Rayne, Sigmund's whole demeanor changed. Soft compassion spilled from his eyes and sadness pulled at the corners of his mouth. He wrapped his free arm around Rayne's shoulders. Rayne shuddered and tried to pull away, but Sigmund was too strong and with his arm draped in a friendly fashion, he said in a comforting tone, "Poor, poor boy. Even now, you don't understand. Your master has lost.

Think about it. His bishop is dead; his scrolls are gone, reduced to ashes. And look at you. Wounded, dying, trapped in that wretched body. Once again in my power.

"He could have stopped all of that, but he didn't. He didn't protect his bishop, or his scrolls, and he hasn't protected you, has he? Bishop Hedrick may be dead, but my mercy and Heinrich's skills can keep you alive."

He paused and glanced at Brayden. "I could hand this weapon over to your cousin right now and let him have some more fun damaging you, and your master can't do a thing to stop it. You've backed the wrong entity.

"Change sides. Bow down to me now and I'll give you back your body. That's what you want, isn't it? To leave this old body behind and live as the teenager you are? I'll pardon your friends, even Ponce, if you wish. Give you Lexi. Just bow down to me. We can serve my master together, you and I. Then you'll see what real power is. I know you, the fire that still burns in you. We can have limitless power together."

"Don't do it," Lexi pleaded. Rayne could hear Mite huffing, "No, no, no." He turned to them, saw the rebellion in Thorvin, Lexi, and Mite. Even Ponce, who now stood shaking his head, said, "Don't do it."

Rayne, strengthened by the unquestioning support of his friends, turned to Sigmund. "The only true power is the One." His breaths came heavy and hard. "And he is not my master through fear and coercion, but he is my Lord, because I choose to trust him and seek to do his will. No. It's you who doesn't understand. The One is the creator and sustainer of everything. He, and he alone, is the source of the fire that burns within me. There is nothing you can offer me that will change that."

Suddenly Rayne found the strength to step away from Sigmund. His voice grew stronger and fuller, rife with authority. "Know this Sigmund; judgement is coming for you and your master. The light will shine. And the darkness will flee before it. You and your kind will be bound by the light and in anguish will you be cast forth from Ochen. For the true light of the Son will be revealed through his chosen and it burns with power you cannot fathom or defeat. These are the decrees of the One and as such are unalterable. What the One has purposed, he will bring to pass."

Rayne felt the force of the blow before he even realized Sigmund had moved. He heard Lexi's scream and Thorvin's struggle. Sorrow flowed from Mite, as Rayne looked down to see the King's sword buried to the hilt in his chest. His body shuddered and began to collapse. There was so much pain. And then there was no pain, only darkness and silence.

49

Π

The darkness was receding. Voices echoed. Rayne wasn't sure what just happened, or what was happening now. Sigmund and Heinrich were arguing. Lexi and Mite were crying, and Ponce was cursing. But it all seemed so far away. As the darkness continued to dissipate, he realized he was looking down on the old man body he had occupied for the last six months. Sigmund was wiping the King's sword clean on the body's crumpled robe.

Grief struck him as he gazed down on Jonathan's body. The bishop had been a good man and he deserved better than to die at Heinrich's hands. With a start, Rayne realized he was hovering near the ceiling, just like when he had been forced from his body in Inverness. The room vanished, and Rayne was in another place.

Awareness of a presence filtered through him. A presence so strong, so inviting, so full of peace it was almost unbearable. He was no longer floating, but being held, embraced. He looked up. The Son smiled down on him, and a love that drove all fear and anguish from him enveloped him. Never before had Rayne felt so complete, so loved.

Looking up into the compassionate face, Rayne asked, "Where am I?"

"You are being held in the infinite arms of love," the Son answered, his face glowing.

"Am I dead?"

"No, but you must re-enter your body soon."

"The old man's body? Isn't it dead?"

"The time has come for you to return to your own body, beloved Light Bringer. The cup of wrath overflows to judgement. You will be the conduit we use to bind the living darkness; that is Sigmund's master and the demons who serve him. In you, the Words and the Light are uniquely united. You have been made a vessel of light, and you have become the repository of the Words."

"But the scrolls were destroyed. I failed you. You trusted me, and I failed."

The Son's face softened. "No, beloved servant. You have not failed. You have become all you were meant to be. You were chosen. The Words are not lost. The power was never in the scrolls; it has always resided in the Words, and the Words now reside in you. United in you, are the Words and the true light of Ochen. When you call up the power of the King's Sword, all that now lives in you will unite with the power in the sword to bind the living darkness.

"Know this, my beloved child, the Light of my Spirit lives within you. It unites the lights of Ochen; the golden light of the Sun Sparrows, the blue light of Neth, and the red light of the desert. It will strengthen you and guide you. But beware, though the demonic darkness will be diminished, as long as individuals seek evil it will never be gone completely, just bound for a time. It will always strive to destroy the Light and the Words within you but search it out and battle against it always."

The Son's voice permeated Rayne's spirit and he knew the voice of the Son was also the voice of the Father One that he had heard so often. It swelled within him. "Beloved Light Bringer, chosen of the One. You have suffered much, and your faith has been tested by fire, refined like fine gold. Are you ready now to be our agent of judgement against the darkness consuming the worlds of Ochen?"

"Yes, my Lord. What would you have me do?"

Love and peace beyond measure flooded Rayne as the Son smiled down at him and Rayne realized things were changing. Once again darkness surrounded him, and the One's words came as from a distance.

Smite the darkness with the Sword and the Word. And the Light will flow from you as water from a spring.

Heavy. I feel so heavy. Cool air caressed his face ... *face?* He blinked. Rayne opened his eyes. The darkness above him was shredding, like tendrils of windswept clouds moving across the backdrop of the cathedral ceiling.

He was back in a physical body. He wanted to cry out to the Son, *don't send me away. Let me stay with you always, please.* But he rested in the knowledge that a part of the presence was within him still. He wasn't alone, had never been alone. And he was chosen. He lifted a hand, turned it, trying to wrap his mind around the fact that he had a physical body that was alive and strong. Rings set with large gems sat on every finger, and at his wrist rested a cuff of fine, white linen with golden embroidery, half covered by a puffy white sleeve.

Sigmund's shirt?

He shot up to a sitting position. *I'm back! In my own body!* His eyes flicked to where he had fallen and saw the old man's body a few feet away, dead. He scanned himself, decked out in the ridiculous outfit Sigmund had been wearing. He blinked and took pleasure in the action. *The One has done it! The broken has been made whole again!*

But if I'm here, where's Sigmund?

Out of the corner of his eye Rayne caught the movement of something not quite solid. Something not right. His spirit cried out a warning. It was the demon that had been Sigmund, now bodiless, nothing more than an animated shadow, moving around him as though it was stalking him. He watched fascinated as the disembodied demon circled, and he suddenly realized what it was after. The King's Sword.

It lunged for the ancient weapon, but Rayne's reflexes

were quicker. In the blink of an eye Rayne's hand was on the sword. In that instant it exploded into a fire of sparkling light so intense, the area surrounding him was lit as if by a bolt of lightning. Rayne ducked his head, closing his eyes. The demon screamed, springing away from Rayne and the blinding light. Blinking his eyes open, Rayne tracked its movement and watched in horror as the thing wormed into someone's back. The body shuddered for a moment then turned to face Rayne. Brayden.

They were finally one, the demon and Brayden. Their spirits melding into an amalgam of evil desire. Looking into its eyes, Rayne knew the thing that was Sigmund and Brayden now existed for one purpose, to stop the One's chosen Light Bringer and destroy the light.

As the creature started toward him, Rayne's spirit shuddered as the sensation of something even more powerful thrummed through the air. A presence of pure evil. Looking up toward the haze-filled, vaulted ceiling, he saw a mass of deeper black tendrils writhe and coalesce into a body. He staggered back from the outpouring of evil emanating from the immense demon now forming before him. This was Sigmund's master. Aware of Brayden now approaching from his left, he stepped back in horror as Sigmund's master looked down on him, its eyes glowing with swirls of obsidian black swimming through the twin pools of blood red.

Rayne swallowed as the hairs on his arms and the back of his neck rose in response to the demon's presence. He watched in disgust as Brayden turned from him to join Heinrich, prostrating themselves on the floor before their demonic master.

How am I going to fight that?

Sigmund's master was immense. Its head crashed against the cathedral ceiling, sending shards of blocks crashing to the floor beneath. Dark, tattered, bat-like wings emerged from behind huge, muscular shoulders, spreading to fill the width of the sanctuary. Long, white hair hung in clumpy patches from the oozing, balding skull, leaving patches of hair and slime on the ceiling. The face looked as if it had melted and reformed multiple times, the gray skin under his eyes sagging, exposing portions of whitened bone beneath the hideous red and black eyes. The smell of death and decay permeated the air around him. Rayne gagged.

As Brayden and Heinrich rose from the floor, the demon master spoke in a voice that vibrated the surrounding walls, deep and powerful. "Well done, my faithful servants. I felt the release of restraint when you destroyed our enemy's scrolls. Many colleagues joined me in coming to this shore and are now spreading through the land, killing, seizing slaves, and plundering without restraint, reveling in the freedom you have won for us. And so is it happening across the worlds of Ochen."

Brayden and Heinrich bowed again, acknowledging their master's words of praise. Rayne slipped through the shadows toward the prisoners. Sigmund's soldiers had joined Heinrich and the Brayden-Sigmund thing, offering obeisance to their master, bowing to the floor. While they were distracted, Rayne moved into position behind Thorvin and removed his gag.

Lexi, Mite, and Ponce huddled closer, and Thorvin whispered, "Is it really you, now?"

Rayne motioned for quiet then pointed toward the door where he had seen Elsie and Boone earlier. "Hurry. Stay in the shadows and go quickly."

All four shook their heads and Mite whispered, "Mite not leave Light Bringer. No, no, no."

Lexi stepped next to Thorvin, her eyes sparking. "We're not leaving you either."

"Be realistic, old man." Rayne glared at Thorvin. "I can't undo your shackles and I can't protect you.

"If you want to help me, do as I ask. Leave now, while you can. Trust me in this. I know what I need to do, but I can't do it if I have to worry about you four."

As if hearing his words, the demon master twisted its head and impaled Rayne with its malignant gaze.

"Go," Rayne hissed. Striding forward, away from his friends, Rayne met the demon's eyes and pulled in a deep breath, swinging the King's Sword as he advanced.

"So," he shouted, his voice ringing, contempt saturating his words. "You're the repulsive thing that holds Sigmund's leash? Not much to look at, are you?" He glanced back over his shoulder and breathed a sigh of relief as his friends disappeared behind some of the shattered pews near the wall, giving them a shadow-drenched, sheltered route to the door.

The demon master spread its wings. "So ... this is this the puny human who thought to defy us."

"Yes, my master," Sigmund spoke through Brayden's lips. "He is the chosen of our enemy, the failed Light Bringer. Now that the scrolls are destroyed, and he no longer poses a threat, I present him to you. A gift."

"Bow to me failed servant of my enemy."

Rayne grimaced as his will was overcome and his body moved into a deep bow. Struggling, he staggered but then forced his resisting muscles upright, glaring his hatred for the evil in front of him.

The demon master chuckled, a growl-like sound deep in its throat, exposing sharp, razor-like fangs. "Very nice. Your diminutive gift still has some fight. Good. I haven't had the pleasure of breaking a chosen servant before."

Breathing hard, Rayne stood his ground. He swung the King's Sword, sensing the bond he had experienced once before. Strength flowed into him and the indwelling light responded with a vast surge of power. Needing to release some of the force building within him, Rayne yelled a challenge and raised the light-filled sword overhead. It flickered and sparked.

The demon master laughed, unleashing a vibration that shook the floor. His followers backed away, leaving an open circle for their master and Rayne at the center of the sanctuary. The sword's light ate away at the dense darkness that had deepened since the arrival of the demon master. Energy coursing through him, Rayne yelled again, a deep guttural challenge born of pain and anger.

The demon looked down at Rayne and grinned, confident. It didn't move toward him, but stood waiting, tall and imposing, reeking of death and evil. It spread its wings and stretching sharp-clawed hands upward, it began to write in the air.

The familiar motions stirred up memories of Sigmund calling forth a weave of power. In response to his need, the sword pulled more energy from the surrounding air and pulsed with power.

Still the demon wove, the air around his talons sparking with dark energy.

Enough. The longer I let him build, the stronger his attack. Must move. Now! Thought morphed into immediate action. Lithe and agile, Rayne rose onto the balls of his feet and shifted toward the monstrous thing. Instincts born from years of fighting kicked in and he focused to block the power he knew the demon would release. He circled, moving even closer, knowing the thing would react to his proximity soon.

With Rayne closing in, the demon master roared its own challenge, then released a bolt of sparking energy. Rayne's reaction was automatic, as natural as breathing. He shifted slightly to the right as he drew the sword across to his left, initiating an upward swing to block the dark magic hurtling toward him. Rayne faltered, aborted his swing.

Someone was there, suddenly appearing between Rayne and the bolt of energy, screaming, "Nooooo!" Ponce. The blast struck him in the chest and he staggered back.

Rayne caught him, lowered him to the ground, cradling his head. "Why? Why did you come back?"

Ponce shivered, and blood trickled from his mouth. "I couldn't let them hurt you again. Too much ... just couldn't. Not again." He coughed and then a slight smile lifted one side of his mouth. "But I'm forgiven, right Light Bringer? I belong to the One now. Freed from darkness." He sighed. "Tell Coralea, tell ..."

Ponce was gone. Rayne swallowed hard around the lump burning at the back of his throat. Ponce had taken the bolt of energy meant for him, had given his life to protect Rayne. *He shouldn't have done it.* But Rayne couldn't change that now, could only move forward. Lifting cold eyes to the demon he groaned; it was already pulling energy for another attack.

"Aren't you going to thank us for ending that loathsome rubiate who caused you such pain?" Sigmund's voice rose from Rayne's right, while Brayden's face split with the wolfish smile that was so much a part of him. There was something obscene about Sigmund's voice coming out of Brayden's mouth and Rayne's stomach revolted at the sight.

Suspecting Brayden's words were a distraction, Rayne sought out the demon master's eyes. *Oh, yeah! Not going to work.* He coiled, flexed muscles, prepared. Rayne pushed off from the ground like a sprinter and leaped forward to cover the distance to the demon before the energy coalesced into another bolt.

The demon released the magic just as Rayne reached it. With a massive downward swing, the King's Sword severed the energy bolt, sending shards of dark magic shooting off to either side of Rayne. He was on the thing. But the demon leaped up into the air, flapped its wings once, and flung itself back, gaining a good twenty feet between itself and Rayne, laughing.

"I see why you have delighted in playing with this human, Sigmund," the demon master said. "He has fire."

Summoning power from the undulating darkness around him, the demon once again sought to pull energy into itself. With a yell, Rayne plowed into the thing, swinging the King's Sword into its legs, driving it back with a rapid flurry of strikes. Every time the King's Sword connected with the demon's flesh, gouts of black energy shot off, tearing chunks of rock from the walls of the cathedral.

Rayne backed off, circling.

Sigmund taunted. "You surprise me, boy. I thought your time in the old man would have weakened you. Yet you seem as strong as ever, my little Wren. But, you forget ..." Sigmund chuckled then wagged a finger at Rayne. "It would appear you are missing something important." He paused and smirked as Rayne cast a glare at him. "That's right. Your precious scrolls are gone. You helped me destroy them. You may have the King's Sword, but without the scrolls, you don't have the power to bind us.

"You've no escape, little slave boy. Any moment now, my master will grow tired of this game. And when he does, he will punish you for annoying him. You belong to us now, as do all the people of Ochen."

"Enough words." Rayne growled, his frustration boiling

within him. Even with the power and speed of the King's Sword, he didn't have the reach to effectively attack the huge demon. Its body was too well protected by the powerful arms. All Rayne had been able to achieve so far, was to strike at its legs. Every time he struck, the demon healed, closing the steaming wounds instantly. And Rayne was tiring.

How do I fight something like this? He backed off, sucking in deep breaths, while the demon master put on a show of exaggerated boredom.

Brayden licked his lips. "Don't say I didn't warn you. Our master grows bored with your little game. Come, Raynie, drop the sword and end this already." He crooked a finger at Rayne, mocking. "Bow to your new master."

Father One, Rayne prayed. *I can't defeat this demon. Help me. Guide me.*

Beloved Light Bringer, you are trying to do this in your own strength. You cannot do this on your own. Let me be your strength.

Trusting in the strength of the One and resting in his peace, Rayne closed his eyes for a moment and lowered his defenses, just as he had done before Sigmund's attack the night he returned to the palace. He smiled.

Blinking his eyes open, Rayne saw the demon glaring at him. "What have you done?" it roared, fear showing in its eyes.

Rayne startled as a narrow shaft of pure white light shot upward from the King's Sword, piercing the remaining darkness and illuminating the area around him. The light within him thrummed in response. It swelled outward in shades of gold, blue, and red, running up his arms and merging with the light from the ancient weapon. The rainbow of colors twisted around Rayne and the sword, flowing in and around each other, causing the ambient air to hum with power.

The beam of pure white light grew and began to solidify, while the colored lights intensified, spreading outward and swirling around the beam. The white beam began folding in on itself, reducing to a narrow, intense shaft centered over the King's Sword. It contracted even more, folding inward and compressing until it was the size of the blade itself. Then, the light and the sword merged. The swirling colored lights became a wind, spinning around the shaft of white that was now the sword, moving faster and faster, shrinking inward like bands of veredium around the heart of impossibly white light, forging a new sword from the light. Then all became still.

Words of prophecy flitted through Rayne's mind. Raising the sword of light, he spoke with a voice of authority that boomed and echoed through the cathedral and swelled, filling the air over the city of Westvale.

"Know me, people of Ochen. I am Rayne Kierkengaard, restored and made whole again by the power of the One. I am the chosen, the Light Bringer of the Blessed One, the Creator Father, the Lord of all. Though for a time the lights of the worlds of Ochen were shrouded and my severed spirit wandered, I found peace in the Words of the One. He was my shelter in the tempest. It is fulfilled. The darkness that claimed victory is defeated. For the One has guided my steps and the cup of wrath overflows.

"Sing for joy people of Ochen, for the broken is restored; the lost is found. The fullness of time has arrived. By the power of the One, the Words and the Light are united, the chosen and the sword are ready. The time of judgement is now."

Rayne's voice softened, and he prayed. "By your will most Blessed One, have these things been accomplished. I beseech you now, Holy One, Creator Father, as you have spoken, so shall it be. Bind now the living darkness."

Again, the colored lights poured from Rayne, flowing and intermingling over the heads of those in the cathedral, joining with the pure light streaming from the King's Sword. The combined light strengthened until the very air in the sanctuary vibrated with light so intense, it billowed outward, pushing back the darkness throughout the city.

The voice of the One thundered and the light fragmented into countless pieces like shattered glass, exploding. Not bound by the constraints of time or space, each shard of the holy light sped throughout all Ochen. And everywhere the light shown, the voice of the One thundered and the beings born of darkness shrieked in fear.

And as the One spoke the words of binding; the demons

were flung from the worlds of Ochen and imprisoned in outer darkness.

As Rayne watched, Heinrich and the soldiers all collapsed, unconscious. The demon master vanished, torn apart as it thundered in frenzied wrath, deep and primal. Then Brayden convulsed and writhed as the command of the One tore Sigmund from him. The dark, nebulous thing that was Sigmund screamed its hatred at Rayne and at the One, as it battered at Brayden, trying to once again gain his physical form. But the One had spoken. With a last, hate-filled screech, Sigmund was gone, and Brayden lay a crumpled heap on the floor. Silence, intense and irresistible, pulsed in Rayne's ears.

Is it over? Is it finally over?

Energy draining from him, Rayne looked around. Seeing Ponce's body, he felt a tightening at the back of his throat; no one was here to mourn the little man who had so resolutely turned his back on the darkness he had known, and embraced the love and forgiveness of the One.

Turning from Ponce, Rayne walked over to Jonathan's body. Kneeling he allowed the pain of loss for the wise bishop to take him. Jonathanh would be mourned. His passing felt by many. Two very different men, yet both loved of the One. Rayne still struggled with the need to forgive Ponce; perhaps in time he would. But the pain of losing Jonathan cut deeply and Rayne bent his head in prayer.

50

The darkness that permeated the cathedral had all but dissipated by the time Rayne looked up. The collapsed forms of the guards were scattered across the floor, and the remains of Ponce's grandfather lay still and cold. There was no trace of Marius or Giles; somehow, in all the confusion, they must have escaped.

Scanning the ruined sanctuary, Rayne caught sight of Elsie, gripping Boone's leash, stepping cautiously into the debris-strewn area in front of the door to the offices. Lexi, Thorvin, and Mite were behind her. Thorvin's shackles were gone. The man looked furious and lethal holding a pilfered sword. Elsie's eyes widened when she noticed Rayne. She released Boone who sprinted to him, barreling into his legs, barking joyously and covering his face with sloppy kisses as he bent to hug her. "Good girl. You're a good girl. You never doubted me, did you?"

Then Lexi and Mite were running toward him, and Rayne's heart burned at the sight. Their smiles suddenly vanished, replaced by looks of alarm. Mite raised his arm and pointed to something behind Rayne while Lexi centered the sword she carried.

Rayne pushed Boone back and commanded, "stay," as he grabbed his sword from where he had dropped it. He raised it in a swift arc as he spun to face whatever Mite was seeing. A split second later, Rayne was rocked by a violent downward strike. The force of the impact sent needles through his hands. The blow would have torn through Rayne's back if Mite and Lexi hadn't warned him.

Brayden's face was distorted, filled with dark hatred. Spittle flew from his mouth as he screamed, "You! Always you! You've ruined everything. Bring him back. Bring Sigmund back."

He lunged at Rayne screaming, swinging wildly. Brayden's attack was messy, driven by emotion. Rayne blocked each blow easily until, tiring, Brayden stepped back, shaking with fury.

"It was always you everyone wanted. You, the golden child. The Crown Prince. The beautiful boy. Even Sigmund! He was my mentor, more of a father to me than my real father ever was. But all he ever saw was you. Even when we were children, all he talked about was you. I ... hate ... you!"

Brayden pulled in a calming breath, reining in his fury. Rayne questioned what he was seeing as his cousin's whole aspect changed in a moment, from uncontrolled fury to cool calculation. Bringing his sword up, Rayne remained alert to any indication Brayden would attack again. But Brayden just stood—unmoving—gathering himself.

When he lunged again, his movements were controlled and precise. Rayne saw the cold evil in his eyes as Brayden pressed him with a flurry of attacks. Even without Sigmund's magic, now that Brayden had gotten his emotions under control, Rayne faced a master swordsman who would stop at nothing to see him dead.

Pushing apart, Rayne shook his head. "I never wanted Sigmund's attentions. They only brought me grief. I'm tired of the blood and the pain and the death. Stop this. I don't want to kill you, Brayden."

"Why?" Brayden snarled. "Because I'm your cousin? No! You hate me as much as I hate you. So you can lord it over me? Tell everyone how you pardoned me, saved me from myself?

Show everyone what a perfect little One worshipper you are? You think you're so much better than I. Well, you're not. Sigmund showed me the truth of you long ago, when we were children. How while you put on a front of being the sweet little innocent, underneath the mask you were just like me.

"He told me what you were like at Coronus's. He bragged about how bloodthirsty you were and how he could count on you for a nice messy kill. You were so good at it because you loved the kill. That was your true nature. Sigmund knew that, and he used it.

"I realized early on, the only way I could compete with you was to grow stronger and even more bloodthirsty than you. Sigmund liked that, he encouraged me to take your place with your parents, put on a better show of innocence than you had while cultivating the desire to shed blood and cause pain beneath the mask. Just like you.

"And in time, Sigmund chose me over you. He promised me even more power. But you ruined that too. Just like when we were children. It had to be all about you. No more! This time I'll be the one everyone fawns over when I finally take you down. Come, cousin, let's finish this."

Rayne growled and shifted the King's Sword, willing it to once again pull in the energy he had released. "You're wrong," he said. "I never wanted to spill blood. I hated it, got sick every time I had to kill someone. Sigmund has been poisoning your thoughts all along."

Brayden plowed into Rayne with a quick series of blows, forcing him back toward where Lexi and Mite were standing. Rayne, suspecting Brayden's motive, began to circle in an attempt to lure Brayden away from his friends.

Laughing, Brayden pivoted and veered away from Rayne, his focus now on Lexi and Mite. And Rayne knew. That was what Sigmund had taught Brayden. Rayne's weakness. His love for his friends. Now, Brayden was using that against him. But this time Rayne wasn't fighting alone. As Brayden was closing on Lexi and Mite he suddenly found himself facing two swords, Thorvin's and Lexi's. Both combatants glared at him, armed, angry.

Rayne pressed in at Brayden's back, forcing his cousin to shift his attention away from Lexi and Thorvin. Brayden responded with a swift upward slash from the side. But Rayne caught the blow and pushing into it, leveraged the sword more sharply upward. Rather than slicing Rayne's chest, it caught his upper arm. Pain blossomed, but the action gave Rayne what he wanted, an open line straight into Brayden's core. Swiftly dropping his sword under Brayden's, Rayne plunged it into Brayden's unprotected middle, angling it upward toward his heart.

The two stood frozen for a moment. Rayne watched Brayden closely as he tried to raise his sword for another swing, but the truth was written in his eyes. As Brayden began to collapse, Rayne followed him down. He could have pulled his sword, but the blood loss from that action would bring instant death.

Instead, Rayne knelt next to Brayden. "Sigmund lied to you, deceived you and used you from the time you were a child. Seek forgiveness from the One before it's too late."

"No," Brayden huffed. "Don't want your false religion. Don't want your phony sympathy. Pull ... your ... sword."

Rayne stared at Brayden for a few seconds; then rising, pulled the King's Sword. Blood flowed from the wound and began to trickle from Brayden's mouth. He breathed again, shuddered and then was still.

For all the harm he had done, Rayne still felt sorrow at Brayden's passing. He wondered how things might have been between Brayden and him if Sigmund had never corrupted his cousin. He didn't have long to think about that as he suddenly found his arms filled with a warm body. Lexi. Oh, what joy to feel her against him. To be himself. To be home. Then Boone barreled into the back of Rayne's legs. He stumbled, almost falling over Lexi while Boone continued to jump and whine.

"Ray-ray!" Mite bounced from foot to foot, his joy palpable. But then he stopped, went still, and looked up at Rayne with anger in his eyes. "Ray-ray left Mite behind. Mite will not forget. Hurt Mite's feelings it did, it did. Never, never, never do that again. No, no, no."

51

R ayne stood with closed eyes, still and silent, as the cold breeze blowing in off the Cameron Sea pimpled his bare arms. He breathed deeply of the salty autumn air, taking it into his lungs and enjoying the feel of just standing still and being alive while the wind tousled his hair. He could hear the waves crashing in front of him, and the calls of seabirds over the sound of the surf.

Three days had passed since the confrontation in the cathedral. Yesterday, Jonathan's funeral was held in the Great Square. Shaw officiated. Rayne felt the familiar lump in his throat and the burning behind his eyes as he pictured Jonathan in his mind, blue eyes looking over his glasses.

Rubbing his hands over the black leather leggings Andrew had dug up for him from somewhere, Rayne opened his eyes and looked out over the water. The air was crystal clear, the sun rising to his left, a white ball surrounded by a halo of yellow and orange, casting a line of silver across the waves, and warming Rayne's skin on that side. He stood in the spot he had run to the morning Jonathan had yelled at him. But now Jonathan was gone. Just like Warren.

And then there was Ponce. Though Rayne was still conflicted about the little man, he had committed to seeing Ponce's and his grandfather's bodies safely to Sorial later today. But for now, he needed to be alone with his thoughts. And his grief. Glancing over his shoulder, he saw Boone, lying on the rock where he had told her to stay. She watched him with focus, as if she feared he would disappear again.

Rayne closed his eyes once more, seeking his center of calm. It had been so long since he had danced with the sword. It was his way of honoring Jonathan, this sword dance. Just Rayne, alone with his memories and prayers. He pulled the King's Sword from its sling on his back, and sensed it awakening to his touch as muted flickers of colored light traveled up and down his arms. And he danced. Every move a joy. Every move a sorrow. He moved to a rhythm that mimicked the crashing waves and tied him to this place that was home. Finally, home.

By the time he stopped, the gooseflesh on his arms had been replaced with a sheen of sweat. He sheathed the sword and bending to pick up the jacket he had brought, saw he was no longer alone. Watching from the rocks where Boone had waited, he saw Lexi, Thorvin, and Mite. He smiled at their concerned faces. "I don't need a bunch of babysitters."

Lexi huffed and jumped down from the rock. "I don't know about that. It seems to me, that someone who can't even keep hold of his own body is in sore need of babysitters."

She skipped up to Rayne and threw her arms around him. "If I have my way, you'll always have someone to keep watch over you."

Rayne looked down into her golden eyes and smiled. *Thank you Father One for the blessings you have given me.*

Mite bounded down the rocks with Thorvin trailing. "Mite happy, happy, so happy. Lexi keep Ray-ray's heart safe always, always."

Thorvin grumbled. "I can't believe after all that's happened, you take off alone. Haven't you learned anything, boy?"

Rayne smiled at the growling Thorvin and said, "I think with the demons expelled and Brayden dead I'm quite safe.

Besides, I have the King's Sword and Boone with me. You worry too much old man."

"With good reason. Giles and Marius haven't been found yet, and there are still large numbers of those scroll-worshipping idiots roaming around. Ever since they started waking up after collapsing when the demons were bound, they've been complaining they can't remember their names, let alone what happened to them. Then there are the ones who didn't collapse; they're pretty adamant about wanting the scrolls. I don't trust them to not take it into their heads to harm the One's Light Bringer. Bunch of trouble-making fools. You've always been a magnet for trouble and I'm not convinced that's changed."

"Is my father still planning to meet with their representatives?" Rayne asked.

"He is, later this morning. Now that you've relinquished the title of emperor and your father's proper rule has been recognized, he's committed to dealing with them on his own terms. With the bishop dead, the church officials are all too busy scrambling for positions to deal with the aftermath of scroll worship themselves. I guess some things never change." Thorvin sighed and shook his head.

"Jonathan will be sorely missed," Rayne said. "And not just by us. His passing has created a void. We can only hope and pray the man selected to fill that void is a man of true faith and strength of character and not just a figurehead."

Lexi shifted to Rayne's side and grabbed his hand. "Anyway, your father wants you to be present when he meets with the scroll worshipers, so you'd better come to breakfast. Elsie's cooking a breakfast large enough to feed an army and she sent us to bring you."

"She shouldn't be working now." Rayne moaned, knowing the depth of sorrow Elsie was feeling at Jonathan's death. "She should take some time to grieve."

"It makes her feel better," Lexi said. "Just like moving with the sword helps you feel better. Baking is her way of dealing with her pain. She moves through the routine, working with her hands, and finds a kind of peace in it.

Besides, I think she needs to feed you. Like the rest of us, she's missed you and wants to show her love for you through her food."

Lexi pulled Rayne forward. "Come on! Everybody's waiting in the church dining room. We've only heard bits of your story and we're anxious to hear the whole thing. And we only have a little time before you have to meet your father. Elsie even agreed to allow Boone in as long as she behaves."

Hearing her name, Boone jumped up from where she had been obediently sitting and ran up to Rayne, barking with joy and wagging her tail.

"What have you people done to my dog?" Rayne said with mock disgust. "I'm gone for a few days and now she obeys you instead of me."

"If you think this is bad, wait till you see her with Andrew," Thorvin said.

Mite called, "Boonie, Boonie, come, come, run with Mite." He took off running toward the cathedral with Boone nipping at his heels, barking her delight with the game, while Thorvin, Rayne, and Lexi walked behind.

Mite was already inside when the three walked through the kitchen door. Elsie was bustling around, giving orders to her assistant while juggling two serving plates. Seeing Rayne walk in behind Thorvin and Lexi, she stopped and let out a little squeak.

"Here, take this." She thrust both platters at her assistant. With her arms free, she came to Rayne and began to cry while wrapping him in a motherly hug. "It's so ..." she mumbled. "Jonathan should ... oh dear!"

"I know Elsie, I know." Rayne murmured, patting her back. He wanted to say something more, something to comfort Elsie, but he just stood, holding her as she sobbed.

When Elsie settled a bit, she looked up and gave Rayne a tearful smile. "Jonathan would have been so proud of you."

She sniffled and then letting go, said, "Get yourself into the dining room Your Highness. I've got some bacon on the stove just for you. The bread and honey are already on the table and I'll bring the bacon in a jiffy."

Rayne smiled at Elsie and then followed Thorvin and Lexi into the dining room.

Except for Jonathan and Captain Fontaine, all those who had met here with Rayne before he left for Sorial more than a year ago were present, including Travis and Deven. Mite was already sitting next to Shaw.

As promised, Elsie allowed Boone into the dining room. She sat at Andrew's feet with her head on her paws until Rayne entered. Raising her head, she watched him closely. Once he sat down, she got up and walked over to him. Lying down, she lowered her head to rest on his feet with a sigh of contentment.

Elsie walked in at that moment and set a platter overflowing with crispy bacon in front of Rayne saying, "Well, what are you all waiting for? Eat!"

Once she was seated between Lexi and Anne, Rayne prayed. Plates were passed, and conversations flowed. The next two hours sped by as Rayne told his story and answered the many questions his friends asked. Then it was his turn to ask questions about what happened while he was imprisoned in the old-man body. Eventually he asked, "And who in the seven was behind the bloody messages?"

"Knowing what I do now," Thorvin said. "I suspect Sigmund and Brayden were behind them. That way, when the time was right, they could execute us without any questions."

"That sounds about right," Travis said. "From what Sigmund said, our execution as traitors was a foregone conclusion."

Rayne listened quietly as the conversation moved forward without him. Looking around the table at his friends as they discussed things that had happened while he was gone he smiled, once again contemplating how good it was to be home.

Rayne held Lexi's hand as they walked back to the palace with Thorvin. When they got to the main hallway, Lexi kissed Rayne on the cheek, promised to meet him for the midday meal, then headed up the stairs to her room.

Rayne and Thorvin made their way to the large audience chamber. The hallway and antechamber were filled with courtiers and wealthy merchants waiting to see the king. Near the entrance to the inner chamber, a group of about forty dirty, scruffy men and women wearing dark robes, waited. The scroll worshipers. Catching sight of Rayne, one of them whispered to his brethren and they all turned to look at the prince as if he had crawled out from under a rock.

"And you wonder why I think you still need a guard?" Thorvin whispered as he held the door to a small inner hallway open for Rayne.

Rayne didn't respond as he led the way to another door where a palace guard saluted before opening it and bowing them through. They entered the large audience chamber on a landing several levels above and behind the thrones where King Theodor and Queen Rowena already sat.

Though Rowena still looked weak and pale, she sat with her back straight. Rayne grinned to see that she and Theodor were inconspicuously holding hands. He jogged down the levels until he was standing next to his mother while Thorvin took a seat on the level where they had entered.

"Good morning Mother. Father." He whispered as he leaned in and kissed Rowena's cheek.

Two sets of guilt-laden eyes glanced up at him before Rowena and Theodor looked away. Rayne wanted them to let go of the guilt, but he realized that would take time. Desiring to ease their discomfort, he said, "I'm so glad you're my parents. I love you both."

The two returned their focus to Rayne and while Rowena looked at him with a teary smile, Theodor nodded his thanks.

Danton approached and bowed. "Are you ready, Your Majesty?"

"Are we?" Theodor asked Rowena.

She nodded.

Looking up at Rayne, Theodor asked, "And you, Son, are you ready?"

Rayne inclined his head. "Yes, Father."

Rayne planned to stay only long enough to hear the complaints of the scroll worshipers. They filed in and stood before King Theodor as a group, then one stepped forward as spokesman. With a quick perfunctory bow and a glancing scowl directed at Rayne he started.

"Your Majesty, my comrades and I have come before you today to complain about the unfair treatment the rulers of Ochen have directed at our religion. For a long time now, those in power have given their protection to the Church of the One. This should not be so. The political power of Ochen should not tie itself to any one church. Until now, no other body has been strong enough to come forward and challenge this tradition. But that is no longer the case. We, the Scroll Worshipers of Ochen deserve to be recognized, and so, we have come before you today to demand you give us the same honor and protection you have bestowed on the traditional church."

"Just what exactly are you asking?" Theodor said.

"We want the Scrolls of Power. They are the focus of our faith and are now in the possession of the Church of the One. By delivering the scrolls to us, you will prove that the political power of Ochen is not controlled by any one church."

Theodor sat pondering for a bit, then turned to Rayne who sat one row behind him. "What say you, Light Bringer of the One? Is this a political question or one that should be dealt with by the church?"

Inclining his head to Theodor, Rayne asked, "May I, Your Majesty?"

Theodor nodded. Rayne stood and descended to the main floor to stand in front of the spokesman for the Scroll Worshipers. The man stepped back and looking to Theodor said, "I protest. This person is a representative of the Church of the One. As such, he should not be allowed to speak to this issue."

With a growl permeating his voice, Theodor said, "And you, sir, are a representative of your church. Should you also not be allowed to speak?"

The man stumbled over his words and uncertainty crossed his features.

Theodor continued. "This *man* is also my son and heir to the throne of Ochen. I will hear what he has to say on this matter."

Rayne took a deep breath. "The original scrolls are no more."

The man gasped. "How can that be?"

"Sigmund destroyed them; all I can offer you is copies. These seven scrolls are as much a part of our faith as yours. The copies of four are as accurate as we could make them. And, though the last three were destroyed before copies could be made, I plan to write out all I can remember, trusting the One's guidance. But, their true power is in the Words of the One they contain, not the physical scrolls themselves."

"Heresy!" The man sputtered. "This is your doing. We won't forget this."

With an oath, the man motioned to his fellows and they stormed from the chamber.

Silence followed their departure until Theodor nodded to Danton who waved for the guards to recognize the next petitioner. Rayne stopped next to his parents as he climbed the levels. "Thank you for allowing me to speak."

Theodor shook his head. "I can't believe those people. After all you've done, to accuse you of heresy." He looked at Rayne, concern deepening the lines around his eyes. "I'm afraid we have not seen the end of this."

"No, we haven't. The One warned me that even though our battle with the living darkness has bound the evil for a time, there will always be those who will seek the darkness, inviting it to grow again in Ochen."

Rayne reached out to place a hand on his mother's shoulder and give her an encouraging smile before he climbed up to where Thorvin was sitting, as the next petitioner began telling the king his complaint.

"Come on, old man," Rayne said to Thorvin. "I need to return Ponce's body to Sorial and I would feel more comfortable if you were with me."

A short while later, Rayne arrived at the portal station with a contingent of guards and Thorvin. He was surprised to see Lexi, Mite, Anne, Shaw, Stevie, Sashi, and Noah all waiting with the coffin.

Noah waved at Thorvin. "As per your orders, Sir, I procured all the passes using the royal family's diplomatic credits."

"Don't think you're leaving Corylus without us," Anne

said as she approached Rayne. "If you're going to Sorial, then so are we. And don't even try to argue with us."

She gave Rayne a quick, sisterly kiss on the cheek. "Come on little brother. Let's get this done."

Emporium City was as hot, odiferous, and noisy as ever when Rayne, his friends, and the contingent of twenty-four soldiers emerged from the Corylus portal. Though the crowd milling through the markets were used to seeing all kinds of activity and usually ignored most of what went on around them, seeing this number of soldiers wearing the colors of the royal family coming through the portal attracted attention.

It didn't take long for soldiers wearing the Andersen family colors to arrive in the square with Jason in the lead. Jason stopped his men, focusing a curious stare at Rayne. Walking forward by himself, he bowed slightly and asked, "Your Imperial Highness? Why are you here?"

Thorvin and Noah moved in front of Rayne while the guards took positions around the remainder of the group. Stepping past Thorvin and Noah, Rayne approached Jason who studied him with hooded eyes.

"We don't want any trouble with you or the other ruling families here on Sorial," Rayne said. "But I am under obligation to deliver the body of a dead friend to those who loved him. Will you allow us to pass unhindered?"

"Are you Prince Rayne?" Jason asked, eyes narrow with suspicion, his voice uncertain.

"If you're asking whether I'm still His Imperial Majesty, no. I've renounced that title. The position of emperor no longer exists. King Theodor and Queen Rowena have been restored to their status as rulers of all Ochen. Does that answer your question?"

For a fraction of a second fear flitted through Jason's eyes, followed by resignation. "How can I serve you, Your Royal Highness? Are you here on behalf of your father? Do you seek to address the issue of Veres?"

"Though that issue does need to be addressed, and will be in the near future," Rayne said, his voice cold and authoritative, "this is not the time or place for that discussion. I have come at this time for the purpose I have already stated. But you can, perhaps, help me. I need to locate a wealthy widow by the name of Coralea."

"Certainly, Your Highness," Jason said with a deep bow. "I'll send out inquiries for her residence immediately. Perhaps you would care to get out of the heat and rest at one of our inns while you wait?"

Rayne shifted and stared pointedly at the Veres portal for a few minutes, but then turned to face Jason. "We appreciate your kind offer."

It didn't take long to locate Coralea. Rayne met with her alone in the sitting room of a large, well furnished suite. Coralea cried as Rayne explained how Ponce died.

"He gave his life to protect me." Rayne finished his story. "He wanted me to tell you how much he loved you. His last words were those of love for you."

As Coralea cried, Rayne moved to sit next to her on the little couch. He put an arm around her shoulders to comfort her. Eventually the sobs subsided and Coralea looked up at Rayne with a slight smile peeking out amidst her tears.

"The whole time I knew him, Marcus had never been able to let go of the guilt he felt over what was done to you, Sire," she said. "Though we spoke much of the One's forgiveness already given, he had never been able to forgive himself. And though I now mourn for him and my heart is breaking, I know at the end, he must have found peace at finally being able to help you."

Rayne hugged Coralea gently as she, once again, allowed her tears to flow.

Holy One. Rayne prayed. *Your ways are indeed such a mystery. That, of all people, Ponce found your love and forgiveness is beyond belief. And yet, I know it's true. Your wisdom is past understanding. Thank you for saving Ponce and being in my life. Be with Coralea now and all your believers here on Sorial. And give my father the wisdom he needs to deal with Jason, Lord William, and the powerful merchants on Sorial in the days to come as we face decisions about the church here and the independence of Veres.*

52

The sun, a large red ball to the east, rose in majestic glory, splashing the waves of the Cameron Sea with crimson as a bank of storm clouds spattered shadows over the coast. It was the morning of the prince's eighteenth birthday. Though he had requested no large festivities, preferring instead to celebrate quietly with close friends and family, gifts from all seven worlds had been pouring into the capital for the past two weeks. Excitement spread through Westvale as every household prepared to help the prince celebrate by hosting their own parties. And even though there would be no big event, the king and queen had declared a holiday and arranged for dozens of food vendors to set up in the Great Square so the people could enjoy the day. The occasion was much too joyous to ignore.

Rayne basked in the warmth of the sun as he sat and watched Bethie and Mite running across the sand, screaming. Andrew chased after them, growling, pretending to be a bear, while Boone jumped at his legs barking at the play. Lexi snuggled in under Rayne's arm, seeking his warmth in the still cool air of the spring morning. He looked over to where Shaw and Anne sat together smiling at the little girl from Amathea they had adopted nearly four months ago. Bethie was such a blessing not only to Shaw and Anne, but to Elsie as well. She had taken on the role of grandmother with great joy.

Catching Rayne's eye, Shaw said, "Well, my lord, how does it feel to turn eighteen?"

At Shaw's question, Anne and Lexi both looked at Rayne in curiosity.

"I don't know yet," Rayne answered. "I guess I want to make it through the day first." He shook his head. "I haven't had much success celebrating birthdays in the past, and I'm looking forward to a quiet, uneventful one this year."

Bethie came running over and plowed into Anne and Shaw laughing. Pulling Anne's hand, she said, "Up, up Mother. I want to see grandma Elsie."

Everyone gathered their things and hiked back to West-vale. When they reached the church grounds, Anne, Shaw, and Bethie split off while Rayne and Lexi headed toward the palace with Mite, Andrew, and Boone following.

"I'm going to stop in to see my parents," Rayne said to Lexi as he stopped on the second-floor landing while Mite and Andrew continued on to his suite with Boone. "Even though my father has cancelled all audiences today in honor of my birthday, he and Mother asked to see me so we could discuss some issues before he meets with delegates from the six other worlds tomorrow."

Rising on tiptoe, Lexi kissed Rayne's cheek. "I'll see you later then, heart of my heart." Turning, she headed off in the direction of the guest wing.

A smile played with the edges of Rayne's lips as his eyes followed Lexi until she disappeared around a corner. Drawing in and releasing a contented sigh, he headed to the King's Chambers.

Once Rowena had regained most of her strength, she had moved from the Queen's Chambers back into the rooms she shared with Theodor and it was there Theodor asked Rayne to meet with him and Rowena this morning.

Rayne waited in the antechamber as one of the guards announced his arrival to the king and queen. Within a couple minutes, the guard emerged, bowed, and motioned Rayne in.

With the remnants of both the blanket and the spike gone, his parents were finally free to be themselves and Rayne basked in the love they showered on him. Six months ago, he could not have imagined how wonderful his life would become. As he walked in, Theodor and Rowena, who had been sitting together on a couch, rose to hug him.

"Good birthday morning, my beautiful son," Rowena practically sang as she planted a kiss on his cheek.

"Good morning, birthday boy," Theodor said. "Would you like some coffee?" Theodor motioned to a silver serving tray set on a low table between two blue leather couches.

Accepting a cup of coffee from his father, Rayne sat in an overstuffed silver and blue brocade chair that flanked the two couches. Once Theodor and Rowena settled, Theodor turned to Rayne. "Are you ready for tomorrow?"

"To face the delegates? Yes, sir, I think I am."

"I don't think we have too much to worry about from the scroll worshipers. In the last few months, they seem to have lost most of their influence." Theodor stated.

"It would be hard to keep that influence once people learn that the basis of it is false belief in a power that doesn't even exist. Their faith was based on the power of the physical scrolls and now, with the scrolls gone, what do they have to offer? The whole thing was a ruse designed by Sigmund and Heinrich to draw people away from faith in the One." Rayne said. "I hope the truth leads people to seek out the true power behind the scrolls instead of just giving up."

"Yes," Rowena said. "And as the Light Bringer we know you have a responsibility to reach out to those who are confused and searching."

"It's something I need to do. I'm working with Bishop Newson to set up a series of talks through all seven worlds. We're hoping to begin in the fall. Bishop Newson isn't Jonathan, but he's got a strong faith and he's working hard. I like him. Elsie likes him and that says a lot."

"Excellent." Theodor said. "I've already met individually with the officials from Arisima, Nemora, Glacieria, and Amathea and they are all pressing me to continue as sole ruler over all Ochen for the next year at least, They insist Ochen needs the stability of a strong ruler after the events of the past year. But I have requested they reinstate the Interplanetary Council and Court to balance Corylus' control once the worlds are ready to elect officials. Although things have become more stable, the chaos resulting from Sigmund's manipulations and the psychological and spiritual damage wrought by the darkness will take time to repair. And, of course there is the aftermath of the civil unrest the scroll worshipers caused on Glacieria, Arisima, and here on Corylus. Though their influence is waning, many people were killed and displaced in the violence they spawned. It will take time for people to move forward and we will do all we can to help them.

"That brings me to the situation with Sorial and Veres." Theodor said. "Apparently, your last visit on Sorial has helped to soften Lord William's hold on the other families, just as you had hoped."

Rayne looked up, his eyes bright. "And my special arrangements? Have the skipping lines to Veres been opened?"

Theodor glanced at Rowena with a smile, then turned back to Rayne. "I don't know how you managed it, Son, but your special guests from Veres arrived yesterday afternoon. And, as you requested, we have kept their presence here a secret. Through your efforts, we will have representatives from all the worlds of Ochen at the conference tomorrow. What I would like to know, though, is what you have planned for this evening?"

"As would I," Rowena said.

Rayne stood and moved to gaze out the glass doors of the balcony before turning back to his parents.

"You know I love you both and I would never do anything to hurt you. But this evening, no matter what happens I need you to trust me, okay?"

Though Rowena and Theodor pressed Rayne to explain, he would say no more. After a bit, he excused himself leaving his parents to worry about what he was planning.

Rayne made his way to the library where he planned to meet with Shaw and Anne. Elsie had agreed to watch Bethie so

Rayne would have some time alone with the couple. Walking into the room brought back memories of their early studies of the Corylus scroll and Rayne felt a pang of loss that Jonathan would never join them again. But like the loss of Warren, the loss of Jonathan was something Rayne was learning to accept. All things passed in time and at some point, he would be the one missed by those left behind. For now, he needed to keep moving forward, as Prince of Ochen, and as the One's Light Bringer. And there was still much for him to do.

Anne and Shaw were seated across from each other at the table with one of the scrolls spread out before them. Looking up Anne smiled. Once again memories rose, unbidden, at Anne's smile. She was his oldest friend and knew more about him than anyone else. But what he needed to discuss with Anne and Shaw now, even Anne didn't know about.

When Rayne stood to leave a couple hours later, Anne rose with him and putting her hand on his arm said, "Are you sure you have to do this?"

"I gave my word," Rayne said simply. Then he leaned into her and kissed her forehead. "I'm sure. It's what I have to do so I can move forward."

She sighed. "I guess you're right. But after all that's happened, I doubt anyone but you even recalls that promise."

"Possibly. But whether or not anyone else does, I do. And that makes me responsible." Looking up at Shaw, he said, "I'm counting on you both to support me this evening."

"Of course, little brother," Anne said.

"With no reservations," Shaw added.

Rayne spent the rest of the day alone with his thoughts. He knew what he needed to do and that he couldn't pursue the second part of his plan until the first was resolved. About an hour before his party was scheduled to start, he returned to his suite and found Andrew pacing with worry.

"Where have you been? Do you know everyone's been looking for you?"

Rayne grinned and shrugged. "I needed some alone time. That's all. So, my little page boy, are you prepared to get me ready for my birthday celebration?"

As usual, Andrew was ready with a bath. Aware of Rayne's distaste of stockings and flamboyant clothing, Andrew dressed Rayne in simple, charcoal-gray knee breeches that ended in a band above tooled black deerskin boots, the kind Rayne preferred. He wore a simple shirt of deep purple with billowing sleeves gathered at the wrists. Over the shirt came a cap sleeved doublet, fitted at the waist and then flowing in a peplum to his thighs, made of black linen embroidered with golden thread.

Once Andrew finished dressing Rayne, he combed his hair and pulled it back into a loose tail, then tied it with a leather thong dyed a deep purple.

As had become his custom since his return, Rayne strapped on the ancient sword Lloyd had given him on Veres, with a simple belt of fine black deerskin.

Stepping back, Andrew let out a breath and just stared for a moment before swallowing. "You look royal, Your Highness. Perfect."

"You're my page, Andrew. I trust you. If you say I look good, then I believe it. Now, get yourself ready. Do you have enough time, or have I cut it too close?"

With a grin splitting his face, Andrew said, "I've been ready since this afternoon. I just need to change my clothes. But you'd better get down there. You're late."

Rayne waited at the door to the formal dining room while he was announced. As he entered his eyes were immediately drawn to Lexi. Her bountiful, golden hair was pulled up on her head and cascaded down her back in an abundance of curls. She wore a gown of gold and burgundy that made her golden eyes shine. She was so beautiful. He moved to her as if in a dream, barely registering the words she was speaking.

"Oh, Rayne, you don't know how much this means to me. I know it's your birthday, but you have given me the best present I could imagine. Thank you."

Standing next to Lexi, holding her hand, was her father, Duke Justus Erland. Behind them stood Ethan, Silas, and Seren.

The next half hour sped by as Rayne greeted his guests with Lexi by his side. It was as he had hoped it would be, a small gathering of the people he cared about most.

When the meal ended, and everyone was talking, Rayne stood. Soon all eyes were on him. He nodded to several servants who cleared an area at the far end of the room where they set a short table and five chairs.

"Lexi, Duke Erland, Ethan, Silas, Seren, please be seated." Rayne gestured to the empty chairs.

At first they looked at him in obvious confusion, but then all five moved from where they had been sitting to the newly set chairs. Without a word, Rayne walked to stand before them. He unstrapped Lloyd's sword and laid it on the floor in front of him. Then with the sound of murmured exclamations echoing through the room, he dropped to his knees.

"More than a year ago, I gave a solemn vow as Crown Prince of Ochen to present myself before this tribunal and accept your judgement for crimes I committed against you and Veres. The time has come for me to fulfill that vow. I will accept as just and right, whatever punishment you declare." Rayne bowed his head.

Theodor made to rise, a protest forming on his lips, but Rowena put a hand on his arm and whispered, "Remember, my love, we need to trust him." Theodor grimaced but settled back down.

At that moment Mite let out a loud groan and then uttering, "No, no, no," moved to stand next to Rayne. Looking down on Rayne's bowed head, he said, "Wrong, wrong, wrong. But if Ray-ray has done something deserving punishment, then Mite will take the punishment. Mite will do this for Ray-ray." He kneeled down, mimicking Rayne's posture.

Anne and Shaw rose quietly together. Holding hands, they approached Rayne's other side saying, "We will take his punishment."

Rayne looked up at the two and whispered, "What are you doing?"

Without another word, but with fierce looks of determination, they knelt. A loud scraping sounded as Bethie, who had been sitting next to Elsie, scrambled to her feet, knocking her chair back. "Mommy, Daddy, me too, me too." She skipped to kneel next to Anne, smiling up at her. "I want to help brother too."

Lexi rose from her seat between Ethan and her father. "Any sentence handed down against Prince Rayne, I will serve in his stead." She moved gracefully to kneel next to Mite and gave him a smile.

Before she had even knelt, Thorvin rose, angry and growling. "Again. He does it again." Shaking his head and glaring at the Verenians, he stomped to stand behind Rayne. "You'll have to go through me."

Stifling a grin, Duke Erland stood, saying, "Though I am not able to kneel with you, I owe the prince my life. If punishment must be served, I will pay the penalty."

And in that moment, the noise of many chairs being shifted filled the room as others, including Silas, came forward, surrounding Rayne and kneeling, saying, "I'll take his punishment."

"Punish me."

Then Seren rose. She stood for a moment, her face unreadable. Then, with slow, even steps, she moved forward around the table. Turning back to face Ethan, she said, "I have forgiven the One's Light Bringer. I release my need for retribution."

Ethan's eyes shifted to Rowena and Theodor, the only two, other than him, still sitting. With a defiant toss of her head, Rowena rose and stepping carefully around the kneeling people made her way to Rayne. When she stood next to him, she said, "He is my son. If he has done anything deserving punishment, let the punishment fall on me." Anne and Shaw shifted to allow Rowena to kneel next to Rayne.

Then, with a grimace, Theodor also stood. "Don't expect me to walk through that crowd, or kneel," he rumbled, looking Ethan in the eye. "But I've learned to trust my son. If he has done something deserving of punishment, I'm certain it was not by his own choosing. I too stand with my son."

The door quietly opened, and Boone scrambled across the room. Skirting around the many kneeling forms, she made her way to Rayne. Sitting in front of him, wagging her tail she let out a yip, then lowered her head to rest on the ground at his knees with a sigh of contentment.

"Well, I guess that makes it unanimous," Theodor said.

Ethan looked over the crowd of people before him and shook his head. "As the sole remaining representative of the tribunal set in place to judge and sentence the assassin Wren, now known as Prince Rayne, it rests with me to decide his punishment." He took a deep breath and in a loud voice proclaimed, "Prince Rayne has kept his vow. Let no one say he did not fulfill this obligation. I, by the power of this tribunal, now declare in front of these witnesses, that his debt has been paid. In respect for all the prince has done in serving the people of Veres and all Ochen, and for all he suffered as an unwilling slave of Sigmund, I now proclaim him free of all obligations to this tribunal."

Rayne held back the burning tears that threatened. He knelt, now surrounded by so many people who loved him so deeply that they were willing to take his punishment. And he was certain he heard in that room, at that moment, voices of those who were gone as well, Warren, Jonathan, and even Ponce. *You are loved,* they said. He was loved! Beyond all expectation, the little boy who had believed he was unlovable, and had been forced to serve the darkness as a slave and a killer, was loved. He had traveled a long path, but he was home now and he was loved. He felt the warmth of the One and the quiet voice spoke into his spirit. *Well done, my beloved Light Bringer.*